Praise for the Ephemera Series

Bridge of Dreams

"With a well-paced mystery, likable characters, and fascinating world building, this is a fun read." —*Booklist*

"[Readers] will find the characters worthwhile and the story satisfying." —*RT Book Reviews*

"An imaginative world.... I wouldn't hesitate to recommend the Ephemera series to anyone who enjoys unique fantasy books with characters you can admire." —Night Owl Reviews

"Strong on world building." —*Publishers Weekly*

"One of Anne Bishop's fascinating worlds.... [She] has a wonderful way of creating new characters, new worlds that are mind-boggling." —The Reading Cafe

"An entertaining tale with an incredible, vivid description of the Bishop mythos and a wonderful self-sacrificing hero ... a super-fast-paced, exciting thriller." —*Midwest Book Review*

Belladonna

"The work of a master ... thought-provoking." —Fresh Fiction

"Bishop tells a powerful and emotional tale set in a land of dazzling complexity and deep magic.... Those who enjoy sophisticated, mature, and original epic fantasy will be well rewarded by spending time in Ephemera." —SFRevu

"Mystifying forces of light and dark continue to rend Ephemera, a shattered world of extraordinary interconnected landscapes that can be altered by strong emotions.... Fans of the preceding installment will revel in Bishop's imaginative powers." —*Publishers Weekly*

continued...

"Set against a unique fantasy background and filled with intriguing characters, [*Belladonna*] is another tale of enchanted worlds." — *Library Journal*

"Bishop excels at characterization . . . compulsively readable." — *Romantic Times*

"Ephemera is an intriguing world, and the skill taken to create it is readily apparent. . . . *Belladonna* is worth reading on so many levels." — The Romance Readers Connection

"Stunning . . . wonderful." — Romance Junkies

Sebastian

"Erotic, fervently romantic, [and] superbly entertaining, *Sebastian* satisfies." — *Booklist*

"Bishop's talents lie both in her ability to craft a story filled with intriguing characters and in her flair for smoldering sensuality that recommends her to fans of Tanith Lee, Storm Constantine, and Anne Rice. Highly recommended." — *Library Journal* (starred review)

"[Bishop's] worlds are so fully realized and three-dimensional, they jump right off the pages. . . . Exotic, original, [and] sensual, there's nothing here I didn't love." — Fresh Fiction

"[An] impressively unclichéd battle between light and dark. . . . Pure originality and lyrical prose . . . will delight fantasy readers." — *Publishers Weekly* (starred review)

"I enjoyed every page of the book from beginning to end and absolutely love the characters that inhabit it." — Romance Reviews Today

"Highly recommended. . . . Glorianna is a fantastic presence, a nascent goddess." — SFRevu

ANNE BISHOP

Bridge of Dreams

A ROC BOOK

ROC
Published by New American Library, a division of
Penguin Group (USA) Inc., 375 Hudson Street,
New York, New York 10014, USA
Penguin Group (Canada), 90 Eglinton Avenue East, Suite 700, Toronto,
Ontario M4P 2Y3, Canada (a division of Pearson Penguin Canada Inc.)
Penguin Books Ltd., 80 Strand, London WC2R 0RL, England
Penguin Ireland, 25 St. Stephen's Green, Dublin 2,
Ireland (a division of Penguin Books Ltd.)
Penguin Group (Australia), 707 Collins Street, Melbourne, Victoria 3008,
Australia (a division of Pearson Australia Group Pty. Ltd.)
Penguin Books India Pvt. Ltd., 11 Community Centre, Panchsheel Park,
New Delhi–110 017, India
Penguin Group (NZ), 67 Apollo Drive, Rosedale, Auckland 0632,
New Zealand (a division of Pearson New Zealand Ltd.)
Penguin Books, Rosebank Office Park, 181 Jan Smuts Avenue,
Parktown North 2193, South Africa
Penguin China, B7 Jiaming Center, 27 East Third Ring Road North,
Chaoyang District, Beijing 100020, China

Penguin Books Ltd., Registered Offices:
80 Strand, London WC2R 0RL, England

Published by Roc, an imprint of New American Library, a division of Penguin
Group (USA) Inc. Previously published in a Roc hardcover edition.

First Roc Mass Market Printing, March 2013
10 9 8 7 6 5 4 3 2 1

ALWAYS LEARNING   **PEARSON**

For
Lorna MacDonald Czarnota
Merri Lee Debany
and
Barb Markello

Fellow travelers in the landscapes

ACKNOWLEDGMENTS

My thanks to Blair Boone for continuing to be my first reader, to Debra Dixon for being second reader, to Doranna Durgin for maintaining the Web site, to Adrienne Roehrich for running the Facebook fan site, to Nadine Fallacaro for information about things medical, to Anne Sowards and Jennifer Jackson for all their help in bringing this story to life, to Pat Feidner just because, and to all the readers who make this journey with me. May your hearts travel lightly.

Long ago, in a time that has faded from memory, a mother's tears forged the bridge that, ever after, connected the power of the living, ever-changing world to the human heart.

—MYTH

Is the sight that matters most the kind that is seen with the eyes or with the heart?

—SAYING IN VISION

"A wonderful book to get lost in." —Romance Junkies

"A fantastic book. Bishop has built a compelling world that is filled with fascinating and complex characters."
—*Romantic Times* (top pick, 4½ stars)

More Praise for Anne Bishop

"Rich and fascinatingly different dark fantasy." —*Locus*

"A terrific writer.... The more I read, the more excited I became because of the freshness of [her] take on the usual high fantasy setting, the assurance of [her] language, all the lovely touches of characterization that [she slips] in so effortlessly." —Charles de Lint

"Lavishly sensual ... a richly detailed world."
—*Library Journal*

"Vividly painted ... dramatic, erotic, hope filled."
—Lynn Flewelling

"A darkly fascinating world ... vivid and sympathetic characters ... lavish and sensuous descriptions, and interesting world building ... many compelling and beautifully realized elements ... a terrific read." —SF Site

"Intense ... erotic, violent, and imaginative. This one is white-hot." —Nancy Kress

"Mystical, sensual, glittering with dark magic."

—Terri Windling, coeditor of
The Year's Best Fantasy and Horror

"[Anne Bishop's] poignant storytelling skills are surpassed only by her flair for the dramatic and her deft characterization ... a talented author." —*Affaire de Coeur*

Also by Anne Bishop

Belladonna stripped away our human masks, revealing the Dark Guides for what we are—the whispering voices that encourage hearts to turn away from the Light and feed the Dark currents of the world with selfishness and greed and, best of all, violence.

While I wore that mask, I walked among the people of Ephemera as a wizard, as one who was feared and revered because I was a Justice Maker for the most prominent citizens in my assigned landscapes—the kind of citizens who, with whispered persuasion, could do the most harm, snuff out the most Light in other hearts.

But Wizard City, the Dark Guides' stronghold, is gone, taken out of the world and locked away with the landscapes that belong to the Eater of the World. Because the city is no longer within reach, the pureblood females we kept as breeders are also gone. Only a few of us were in other landscapes when Belladonna did that reshaping of the world. Only a few of us escaped that cage. So few of us, hiding now in the pieces of the world.

Of course, we still have some wizards—those descendants of Dark Guides who polluted the bloodlines by mating with humans. Despite that pollution, wizards have the powers that were the gifts from the Dark aspects of the world and, more important for my purpose now, they still look human.

When my true face was revealed, it was the wizards, eager to prove their loyalty to me, who found and booked passage on the various ships that eventually brought us to this city. It was the wizards who found us lodgings that allowed me to study the particular nature of this city and understand how to use it to our advantage.

I can create another stronghold here, another place like Wizard City. Quietly, carefully, I can take part of this city away from its present guardians and turn that piece into a dark landscape where we can rule again.

In the pieces of world we knew, Landscapers were Ephemera's bedrock—the hearts through which the currents of Dark and Light flow, the sieves that keep Ephemera from manifesting the turmoil in all the other hearts. Here the Landscapers are called Shamans. They guard and guide all they can see with the complacency of those who believe they have no rivals.

They don't know about Dark Guides or wizards. They don't know what to look for. Blinded by that ignorance, the Shamans will be able to do nothing but wonder why pieces of their city are slipping beyond their sight and control.

We have a foothold in two sections of this city. Soon entire streets will be under the control of my wizards. The Shamans will not find us.

And neither will Belladonna.

—an entry in the Book of Dark Secrets

Chapter One

Following his cousin Sebastian, Lee stepped off the stationary bridge that connected the Island in the Mist to the rest of Sanctuary. A few months ago, the island had been almost impossible to reach. It still wasn't easy—Ephemera made sure of that—but now family and a few special friends could reach the place Glorianna Belladonna called home.

"We could have used my island to get here," Lee grumbled. His little island was always with him, a piece of land he could impose over any other landscape, Dark or Light. As a Bridge, he created connections between the broken pieces of the world, and his work sometimes took him to faraway—and dangerous—places. But his island, anchored in Sanctuary, was the assurance that he was never more than a few steps away from home.

"We could have used your island," Sebastian agreed. "And we would have if I had been accompanying you on this visit. But since you're accompanying me, I chose to use the bridge."

"Oh, that makes sense." Lee took a couple steps toward the two-story stone house that Glorianna and Michael now shared. Then he stopped and rubbed his left forearm.

Michael had broken that bone during the fight to keep the family away from the terrible landscape Glorianna had made to cage the Eater of the World. The rest of the family had forgiven the Magician for the part he'd played in making that cage—especially after he found a way to bring Glorianna back—but Lee's arm always hurt when he visited the Island in the Mist. He couldn't say for sure whether it was the bone that bothered him or if it was being around the man who broke it.

"Can't tell from here if they're at home," Sebastian said.

"Where else would they be?" Lee asked bitterly. "Glorianna hasn't left this island since she . . . came back."

"It's been only a few weeks," Sebastian said softly. "We don't know what happened to her while she was in that place."

And if the Magician was right and she became the monster that Evil feared, we don't know what she did while she was in that place, Lee thought.

"She needs time to mend, Lee. Time to heal."

"Do you really think she's going to *heal*?" Lee spat out the words. "It's all hugs and kisses for you, isn't it? Some part of Glorianna came back. Aren't we the heroes?"

Sebastian's right hand clenched, reminding Lee that the wizards' lightning, a magic that had been dormant in Sebastian until the previous year, was now a power the incubus-wizard could wield with deadly effect.

"Suit yourself," Sebastian said as he headed for the house. "But if this little discussion produces weeds or stones in Glorianna's gardens, *you're* cleaning them up."

Lee headed toward the walled garden that held Glorianna's landscapes, the pieces of the world that she kept balanced through the resonance of her own heart. Then he saw Sebastian veer toward the sandbox Glorianna called the playground and hurried to catch up.

The playground was a wooden, calf-high box that was about the size of a marriage bed and was filled with sand. Attached to it was another wooden box, about half that length, that was filled with gravel and had a bench to sit on. Glorianna had made the box as a place for Ephemera to play without there being any consequences in the landscapes where people lived. It was also the means that Sebastian and Michael had used to reach Belladonna.

Michael was in the box, one knee resting on the gravel, a shapeless brown hat shadowing his face from the summer sun. Maybe it was the brim that kept the man from seeing them approach, but Lee thought it had more to do with the

Magician being focused on the items in the playground's sand.

"Ah, come on, wild child. Come on," Michael said. "I wasn't meaning it like that, so you have to stop bringing me such things."

Sebastian grinned as he looked at the handful of pocket watches poking out of the sand. Then he laughed out loud when a mantel clock that was missing its hands pushed out of the sand.

"Guardians and Guides," Lee exploded. "What are you doing?"

Startled, Michael almost tipped over. He gave them a sour look as he stood up and carefully stepped out of the box. "It's just a misunderstanding. We'll get it cleared up. Eventually."

Lee stared as another pocket watch poked out of the sand like a shiny gold clam. "You're teaching the world to *steal* things?"

"No," Michael said, looking flustered as he pulled off his hat.

"Then what is that?" Lee pointed to the playground.

"A misunderstanding." Now Michael's voice carried a hint of temper.

"You taught Ephemera to be a thief," Lee said. Then he gave Sebastian a hard look. "I guess the two of you are more suited to each other than I thought."

"Have a care," Michael warned.

Lee swore under his breath. He shouldn't have needed a reminder that Ephemera shaped itself by manifesting the resonances of the human heart. And on Glorianna's island, the world was more responsive to people's emotions than anywhere else.

Moments later, all three men clamped hands over their noses and backed away from each other.

"Daylight, Magician!" Sebastian said. "Did you just fart?"

Michael huffed and pointed to the sand in the playground. "Stinkweed. The wild child has started making it in response to swear words. And if you're wondering who influenced Ephemera so that it creates a weed that smells like farts every time someone swears, all I can tell you is it wasn't me." Turning, he pointed at the stinkweed plant. "But

Lee wasn't standing in the box to play with you, so you shouldn't be listening to him so closely that you turn his words into plants."

The stinkweed sank into the sand. Since the smell didn't disappear as fast, the men walked away from the playground.

"So," Sebastian said, wheezing a little. "*Did* you teach the world to steal?"

"No," Michael said firmly. Then he faltered. "At least, I don't think I did. I just said . . ." Taking a couple more steps away from the playground, he lowered his voice. "I just said I'd like to steal a little time so that Glorianna wouldn't feel she has to take up her work as a Landscaper so soon and could rest a while longer."

"And Ephemera has been bringing you timepieces since then?" Sebastian laughed long and loud.

"It's amusing as long as you're not the one trying to explain why you have a basket of broken pocket watches," Michael grumbled.

"All broken? So the world isn't sneaking into people's houses and—"

"Don't even be *thinking* that," Michael said. "No, I'm fairly sure it's been finding these things in the dumping grounds of various landscapes. At least, I'm hoping that's what the wild child has been doing."

"I could talk to Dalton and ask if anyone in Aurora is missing a pocket watch or mantel clock," Sebastian said. "As a law enforcer, he'd have heard about a mysterious thief."

"Oh, sure," Michael said agreeably. "And with a handful of diamonds and a couple of emeralds the size of sparrows' eggs, I'll be able to pay for whatever the wild child took without permission."

Things popped out of the ground with enough force and speed to zip past their faces. Sebastian caught one. He opened his hand, stared at the emerald, then handed it to Michael. Without saying a word, he hunted in the grass and found the diamonds and the other emerald.

He gave the emerald and most of the diamonds to Michael, then dropped one diamond in his shirt pocket. "Finder's fee," he said with a grin.

"You're welcome to it," Michael sighed. "If I'd known I

could have gems for the asking, I could have been a wealthy man."

"You wouldn't have asked for more than you need," Sebastian said.

"Maybe. Maybe not. Truth is, the wild child didn't start giving me such things until I made my bit of a garden inside Glorianna's."

Having heard all he could stomach, Lee walked away from them and went to the gate in the two-acre walled garden. Slipping through the gate, he followed the paths to the beds that represented Sanctuary, the landscapes that nurtured and protected Ephemera's currents of Light. Each of those places had been alone once, isolated by distance and the nature of the world. Then Glorianna brought them together, connecting them to give the Guardians of Light access to each other. Most of those places still kept themselves apart from the hurry and scurry of people's lives, but the landscape most people thought of as Sanctuary was an open place where anyone could come to rest and renew the spirit.

Anyone whose heart resonated with Sanctuary, that is.

Did Glorianna still resonate with the Places of Light? If she walked across the stationary bridge that connected her island to Sanctuary, *would* she end up in the right place? Or would Ephemera send her somewhere else?

If she found herself in a different place, would she take the step between here and there and return to her garden? Or would she disappear into a landscape that appealed to Belladonna?

All their lives, Lee had been her working partner and her closest friend as well as her brother. He'd had few friends outside the family because he'd needed to be so careful of what he said, whom he trusted.

He'd had plenty of acquaintances once he left the school and began traveling to check on the stationary and resonating bridges that allowed people to cross over from one part of Ephemera to another. And he hadn't lacked for casual lovers. But there had been no one he could share his life with, no one he had dared trust with his family's secrets—and bringing anyone in close enough to know his family meant letting them get close enough to learn at least some of the secrets.

Lee sighed and rubbed his forearm. It wasn't just a bone

Michael had broken. The Magician had also broken the friendship that had been forming between them, had broken the trust. The feeling of betrayal had hurt as much as the broken arm.

What hurt even more was that Michael had asked for Sebastian's help to find a way into a landscape that no one should have been able to reach. Michael had asked Sebastian, the cousin, and didn't mention the plan to the Bridge, the brother, the one who had put aside his own life to support Glorianna.

And the Magician and the incubus-wizard had done it—they had created a bridge out of memories, heart, and music that was strong enough to draw Belladonna back to the Island in the Mist and the part of her that belonged to the Light. The part of her that was Glorianna.

Rubbing a hand over his chest, as if that would ease the ache in his heart, Lee turned away from the access points that led to the Light and headed for the part of the garden where he knew his sister would be.

She spent hours sitting on a small bench she'd placed in front of the beds that were the access points to her dark landscapes. She didn't even weed the other parts of her garden unless someone was with her, but the beds for the dark landscapes she tended with meticulous care.

He approached her, his footsteps loud on the gravel path. At least, it sounded loud to him, but she didn't turn her head to see who was coming.

"Want some company?" he called.

Now she turned her head and he saw Belladonna, the woman who had cast out the Light in her own heart to become the monster Evil feared. In that moment, he saw cruelty in her eyes, a dark, rich desire to send him into a landscape where suffering was a man's only lover.

Then the look faded, and Glorianna smiled at him and said, "Sure."

She shifted on the bench, making room for him.

He hesitated before sitting so close to her—and hated himself for it.

"Something interesting?" he asked, trying to remember how easy it used to be to talk to her.

"Yes," she replied as she pointed to a grass triangle.

He studied it and frowned. "Why did you rearrange the

access points for the other dark landscapes to have that triangle close to the Den?"

"I didn't rearrange anything. Ephemera did." Glorianna also frowned. "The Den of Iniquity is still at the center of the dark landscapes that resonate with me, but Ephemera shifted their access points to make room for this new connection."

"But it's only connected with the Den," Lee said.

"The other dark landscapes aren't connected to each other either except through the Den, so that's not strange. Besides, demon landscapes aren't exactly hospitable."

"The Merry Makers are hospitable. They're always willing to have someone for dinner." Of course, the hapless person who stumbled into the Merry Makers' landscape usually ended up *being* dinner.

She didn't give him a disapproving smile or an elbow jab.

His sister would have. Before she split her heart to save the world, she would have.

"So where is this landscape?" Lee asked.

"I don't know. That's why it's so puzzling. It doesn't resonate with me yet, but Ephemera seems to think it wants to. It's like only one part of it has begun resonating with me, but that's not enough to—"

"You're not crossing over!" he shouted as he shot to his feet. "You don't know anything about that place except it's a dark landscape."

"That's right. I don't," Belladonna said. She turned her head away from him. "You should leave now."

"Glorianna . . ."

"*Please,* Lee. Get out of the garden. *Now.*"

He took a step away from her. Took another. It hurt him to ask, but he asked because she was his sister and he still loved her. "Do you want Michael? Or Sebastian?"

"No. I don't want anyone in this garden right now."

His own heart had soured this time together. His own hurt at what she had done to save them all and how she came back kept getting in the way. Would it get in the way one time too many?

"I'm sorry, Glorianna," he said.

"So am I."

As he walked away from his sister and her dark landscapes, he heard her say, "Ephemera, hear me."

He wasn't sure who had summoned the world—the Guide who belonged to the Light or the monster who ruled the Dark.

She had walked those landscapes, folding them into each other, turning them into mazes that celebrated her Dark purity, altering them into labyrinths that offered no peace, no comfort. Those things did not exist in her world. She created out of the brutal beauty that came from the undiluted feelings that lived in the dark side of the human heart. She was sublime madness, magnificent rage, divine indifference.

In that place, she had been Belladonna.

Only Belladonna.

Setting her feet on the bench, Glorianna dropped her forehead to her knees and trembled with the effort not to give Ephemera a command as the world's currents of Dark and Light swirled around her, waiting to resonate with whatever her heart wanted.

Unfortunately, when she wasn't vigilant, she craved the undiluted power she had wielded in the dark landscape she had made for the Eater of the World. She wasn't supposed to leave that landscape. The Warrior of Light must drink from the Dark Cup and cast out the Light from her own heart. Once she had done that, she became the greatest danger to the people around her.

But Michael, Sebastian, and Ephemera had found a way to reach her, made her remember who she had been, and hearing the music in Michael's heart, she had used the access point Ephemera had created and taken the step between here and there.

And in taking that step, she had taken back the Light she had cast out of her heart. But she wasn't whole. She wasn't Glorianna Belladonna anymore. She was Glorianna and she was Belladonna. Separate. Opposite. Much like her dark landscapes and Sanctuary. The problem was that the middle ground was missing inside her, and she didn't know how to fix that. Didn't know if anyone could fix that.

Now she had this mysterious landscape that wasn't yet hers. She *thought* its resonance might be enough for her to cross over and find out what the place was—and where it was. Only it didn't feel like a dark landscape, despite Ephemera thinking it should connect with the Den, and it didn't feel like a landscape that belonged to the Light.

And she wasn't sure if that piece of the world called to Glorianna or to Belladonna.

Something rippled through Ephemera's currents of power. Then it washed through her. Both parts of her.

"Maybe it's not the landscape that's calling to me," she whispered as she raised her head to study the triangle of grass.

Someone from that landscape wanted something so much, a heart wish had gone out through the currents of power—and had found her because she wasn't just a powerful Landscaper; she was also a Guide of the Heart.

Glorianna swung her feet off the bench, then lifted them again, startled by the gravel suddenly moving between her feet. A moment later, a pocket watch poked partway out of the gravel.

Oh, that can't be good, she thought as she reached for the watch with the same enthusiasm a person feels when picking up a mouse the family cat left as a gift.

Before she could touch it, the watch wiggled back under the gravel.

She stared at the gravel, then at the triangle of grass. "It's not time for me to go there?"

yes yes yes

At least she understood Ephemera's message.

And she thought it best not to ask her lover where—and how—the wild child had acquired the watch.

Then she heard the music. Michael, tending to the garden he had made within her garden by playing his tin whistle. He heard the song of a place and kept his pieces of the world balanced with tunes—along with the ill-wishing and luck-bringing that were the ways a Magician's power connected with the world.

Giving the triangle of grass a last, thoughtful look, she followed the sound of the whistle until she reached Michael's garden.

He finished the tune and gave her a sheepish smile.

"So what have you and the wild child been up to today?" she asked.

"That depends," he replied. "How do you feel about diamonds and emeralds?"

yes yes yes

Knowing better than to answer when Ephemera was so eager to please, she said, "Play another tune, Magician."

"Lee."

Swearing silently, Lee turned to wait for the man striding from Sanctuary's guesthouse. If he hadn't stopped for some food to add to his pack, he could have slipped away from Sanctuary like he had slipped away from the Island in the Mist after he left Glorianna's garden.

"Honorable Yoshani," he said. "Have you come to argue with me too?"

"Who have you argued with today?" Yoshani asked.

Lee saw nothing but compassion in the holy man's dark eyes. "Michael. Sebastian. Glorianna." He looked away, not wanting to meet Yoshani's eyes. "You all think I'm wrong, that I should accept she will never be the same, and that I should make some kind of peace with Michael because I'm Glorianna's brother and he's as close to being her husband as a man can get without the formal vows."

"He would speak those vows without hesitation. It is Glorianna Dark and Wise who is not ready to take that step." Yoshani hesitated. "You have not asked for my advice, but as we are standing in Sanctuary, I will offer it anyway. There is much hurt and anger in your heart. It clouds your ability to see the people around you for who and what they are now. Perhaps you need this, but a man who does the work you do cannot afford to hold that much hurt and anger in his heart. People change, Lee. And the world changes. You know this better than most. Don't let these dark feelings change you so much that you can't find your way home again."

"I'll always be able to get back home," Lee said, his voice turning sharp as a way to defy the odd shiver produced by Yoshani's words.

"Will you?" Yoshani asked gently. "If you refuse to see the Landscaper, will you be able to find her landscapes?"

Lee took a couple of steps away from Yoshani. "I have to go."

"Do your friends and family a kindness. Every two days, return to Sanctuary and let us know you are well. There are still wizards and some Dark Guides hiding in the landscapes beyond your mother's and sister's control. And the Bridges who survived the Eater's attack haven't stopped creating bridges for people who need to leave where they are."

Which was why he needed to patrol and stay vigilant. But he couldn't deny that Yoshani's suggestion was prudent.

"All right," he said. "I'll use my island to reach Glorianna's and Mother's landscapes so I'm not spending a lot of time on the roads alone. And every second day I'll return here and give you or Brighid my itinerary for the next bit of journeying."

"Fair enough." Yoshani smiled. "Travel lightly, Lee."

Giving the man a terse nod, Lee walked to the stream and the small island that sat in the middle of it. His own personal landscape, it existed on the bridge of his will when he imposed it over other landscapes. Because of that, Sanctuary—and safety—was never more than a step away.

Nimbly walking across the stepping stones, he jumped to the island and staggered, off balance.

Had there been a moment when the island hadn't been under his feet? But he was in Sanctuary, where the island actually existed. How was it possible for it *not* to be there?

Lee went to the center of the island and left his pack near the fountain—a bowl of black stone with a hollowed-out piece of cane that drew fresh water from the stream. He carefully inspected every section of the island to be certain nothing about it had changed. Then he shifted it to a landscape held by his mother.

Let your heart travel lightly. Because what you bring with you becomes part of the landscape.

Heart's Blessing was one of the first things he had learned, but this was the first time in his twenty-nine years that the words made him uneasy.

Chapter Two

Danyal felt his heart lift as he looked at the two females who were now the center of his nephew Kanzi's life. Four years ago, he had nudged Nalah toward this community of artists and artisans, hoping she was the one who could fill the empty place in Kanzi's life.

She had done more than fill it. That empty place in his nephew now overflowed with energy and joy.

Holding his hands heart-high, Danyal pressed his palms together and spoke the blessing for newborns. "May she give you a hundred tears and a thousand moments of joy."

"Thank you, Uncle," Kanzi said.

"Have you decided on a name?" he asked.

"Nali," Kanzi said at the same moment Nalah said, "Ephyra."

Danyal laughed. "Ah, well. You have a little time yet before the Naming Day to decide."

"We've already decided," Kanzi said.

Nalah followed those words with, "We just don't agree." Then she smiled at Danyal. "What about you, Uncle? Wouldn't you like one of your own? Or perhaps just a wife, someone to be companion and partner? I have some friends who . . ."

Startled, he rocked back, which made her laugh, and that laughter helped him hide the ache produced by the truth in her words. He *would* like to have a partner, to *be* a partner. But Shamans weren't ordinary people. While he'd enjoyed being a lover whenever time and circumstance allowed, he hadn't yet met a woman who was comfortable for long with the way he saw the world—or saw the core of people's hearts. And lately he'd begun to wonder when he'd stopped associating the words "companion" and "partner" with sex.

He'd been wondering about too many things lately.

"No response, Uncle?" Nalah asked, her voice still full of teasing laughter that also held love.

"Nalah," Kanzi said, looking flustered.

"Be easy, Nephew," Danyal said. "I won't admit to playing matchmaker where the two of you are concerned, but I'll allow that I deserved that tease." He playfully shook a finger at Nalah. "But only once."

"Only once," she agreed.

"Why don't I slice some fruit for all of us?" He retreated into the airy kitchen, wanting solitude. He barely had the sense of being alone before his nephew joined him.

"Nalah meant no harm," Kanzi said.

"And no harm was given," Danyal replied quietly as he selected the ripest fruit from the bowl on the table. "Would you loan me your daypack, Nephew?"

"Of course, but . . . You're not staying?"

"My mind needs to think, and my feet need to walk. Your house will be crowded tomorrow." *And having a Shaman here will make your other guests uneasy about being themselves,* he finished silently.

But Kanzi heard what wasn't spoken. "You're always welcome in my house, Uncle. You know that, don't you?"

Danyal smiled as he sliced the fruit and arranged it on a plate. "I know. Being here with the three of you is cool water on parched land, but I would like a day of solitude in the village where I grew up, a day to listen to the land." He put a small bowl in the center of the dish holding the sliced fruit and began cracking nuts.

"Then you'll have your solitary day." Kanzi hesitated. "I'm glad you're here. Nalah is too."

The words were said too heartily to hide the worry. A forty-one-year-old Shaman might take a season's rest after a demanding assignment, but he didn't take a year's leave without a serious reason.

"I am glad to be here." Danyal picked up the dish of fruit and nuts, a clear signal that the conversation had ended. "Let's return to the other room and admire your daughter."

*   *   *

The next morning, Danyal slipped out of Kanzi's house at first light. The daypack held a slender, stoppered jug of water and a rolled flatbread filled with a mixture of dates, chopped nuts, and sweet cheese. It also held his box of pencils and the sheets of paper he used for quick sketches.

Today that was all he needed.

He walked the familiar streets, relieved so few people were up yet. He'd grown up here, and he still loved the feel of the land in this part of Vision. But he'd known early on that he wasn't like the rest of the people in this community, wasn't like his parents or older sister, wasn't even like the young men and women who were called to the village temples and a spiritual life. He was a Shaman, a voice of the world. Someone who wasn't quite human—or was a bit more than human. Someone *different* because of something that emerged in particular bloodlines every generation or so.

It was considered a blessing to have a Shaman in the family, but blessings were often mixed, and many people felt such a relation was best enjoyed at a distance.

Don't fill your pockets with sorrows, he scolded himself.

After taking a long drink of water, he changed direction to refill the jug at the market well. People were up and about now, opening their booths and setting up their merchandise. Soon the market would be packed with people.

As he walked to the well, he was aware of the bold, assessing looks some of the women gave him—until they looked at his face, at his eyes. Then they turned away, their faces filled with shame and fear, hoping he hadn't noticed.

What a body wants isn't always what the heart needs, his mentor Farzeen had said once. *Even among Shamans, your eyes are unusual. When a woman can tell you the color of your eyes, you'll know she sees the man and not just your bond to the world.*

"Something I can do for you, Shaman?"

The man's voice was hearty, but his brown eyes held worry.

Danyal suppressed a sigh. A Shaman put aside his name when he put on the white robes. But he wasn't wearing the white robes today, wasn't working as a voice of the world. That didn't matter to most people, even to a man he'd gone to school with as a boy.

"I'm just refilling my water jug," Danyal said.

"Let me give you a hand with that."

He didn't need a hand, but he let the man haul up the well's bucket and pour the cool water into the jug.

"My thanks," Danyal said as he put the stopper on the jug. Because it would matter, he added, "May your heart travel lightly."

The man flushed with pleasure—and relief. Those words, said by a Shaman, were a blessing heard by the world.

Danyal slipped the jug into the daypack, settled a strap over one shoulder, then headed away from the market, choosing the narrow western road that passed through woodland and fields. A couple of miles down that road was a bridge, and just beyond the bridge was a large tree where he could sit in the shade and enjoy his simple meal.

He wanted to travel, *needed* to travel. He wanted to spend some time in a place where he could be Danyal instead of Shaman. And he needed to find someone who could help him understand why, over the past few weeks, he felt more and more as if someone was always watching him, always aware of him through his connection to Ephemera. Not a malevolent mind, but not a passive, comfortable one either. Some days he wasn't sure if that feeling was real or if his mind was breaking in some way.

Only Farzeen was privy to that worry about his mental health and emotional stability; it was the reason Danyal's old mentor had arranged for him to have a year's leave from all duties.

He saw the bridge that spanned the stream and, beyond it, he saw the big tree where he would have his meal. His stomach rumbled. He laughed softly and lengthened his stride.

Halfway across the bridge, he wasn't laughing anymore. The light dimmed and the air cooled with every step he took. The tree faded until it was no longer there. And a voice suddenly whispered, *not yours.*

Cautious now, and unwilling to believe he'd heard what he'd heard, Danyal took two more steps closer to the other side of the bridge.

A breeze sprang up and pushed at his face, at his chest.

He took another step—and a gust of wind knocked him back.

not yours

A stubborn need to prove that his mind wasn't playing tricks made Danyal lean into the wind. He regained the step he'd lost and took the last step on the bridge. His hand closed over the railing in a painfully tight grip as the land in front of him swam in and out of focus, making him feel dizzy and a little sick.

"What *is* that?" he whispered. Light, dark, shadow. The same, but not the same. And . . .

not yours!

The next gust of wind almost knocked him down.

Danyal carefully backed away from that end of the bridge. The wind swirled around him, pushing until he'd reached the halfway point. Then it vanished.

He stopped and stared at the big tree on the other side of the stream. It had faded when he tried to cross the bridge. Now it was back.

He didn't think the strange land he'd seen on the other side of the bridge was evil, but it wasn't part of the city, wasn't part of anything his people knew. And something wanted him to keep his distance from it.

Retreating to his side of the bridge, Danyal sat on the bank of the stream and forced himself to eat his meal.

What had just happened? Why had land he'd known all his life faded, only to be replaced by something else?

heart wish

Danyal felt currents of power flow around him, through him. He sprang to his feet, alarmed. Then he forced his breathing to slow down. *This* was the awareness that had been watching him for the past few months. Maybe he could get some answers.

"Who are you?"

A hesitation that held hope and disappointment in equal measure.

world

"Ephemera?"

yes yes yes

Ephemera, the living, ever-changing world was actually *talking to him*? How? Why?

Danyal did nothing but breathe as he considered what was happening. The voice that whispered to him might be the world, but in his head it sounded like a child, and like a child, it might flee from anger or demands.

He had asked a question. Ephemera had tried to answer.

"What heart wish?" he asked gently. And what, exactly, *was* a heart wish?

not yours heart wish. danyal heart wish. she will know.

Know what? he wondered. "Who is she?"

Instead of answering, the currents of power drifted away, leaving him shaken.

He needed to tell the Shaman Council at least some of what had just happened. He needed to tell Kanzi not to use the bridge on the western road. And, privately, he needed to ask Farzeen if the Elders knew anything about heart wishes—or had ever heard of the world *speaking* to a Shaman instead of manifesting emotions into tangible pieces of itself.

Danyal tore up the rest of his meal, scattering it for the birds and other creatures. Then he settled the daypack on his shoulder and hurried back to Kanzi's house.

When he reached the house, his nephew took the daypack, handed him a sealed letter, and gave him privacy.

Danyal broke the seal and read . . .

Danyal,

A darkness has come to the city of Vision. We do not know its name or its nature, but now we are certain it is there. Shamans who tend pieces of the northwest and southern parts of the city are reporting that they can no longer see some streets they had walked last season, can no longer sense what is taking place in the hearts of the people who live there—can no longer be a voice for the world because something is making us blind and mute.

We promised you a year to rest from your duties and search for what your own heart seeks. We are breaking that promise, and it grieves me that you will have to end your visit with your nephew and return immediately to take up your new duties as the Keeper of the southern Asylum.

We know you are tired, and we know this is a diffi-cult task—and I alone understand the cruelty of asking this of you when you are concerned about your own sanity. Shamans are not usually Asylum Keepers. We are too attuned to the inner landscapes of the people

*around us, and being around the broken day after day
eventually breaks us too. But the bone readers and fortune tellers are all sending us the same message: there
will be a convergence of allies and enemies in a place
of shadows—a madman and a teacher, a guide and a
monster. The madman is the reason we want one of
our own as Asylum Keeper.*

*The council considered every Shaman, regardless
of age, and we all agreed. It comes down to you, Danyal. You are not like other Shamans. You never were,
and what your own heart needs is something the Elders cannot give you. Because of that and your unusual ability to see the hearts of others so clearly, you
are the one chance we have to save Vision. As much as
you love this city, you are seeking something beyond
what you can find here. We are hoping the needs of
your own heart will lead you to the person who can
help us see and understand the enemy.*

*We will give you every assistance we can, but in the
end, it is your voice that will speak for us all—and for
our piece of Ephemera.*

Travel lightly,
Farzeen, on behalf of the Shaman Council

Danyal folded the letter. Yesterday he would have wondered if they were sending him to the Asylum to find a madman or because they believed he was one. Now that he
knew he was sane, he couldn't tell the council about what
happened on the bridge, couldn't tell them the world had
spoken to him. He didn't want this assignment, but he
needed to be the one who took it because Ephemera's
words floated through his mind: *not yours heart wish. danyal
heart wish. she will know.*

The world communicating with him now wasn't a coinci-
dence. Not when parts of the city were changing and a
strange piece of land appeared and disappeared.

"Let your heart travel lightly, because what you bring
with you becomes part of the landscape," he whispered.

Then he left the room to find Nalah and give his
excuses—and to find Kanzi and warn him to stay away from
the bridge on the western road.

Chapter Three

L ee followed one familiar road after another, maintaining an easy walking pace that covered a good bit of ground in a day. He'd been using his little island to travel between landscapes, as he'd promised Yoshani he would do, but the weather was fine and the walking helped soothe the restless unhappiness he couldn't shake. Just like he couldn't shake the feeling that he should be somewhere else.

But where was that somewhere else? That was the main reason he was walking so much instead of using his island to shift from one bridge location to the next. He'd been keeping a log for the past nine years. He knew where his bridges were located. But keeping an eye out for connections *other* Bridges had made with his mother's or Glorianna's landscapes required being close enough to feel their resonance. Therefore, he was walking so he could check out anything that caught his attention.

It was a good cover story, and he was going to stick to it—especially since it gave him an excuse to avoid his family as well as friends like Teaser, who lived in the Den of Iniquity. The incubus had spent an hour the other night telling him about a girl he had *befriended*. No sex, just walks and a little talk and holding hands. For an incubus, such behavior was unheard-of unless it led to the kind of steamy dreams the incubi fed on.

A couple of years ago, Teaser wouldn't have considered doing such a thing, but a lot of things had changed in the

Den when Sebastian fell in love with Lynnea and opened up possibilities that hadn't existed.

Everyone has a chance to change except me, he thought, struggling to push away the anger and bitterness that often filled him.

All his life, he'd never doubted that keeping Glorianna safe from the wizards was worth the things he didn't dare want for himself—like a real lover or having a piece of his life that wasn't defined by what his sister needed. Lately, he'd begun to wonder if anything he'd done had ever mattered. Did anyone in his family realize how frightened he'd been during those years at the Bridges' School? The instructors had watched him, always ready to report him to the wizards if he manifested some oddity in the power that allowed Bridges to connect pieces of Ephemera. They had watched for any sign that he might be in contact with his sister.

Even after he left the school, he had to report back a couple of times each season to list the bridges he'd created or broken or reinforced. He reported the bridges in his mother Nadia's landscapes and those he'd made in other Landscapers' pieces of the world, but he never admitted to traveling in any of Glorianna's landscapes.

Nine years of being friends and partners as well as siblings. Nine years of being the person she trusted with the landscapes in her care as well as being one of the few people who knew how to find her. Then Michael, a Magician from a country called Elandar, walked into her life and everything changed.

Why have a brother for company when she could have a lover?

You're jealous because you have to share? Sebastian had said, sounding pissed off and appalled. *Grow up, Lee.*

Easy enough for Sebastian to say. He hadn't been in the thick of it day after day. He'd been the Den of Iniquity's premier bad boy, an incubus who could pick up lovers just by strutting down the Den's streets.

Lee sighed as he reached the bridge he wanted to check. That wasn't a fair assessment of Sebastian or the incubus's life. "I wasn't pissed off because I have to share," he muttered. "I *want* Glorianna to be happy. I just—"

The bridge in front of him blurred. Light, dark, and in

between. One moment it was a stationary bridge that linked two of his mother's landscapes, and the next it was resonating wildly in a way he'd never felt before—as if something were grabbing blindly in a desperate attempt to find a handhold anywhere.

Then the blurring stopped and the bridge was back to being a stationary bridge.

"Guardians and Guides," Lee whispered, feeling as if he'd been spun around and shaken. He'd felt something like this only once before, when Michael's sister, Caitlin Marie, had yearned for someone who could understand her. That yearning had resonated through the currents of power so strongly, he had been able to follow the resonance and find her. But Caitlin had been a single resonance. This almost felt like three that were entwined somehow.

What—or who—was he supposed to find this time?

Currents of power swirled around him once, twice, thrice.

When the ground felt steady again, Lee turned away from the bridge and reached for one of the trees that bordered the path to the center of his little island.

No bark under his hand.

Alarmed, he took another step. Then another. *Where . . . ?*

Exerting his will, he resonated with the island—and finally felt it on the other side of the road, a dozen paces from where he stood.

Sweating now, he hurried to the island and stepped up onto ground not too dissimilar from the land he'd just left. Getting a firm grip on the tree in case he became dizzy, he closed his eyes and thought, *Sanctuary. Take me to Sanctuary.*

He heard water. When he opened his eyes, he saw the stream and the stepping stones that led from the island to the bank. He saw the guesthouse where he had a room that was always ready for him—a courtesy, since Sanctuary was one of Glorianna's landscapes.

Picking up his daypack and his large travel pack, Lee stepped off the island, crossed the stones, and headed for the guesthouse. He slipped up to his room quietly, glad he'd avoided Michael's aunt Brighid as well as Yoshani, who acted as host and counselor to the people who, in need of peace or guidance, found their way to this part of Sanctuary.

Glorianna also had a room here, connected to his by the

shared bathroom. But she hadn't left the Island in the Mist since she'd returned from *that place*.

He shook his head, unwilling to think about that right now—especially when his skin felt clammy all of a sudden.

A bath and some sleep. Later he'd go downstairs and get something to eat.

As he ran water in the bathtub, he looked in the mirror over the sink. Tired green eyes looked back at him. His black hair had gotten long enough to look shaggy. He'd have to stop at a barbershop soon and get it cut. His skin was browned a bit from all the time he spent outdoors, but it wasn't leathery or lined, so he didn't look older than his almost thirty years. He wasn't dangerously handsome like Sebastian, but women thought he was attractive, and that was good enough for him.

This was the second time in two weeks that his island hadn't been where he thought it should be, the second time he had felt a resistance when he tried to bring it to him. The island was attuned to him, so that shouldn't happen—unless something was interfering with his connection to it.

Glorianna? No. She knew how much he depended on being able to impose his island over other landscapes in order to tend all the bridges. She knew the value of having fresh water available and being able to camp out overnight without worrying about thieves or anyone else who might want to prey on a lone traveler. Glorianna knew these things. But what about Belladonna?

It was anyone's guess what Belladonna knew.

It was anyone's guess what Belladonna might do.

He still loved his sister. He did. But he was tired of not having the things other men took for granted: a partner, a home. He was tired of being a traveling Bridge. He wanted to do something more with his life, wanted to *be* more.

He didn't know how to do any of those things without feeling like he had abandoned the people who needed him most—his mother, his sister, the rest of the family.

Currents of power swirled around him once, twice, leaving him a little off balance.

"Those are troubles for another day," he sighed as he turned off the taps and stripped out of his dirty clothes. Settling into the water, he leaned back, closed his eyes, and tried to ignore the confusion filling his heart.

They call themselves Tryad, children of the Triple Goddess. They crept into the city of Vision, pathetically hoping to gain a foothold here, but my wizards caught two of the creatures for my examination.

A Tryad is three beings who inhabit a core body, which consists of the brain (but the mind is distinct to each), the internal organs, and bones. Height doesn't change, and there is no significant difference in weight between the aspects, as they refer to themselves. However, there are sufficient differences in muscle and body shape to be noticeable, especially between the weakest and strongest of the three. Each has a distinct face, and features like the color of skin, eyes, and hair can vary widely. Each has its own personality, its own memories, although they can share an experience to some degree.

One member of a Tryad has a brand on the left arm—a heart within a triangle. This allows them to identify others of their race, since they are never open about their presence in a city.

This ability for only one of them to bear the proof of a physical change fascinates me, so I have conducted some tests. Violations like burns or cuts on one have no effect on the other two. Despite being part of the shared core, a broken bone, if it is a clean fracture, only hobbles the one on whom the injury was inflicted, although the other two experience weakness and pain in that limb and are severely limited in its use. A fever produced in one will weaken the other two to some degree, or they may suffer a minor version of the same illness. However, if a hand is amputated on one, that hand is lost to all three. Interestingly enough, removing the eyes from one of the aspects does not blind the other two. Neither does destroying the eardrums carry over to a loss of hearing in the other two aspects. On the other hand, the teeth and tongue appear to be part of the core, and if lost in one are lost in all.

It took me some time to recall what I had learned during my training, but as I experimented with my specimens, I remembered the reports about this demon race.

Dark Guides found these creatures generations ago, before the world was broken during the war between the Guides of the Heart and the Eater of the World. Some of the Dark Guides sowed their seed in females whose hearts already fed the Dark currents of the world, so that offspring would be born with an instinct for discord—and maybe even some portion of the wizards' gift of persuasion.

We helped them turn against their own kind. We helped them break their piece of the world away from the rest of Ephemera, and then salted their hearts with guilt and blame that soured their land, spreading those feelings like swift-growing weeds. Even after we abandoned them, our resonance in their hearts helped them crush their own hope, their own future. There is so much destruction a Dark Guide can accomplish when the hatred in one sibling is nurtured and disguised as love.

Yes, we have seen these creatures before. We have used them to change the resonance of other landscapes into something darker. When a race is so different, it becomes easy to blame them when things begin to go wrong, as things will when wizards put some effort into reshaping a place.

They call themselves Tryad. We call them scapegoats.

—*an entry in the Book of Dark Secrets*

Chapter Four

Zhahar hurriedly cleaned her teeth, then wet a cloth and washed her face and under her arms—and sent a prayer to the Triple Goddess to help her stay downwind of anyone important.

"Can't be late," she muttered as she grabbed underclothes out of drawers. "Not today." She found a clean pair of trousers suitable for work, but the only short-sleeved tunic left in the closet was Sholeh's. Fortunately, that shade of green favored her complexion and brown hair as well as her sister's fairer skin and auburn hair.

One of them would have to do some washing this evening—and it would probably end up being her, since Sholeh had to keep up with her studies. Maybe Zeela?

She would have a better chance of teaching a pig how to fly.

=I'll wash the clothes tonight,= Zeela said.

Startled by the offer, Zhahar almost missed a step as she rushed to the alcove that served as their kitchen. It was tempting to grab her daypack and run to catch the omnibus, but Sholeh tended to get shaky and disoriented if they didn't break their fast in the morning and eat light meals throughout the day.

Sholeh? Zhahar called as she stuffed a couple of dates into her mouth and slathered soft sweet cheese over a piece of flatbread. *I had to wear your last clean tunic. I'll try not to get it dirty, so you'll be presentable for your class later.* When there was no answer, she stopped her hasty attempt to rush off to work. *Sholeh?*

=Leave her be,= Zeela said.

Zhahar's hands began to shake. She put the flatbread on the counter. Zeela had *that* edge to her voice only when one of her sisters was hurt. *What happened?*

=She was dismissed from the school.=

Why? She worked hard because she wanted this so much!

=They said she missed too many classes.=

But she did the work!

Bitterness filled Zeela's voice. =She couldn't play by the one-face rules and be where they wanted her to be when they wanted her to be there. So she can't study at the school anymore.=

But we paid all that money. Zhahar looked around. She and her sisters did their best to make it a home, but it didn't change the truth. They lived in that shabby little room, eating cheap foods and wearing secondhand clothes to pay for Sholeh's studies. *If they won't let her study, will they give back the money?*

=Is that all you care about? The money?=

No! Zhahar snapped. *But we can't afford to find another place for her to study unless we get it back!*

::Don't fight. Please.:: Sholeh sounded broken, beaten. ::Zhahar, you have to get to work. We can't afford to have you fail too.::

=You didn't fail!= Zeela shouted.

::Let me rest. I don't want to be in view today.::

Nothing to be done, especially because Sholeh was right: if they were going to stay in the city of Vision, one of them had to earn wages.

Zhahar grabbed her daypack and rushed for the door. Then she went back, folded the flatbread and cheese, and wrapped it in a napkin. If she wasn't *too* late, the new Asylum Keeper might not notice her absence, and she might have the few minutes she needed to finish her simple meal.

Zhahar twitched with impatience as she waited her turn to exit the omnibus. Some drivers were more interested in maintaining their schedules than giving people time to get off at their stop. Fortunately for her and other passengers, the teams of horses that pulled the omnibuses knew what the bell meant and planted their feet when they reached a stop, regardless of what the driver wanted.

As soon as she stepped down, Zhahar hurried across the street, then trotted along the path through a weedy, overgrown piece of land that was supposed to be a small park for those whose minds had healed enough to meet the world partway. Since the people in the city were supposed to maintain the park as a kindness to those who had been hurt in mind or spirit, the neglected land felt like a shouted warning that *her* kind would never be accepted.

The one time Zeela had seen this park, she'd thought it was a sign that they were in the wrong place. But in the city of Vision, you could find only what you could see, and this piece of it was the one place they had found when they arrived that offered something for each of them.

Other parts of Ephemera where it had been safe for Tryad to work or trade—albeit showing only one face and never admitting they were a "demon" race—had turned dangerous or had disappeared completely. And the last time the moorings failed to hold a connection between their land and another place in Ephemera, parts of Tryadnea had vanished, along with the Tryad who hadn't returned to the homeland in time.

A few months ago, Morragen Medusah a Zephyra, the leader of the Tryad, had sensed the presence of another land that was within reach. Using her magic, she twisted a little of Ephemera's currents of power into six moorings between Tryadnea and the city of Vision. Then she asked some of her people to brave the unknown city in the hopes that the Tryad would be able to secure the moorings and provide a stable connection between Tryadnea and that piece of the world.

Sholeh speculated that what the a Zephyra Tryad could do with the currents of power was the equivalent of people putting down the gangplank on a moving ship and rushing down to the dock to secure the lines before the gangplank fell into the water and the ship drifted away. A risky business, since those securing the lines could be left behind, and those left on the ship might not have enough supplies remaining to survive until they found another port.

But that was the truth the people of Tryadnea had faced for generations, so Sholeh Zeela a Zhahar and five other

Tryad had crossed over to the city of Vision. Despite its vastness, the city had held little promise for her kind so far—and time was running out. The other five Tryads, perhaps feeling too desperate to be careful, had revealed too much about themselves. According to the letters Zhahar had received from the Zephyra aspect, the Tryad who weren't dead and had managed to get home were too wounded, physically or emotionally, to return to Vision.

Now Zhahar and her sisters were the only Tryad left. Despite their best efforts to live in a way that secured Tryadnea to Vision, the mooring the a Zephyra Tryad had spun for them kept slipping, and that connection, the *last* connection, was now in the northern part of the city. If it slipped to a place beyond Vision or snapped completely, they would be left here with no way to get home.

She couldn't think about that. Every day the a Zhahar Tryad remained here created another tiny thread that helped Tryadnea retain its connection to Vision—and that, in turn, gave Zhahar and her sisters another day to find *something* that would end a cycle that was tearing the hearts out of the Tryad people. Their homeland needed the sustenance of connection to another part of the world. When they were adrift, rivers and streams dried up. Rain was sparse if it fell at all. Crops withered in soil that couldn't nourish them. Little by little, Tryadnea became a desert that couldn't sustain its people. The only time there was a sign of the land restoring itself was when they were anchored to another piece of the world—and every time less of Tryadnea bloomed.

We'll stay here until autumn, Zhahar thought. *If we don't find some occupation for Sholeh and Zeela by autumn, we need to move to another part of the city. Maybe head north so we have a chance of getting home before the mooring fails.*

Of course, if she lost this job, they would have to move much sooner.

Zhahar pulled a ring of keys out of her daypack and unlocked the gate that separated the Asylum's grounds from the weedy park. Pushing open the gate just enough to slip through, she locked it again before running to the staff room in the main building, where she could store her pack and pick up the blue jacket that indicated she was a Handler.

Putting the keys in her trouser pocket, she had almost

closed her daypack into the lock bin assigned to her when she remembered the flatbread. Pulling it out, she locked her bin, unwrapped the napkin, and bit into the simple meal, filling her mouth with bread and sweet cheese.

Naturally, the moment her mouth was full, the door opened.

"Where have you been?" Kobrah asked as she hurried into the room. She eyed the flatbread for a moment before looking away.

Not damaged enough to be an inmate, but too damaged by her past to see anything but the darkest pieces of the city, Kobrah had been found by Zeela in the weedy park one night, unconscious and beaten. After shifting who was in view, Zhahar had alerted the Handlers who tended the inmates at night.

Uncertain if Kobrah should be made an inmate or sent to The Temples for some kind of heart healing, the former Keeper allowed her to stay until he could decide. Zhahar had given Kobrah small tasks—weeding in the garden, sweeping a floor—while the young woman healed physically. By the time the Keeper made up his mind, Kobrah was working as Zhahar's Helper. Instead of being locked up or sent away, she was given room and board and token wages—not quite an inmate, but it was understood that Kobrah couldn't leave the Asylum alone.

That was six months ago. The only clue to Kobrah's past was that she looked at every man who worked at the Asylum with suspicion bordering on hatred and called them all Chayne—the name of the man who had damaged her.

Saying nothing, Zhahar divided the flatbread and gave Kobrah half. When the woman was upset, she wouldn't eat, and the uncertainty swirling around the arrival of the new Keeper had put everyone on edge.

"*He* was looking for you," Kobrah said. "He's already spoken to the other Handlers. And I wanted to talk to you about something else."

Zhahar heard the fear in Kobrah's voice, watched the way the woman's hands trembled. But she wasn't sure the fear and trembling were caused by the same thing—especially when Kobrah took a bite of the flatbread.

Then the door opened again, and the new Asylum Keeper walked into the room.

Zhahar choked down the mouthful of food. Anyone might wear white trousers and a lightweight, collarless shirt. But only one group of people wore the long white robes.

The new Keeper was a *Shaman*?

"You are Zhahar?" he asked.

His voice held the song of a mountain stream and a whisper of summer grass. His dark hair was grizzled. His face was unlined, giving her no clue to his age. And he had the most beautiful eyes she had ever seen.

Kobrah elbowed her, a sharp reminder that she hadn't answered the man—and a Shaman wasn't someone she wanted looking at her too closely.

"Yes, Keeper," she replied. "I am Zhahar."

He glanced at the flatbread. Then his eyes returned to hers.

"Do you value your work?" he asked.

"I want to keep this job."

"That isn't what I asked."

His smile was gentle, but it held regret—and a decision.

She spoke before he could. "I'm sorry I was late, sir. My sister received bad news and was distressed this morning, so I stayed a few minutes too long to comfort her."

"Ah." He reached out and touched her arm. Just a brush of fingertips, but she felt the warmth of that touch. "Does she need you with her today?"

Sympathy. Understanding. Genuine concern.

"No, sir. My other sister will be with her today. And we'll all be together this evening." Not quite a lie, since they *would* be together that evening. The words just didn't acknowledge that her sisters were always with her.

Nodding, he turned his eyes to Kobrah. "You are a Helper?"

"Yes. I mostly work with Zhahar, Keeper."

He looked uncomfortable. "'Keeper' is a title I must use when I deal with other officials, but it is not what I am. So I will tell you what I told the other Handlers and their Helpers. When we are private as we are now, you may call me Danyal. Out there"—he made a graceful move with one hand to indicate the grounds—"you should address me as Shaman."

She wasn't going to be dismissed. Knowing she would still have a job made her momentarily dizzy.

Which the Shaman noticed, of course, because Shamans noticed everything.

Please, Zhahar thought. *Let my secret remain secret.*

"Break your fast," Danyal said. His smile was a bit apologetic. "You had good reason to be tardy today, but I must set an example. The others have their assignments. There is only one task left, and it is hard, dirty work. Meet me outside in ten minutes."

He walked out of the room.

Zhahar looked at Sholeh's tunic and sighed.

"Do you think he really gave the other Helpers permission to call him Danyal?" Kobrah asked.

"No." She took another bite of bread and cheese. It would probably sour her stomach, but she needed the food if she was going to spend the day laboring. "But I doubt any of the Helpers were present when he talked to the Handlers. What did you want to tell me?"

Kobrah nibbled her piece of flatbread before answering. "I made a friend. He's not like anyone I met before. He doesn't dress like us or talk like us. We take walks and hold hands, and he doesn't mind just being friends. He's met me a few times now, and he's going to come back. I don't know when, but he's going to come back."

Startled, Zhahar ate the rest of her bread. Kobrah, taking a walk with *a man*? What man? Kobrah wasn't allowed to leave the grounds. She couldn't stand the male Handlers, and becoming involved with an inmate was foolish as well as dangerous. So who could it be?

"Where did you meet him?" she asked.

Kobrah hesitated too long. "In a dream. He says we meet in the twilight of waking dreams."

She sucked in a breath. A couple of the inmates had talked about dream lovers. The woman had become calmer, more lucid, but the man had become violent when he wasn't allowed to leave in order to "cross over" and meet his lover in the flesh. If this was a new symptom of madness . . .

"What does he look like?"

"He has pale hair and blue eyes. His name is Teaser," Kobrah said.

Zhahar wiped her hands on the napkin, offered it to Kobrah, then folded it and put it in her pack.

"We had better find the Shaman and get to work," she said.

"I'd like to hear more about your friend, but I think it best that this remains between the two of us. At least for now."

Kobrah studied her, then nodded.

They hurried outside and found the Shaman waiting for them. There were Handlers, Helpers, and inmates all over the grounds, washing windows, weeding flower beds, draining the murky water out of a reflecting pond. But the worst job was on the other side of the pond from the main building—a small, two-room building that hadn't been used in years.

"We're supposed to clean this?" Kobrah asked when Danyal led them inside.

"Yes," he replied.

"How clean?" Zhahar asked.

"What is precious to you will be held in this room," Danyal said. "How clean does it need to be?"

Zhahar sighed. "I understand."

He smiled. "Then I'll leave you to your work."

She and Kobrah did work. They swept and washed and scoured and polished. By the end of the day, the small building was clean and the grounds showed noticeable improvement. Through it all, the Shaman walked among them, helping, listening, being.

When she got home, she was more than ready for Zeela to come into view. She sank into a deep rest—not quite full sleep, but not participating with the others. True sleep came only when all three of them were at rest, and was something they needed at least once every third day.

As memories of the day drifted through her mind, one realization brought her back to the surface.

=What's wrong?= Zeela asked.

Nothing. When you were one who was three, you really couldn't lie to your sisters. *Something I just realized about the Shaman.*

=What is that?= Zeela sounded wary.

He has the most beautiful eyes, but despite all the times I spoke with him today, looked into his face, into those eyes . . . I can't tell you what color they are.

Too restless to sleep, Danyal followed the lit walkways between the buildings. He had been at the Asylum only a day and already felt the weight of this place seeping into his body, into his heart. If he'd come here with any lingering doubts about his own sanity, this place would have crushed him. And it still might.

Some of the inmates were truly ill beyond changing. However, many of them had simply lost their way, confused by the nature of the world. But until their minds were able to gain some peace and clarity, those people would remain in the Asylum, unable to see a future in a city that should have held boundless futures.

Zhahar disturbed him. He had sensed nothing unusual about her until that brief touch of his fingers against her arm.

Light, dark, shadow. Just like that strange place on the other side of the bridge.

Then it was as if he'd touched three people, had picked up the feel of three distinct heart-cores. That shouldn't have happened with one person. Unless she wasn't a person at all. Unless she was something else.

Was she, or something like her, the reason some of the streets had disappeared from the Shamans' sight? Was she working at the Asylum because it benefited her plans in some way?

"Why is this place so important?" he whispered, looking around at shabby buildings and unkempt grounds.

heart wish

He shivered despite the lingering heat. That voice again. Those words again.

He was exhausted from the demands of his first day as Keeper and the rushed journey to reach the Asylum after receiving the letter from the Shaman Council. Throughout the two days of travel, he had thought the council had been foolish to send him here on the advice of bone readers and fortune tellers.

Now he knew they had been right. All of them had been right. Something was going to happen here. Something that required a Shaman's presence. When it came, he had to be ready.

He hurried to the apartment that would be his home for the next year. After locking up for the night, he took the sleeping draught he used occasionally when he needed to block out everyone and everything for a few hours.

Chapter Five

Lee frowned at the footbridge that spanned a narrow creek. It *should* have been a stationary bridge that connected two of his mother's daylight landscapes and one of Glorianna's. And it did. But the bridge now also resonated with Foggy Downs, a dark landscape tended by Michael.

This wasn't the first bridge he'd come across in the past two weeks that suddenly provided access to one of Michael's pieces of Elandar, but he was getting tired of dealing with this weird piggyback. Seemed like there couldn't be a landscape connected to Glorianna anymore without there also being access to something connected to Michael. That meant someone crossing over a stationary bridge they'd used for years could suddenly end up in another part of the world because the Bridge—meaning him—couldn't unravel the resonance of Michael from Glorianna.

Damn Magician. Just another way he had fouled up their lives.

He lied, something dark whispered inside Lee. *You thought Michael wanted to be your friend, but it was just an excuse to get close to your sister, to use her for his own purpose. Caitlin Marie is a Landscaper too. She could have been the bait used to trap the Eater of the World. But the Magician chose to sacrifice your sister instead.*

Lee rubbed his forehead, trying to ease the ache between his eyes. Yes, Michael had lied to all of them, had known from the beginning that Glorianna could stop the

Eater of the World. But he didn't tell any of them, didn't give the family a chance to discuss what they should do. He waited until he and Glorianna went to one of his landscapes. *Then* he told her that damn story about the Warrior of Light and convinced her to throw her life away to save the world.

"I could have reached her, you ripe bastard," Lee whispered as he stared at the bridge. "There had been time to get into that landscape before she locked it tight. I could have gotten in and gotten her out if you hadn't entangled us all in a fight, hadn't broken my arm. Damn you, Michael. She wouldn't have suffered in that place for so long, wouldn't have come back different. If you hadn't stopped me, I could have reached her."

He sneezed twice, then felt the burn in his chest. *Sick? Now? Damn it!*

Well, a cold wasn't so bad.

Then again, a cold could make a man fuzzy-headed enough to impair judgment, and a man working alone and trying to make decisions about the resonance of bridges that connected one piece of Ephemera with another couldn't afford to have his judgment impaired.

Nothing he could do about this footbridge, so he would check out the other bridge he sensed was nearby and then rest for a day or two.

Where to go for that rest? Ah, that was the question. If he went back to Aurora, he could stay in his own cottage, using his illness as an excuse not to socialize. He'd get sympathy—and plenty of food—from his mother and Lynnea, Sebastian's wife. Food and sympathy and quiet when he didn't want company.

Or he could go back to the guesthouse in Sanctuary. There would be food and sympathy there too. But there was also a chance Glorianna would be visiting Sanctuary, and he wasn't ready to see her again—especially if he looked into her green eyes and saw Belladonna looking back at him.

She scared him now in ways she never had before, and he didn't know what to do about that.

Aurora, then. Or maybe the Den. Sebastian would let him use the room the Justice Maker still kept at the bordello and wouldn't be inclined to fuss over him.

First he would check out the other bridge. It wasn't in his

notebook, so it wasn't a bridge he had made. Which meant another Bridge had created a means of reaching Nadia's landscapes, and anyone who could reach Nadia's landscapes had the potential of reaching Glorianna's.

He coughed again and felt the congestion in his chest break. He bent over and spat out phlegm. When he straightened, he had to wait for the dizziness to pass.

He'd been pushing too hard. Too little food, too little rest. Feeling too stubborn to return home after getting soaked during a storm last week. The urgency to check all the bridges that connected to his family's landscapes was of his own making, an excuse to avoid the very people his diligence helped protect. He kept pushing himself because he was angry with Michael and Glorianna and even with Sebastian, and his own feelings resonating through Ephemera's currents of power had come back to bite him in the ass—or in the chest—when a summer shower had turned into a cold storm.

"One more bridge," he said, his voice crackling. He turned toward the spot where he'd left his little island imposed over this landscape and wondered if it would be there. It drifted every time he left it to inspect a bridge. Never far, but the certainty of the island never being more than a step away when he needed it had been a safety line when he worked alone in the dark landscapes.

He didn't have that certainty anymore. He could make a one-shot bridge out of a small stone and get home if he found himself in a dangerous situation, but that wasn't the same.

He felt the island's resonance and knew he was almost beside it. As his fingers brushed against one of the trees, someone hailed him. He lowered his hand and turned, still only a step away from safety.

"Guardians and Guides," the young man said as he hurried up to Lee. "Are you a Bridge? I haven't seen another of us since the School. . . ." He trailed off.

"Since the Eater of the World destroyed the Landscapers' and Bridges' Schools." Lee studied the stranger. Maybe old enough to have finished his training. "I'm Lee." No reason to hide it or deny it.

"I'm Mason, but mostly I go by Mace. I guess you escaped too?"

"I wasn't at the School when the Eater attacked."

"Me neither," Mace said. "I was working with one of the instructors, and the resonance of the bridge just *changed* to resonate with a dark landscape. My instructor thought I'd done something, so after he stabilized the bridge, he crossed over to make sure it still connected the landscapes it was supposed to, which included access back to the School. As soon as he stepped off the bridge and disappeared into another landscape, I started across." Mace swallowed hard. "I think I heard him scream. I think I did. Next thing I remember is running until I came to another bridge. I ran across that one."

"Where did you end up?" Lee asked.

"Not sure. Wasn't anyplace I knew. I've been wandering since then. Finally reached this landscape a couple of days ago." Mace looked around. "First place I've been in a while that looks close to home."

Why don't I believe him? Lee thought. *What is it about his story that doesn't feel true?* "So you've been wandering. I know parts of this landscape fairly well. You must have been on the other side of that rise. I would have seen you sooner otherwise. Why didn't you head for the other bridge? It would have been closer."

Mace shrugged. He continued to look around, but there was less innocence in his eyes now. "I was hoping to find a village or even a farmhouse." His eyes widened. "Guardians. Do you think this is one of Belladonna's landscapes?"

False note in the voice. Calculation in the eyes.

"You're not even close," Lee lied, turning his voice into a slap. "Can't you feel the difference between a dark landscape and a daylight one?"

Mace hunched his shoulders and looked embarrassed. "Sure, I can. It's just . . . Well, wouldn't you want to see Belladonna?"

"I've seen her." Remembering the pure malevolence that sometimes filled his sister's eyes since her return from the landscape that caged the Eater of the World, Lee shuddered. "Trust me. You don't want to."

"I think I do," Mace said. "I've never seen a Dark Guide. . . ."

"She's not a Dark Guide!" Lee snapped. Turning away from the footbridge that *could* bring Mace to one of Glorianna's landscapes, Lee headed for the other bridge.

Like the Guardians of the Light and the Guides of the Heart who, long ago, were created as a response to human hearts crying out for help and guidance, the Dark Guides had been manifested by Ephemera in response to the darkness that dwells within the human heart. Glorianna wasn't just a Landscaper; she was a true Guide of the Heart. Even if Belladonna reveled in dark emotions, she was still one half of Glorianna Belladonna and *couldn't* change into a Dark Guide. Nothing and no one could *change* into a Dark Guide. Not even the wizards who were descended from them but weren't purebloods.

Are you sure? a sly voice whispered in his mind. *Are you really sure? She's done so many things the rest of you can't do. Would you be afraid of her if you were sure?*

"Do you mind if I walk along with you?" Mace asked, hurrying to catch up to him. "It's been a while since I've had another Bridge to talk to."

"Suit yourself," Lee replied. "I'm going to check out that other bridge and see if I can determine who made it and what landscapes are connected by it."

"You can do that? Tell who made a bridge?"

Can't you? Too many questions about this man and none of the right answers. "Sometimes I can recognize the resonance of a Bridge I know." And he wondered if that unknown bridge would resonate with Mace.

"That's interesting," Mace said.

Lee started coughing again. He wished he hadn't responded to that hail, wished he'd stepped onto the island and gone back to Sanctuary, or at least been standing on safe ground while he observed the man. Now that he'd spoken to Mace, he didn't want to leave the other Bridge alone in one of Nadia's landscapes.

"You don't sound good," Mace said. "You sure you're up to more walking?"

Lee struggled to draw in the air he needed without starting another coughing fit. "Do you see a village or farmhouse where I could ask for shelter?"

"No."

"Then I'm going on to the next bridge to see if it will lead to a place where I can stay for a few days."

"What if we cross over into one of Belladonna's landscapes?"

"We hope whoever finds us doesn't want to eat us."

Mace didn't say another thing all the way to the next bridge.

Lee saw the men clustered around a small fire near the bridge and slowed down. The other reason he wanted to buy some time before getting closer was walking beside him.

While the majority of people weren't sensitive enough to Ephemera to notice such things, a landscape did hold the signature resonance of the Landscaper who kept it balanced, and a bridge held the signature resonance of the Bridge who created it. He was close enough to that other bridge now to be certain that it connected to a landscape he didn't know—and that Mace had been the one who created it.

Did the other man cross my path by chance? Lee wondered. *Or had it been Mace's intention all along to get me close to this bridge and these men?* He wasn't carrying a pack because he'd left it on the island. Mace wasn't carrying anything either, and if the man had been wandering as he'd said, he should have picked up a water skin and some kind of pack that would fit a change of clothes and a day's worth of food.

Unless Mace had left his gear at a camp.

"Maybe they'll share their fire and a bit of food," Mace said, raising a hand in greeting.

"Don't call attention to yourself," Lee said as he slipped a hand into his trouser pocket. "Don't you remember any of your training? Those are rough-looking men. I didn't get the impression you knew much about this landscape, so we don't have anything between us worth stealing and no information to trade."

"Don't you know this landscape?" Mace asked.

"Like I said, I know parts of it, but not this area," he lied. His fingers curled around three smooth stones in his pocket. Infusing the power of a Bridge into the stones, he could create one-shot bridges that would take a person to a specific landscape—if the person resonated with that landscape. Or he could make resonating bridges from the one-shots, which would send a person to one of the landscapes that resonated with that person's heart.

Something about the way those men stood up and

watched him and Mace made Lee wonder how they had been able to reach one of Nadia's daylight landscapes in the first place.

He took a step to the side, putting a little distance between himself and Mace as he rubbed the stones and began turning them into resonating bridges.

"What's wrong? They might be able to help us." Mace's face held an expression of hurt puzzlement.

The expression was perfect. Too bad it didn't match the look in Mace's eyes.

"Help us do what?" Lee asked. Holding the stones, he pulled his hand out of his pocket. His other hand reached back for his island. For a moment, his fingers brushed against the bark of one of the trees that grew near the path. Then he felt nothing.

Come on, he thought as he shifted another step away from Mace, who now watched him with predatory interest. *Come on. Why aren't you there?*

The men were moving toward them, and two of them . . . Oh, he'd seen enough of them in his life to recognize *that* resonance.

"You bastard," Lee said softly. "You're working for the *wizards*? Don't you know what they are, who most of them serve?"

"They're going to save Ephemera," Mace said. "*We're* going to save Ephemera. And you're going to help us."

Lee glanced at the men approaching too fast. Guardians and Guides! Why couldn't he find the island? All he needed to do was stay free long enough to take that step. Then he would be out of reach and could shift the island back to Sanctuary. But the island kept fading, as if it couldn't be *here* long enough to hold him.

"What did they offer you?" he asked, stalling for time.

"I'm going to be the wizards' personal Bridge," Mace said. "They know about places you haven't imagined, but *I've* seen those places. *I'm* going to be the most important person in the world. After the wizards, of course."

"What about the Dark Guides?" Lee took another step back. "Don't you think they're important?"

"*Belladonna* is the *only* Dark Guide," Mace said earnestly. "And once she's destroyed . . ." He shrugged and gave Lee a happy-child smile.

He's insane, Lee thought. *Or else he's controlled enough to be a danger to everyone Glorianna tried to protect from the wizards and the Dark Guides. If he finds a way to help those bastards reach Sanctuary and the Places of Light . . .*

The Warrior of Light must drink from the Dark Cup. What Glorianna had become in the dark landscape she had created to hold the Eater of the World had changed her. He couldn't accept the woman who came back because she had made that terrible place from the darkest parts of her own heart—and he still saw that darkness when he looked into Belladonna's eyes. But she was still his sister, and he still loved her, and this he could do for her and their mother.

Guardians of the Light and Guides of the Heart, keep my family safe.

Clenching the three stones that just needed to connect with another person to become active, resonating bridges, Lee held out his other hand to Mace and said urgently, "Take my hand. The magic that will take us to one of Belladonna's landscapes lasts only a moment."

If Mace had been in his right mind, the words would have made no sense. But he held out his hand without hesitation or question. Grabbing Mace's hand, Lee ran toward the men, his chest and lungs burning.

I reject all that is Belladonna. I deny all that is Glorianna. I have no place in her landscapes. I do not belong to any place that resonates with her. I WANT NO PART OF HER!

A moment of pure anger, of truth unfettered by a lifetime of love.

Lee felt something snap inside him, felt the change in the resonance of his own heart. Felt the pain of losing something he had counted on existing forever.

He slammed into the other men, knocking two of them down and yanking Mace off his feet to add to the tangle. The other men fell on him, and the two wizards were grabbing and yelling, "Don't kill him!"

Ephemera, take me to the landscape farthest from this place. And take these hearts with me.

He wasn't a Landscaper and had no reason to believe Ephemera would listen to him the way it listened to Glorianna or Michael. But as the wizards grabbed him, Lee opened his hand, and the three stones that were now resonating bridges fell into the tangle of bodies and limbs.

Then he screamed as Ephemera pulled them all into a whirlwind as it tried to find a place that resonated with all their conflicting hearts.

Glorianna sat on the bench near the koi pond and breathed in the peace of Sanctuary. She had shaped this place to protect some of Ephemera's Places of Light. She had also wanted to help the people who tended those places reach one another, learn from one another. Sanctuary was beautiful, and there were many small spots that gave more than they took from her. But out of all of those small pieces, the koi pond was her favorite.

Was it because the koi's world, with water that glistened in the sunlight and yet was partially shadowed by the plants, so clearly illustrated the simple lesson that there had to be Dark and Light in all landscapes? Even here, in a Place of Light, there were threads of Dark power that flowed in unity with the thick currents of Light. A piece of the world that belonged on one side of the scale of Dark and Light still needed a touch of the other side to stay in balance within itself.

That was also true for a person, although finding that balance again after it was destroyed in a human heart was much harder.

Or was she often drawn to the koi pond when she was tired or troubled because, like the koi, the whole of a Landscaper's world was bound within walls?

Landscapers were women who acted as the bedrock for pieces of Ephemera and the sieve through which the world manifested all the wants and dreams and wishes, for good or ill, that came from all the hearts that lived in those places. In her part of the world, those women had built walled gardens where they kept access points to landscapes that could be as close as the next village or as far away as part of a distant land. They tended that ground, watering and weeding, turning the soil, and through those simple tasks they remained aware of those places in between the times when they used their access points to cross over to those pieces of the world and interact with the place and the people.

There were seven levels of Landscapers. Some could do no more than act as a sieve that kept the world from manifesting every person's wishes and feelings. Others were stronger and could, by their presence, provide opportunities that would help a person take another step toward a true heart wish—the kind of wish that changed lives.

There were seven levels of Landscapers. And then there was Glorianna Belladonna, who was a Guide of the Heart—a descendant of the Guides who had originally defeated and caged the Eater of the World.

And like those first Guides, she learned that there were all kinds of cages.

Everyone lives within the walls built by their own hearts, she thought. *But most people aren't aware of that, so they're also not aware of the boundaries—or that some things, no matter how much they are loved, can drift out of reach.*

"Should I be offended that the koi receive a visit from you before I do?" a male voice asked, the sound like warm silk over skin.

Smiling, she shifted on the bench to make room for him. "Honorable Yoshani."

He sat beside her, returning her smile but saying nothing.

"That pond makes up the koi's world," Glorianna said. "Do you think they know there is something beyond the sunny parts and the parts shadowed by water plants?"

"They know that when the shadow of the heron falls across their world, they must hide or be eaten. Just as they know the people who sit on this bench bring them food," Yoshani replied. "Why are you are wondering about the koi?"

"I was actually thinking about how a Landscaper's life is contained within the walls of her own garden." *And how a heart can become caged by duty,* she added silently.

Yoshani looked thoughtful, then shook his head. "Your work is contained within the garden, but not all of your life. You spend time in some of your mother's landscapes—the village where you grew up resonates with her, not you. You travel with Michael to some of his landscapes, and you visit Caitlin Marie in Darling's Harbor. That is not a constricted life."

No, it isn't, she agreed silently. *But it's not my life I'm really wondering about.*

"What are you thinking, Glorianna Dark and Wise?"

Nothing she wanted to share yet, so she said, "Glorianna is not much of either anymore. And Belladonna . . ."

"Do you still feel split asunder?"

"I am split asunder." She looked into the dark eyes that held so much warmth and listened to a heart she knew well. "Were you asked to watch over me while Michael checks his landscapes?"

Michael had created a simple garden within her garden so that he could travel quickly to the parts of Elandar that were in his keeping. Before he met her and learned more about his own heritage and connection to Ephemera, he used to spend weeks on the road, traveling from one place to the next.

Yoshani smiled. "Yes, and I'm glad to have the opportunity. The last time I was asked to watch over you, the experience changed my life. Perhaps it will again."

"Perhaps you shouldn't wish for such a thing."

He took her hand. She flinched at the touch, then chose to accept it. Michael's touch, whether it was casual or in the heat of lovemaking, felt natural. So did her cousin Sebastian's touch. Maybe because they were the ones whose hearts had found a way to reach hers. But with everyone else, even her mother, Nadia, there was still a moment when dark feelings wanted to rise in response to a touch— because where she had been, in that landscape she had created, anything that could touch would most likely also kill.

"Michael wouldn't say why he didn't want you to be alone on your island. Will you tell me?"

She studied the holy man who had been her friend since she was fifteen years old, who had helped her shape this part of Sanctuary into a place where people could come to find peace and renew their spirits. He had crossed over to an unknown landscape with her when the hearts living there had called out so strongly she had to respond. He was a trusted counselor to many who visited Sanctuary. And he was the person she trusted to be a guide for a Guide of the Heart.

"A landscape is calling to me," she said, watching the koi. "A dark landscape." She felt the sudden tension in his body, but he said nothing, so she could give him more words. "Its access point appeared in my garden a few weeks ago."

"In the same way Lighthaven first came to your attention?" he asked, referring to a Place of Light she had saved from the Eater of the World.

"Yes." Ephemera had brought a bowl-shaped stone and a silver cuff bracelet from Lighthaven to act as an access point she could use to cross over. Taking that step between here and there had begun her connections to the White Isle—and to Michael and his sister Caitlin Marie, a gifted young Landscaper who had been condemned as a sorceress because no one in her village had understood her power. "But for this landscape, Ephemera has brought a triangle of grass as an access point. It calls to me, but there isn't enough of a connection yet for me to cross over."

"So you wait to see if the connection grows or fades, yes?" Yoshani asked. "You've done this before."

"I've done this before," she agreed.

"Then why is it different now?"

She turned her head and looked at him. Her fingers tightened on his, giving him no escape.

"Because," Belladonna said, "Michael is afraid I'll disappear into a dark landscape and not come back."

She looked into Yoshani's eyes. They held alarm now. His heart hammered; she could feel his pulse through his fingers.

"Say it," he said quietly.

"I want to call Ephemera." Her voice was malevolent and dreamy. "I want to call Ephemera and have it wrap you in vines as thick as tree limbs. Wrap you in vines full of thorns that will pierce your skin so you hang over the koi pond like a succulent, bloody fruit. I could have done that *there*. I did that *there*. There was nothing I couldn't do when I was *there*."

"Is that what you want to do to me?" Yoshani asked.

Did she? Desire swept through her. . . .

???

. . . and Ephemera trembled, but the world wouldn't disobey her. No matter what she asked of it.

She took a deep breath, willing the side of her that belonged to the Light to be the part of her sitting by the koi pond with a friend.

"No," Glorianna said. "I don't want to do that."

"Yes, you do." Yoshani placed his other hand over their

clasped ones. "But today you choose not to. Isn't that how a life is shaped? By all the choices that we make each day?"

"How did you get to be so wise?"

"I watch the koi and the clouds, and I learned from you."

They sat in companionable silence. Then Glorianna said, "Did Brighid bake today?"

Laughing, Yoshani pulled her to her feet. "So that was the reason Michael's journey began today and you agreed to visit."

"Maybe. It seemed a shame to ignore fresh bread."

"Indeed."

As they headed for the guesthouse, currents of power swirled around her, through her. She stopped and looked toward the small island that divided a stream.

Something is changing, she thought. *Has already changed.*

"It appears someone else has kept track of baking day," Yoshani said.

"No." Glorianna headed for the island. "Something's wrong."

Nothing is wrong. The heart has no secrets from you. You just haven't wanted to acknowledge what you felt in Lee's heart the last time he visited the Island in the Mist. Wasn't that one of your own sorrows all of these years? That he never had a life of his own because you needed him? But . . .

"Lee?" she called. "Lee!" She ran across the stepping stones. The moment her feet touched the island, she knew.

"Glorianna!" Yoshani rushed up behind her.

"He's not here." She walked to the center of the island where the fountain drew fresh water from the stream. Lee's pack was sitting there, unbuckled, as if he'd intended to come right back.

"I'll look around," Yoshani said, sounding calm yet grim.

She sat on the bench by the fountain and closed her eyes. She had created this island, had intended it to be a private sanctuary within Sanctuary. But the island had resonated with Lee the moment he set foot on it. It had become a small landscape that he could impose over any other landscape. Safe ground.

The grief swelled up inside her—and a painful joy. Her eyes filled with those feelings until the feelings spilled over as tears.

"Travel lightly, brother," she whispered. *Ephemera, hear me. Give him opportunities to find the life he seeks. But if he wants to come back, help him find his way home.*

"Glorianna." Yoshani went down on one knee in front of her.

"He doesn't resonate with me anymore," she said. "He doesn't belong in my landscapes anymore. He crossed over to somewhere else."

"Where would he go?" Yoshani asked.

"Somewhere I can't." She swallowed tears. "I need to return to the Island in the Mist and leave a message for Michael. Then I need to get messages to Sebastian and my mother. Will you help me?"

He let out a pained sigh as he started to rise. "Yes, of course." He froze, then sank back down. "Your mother's landscapes are held protected within your garden. And so are Michael's."

"Yes."

"If Lee no longer resonates with your landscapes, he won't be able to reach theirs either, won't be able to reach Sebastian in the Den or Nadia in Aurora."

"No. He won't."

"What about Caitlin Marie's landscapes?"

"Her garden isn't held within my garden, so he should be able to cross over to her landscapes if he wants to."

Yoshani bowed his head. "But he won't."

"No, he won't."

"Then he's left all of you."

Because of me, she thought. *He left everyone he knew because of me.*

"Come away," Yoshani said, rising to his feet. "We'll take the pack and store it in his room at the guesthouse. Unless you think he'll call the island to him and would want the pack?"

She rose, wishing they'd had one more of those silly sibling quarrels so that she could smile about it when she thought of him. "Lee can't call the island. It doesn't belong to him anymore."

Chapter Six

Friends and family gathered at Philo's Place in the Den, using the indoor dining room for this private meeting. Glorianna wasn't sure why she'd chosen the Den instead of Nadia's house in Aurora. Maybe because she needed to say these words in a landscape that was hers instead of one held by her mother?

She and Yoshani had left a message for Michael where he would find it the moment he returned from Foggy Downs, the village that was first on his list to visit. After leaving a message at Nadia's house, she and Yoshani had gone to the Den.

She had created this landscape for Sebastian when they were fifteen years old. He had needed a place where he would feel welcome, would feel at home. She had taken a dark piece of a city and reshaped it into this carnal carnival out of the wants and dreams and needs of the young incubus Sebastian had been.

The Den and the man had changed over the years, had matured. Had almost parted ways. In fact, she had almost lost her cousin when he'd been captured and taken to Wizard City, but he was still here. She needed to remember that a person could find his way home if his heart still belonged to a place or the people who waited for him there.

She managed to remain seated until Teaser walked into the room and grinned at her.

"Hey-a, Glorianna. I wanted to tell you—"

"Not now, Teaser," Yoshani said quietly.

Glorianna pushed away from the table and began to pace. Being a Guide didn't make her any less unhappy as a sister.

Teaser looked from one to the other, his grin fading. "Has something happened?"

"Yes," Yoshani replied, "but let's wait for everyone to arrive before we discuss it."

"Daylight," Teaser muttered. "I'll go see what Philo has to drink." He walked through the door that led to the kitchen.

Before he returned, Sebastian's wife, Lynnea, entered the dining room. "Glorianna! It's wonderful to see you here."

"No, it's not," Teaser said as he swung back into the room with a tray full of bottles and glasses. "Well, it is, but she's not here to play cards with the bull demons and win a jar of olives."

"You play for olives?" Yoshani asked.

"*I* play for money most of the time, but Philo will trade meals for jars of olives or olive oil, so . . ." Teaser shrugged.

"Is something wrong?" Lynnea asked. "Where is Michael?"

"Foggy Downs," Glorianna replied. "I left a message for him to meet us here, but we won't wait for him."

She saw the alarm in Lynnea's blue eyes, but before Lynnea could ask any questions, Nadia and her husband, Jeb, walked in, followed by Sebastian.

Dressed in a moss green shirt and snug black denim pants, Sebastian had a body that would earn him a second look from any female old enough—or young enough—to dream about a man. The sable hair, sharp green eyes, and sinfully handsome face guaranteed he could have his pick of lovers. And he'd had his pick until he turned in his membership in the "I'm a badass incubus" club, married Lynnea, and became the Justice Maker for the Den. Of course, learning that he had inherited the deadly powers of a wizard from his father and was the heart Glorianna had used as the anchor for the Den might have had something to do with his decision to change careers.

Sebastian looked around. Anticipating him, Glorianna said, "Michael will be back as soon as he can. I didn't ask Caitlin to join us. She'll need to be told, but she doesn't need to be here right now."

"Told what?" Nadia asked at the same time Sebastian said, "Where's Lee?"

Glorianna took a deep breath and let it out in a sigh. "Lee crossed over to another landscape, one that doesn't resonate with me—or with anyone else in the family."

"What do you mean?" "When did this happen?" "Glorianna . . ." Protests and questions from Nadia, Jeb, and Lynnea.

"Wait," Sebastian said sharply. Nudging Lynnea out of his way, he walked up to Glorianna and studied her. "Why do you think he crossed over?"

"I don't think it; I *know* it," Glorianna said.

"He's a Bridge and your brother. He wouldn't leave."

"You're my cousin and you almost did."

"*No.*"

"Yes." *This* was why she'd come to the Den to tell the family about Lee. Because she'd almost lost Sebastian too, and she was hoping he would help the others understand. "You had grown away from the Den, had begun to want something else. If the Eater of the World hadn't escaped when It did, if Lynnea hadn't come to the Den when she did, you would have crossed over one night to rendezvous with a woman you had met in the twilight of waking dreams—and you wouldn't have come back. Even if you'd intended to return to the Den, you wouldn't have found your way back."

"But I did stay," Sebastian protested.

"Because things changed," Glorianna said. "*You* changed. You realigned with the Den in a new way and opened your heart to the daylight landscapes in order to make a life that included the woman you love."

"What does that have to do with Lee walking away from his family?"

"I'm not sure he walked away from everyone." It hurt to admit that.

"Nadia's landscapes are in your garden," Yoshani said quietly. "While we made arrangements for this meeting, you seemed certain that Lee couldn't reach the landscapes held by your mother."

"I did think that at first. But Mother's landscapes don't resonate with me; they resonate with her." Glorianna looked at her mother, who was a Fifth-Level Landscaper.

"Lee is a Bridge. He can pick up a stone and make a one-shot bridge to Aurora anytime he wants to without going through any of my landscapes. So I think he'll still be able to reach you."

"Or he could use that island of his, right?" Jeb asked.

She shook her head, her eyes still on her mother. "That island doesn't resonate with him anymore."

Nadia sucked in a breath and pressed her fingers over her lips.

"Damn the daylight, Glorianna," Sebastian snapped as the door opened behind him. "Why did this happen?"

"Why did what happen?" Michael set his daypack by the door. He hurried over to Glorianna and wrapped an arm around her waist.

Sebastian stared at Michael, whose brown hair was always a little shaggy and whose smoky blue eyes usually held a friendly look and missed little about the people around him. He was a Magician, ill-wisher, and luck-bringer—and he was learning to be a Guide to the world. Ephemera called him the Music because he used music to reach people's hearts and keep his pieces of the world in balance.

After a long moment of staring at Michael, Sebastian's sharp green eyes fixed on Glorianna. "He's acting like a brat because you and the Magician are playing house?"

"Don't be snide about a heart's journey," Glorianna warned. "And Michael and I are *not* playing house."

"Will somebody tell me what's going on?" Michael demanded.

"Lee's gone," Teaser said. "Crossed over somewhere and poofed. Even abandoned his little island."

Michael looked thoughtful. Then he shook his head. "No. He doesn't want to be around me, and I'm sorry to say it, darling, but he's a fair ways out of tune with the darker side of you these days. But he's not out of tune with the Light. The music in him is still in tune with Sanctuary."

"The island that was his personal landscape doesn't resonate with him anymore," Glorianna said.

Michael looked grim. "It should."

She pulled away from him. Couldn't they see she was struggling to accept this? Why wouldn't they let her accept this? "But it doesn't. Because he's had enough. Don't you see? Lee is twenty-nine years old, and he has never had a life of his own because of me."

"Glorianna!" Nadia said sharply, rising to her feet.

"It's true, Mother. You know it is." Feeling desperate, she took a step away from them all. "He trained at the School in order to be a Bridge *for me*. He avoided making friends because he couldn't trust anyone *because of me*. He's never had a lover, never been a lover in the fullest sense, because he wouldn't take the chance of the woman *betraying me*. Then I walked away from him, walked away from everyone. Well, now *he's walked away from me*."

Silence.

"That was quite a performance," Nadia said. "Should we pass a hat and throw in some coins?"

Stunned, Glorianna stared at her mother.

"We are not the only family in Ephemera who has had secrets," Nadia said. "We're not the only family who has had to take some care in what we say and how we live. Your brother wasn't a Bridge for you out of some sense of family duty, Glorianna. He *chose* to work with you. He *chose* to stand with you. If he'd found a woman he loved as deeply as Sebastian loves Lynnea or Michael loves you, he would have brought her around to meet the family, to meet *you*. Lee isn't alone because of you."

Glorianna's eyes stung with unshed tears. "Then why is he gone?"

"When was the last time Lee used the island?" Sebastian asked.

"He was doing a circuit, checking bridges," Yoshani replied. "He returned to Sanctuary every two or three days to replenish his food and check in. When Glorianna noticed the island, I thought Lee had returned." He tried to smile. "It was baking day, and Brighid always set some treats aside for him."

"The music in a man's heart doesn't change that much that fast," Michael said quietly. "I'm not saying Lee didn't find a place of interest to him that isn't within reach of the rest of us, but a man doesn't change that fast."

"Unless something happened to him," Sebastian said.

"Or someone happened to him?" Teaser asked.

Glorianna stiffened. Why hadn't she thought of that when she'd *known* it could happen?

"All right," Michael said. "Who could change a man that fast?"

"Wizards," Sebastian spat. "When I was held captive in Wizard City . . ."

"Your resonance changed," Glorianna finished softly. "Because of what they did to you. We almost lost you, Sebastian."

Michael turned to Yoshani. "You said Lee would check in. Do you know where he was?"

Yoshani picked up a small book from the table beside him. "Lee kept meticulous notes about the bridges he created—where they were, what kind, and what landscapes they connected."

Glorianna pushed her long black hair away from her face and held out a hand for the book. "Let me see that. If he was avoiding my landscapes, he would have been checking bridges in Mother's pieces of Ephemera." She riffled pages until she reached the last notation, then tipped the book when Nadia came up beside her so that her mother could read it too.

"I know that bridge," Nadia said. "It's in the landscape that borders Aurora. It spans a creek near a village called Tully and provides a way to cross over to two of my other landscapes and one of yours."

"So this bridge is in one of your landscapes, Aunt Nadia?" Sebastian asked.

"Yes." Nadia paled. "If Lee ran into trouble . . ."

"Then an enemy may have found a way in," Sebastian finished. "Do you think Michael and I resonate with that other landscape enough to cross the border and visit? What about Dalton and Addison? I'd like to take a look at the bridge Lee was checking, and I'd like to have trained guards coming with us."

"I—" Nadia took a deep breath and squared her shoulders. "I don't think any of you would have trouble, but if something has changed . . ."

"Lee gave me a couple of one-shot bridges that would bring me back to the Den," Teaser said. "I asked for them so I'd feel easier about crossing over to . . . ah . . . visit a new friend."

"I have a couple of one-shots for the Den," Sebastian said.

"If I get separated from the rest of you, I can just take the step between here and there and return to my bit of garden on the Island in the Mist," Michael said.

Sebastian nodded. "Then let's send word to Dalton and Addison. The sooner we figure out where Lee has gone, the better."

Dalton, a law enforcer in Aurora, had his own horse. So did Addison, who worked as a guard in the Den. Since Sebastian wasn't sure the demon cycles that lived in the Den would be able to cross over to the landscape they needed to reach, he and Michael borrowed horses from the law enforcers' stables in Aurora.

Following Nadia's directions to the cairn that marked the border between Aurora and Tully, the four men reached the bridge without incident, but they didn't see any sign of Lee and couldn't find any indication that they were on the *right* side of the bridge.

"If Lee crossed over to check on this bridge from the other side, he could have run into trouble there," Dalton said, shifting in his saddle. "Even a daylight landscape has dark hearts in it. He could have been robbed and left somewhere, wounded."

Sebastian shook his head. "Why would thieves be interested in him? He wasn't carrying anything. His pack was on the island. If he'd felt threatened, he would have stepped back on the island. That's all he needed to do to be in a place thieves couldn't reach."

"Except the island isn't answering him anymore, is it?" Michael said quietly. "So maybe he thought the danger couldn't reach him, but it did."

"Maybe." Sebastian dismounted, glad to feel his own feet on the ground. Ordinary horses wouldn't try to kill you for fun—or eat you—but if he had to depend on something besides his own feet, he still preferred dealing with the demon cycles.

Michael, Dalton, and Addison dismounted. Dropping his reins to ground tie his horse, Addison moved away from the others, studying the ground.

Dalton ground tied his horse, drew his short sword, then tipped his head toward the bridge. "I'll cross over."

"No," Sebastian said. "You have a wife and children."

Dalton gave Sebastian an odd smile. "Justice Maker, this is a stationary bridge between known landscapes. This is as safe as a man can be in Ephemera. And I have the one-shot bridge you gave me that will get me back to the Den."

"All right, then—"

"Captain!" Addison called. "Found something." He pointed at the ground just ahead of where he stood.

They hurried to join him. Addison shook his head and took the reins from Michael and Sebastian.

Sebastian hesitated, then picked up the pocket watch, tugging the chain out of the soil.

"Is that Lee's?" Dalton asked.

Michael muttered under his breath about the wild child.

Sebastian smiled as he handed the broken watch to Michael. "It belongs to the Magician, in a manner of speaking."

Dalton walked ahead of them for a few paces, then stopped and pointed. "Here's another one."

"I'd best fetch the other horses." Addison handed the reins to Michael.

They found two more broken pocket watches while they were still in sight of the bridge.

Sebastian looked at Michael. "Looks like Ephemera is giving us a trail. Should we walk for a bit?"

Michael nodded. "If we keep the creek on our right, we'll be able to retrace our steps."

They walked for several minutes at a brisk pace, Dalton in front and Addison in the rear, leading the four horses.

"Haven't seen another of those watches," Dalton said. "Maybe Lee—"

The wind shifted.

"Guardians and Guides," Dalton said, choking. "What's that smell?"

"Stinkweed," Sebastian and Michael said as they broke into a run.

They slowed when they spotted pieces of broken planks floating in the creek. Holding a hand over their noses and mouths, they cautiously approached what was left of a rough footbridge. At Dalton's signal, Addison hung back with the horses.

The stinkweed spread two man lengths in front of the

bridge. What was left of the planks had been crushed by some kind of thorny vines. Five plants with leaves so dark a green they looked black grew around the area where someone had built a campfire. As they stared at the plants, a flower began pushing out of a fleshy pod.

"Shit!" Dalton yelped, taking a step back.

"A turd plant?" Sebastian asked as he too stepped back. The smell made his eyes water.

"The wild child has been more expressive since Glorianna returned," Michael said.

"Meaning what?" Sebastian backed away from the plants. "That there were five people here the world didn't like?"

"Or didn't like being here," Michael said grimly.

"There's a bit of a rise there," Dalton said. "Enough to hide a small camp. Stay here. I'm going to take a look." He headed toward the rise.

Sebastian studied the ground around the creek. Not that he could tell much beyond the obvious. "Lee didn't make that bridge."

"No," Michael agreed, "but somebody did—and *that* person managed to bring over others who shouldn't have been able to reach a place held by Nadia."

He could think of one kind of person who had been able to travel in the daylight landscapes, regardless of the foulness in their hearts. Wizards. Not just the wizards who were Justice Makers, but the ones who acted on behalf of the Dark Guides.

Dalton whistled, pointed to them, and made a "come along" motion. Another hand signal to Addison had the other guard tying the horses to a couple of young trees before pulling out his short sword and joining them.

Sebastian and Michael hurried up the rise.

"What?" Sebastian asked.

"I've made enough of both kinds of camps to know the difference between making an overnight stop and settling in," Dalton said, looking at Sebastian.

Dalton had been the guard captain who had helped Koltak, Sebastian's wizard father, capture him and bring him to Wizard City—and had protected him when Koltak tried to kill him after Sebastian maimed the wizard's foot. Dismissed and stripped of his rank because he'd protected the incubus, Dalton and his family had ended up in Aurora.

Now Sebastian and Dalton were both law enforcers in their own ways—although the incubus-wizard's interpretation of those duties didn't tend to match the former captain's.

"They waited here for someone?" Sebastian asked, wanting confirmation.

Dalton nodded. "And whatever happened here happened fast enough that they left without breaking camp."

"Then let's take a look around." Michael headed down the rise. He stopped when he reached the tents and tipped his head toward one, then the other. "Sebastian, give me a hand with this."

Moving to the back of the tent, Michael wrapped a hand around the tent peg and waited until Sebastian held the front tent peg. They pulled out the pegs and flipped up that side of the tent, revealing the contents stored inside.

Blanket rolls. Packs. Water skins. Nothing Sebastian wouldn't expect to see. Nothing Lee didn't keep on the island when he was planning to sleep out for a few days while checking the bridges.

When they flipped up the side of the other tent . . .

"Guardians and Guides," Dalton said.

A man lay on the ground, his body blackened. He might have been a young man, but his face and body were so broken, it was hard to tell.

"What happened to him?" Addison asked.

"Wizards' lightning," Sebastian replied, rubbing his thumb against two fingers. "He was struck by wizards' lightning. Looks like he was beaten first, but he was killed by the lightning."

"Maybe he was trying to help Lee fight off a wizard," Dalton said.

"Whatever he was doing here, I'm thinking he wasn't a friend to Lee," Michael said, pointing to the small plants that began poking out of the ground around the man's head.

Even when they were tiny plants, stinkweed was *vile*.

The men backed away.

"All right," Sebastian said. "Assuming the world knows how to count"—he looked at Michael, who shrugged—"five people crossed over to this landscape—one of *Nadia's* landscapes—and made camp. At least one of them was a wizard. Now they're gone. So is Lee. And the only one left in their camp is a dead man. How did they get here, and how did they leave?" He had his own ideas about *how*, but he wanted to hear what the other men had to say.

"Those planks over the creek," Dalton said thoughtfully, looking in that direction. "The bridge that linked Wizard City to the landscape Wizard Koltak traveled through to find you wasn't any different. If that fellow was a Bridge, that could explain how the wizard and his men got here, but not why they stopped here. The wizards who are roaming free in the landscapes still want to destroy Belladonna. Why stop here?"

"Maybe this is as close as they *could* get," Sebastian said. "It took Koltak days to reach me in the Den, and I don't think any wizard or Dark Guide has been able to reach any place held by Glorianna Belladonna since then."

Dalton stiffened. "But if they had someone like Lee, a Bridge who *could* get them into her landscapes . . ."

Sebastian nodded. "A Landscaper, a Bridge, even the thrice-damned wizards would know bridges are checked regularly. Wouldn't be hard to guess that Lee had made most of the bridges in Nadia's landscapes. All they needed to do is find one and wait for him to show up."

"Doesn't explain what happened to them," Addison said.

"One-shot resonating bridge," Michael replied quietly. "When Lee and I were in Raven's Hill, he tossed a stone at a man who was about to start a tavern brawl. The man disappeared before our eyes. Lee didn't know where the man had gone, just that he'd gone to a landscape that resonated with his heart at that moment."

"Probably not a good place if he was about to start a brawl," Sebastian said.

"Probably not," Michael agreed. He shifted his weight from one foot to the other. "Whatever problems Lee has with Glorianna and me, there's one thing about the man I'm sure of: when he realized there was a wizard among those men, he did whatever he could to protect his mother and sister."

"He couldn't get to the island," Sebastian said softly. "Couldn't get away."

"So he grabs some stones and puts enough of the

Bridges' power into them to make them one-shot resonating bridges, trying to get those men away from here," Michael said.

Sebastian nodded. "You throw a few resonating bridges into a tangle of limbs and angry hearts ... Guardians and Guides, Michael. Lee could be anywhere now."

"He could be anywhere," Michael agreed. "And he probably didn't go with those other men willingly."

Sebastian sighed. "We need to get back and tell the others."

"You go on," Michael said. "I'll meet you at the horses."

Sebastian, Dalton, and Addison walked away from the tents. As they approached the broken planks, the stinkweed and turd plants sank into the ground, leaving bare earth.

A few minutes later, Michael joined them.

"We saw what we were supposed to see," Michael said. "Didn't seem right to leave those nasty plants in Nadia's landscape—or to leave a body aboveground, no matter what part he had played in Lee's disappearance."

No, it didn't seem right, Sebastian thought as they mounted and rode back to the cairn and the border that would bring them closer to home. None of it seemed right. But even if Lee *had* been taken by a wizard or was just lost in the landscapes somewhere, he had an idea how they might find him. And judging by Michael's thoughtful expression as they rode back to Aurora, the Magician had the same idea.

Chapter Seven

Danyal removed the broom from the storage cupboard and began sweeping the floors of the two-room building he'd named the Temple of Sorrows and Joy.

It had been a month since his arrival at the Asylum, and it had taken some time for the Handlers and Helpers, as well as the inmates, to adjust to having a Shaman as the Asylum's Keeper. He didn't want this Asylum to be just a place of containment. He wanted it to be a place of healing, providing some of the same assistance to the inmates here as the Shamans gave to people who came to The Temples, the enclosed community in the heart of Vision that was the Shamans' home and training ground.

At his request, his mentor, Farzeen, had sent him a set of gongs and chimes—the tools he had used when he had served in the Temple of Sorrow. And some of the inmates *were* beginning to find relief from their mental or emotional confusion by using the gongs. The release of anger, pain, disappointment, and life's sorrows was starting to provide some peace, was allowing these people to give a voice to heart wounds that had been left untended.

Would that change the balance of Light and Dark in this part of the city?

Danyal paused as he felt the world's whispers shiver through him.

The Asylum was in a part of Vision that was considered a shadow place—a place that was neither light nor dark because it was both and could be found by almost anyone. But no two shadow places were alike. Some were the cool, deep shade found beneath old trees. Some were caverns that could reveal wonders. And some were cold, stagnant places full of creatures with poisoned stingers.

The Shaman Council was right. Something had come to Vision and was scratching around the shadow places, turning some of them dark in a way that hid them from Shamans' eyes. He wasn't familiar with this part of the city, so he didn't know what he couldn't see, but as he walked the streets around the Asylum to become acquainted with the shops and the people, he sensed disturbing pockets of *absence* that made him think a building or even a whole street was beyond his ability to see it and, therefore, protect it.

Peace, Danyal thought as he resumed his sweeping. *If you can't guide your own heart to peace, how can you show the path to others?*

He heard someone running on the path toward the building, heard the clatter on the stairs. Then Kobrah burst in. Her already flushed face turned redder when she saw him.

"Shaman Danyal," she said, flustered. "I'm supposed to sweep the floor."

"Yes, you are," he replied calmly. "But today I'm sweeping the floor. You can do the dusting, then help me set out the mats and gongs."

Her hands fisted in her ankle-length skirt. "I'm sorry I'm late."

He glanced at her. She should have been a well full of sweet, clean water. Instead, she was a broken well full of sharp stones hidden under a few inches of dark, frigid water. Through correspondence with Nalah, his nephew Kanzi's wife, he had learned some things about Kobrah and the pain that had shaped her. What he couldn't tell was how much of the darkness in her had been there before Kobrah, Nalah, and two others had escaped their village. And yet . . .

He didn't stop sweeping, didn't break the rhythmic sound of broom on floor, but he glanced at her again.

Something different. There was a little more water now at the bottom of that broken well, and it wasn't as frigid.

"Have you made a friend?" he asked casually.

Kobrah had been dusting the gongs and the shelves built under the windows. Now she stopped and turned—and

Danyal felt the stones in her well shifting and becoming sharper.

"She told you?" Kobrah's voice was harsh, hateful. Pained.

Danyal stopped sweeping and gave her his full attention. "If you have confided in someone, your trust was not betrayed. I asked because you seem happier." He gestured to the gongs. "I would like to take credit for lifting some of the weight from your heart, but I don't think I'm the reason you've been smiling lately."

Kobrah stared at him, want and wariness in her face.

"I am a Shaman," he said gently. "I know how to listen."

When she continued to stare, he went back to sweeping.

She watched him for a minute. Then, "His name is Teaser. He comes from a place called the Den of Iniquity. He says it's a dark landscape, but it's not a bad place."

She clearly wanted—or expected—him to react badly, so Danyal just went to the cupboard for the dustpan. "What else does Teaser say?" he asked.

She studied him a while longer before she told him that Teaser was from a race called incubus and his best friend was an incubus-wizard named Sebastian who was also the Den's Justice Maker.

Strange words. Mostly likely this friend was someone she had imagined, since Guards did walk the Asylum's grounds at night and would have noticed Kobrah and a stranger—or an inmate—taking a walk in the moonlight.

"How does he reach the Asylum?" Danyal asked.

"Through the twilight of waking dreams."

A little breeze brushed the back of Danyal's legs like a friendly cat, as if to encourage him to believe the words.

A shiver ran through him. That breeze seemed too *aware* to be something natural.

With effort, he pushed that thought aside and focused on Kobrah and what she had told him.

He would send a note to the Shaman Council this evening, but he didn't think this den of iniquity was a part of Vision. That left the question of *where* it was and how someone could travel through dreams.

Many roads led to this city, but few things beyond the city seemed able to set hooks deeply enough to bring in something alien. At least until now.

Which made him wonder again about Zhahar and why he often felt three heart-cores in her instead of one—and why he usually felt the three when she was tired or distracted and, therefore, less able to keep some truth hidden from the one person who sensed she was different. Him.

"He sounds like an interesting man," Danyal said as he set a gong in front of each mat Kobrah had positioned in a circle.

"Yes."

There was no trust in Kobrah's voice. She had confided in him. Now she would wait to see what he did with her words.

Having prepared the room he used to help people release sorrow, he and Kobrah went into the room set aside for joy. In silence they swept and dusted, and the wind chimes sang at their touch.

As part of his morning and evening ritual, he chose a wind chime that had a particular sound. Then he walked the grounds, letting it ring with his movement. Bright notes to encourage bright thoughts and lift hearts toward the Light.

Today he chose one of the larger wind chimes.

"Could I . . . sometime . . . ?"

He looked at Kobrah. Her eyes were fixed on the chime. That gave him hope for her, so he held it out.

When she smiled at him, he saw the girl she had been before dark acts had twisted her life.

He waited until he heard the chimes moving away from the temple. Then he walked over to the main building and went into the room that held the Handlers' lock bins—and saw a strange woman standing in front of Zhahar's open bin, pulling out her blue work jacket.

She had dark brown hair and dark eyes. There was a jagged, raised scar that ran down her left forearm from elbow to wrist. On her left bicep was a tattoo of a heart inside a triangle.

"Who are you?" he asked, his voice ringing with the authority and power of a Shaman.

Storms. Floods. Landslides. That's what he felt when her eyes locked with his.

Dangerous. And somewhat familiar.

"I'm Zeela," she finally said. "Zhahar's sister."

Her answer left him caught on a frozen pond, with the

ice suddenly cracking beneath his feet. A careless move would destroy more than his own life. He was sure of it.

He took a step toward her—and felt the calm summer lake he associated with Zhahar as well as brooks full of bright water.

He had never experienced such confusion in a person who was supposed to be sane. And yet it didn't *feel* like confusion. Which made no more sense than a person with three heart-cores.

"Has something happened to Zhahar?" he asked.

"No," Zeela replied. "And nothing will while I'm around."

He glanced at her boot. "Is that why you carry a knife?"

"I carry more than one." She tipped her head toward the sliding door that closed off a washroom and toilet. "She's in there."

"What happened?" he asked. He had loaned a book to Zhahar for her sister, but he didn't think this woman had much interest in books.

Those dark eyes studied him, and he felt the storms getting closer.

"A woman down the street from where we live was attacked last night. She isn't expected to live through the day. She might have survived the violence done to her body, but her mind was damaged as well, and in the end that is what will kill her. Zhahar can be tough when she needs to be, but Sholeh . . ."

"There are three of you?"

Zeela gave him an edgy smile. "Not unusual in our family. Zhahar is the eldest by a few minutes. Sholeh is the baby, since she left the womb after me."

Danyal rocked back on his heels. Triplets? Was that why he sensed an overlapping of heart-cores? He'd never heard of such a thing happening, but he supposed it could if the emotional attachment between the sisters was strong enough.

Did that mean Sholeh was the bright water?

"Sholeh is the scholar?" he asked, hoping to find out a little more about Zhahar's family.

"Yes." A clipped answer that didn't invite further curiosity.

And you're the warrior. Danyal looked at the sliding

door, then back at Zeela. "Tell Zhahar I'd like to speak with her. It was a pleasure meeting you, Zeela. I hope to have a chance to meet Sholeh someday."

"Shaman."

It sounded like a dismissal.

Danyal went to his office and sat at his desk, determined to review the nighttime reports from the Handlers. But after a minute, he rose and stared out the window.

Storms. Floods. Landslides. Zeela made him uneasy. She was capable of great violence. The scar on her arm wasn't as much proof of that as was the look in her dark eyes. She would do anything to keep her sisters safe, and that was something he couldn't afford to forget if he was going to pry into the mystery of why he could sense all three heart-cores when only one of the sisters was present.

He should report her presence to the Shaman Council. She was a mystery, an unknown that might be the source of Vision's troubles. But if she wasn't the source, if she was only a mystery because he didn't understand some simple truth, he could set some changes in motion that would not be undone easily, if at all.

So he would watch and wait and see if he could gain her trust enough to tell him what made the connection between her and her sisters unusual. And he would ask Farzeen— carefully—if the older man had ever heard of anything like what he was sensing.

A tapping on the door he'd left open. He turned and saw Zhahar, straightening her Handler's jacket.

"You wanted to see me, Shaman Danyal?"

"I met your sister," he said, giving her a gentle smile.

"Yes, she mentioned that when I came out of the washroom."

Was he seeing wariness in Zhahar's blue eyes? "She told me about the woman who was attacked. Perhaps I should have a Guard escort the female Handlers to the omnibus stop from now on if their shift ends after dark."

Zhahar nodded. "That would be wise—and, I think, welcome by all the women who work at the Asylum, not just the Handlers."

Her answer surprised him, because he'd thought she would tell him Zeela was sufficient escort. But the surprise lasted for only a moment. It had become apparent to him over the past month that when it came to dealing with other people, whether they were her colleagues or her assigned inmates, Zhahar was highly intuitive and tended to lead with her heart. She might have a sister who could protect her against would-be attackers, but the other women didn't. Therefore, she would show approval for an escort even if it was inconvenient to her to have someone observing her once she was off the Asylum grounds.

And what had given him the impression it *would* be inconvenient?

"What do you know about the twilight of waking dreams?" he asked, deciding to pursue the other subject that was bothering him. She looked almost fearful until he added, "Kobrah mentioned the phrase, and I wondered if you had any thoughts."

Zhahar licked her lips. "I'm comfortable that whatever Kobrah is experiencing is doing her no harm, and the female inmate who had mentioned being visited by a dream lover was also not being harmed. In fact, her clarity of mind seemed to be improving until . . ."

"Until?" Danyal prodded when it became apparent that she didn't want to say anything more.

"Until the previous Keeper ordered Meddik Benham to give her a sleeping draught that would put her under deeply enough to silence any dreams."

Danyal studied her. "You don't agree with that decision?"

"She was improving," Zhahar said, a touch of stubbornness—and anger—in her voice. "Even if no one else will acknowledge it, she's been declining daily since the dreams stopped."

"Why wasn't I informed of these dreams if they were unknown before?" Danyal asked. "This inmate as well as Kobrah is my responsibility now, Zhahar. I may not be a physician or a mind healer or even a general meddik, but I *am* a Shaman and I am the Asylum's Keeper. As such, I should have the final say on the treatments the inmates receive."

Zhahar lifted her chin and straightened her shoulders, and he saw—and felt—some of Zeela in her body language. "Kobrah isn't an inmate, and what is said to a friend should remain with that friend when no one will be harmed by word or deed. As for the other woman, I'm sure the Handlers on duty made a notation about her 'friend,' especially after a male inmate had to be restrained when he tried to escape in order to 'cross over' to meet *his* dream lover. Deep sedation might have been the right decision for dealing with him, but it damaged the woman. As for why you weren't informed, this happened just before your arrival. We're all still learning what you expect of us. I am not a senior Handler, Shaman Danyal. It is not my place to offer opinions about the Keeper's or the Meddik's decisions."

And yet I heard several opinions about the Asylum and the people who make decisions for those not capable of making choices for themselves. "Is there anything else I should know?" he asked mildly.

She didn't have a chance to answer because another Handler ran in, his jacket splotched with blood.

"Shaman! One of the inmates just attacked Kobrah and bit off one of her fingers!"

Zhahar was the first one out the door, but Danyal was close behind her. Together, they burst out of the building and ran toward the tangle of people on the lawn.

Three Handlers were struggling to secure a restraining jacket on an inmate. Kobrah stood to one side, pale and shaking. Her left hand bled untended; her right still held the wind chimes.

"Damn you for bringing the Light!" the man screamed. "We don't deserve the Light! We don't deserve anything!"

Zhahar rushed over to Kobrah, bunched the bottom of the Helper's gray jacket around the woman's left hand, and held it while Danyal grabbed the man's hair to prevent him from biting the Handlers trying to subdue him.

"We should be drinking pus and eating worms!" the man screamed. "Snuff out the Light before it grows any stronger!"

He didn't like it, but after the Handlers strapped the man to a bed in an isolation cell, Danyal gave permission to use a mouth restraint, as much to protect the Handlers as to prevent the man from biting off his own tongue.

Going to the infirmary wing, he found Kobrah sitting on one of the narrow beds, dressed in a clean white shift. Her left hand was thickly bandaged. She had the groggy look of someone heavily sedated, but her right hand still clenched the short chain attached to the wind chime.

"Kobrah?" Danyal sat on the wooden stool next to the bed. It took her so long to focus on him, he wondered if Meddik Benham had been too generous with the sedative.

She held out the wind chime. "I kept the Light safe. It's important to keep the Light safe."

He took the wind chime. "Yes, it is."

Zhahar breezed into the room, her effort to be cheerful producing whitecaps on her usually calm lake. "I brought you a glass of water, and I found some twine so we can ... Oh. Shaman." She glanced at the wind chime in his hands, then sat on the bed beside Kobrah. "Drink some water. Then you should sleep for a while."

Danyal held out his hand. "Give me the twine."

She pulled a length of twine from her jacket pocket.

He knotted one end of the twine to the wind chime's chain. Pushing aside the gauzy curtains, he secured the other end of the twine to the curtain rod. The light breeze coming in from the fully opened window made the chimes sing.

Kobrah looked at the chimes but was too drugged to respond. Zhahar, on the other hand ... Those blue eyes told him hanging the chimes to comfort Kobrah had earned another level of her trust.

Then he looked down at her boots—and another shiver ran through him.

Why was she wearing the boots that held her sister's knife?

"Get some rest," he said, gently touching Kobrah's shoulder. Looking at Zhahar, he tipped his head and walked out of the infirmary. She joined him a few minutes later.

"The Handler who informed you saw the blood but not the actual injury," Zhahar said. Holding up her left hand, she pinched the bit of finger between knuckle and joint. "The inmate took a chunk of skin and meat, but not bone. More blood than damage."

"Do you know why this happened?"

"He wanted to destroy the wind chime because it called to the Light. Kobrah wouldn't give it to him, so he attacked her. He said ..." She hugged herself. "He said the Dark

Guide would stop tormenting him if he helped destroy the Light."

Dark Guide. Drought. Famine. Death.

"Shaman?"

Danyal didn't realize his eyes were closed until he opened them. "I'm fine. I'm just concerned, and I have much to think about." He touched her arm, fingertips on her jacket at the spot where he'd seen her sister's tattoo.

Storms. Summer lake. Bright water.

"I want to be kept informed about Kobrah's condition—and if there is anything I can do to help."

"You let her keep the wind chime," Zhahar replied softly. "That helped."

Instead of returning to his office—and all the confused hearts wanting counsel—Danyal went to the apartment on the administration building's top floor. Some of the Handlers had rooms in another building on the grounds, but he and Meddik Benham were the only occupants on this floor.

He unlocked the apartment door, relocked it, and made a careful inspection of his home before settling into a chair. He felt vulnerable, and a Shaman, being the voice of the world, should not feel vulnerable. Ever.

Something had entered that poor, addled man, making him an instrument of evil. Another whisper of proof that something was very wrong in this part of the city.

Allies and enemies. A madman and a teacher. A guide and a monster. He'd been sent here because the council believed he could find these things.

But would he find them in time?

Chapter Eight

Sometimes the hated voices whispered in Lee's ear.

You need to get back to your sister. There's danger coming.

All you need to do is cross over to one of Belladonna's landscapes. We'll help you.

You need to get home before it's too late.

Sometimes the hated voices scratched against his mind.

Belladonna needs you. You have to reach her.

Your mother is in danger.

Don't you want to go home?

His answers—whispered or screamed or trapped in his mind—were the same.

I don't have a sister.

My mother is gone.

I have no home.

I don't know Belladonna.

Every time he denied knowing her, he felt the last little heart thread that connected him to Glorianna thin a little more. The day would come when he denied knowing her one time too many and that thread would break completely—and he would never be able to find his way back home.

When the soft persuasion didn't work, they began using the needle that poured fire into his brain and sent his body into thrashing, screaming panic. They laughed as they strapped his head down, forced his eyes open, and put in the drops of poison that clouded his eyes a little more each day until he couldn't see his tormentors, couldn't see anything.

Here in the city of Vision, you can find only what you can see. What do you think a blind man can find here, Bridge?

Nothing. No one. How many times had he said to Nadia, "I don't want to see her!" when she suggested he go to the Island in the Mist to visit Glorianna? Now he *couldn't* see her.

Now he pushed her away with all the strength and love in him. To save her from her enemies.

The words they whispered changed, became as painful as the needle and the drops they put in his eyes.

You want to be hurt, want to be punished for not loving your sister enough. That's why you ended up with us. That's why we punish you. It's what you want.

You can't escape us. We're always with you, always watching. If you try to go home, we'll be close enough to grab you, go with you.

There is no one you can trust because you're surrounded by people loyal to us. No escape, Bridge. We're always with you because you want us with you, want us to punish you for not loving your sister enough.

The words they whispered became as painful as the needle because, after a while, they became true.

Chapter Nine

Zhahar grabbed Kobrah's arm and pulled her out of the way of the male Handlers running into the building toward the sounds of fighting and a man's raging screams. "Stay out here."

"What's going on?" Kobrah asked.

"New inmate. A violent one." Squeezing Kobrah's arm, Zhahar joined the other Handlers.

"Warn the Landscapers!" the man screamed. "Wizards and a Dark Guide have come to this place. *Warn the Landscapers!*"

"What are wizards?" one of the Handlers asked as he tried to muscle closer to the isolation cell.

"Don't know," another said. "And unless one of them drops his pants and takes a dump on a path, why would the groundskeepers care?"

Zhahar tried to slip into the hole left by the two men, but a hand closed on her arm and pulled her back, just as she had done to Kobrah moments before.

"Stay here," Danyal said. "There is already too much help in that room."

Surprised by the anger in his voice, Zhahar looked at him—and shrank away from the storm she saw in his eyes.

He released her arm and moved toward the pack of Handlers trying to get into the room.

Thunder shook the building as if the world had given voice to someone's anger. Handlers looked around and scrambled to clear a path for the Shaman.

Within a couple of minutes, the new inmate was strapped to a bed in the isolation cell, still screaming about wizards and lightning and dark guides.

A couple of minutes after that, Shaman Danyal left the cell with two dark-haired men who looked disheveled and distressed.

As he passed her, Danyal gave her a slashing look that warned her to stay away from that room.

Despite the warning, she waited until she was sure he'd taken the two men up to his office in the administration building. Then she crept to the doorway of the isolation cell.

Two brawny men she hadn't seen before were bending over the bed, whispering to the inmate who still struggled despite the straitjacket and ankle restraints that were secured to the bed's metal railings. One of them reached down and pinched the inside of the inmate's thigh hard enough for the man to cry out in pain.

The other, glancing up and noticing her, mumbled something to his companion. They both looked at her and gave her smiles that made her cold.

::I don't like those men,:: Sholeh said.

=Let's get out of here,= Zeela growled. =It would be too hard to explain my sudden appearance or why I got into a fight with these men.=

They hurt him, Zhahar replied, squaring her shoulders. *On purpose.*

"We're just making him comfortable," one of the men said. The heat in his eyes as he looked at her body . . .

=Get out of here *now*!= Zeela shouted.

"I'll put that in the daily notes for Shaman Danyal," Zhahar said. "He expects to be informed of the care given to all the inmates." And as much as she quailed at the thought of admitting she hadn't followed his command completely, she *was* going to tell Danyal about that pinch—and about that look. If any female at the Asylum was violated by those men, she wouldn't forgive herself for the cowardice of silence—and neither would Danyal.

She turned and walked away, feeling one of the men moving behind her. Then Kobrah stepped in from the outside doorway, a chilling look in her eyes as she stared past Zhahar.

The footsteps stopped, retreated back to the isolation cell.

Hurrying to the outside door, Zhahar left the building, relieved to breathe in dusty, heated air.

"We have a new Chayne?" Kobrah asked.

"Two of them," Zhahar replied. Kobrah's word for men who had power over other people certainly fit the new Handlers.

::I don't like those men,:: Sholeh repeated.

=I'll come into view when it's time to go home,= Zeela said.

Yes, Zhahar agreed. Their middle sister was the strongest of them. She carried knives and brass knuckles when she was in view, and had won the bar fight that had given her the jagged scar on her left arm. Most men weren't foolish enough to look at Zeela the way those new Handlers had looked at Zhahar.

"Isn't your shift over?" Kobrah asked.

"Yes, but I need to speak with Shaman Danyal before I go," Zhahar replied. She looked around, feeling too exposed, too close to the men who made her uneasy. "I'm going to the temple for a few minutes. Do you want to come with me?"

Kobrah stared at the doorway as if her vigilance was the only thing keeping those men in the isolation cell. "Yes, I'll come with you."

They hurried across a lawn that was turning brown and crisp in the late-summer heat, skirted the reflecting pool that turned rank every time Teeko, one of the groundskeepers, filled it with water, and entered the small temple. The gongs that gave a voice to sorrow were always set out in the same order and each had a subtly different tone.

Zhahar knelt on the cushion behind the gong she usually preferred, but hesitated when she reached for the mallet. She thought a moment, then shifted one cushion to her left. A deeper sound. Even struck softly, its resonance reminded her of the thunder that had rolled over the building—and fit the itchy anger and sympathy that the new inmate's screams had stirred in her.

She didn't strike the gong softly the second time. He had fought, so they had to subdue him, but a man who was mind-sick shouldn't be treated with such cruelty.

She struck the gong again. This time Kobrah struck a gong as well, and the sound seemed to wrap around anger and uneasiness, drawing them out of Zhahar.

The next time, Kobrah's voice rose in a wordless sound that conveyed the feelings produced by the strangers.

When the gongs were struck again, Zhahar added her voice to Kobrah's — and hoped the sound now resonating through the room covered the fact that there were four voices expressing their feelings instead of just two.

Standing in front of the desk in his office, Danyal studied the two men and struggled to hide his revulsion of the images that came to him from their heart-cores. Maggots so bloated they burst. Spiny worms crawling under the skin before turning to lightning that would silence a heart or mind.

Despite his ravings, the inmate felt like clean summer rain. These men felt like a festering cesspool.

"Why did you bring him here?" Danyal asked.

"He is our nephew," Styks, the taller of the two men, replied. "Our poor sister's only son. He lost his way in our great city and sought out places that damaged his mind and roughened his heart. It was no longer prudent to try to care for him ourselves. Bringing him here became necessary."

"But why this one?" Danyal persisted. "You told me your sister lived in the northern part of Vision."

"The northwestern part," Pugnos, the shorter man, corrected.

"Which is my point. Why didn't you take your nephew to the Asylum closer to his home? It will be a two-day journey for his mother to come visit him here."

"Ah," Styks said, looking unhappy. "That is one of the reasons we chose this particular place. She tried to help him, but he was drawn to the city's unsavory streets, and his behavior became so degenerate, he attempted to have carnal relations with her."

Danyal stiffened, certain he had misunderstood. "With his mother?"

"Yes," Pugnos said. "They were found, and he was stopped before . . . Well. If he was nearby, she would feel obliged to visit him, and, frankly, we fear for her mind now.

And her physical health has become fragile since that unfortunate episode. Knowing she could not make an arduous journey will allow her distance from her son without guilt. We will encourage her to write to him, of course."

"There are two other reasons we choose this Asylum," Styks said. "One is that I live in the southern part of the city, no more than a mile from here. My brother is staying with me for the time being, so we will both be available to visit often and do whatever we can to help restore our nephew to his right mind."

"That is also why we hired two men to take care of him," Pugnos said. "We did not want our family troubles to take your Handlers and Helpers away from the other inmates."

How convenient, Danyal thought. *A mother who is too fragile to travel and, therefore, will never be seen. And the men they've hired as personal Handlers are better suited to rough work in some of the shadow places than dealing with a man who has a damaged mind.*

Before he could push for more information about the Handlers, he felt a pressure at his temples—and the thought drifted away.

"And your other reason for bringing him here?" Danyal asked, feeling off balance and wondering if he should stop by the infirmary and see Benham.

"Why . . . you," Styks said with a smile. "No other Asylum has a Shaman as its Keeper. We are hoping that you can do what another Keeper could not: restore our nephew's mind. Or at least keep it stable while we wait to see if the medicines our physician provided can cure the disease that's festering in his brain."

"We must be completely truthful about what that disease has done to the boy," Pugnos said, giving his brother a sad look. "The Shaman must be prepared."

"Yes," Styks agreed, not meeting Danyal's eyes. "You heard some of his ravings. He thinks people can disappear just by crossing a bridge. Or that he can make people disappear by throwing a stone at them."

"He insists the world is full of demons and that he has never heard of the great city of Vision," Pugnos said. "He began claiming he came from a different place when his eyesight began to fail. We think it's because a blind man has no future in a place like Vision."

There is more than one way to see, Danyal thought. *You would know that if you came from here.* "Anything else?"

They both lifted their hands as they shrugged. "More than we can think to tell you," Styks said. "But if you can help our sister's boy find his way back home, we will be in your debt."

He didn't want their gratitude or their assistance or their hired muscle. He wanted them off the grounds he tended and away from the people under his care.

Danyal walked around his desk, sat down, and reached for a clean sheet of paper—the first of many that would fill a folder and define a man's life. "I'll need some information about your nephew."

"Of course," Styks said as he and Pugnos settled in the visitors' chairs. "His name is Lee."

Chapter Ten

Michael tossed a few broken pocket watches on the sand inside Ephemera's playground on the Island in the Mist. Then he settled on the bench in the gravel section and pulled out his tin whistle.

"We're going to play the Lee-heart game," he said cheerfully. "Take those pieces of time and leave them where the Lee-heart can find them."

The only response he got was sharp bits of stone jutting up from the sand, as well as patches of bog and some foul-smelling water. He wasn't sure if that was a location or a message—or just Ephemera's effort to bring him *something*.

Closing his eyes, Michael played the last tune he'd heard in Lee's heart. It wasn't the same tune as when he'd first met the man. There was more hurt now in Lee than there had been a year ago, more shadows and sharp edges. While it was tempting to play the tune he remembered, he needed to give Ephemera the heart music of who Lee was *now*.

So he played the music and sent it out through the currents of the world to guide Ephemera to the heart that matched the tune.

He and the wild child had done this once before. He had sent the music in his heart and Sebastian's into a place that couldn't be reached in any other way. By doing that, he had reached Belladonna, the Warrior of Light who had become the monster that Evil feared. He had reached the woman he loved and found the way to help her come home.

Now he was trying to reach out again. Ephemera hadn't found Lee yet, and that was a worry because it meant Lee had changed so much the wild child couldn't match heart to music—or it meant Lee was dead.

No one in the family said those words, but after so many weeks without any kind of news, it was a possibility.

Possible, Michael thought as he began the song again. *But I'm not giving up on you yet, you ripe bastard. I'm not giving up on you.*

He played the song a third time, then lowered the tin whistle. The pocket watches were gone. Ephemera was following the music through the Light and Dark currents of power and had taken the physical messages with it.

Hoping that this time they might get a message in return, Michael went up to the house where Glorianna waited for him.

Chapter Eleven

Zhahar watched the brawny man, that so-called Handler, slip out of the isolation cell and head for the staff toilets on this floor of the inmates' building. Picking up a jug of water and a dipper, she walked briskly across the common area that separated the isolation cells from the rest of the rooms.

The cell's door wasn't locked. Wasn't even secured by the outside chain, which was against the rules.

Her heart hammered, but she didn't look around to see if anyone was watching her. Giving anyone a reason to doubt she was allowed to enter that room would get her into trouble.

::We shouldn't be here,:: Sholeh whispered.

Zhahar opened the door, slipped into the room, and moved to the narrow bed that had strong metal bars where the Handlers could fasten restraints. *I just want to make sure he's all right. Besides the Handlers his uncles hired, no one but Meddik Benham has seen him, and only with one of the uncles present.*

=Has Meddik seen him lately?= Zeela asked grimly. =Not only has he soiled himself, but he hasn't been washed in so long, he reeks.=

I don't know, Zhahar said doubtfully as she looked at the inmate. *I *do* know Shaman Danyal isn't aware of how badly those Handlers are treating this man. He wouldn't allow this.*

Her sisters were silent, which made her nervous. But seeing the inmate, she wondered what was really going on.

Why was Meddik Benham ignoring this man's condition? Why was Danyal?

::The Shaman won't be happy that you're in here,:: Sholeh finally said. ::Not after he told you to stay away so that you don't draw the Chaynes' attention.::

*I know, but . . . *

She looked at the man on the bed and felt her heart clench because of the mistreatment he'd been enduring. And then she felt her heart lift and soar as if someone had just fulfilled a cherished wish.

I've been looking for you, she thought. She couldn't explain the words, but they felt true. They also frightened her because she understood what she was—and what he was.

Having a more personal interest now, she studied his face. His black hair was tangled and greasy. His skin looked pasty sick, and his lips were so parched they had split in a couple of places. She thought the unfocused eyes were green, but they were so cloudy, she wasn't sure.

"Who's there?" he said in a hoarse voice. "Who's there?"

"Shh," Zhahar said, pressing one hand against his shoulder. "I'm Zhahar. I'm one of the Handlers who works here. I've brought you some water." She pulled the small dipper from her pocket, filled it, then set the jug on the floor so that she could raise his head. "Let me dribble the water into your mouth. Easy, now. Easy."

She got a second dipper of water into him before he began to thrash and make vicious sounds.

"Help me," he said. "Please help me." Then he swore at her with such savagery, she took a step back from the bed. "Help me."

The plea, combined with the thrashing and swearing, made her angry, so she stepped up to the bed.

=Let me,= Zeela said.

That brute of a Handler could return at any moment, Zhahar protested. But having Zeela's aspect so close to the surface lent Zhahar strength her arms didn't usually have. She grabbed the man's hair and yanked before saying in a harsh voice, "If you don't want to be treated like a madman, stop acting like one."

"Can't," he gasped. "What they put in the needle . . . does this . . . to me. Please."

=I believe him,= Zeela said. =The Apothecaries who have shops on the shadow streets could make such a thing.=

::I believe him too,:: Sholeh said.

So do I, Zhahar thought. "I'll talk to Shaman Danyal and see what he can do." Releasing the man, she grabbed the water jug and slipped out of the cell. She walked across the common area and caught sight of the hired Handler returning to his post. Unfortunately, he caught sight of her too and gave her—and the cell door—a look that held too much meanness.

As Zhahar set the water jug and dipper on a rolling cart, she heard the man in the isolation cell scream.

Danyal felt a storm of anger roll through him as he stared at Zhahar. She stared back at him, her face set and her hands clenched. Until five days ago, Zhahar had been one of the best Handlers at the Asylum. Yes, there was the oddity about the way her sister Zeela showed up to help, and that overlap of heart-cores made him uneasy, especially after Farzeen's reply to his carefully worded letter indicated that the other Shamans had never heard of such a thing in one person. But he'd been able to count on her—until the new inmate arrived.

Something about that man scratched at him too—at least on the days when his uncles didn't come to visit. That was the main reason he wasn't dismissing Zhahar right now for disobeying his orders again.

"Have you seen him?" Zhahar demanded.

"Meddik Benham—"

"Is either lying or he's being fooled somehow," she snapped.

"Be careful," he warned.

"Shaman, the inmate is parched from lack of water. He's lying in his own excrement. He hasn't been washed since he's been here. Who knows what kind of bruises or raw skin might be under that straitjacket or the other restraints?"

"He's a very sick man." The words didn't sound quite true, didn't feel quite true. And when he'd said them just now, he could have sworn he heard them spoken by the voice that had been whispering in his dreams lately.

"Is he, Shaman?" Zhahar replied. "He says they're doing

this to him, that whatever is in those needles they give him is causing the raging. What if that's true?"

"Why would his uncles do that?"

"I don't know. What if he inherited money and his uncles want control of it? Or they have some other reason to want him out of the way?"

Danyal shook his head. "You've been reading too many stories. I doubt their reasons are that dramatic." *Or that simple,* he added silently.

Then he stiffened as another thought finally came to him. Had he found the madman the bone readers had foretold?

"Aren't we supposed to help the people who have lost their way?" Zhahar argued. "Aren't we supposed to help them go back to the world? Do those gongs in your little temple have some magic power to drain sorrow on their own, or is the belief in the gongs the real magic? If he believes the reason he's insane is because of what they pump into him, will he ever get better as long as he feels those needles being jabbed into him?"

"His name is Lee," Danyal said quietly. "I haven't seen him since that first day because I cause him distress, and I didn't want to add to his burden." Had that really been his own decision or was the idea that he caused the man distress something else that had been whispered in his dreams?

Landscaper! Beware of the wizards! A Dark Guide is near!

Summer rain. Sometimes fierce, sometimes gentle, but always in harmony with the world.

Unlike the men claiming to be Lee's uncles.

Danyal studied Zhahar. "Why is this man so important to you? Out of all the men you've cared for since you began working here, why does this one spur you to defiance?"

Zhahar studied him in return. "It feels like if I don't at least try to help him, something will pass me by. I'll catch hold of the edge of it, but it will be too wispy to hold on to. And then, when it has passed, I'll realize how important it was—and how much I lost."

"This isn't some romantic daydream, is it?" What he was about to do would have the Directors of the Asylums *and* the Shaman Council demanding an explanation. He didn't want to cause that kind of commotion, only to discover Zhahar's feelings were the result of girlish fantasies.

She shook her head.

He wasn't sure he believed her, but he rounded the desk and stopped beside her. "We'll remove him from the care of the men his uncles hired. You will be his Handler and give him the same treatment the others receive. If there is measurable improvement, I will continue to override the treatment his uncles initiated."

"Thank you, Shaman."

For the first time since she stormed into his office, he saw her relax.

"Don't thank me yet," he replied as he headed for the door.

Blinking back tears, Zhahar squared her shoulders and kept her mouth shut.

"I-I don't understand this," Meddik Benham stammered as Nik and Denys, two of the male Handlers, pulled down Lee's shit-soiled pants and revealed the needle marks, bruises, welts, and raw skin. "This couldn't have happened in a day, and I saw no evidence of abuse when I last examined him."

Shaman Danyal studied the Meddik, those beautiful eyes as cold as deep winter. "I believe you. How you were deceived is still a mystery. That you were deceived brings into question all we've been told about this man and about the medicines that were given to him."

Lee began to thrash and scream.

Zhahar stepped forward and gave Nik and Denys an apologetic look. "Shaman, I don't think he's going to respond well to being handled by men. At least for a while."

Danyal hesitated.

"Let me see what Kobrah and I can do. We'll call for assistance if we need it."

Another hesitation, but that was probably due to the hatred on Kobrah's face as she stared at Lee's genitals.

Finally, Danyal nodded. "Clean him up as best you can without removing the restraints. I want a catalog of his injuries. When he's more lucid, he can have a proper bath."

Zhahar waited until the men left the room before turning to Kobrah. "Can you be my Helper with him?"

Something dreadful slipped into Kobrah's eyes.

::She scares me,:: Sholeh said.

=Don't leave him alone with her,= Zeela said. =Not when he's naked.=

"Kobrah?" Zhahar said.

"I won't touch him if he gets a stiffy," Kobrah said.

"All right. Anytime you feel uncomfortable, you tell me."

Kobrah nodded. "I'll get a cart and bring one of the big basins and jugs of warm water."

"Sponges and soft cloths too."

As soon as Kobrah left to fetch the supplies, Zhahar closed the door most of the way. She hurried back to the bed and took Lee's face in her hands—then jerked back when he tried to bite her.

"Lee," she said urgently. "Lee, can you understand me?"

He thrashed a bit more, then seemed to make an effort to hold himself still. "Who . . . ?"

"Zhahar. Do you remember me?"

He turned his head as if focusing on the sound of her voice. "You gave me water."

Relief washed through her. She wasn't sure he'd been aware enough to remember that. "Yes. I'm going to be taking care of you now. The Keeper agreed to give you some time without the medicine—without the needles. But you have to help me. You have to show him you can get better without the medicine."

"I'll . . . try." His face was turned toward the side of the bed where she stood. "Who's with you?"

"My Helper's name is Kobrah. She's gone to fetch some water so we can clean you up a bit."

"No. Who's with you now?"

A chill went through her. "No one is here except me."

His body relaxed so suddenly, she wondered if he'd had some kind of seizure. Then she realized he was falling asleep.

"Lee?"

"Funny," he mumbled, "I was sure there was more than you in the room. I keep hearing three voices speaking in unison."

::He's a one-face,:: Sholeh said. ::It's not possible for him to sense all of us, even when we're all close to the surface.::

And yet he did, Zhahar thought. He'd heard Sholeh's and Zeela's voices in hers when they weren't in view.

=The Shaman senses us,= Zeela said.

::But that's because he's a *Shaman.* And even he doesn't *hear* us.::

Zhahar stood by the bed and watched Lee sleep until Kobrah returned with the cart full of supplies, including some basic ointments for the bruises and raw skin.

Lee wasn't a Shaman, but he was different from other humans. As Zhahar washed the parts of the man she could reach without undoing the restraints, she wondered what he was.

Fever raged through his mind, turning memories into strange landscapes. Convulsions shook his body until he was certain his bones would break apart. Firm but gentle hands draped a cool cloth on his forehead and washed the sweat from his body.

Zhahar. Her name was Zhahar.

Found you, he thought, trying to tell her the simple truth that the fever kept locked in his mind. *Didn't even know where to look, and yet I found you. Like Sebastian found Lynnea. Like Michael found Glorianna.*

Sometimes her voice was a single note; sometimes he heard an intriguing chord that spoke in perfect unison. When she talked to him, she resonated with the conviction that he could get well, and despite the pain and fever, her resonance tugged at him enough to make him listen—and believe. Of course he would get well. Now that he'd found her, he *had* to get well.

He told her about the pain, about the heat. Things she could ease.

He didn't tell her about the nasty voices scratching at his mind, whispering their poison—voices that sounded like the wizards who claimed to be his uncles.

We'll always be with you, one voice snarled. *We'll always be close by. The day you're well enough to leave the Asylum, we'll be waiting. And the next time, we'll take more than your sight, Bridge. Much more.*

We'll always be with you, the other voice crooned, as if offering comfort. *We'll always be close by.*

I know, Lee thought as he shook from the latest convulsions. *There's no escape.*

Before he could decide if he felt troubled or relieved by that truth, the fever took him again and burned all thoughts from his mind.

Chapter Twelve

Danyal watched fury flicker across Pugnos's and Styks's faces before they regained control.

Bloated maggots. Spiny worms under the skin.

"Why were we not informed before this decision was made?" Styks asked.

"The men you hired to take care of your nephew deceived you," Danyal replied.

They hadn't been deceived. He saw that truth in their eyes despite the effort they were making to hide their heart-cores from him. They had hired those men precisely for the harm that would be done.

"The abuse they inflicted on Lee can't be undone completely," he added.

"What does that mean?" Pugnos asked.

"If he wasn't truly mad before, he is now." Danyal laced his voice with regret. "I am confident that we will be able to bring him to a point of being calm, even docile, within the confining environment of the Asylum, but the damage that was done to his mind cannot be repaired. He may be lucid in his madness, but he'll never be able to participate in the real world."

"Then we will take him home again," Styks said. "Care for him there."

"No," Danyal said gently. "Placing him in the Asylum was your choice, and given what I have seen of him, it was the right choice. But when—or if—he ever leaves the Asylum is now my choice. You relinquished all rights to make decisions for your nephew the moment I accepted him as an inmate here."

"We weren't aware of that," Pugnos protested. "We weren't told we couldn't take him away again."

They hadn't been told because it wasn't quite true, but until he discovered who Lee was and heard his side of the story, Danyal wasn't giving him back to these men. "That is regrettable, but it makes no difference. As the Asylum's Keeper, I now have control over Lee's life. However, if this is difficult for you to understand, the Directors of the Asylums hold an audience at The Temples on the day of the new moon. Perhaps you should discuss your nephew's case with them."

Styks tried to mask his fury. Pugnos didn't even try.

"What about the Handlers we hired?" Styks asked.

Danyal shook his head. "As I said, the men you hired deceived you. When their ill treatment of your nephew was discovered, I demanded that they produce the letters that verified their credentials and proved they were qualified for such work." He sighed. "Forgeries. Nothing you gentlemen could have detected, but clear enough to those of us who must be vigilant about such things. I should have demanded to see their credentials when they arrived, but since they were already in your private employ, I was lax in that particular duty. But I have made up for that lapse by filing an official complaint with the city guards, since forging credentials is against the law. I also gave the guards careful descriptions of the two men, who were gone by the time the guards answered my summons. When they're found, they will be questioned. Eventually we will know everything they have done to your nephew."

"We had not expected such diligence," Styks said after a pause.

"Vision is a very large city, but it is also a patchwork of small communities," Danyal said with a smile. "When it comes to keeping the people safe, the city guards, like the Shamans, are always diligent. Isn't that why you brought Lee to this particular Asylum?"

Lightning, quicksand, and foul bogs swirled in their heart-cores. They understood now that he wasn't a tool they could use—and that made him an enemy.

"I have your location," Danyal said, noting how they

both twitched at the words. "When the men who deceived you are found, I'll send word."

"Thank you," Styks said. He hesitated. "Will you also keep us apprised of our nephew's condition?"

"Of course. And may those reports give you hope that Lee will recover enough for you to see some measure of the man he had been."

"Easy now," Zhahar said as she and Kobrah led Lee down the corridor. "One step at a time."

"What . . . ?"

"You've been calm for a whole day. We're taking you to the bathing room so you can have a proper bath. It's going to be a hot day and you still have a touch of fever, so we'll keep the bathwater cool."

She wasn't sure he understood her. He still tended to fight when one of the male Handlers tried to touch him, because he didn't seem to hear her when she told him the men who had mistreated him were gone. But he'd become docile enough when she or Kobrah fed him or gave him water or helped him use the portable commode.

She suspected embarrassment had been a strong incentive for getting well enough to be kept without restraints and, therefore, being able to use the commode by himself.

They had put him in a short robe for the walk to the bathing room, but as soon as Kobrah filled the bath, Zhahar tipped her head toward the door.

"You're not supposed to be alone with him," Kobrah said. "Shaman Danyal said so."

"I'll be fine," Zhahar replied. Kobrah, on the other hand, wouldn't be—although the moonlight walks with her dream friend *had* raised her tolerance for dealing with men. "You supervise getting his room cleaned. And check with house-keeping about replacing that mattress."

Giving Lee a long, somewhat hostile look, Kobrah slipped out of the bathing room and closed the door behind her.

Breathing a sigh of relief, Zhahar matter-of-factly stripped the robe off Lee. "Let me help you into the bath."

"I can do it."

"Next time you can do it," she said tartly. "This time

you're going to accept help so you don't slip and crack your head."

"Daylight," he muttered.

He made the word sound like a curse.

"There are handholds on the wall. Here. Got it?" She guided his hand to the handhold. Her muscles bunched as she offered support on his other side while he eased his weakened body into the water.

His sigh of relief when he settled in the water made them relax. They stripped off the Handler's jacket and set it aside, glad to have their arms bare for a little while. As they turned to reach the basket that held the soaps and sponges . . .

=Zhahar!= Zeela shouted.

. . . Lee lunged, grabbing the left arm. His other hand just missed locking around a throat and, instead, grabbed a fistful of the sleeveless tunic.

"Who are you?" he snarled. "What did you do with Zhahar?"

Shock. They had never been this careless at the Asylum. *Never.* But they'd been so focused on getting him safely into the bath, Zhahar had submerged without conscious thought so that Zeela could come into view and provide the needed muscle.

That kind of casual submergence/emergence was something they only did in the privacy of their own rooms.

::He knew the difference before he touched us,:: Sholeh said, taking on a tone of scholarly curiosity. ::He can't see us, so how did he know?::

=Not now, Sholeh,= Zeela snapped. "I'm Zeela. Zhahar's sister. I help her sometimes."

His hold on her tunic and arm didn't ease. "I didn't hear you come in."

"I came in when Kobrah left." More or less true.

His grip didn't lessen, but his expression was thoughtful. "I've felt your resonance before, heard your voice before. With Zhahar."

By the triple stars, what does that mean?

Now his grip on her arm eased, and his thumb brushed over the scar. "Accident?"

"Knife fight in a tavern. I won," Zeela replied.

His cloudy eyes seemed to stare at her face. "Prove you're Zhahar's sister."

"How?"

"Describe her."

"It's against the rules to participate in inmates' sexual fantasies."

His thumb brushed over the scar again. "'Physical description' to 'sexual fantasies' is quite a jump. Describe yourself, then. You have any other distinguishing features besides this scar?"

"A tattoo on my left bicep. It's a heart inside a triangle."

Why did she tell him that?

"What does it mean?"

She could feel Zhahar pushing to come into view and tell him. Their core sister had been intrigued by this man from the first time she'd seen him, spoken to him. Intrigued enough to be too trusting? Was Zhahar's willingness to trust lowering *her* guard as well?

"If you have to ask, you're not meant to know," Zeela said.

He cocked his head, as if he'd heard more than he should have. "One more question. Are you the older sister?"

"I'm the middle sister. Zhahar is the oldest."

He released her and settled back in the water. "Ah. I thought I recognized that particular tone of bossy when she was ordering me around."

*I am *not* bossy!* Zhahar said.

=Ha.= "You have an older sister?"

Naked grief, there and gone. "You have any soap?" Lee asked, his voice subdued.

"Yes. First, lean back so you're on the headrest. There's a secondary basin for washing hair. I'll do that first."

"Couldn't you just cut the hair?"

Zeela hesitated as she reached for the jar of hair cleanser. "Why do you want to cut it?"

"Short hair will be cooler in a hot climate like this."

She narrowed her eyes as Sholeh piped up, ::How does he know it's not just a hot summer?:: She repeated the question.

"It doesn't feel like a hot summer in a cooler climate," he replied.

Ask him, Zhahar said, while Zeela washed Lee's hair.

"We— I haven't been there, but I've heard Vision's northern communities have cooler weather than here in the southern part. Is that where you're from? One of the northern communities?"

"Never heard of the city of Vision until I landed here a few weeks ago—or however long it's been."

Zeela hesitated before asking Zhahar, =Isn't that part of his mind-sickness, thinking he's from a place beyond the city?=

I'm not so sure he isn't, Zhahar said. *After all, *we* aren't from the city either.*

"Where are you from, then?" Zeela asked.

Lee hesitated. Then he smiled. "I'm a madman. How would I know?"

I cast out the Light.

Glorianna Belladonna had built her cage with five words. *I'm a madman. How would I know?*

He had built his with seven. As long as he played the madman, he would be kept at the Asylum—and kept out of the hands of the damn wizards who were trying to gain a foothold in this city. As long as he didn't play his part too well, he would, eventually, be free of the restraints and be allowed to move around the grounds. Not that a blind man could go anywhere or do anything. Maybe that should bother him, but it didn't. If nothing else, it gave him time to solve the mystery of Zhahar and her sister. Sisters? Sometimes he heard three voices in unison when she spoke to him. One of the voices was Zeela's. The other voice wasn't the Helper's, so whose was it?

A man with a loose grip on sanity could ask all kinds of questions without giving offense. Couldn't he?

I'm a madman. How would I know?

Seven words that equaled a strange kind of freedom. Or would once they let him out of the restraints that secured him to the damn chair.

Danyal paused at one entranceway to the porch and watched Zhahar cut Lee's hair. His wrists and ankles were strapped to the chair, and Kobrah and Nik, one of the male Handlers, were standing nearby, ready to assist or restrain.

Lee's muscles twitched and his face looked tight, but there was control. A lucid madman.

Was he truly mad or simply a troubled man who had gotten lost in the world? Or was Lee something more?

Danyal silently stepped over the threshold. Lee immediately turned his head, although those cloudy eyes didn't quite look in the right direction.

"Hold still," Zhahar scolded lightly.

"May I join you?" Danyal asked quietly.

"Of course," she replied.

Lee said nothing, and Danyal had the impression that not offering an opinion was unusual—especially when he had the equally strong impression that Lee didn't want him there. And that was why he needed to be there. To observe. To try to understand.

"How long have you been blind?" Danyal asked.

"For as long as I've been in this city," Lee replied.

Which either meant all his life or not that long.

"The southern part of the city is hot for most of the year," Danyal said, keeping his voice pleasant. "That's why there is this wide, screened porch that runs around the outside of the building on all four sides, only broken by the two outside doors. The isolation cells are inside rooms that are completely enclosed, but the rooms inhabited by the less-troubled inmates have a window that opens onto the porch."

"What are you telling me?" Lee asked. "To enjoy the fresh air while I can? Or that if I behave I'll be given a room with a view?"

The sharpness in the question surprised Danyal. Not just clean summer rain now in Lee's heart-core. There was a storm building.

"All done," Zhahar said brightly. She handed the scissors to Kobrah, who slipped them into a jacket pocket. Then she began undoing the restraints that held Lee to the chair—a sensible precaution when she'd held a potential weapon. "Would you like to sit out here for a while longer?"

"I have something else in mind," Danyal said. He stepped closer and saw Lee tense. "I think it will help you."

He closed his hand around Lee's arm, then waited for Lee to accept the contact. When Zhahar put her hand on the other arm, there was no resistance, no tension, no hesitation to accept.

"Where are you taking me?" Lee asked once they left the building. His steps were hesitant at first but grew more confident.

How many times had the hired muscle let Lee stumble around, walking into walls or tripping over furniture? How many times had they frightened him into trying to escape and deliberately put him in harm's way?

"I am a Shaman," Danyal said. "When I came here to be this Asylum's Keeper, I set up a small temple. That's where we're going."

"Shaman," Lee said softly. "That explains why I've been sensing a Landscaper's presence, but no one knew what a Landscaper was."

"While I enjoy being outdoors, Shamans tend to the city and its people, not its gardens."

"Shaman, Landscaper, Magician, Heartwalker, Heart Seer. Different words for the same thing, although how the power manifests in them reflects what their piece of the world needs."

"What do you think these people are?" Danyal kept his tone politely curious, but his heart began to pound, especially when he noticed how Zhahar was glancing between him and Lee.

"Someone who has a special connection to the world," Lee replied. "Someone who acts as a landscape's bedrock, as the sieve through which Ephemera responds to all the other hearts in that place. And a rare few are true Guides of the Heart and have such a strong bond with Ephemera, they can reshape the world."

"They don't sound human," Zhahar said softly enough that Danyal was sure she hadn't meant to say it out loud. It was one thing to think that about the Shamans; it was another thing to say it to one's face.

"They aren't human," Lee said. "Ephemera made the Guardians of the Light and the Guides of the Heart. And it made the Dark Guides too."

"How do you know all this?" Zhahar asked.

Danyal didn't look at Zhahar, but it took effort. One moment he sensed the summer lake of the heart-core he identified with her. The next moment he sensed the summer lake *and* the bright water, meaning another of those unexplained heart-cores had suddenly appeared, making it feel as if he were addressing two women when only one stood before him.

And the way Lee cocked his head made him think the madman was sensing something too.

"How do you know?" Zhahar repeated.

A long pause. Then Lee wrinkled his forehead. "Know what?"

"Hold for a moment while I open the door," Danyal said as he released Lee's arm.

A lucid madman or a cunning man playing a strange game? Were the men claiming to be Lee's uncles his enemies or were they his accomplices?

To speak an unspoken truth about Shamans so matter-of-factly . . .

The Shamans, as the voice of the world, were not human as others were human, despite coming from human families that had no touch of demon, and there was nothing in the city's history to explain how or why that could be. In order to earn a place for themselves—and a piece of the city in which to form their own community—they became Vision's spiritual guides. And sometimes they channeled their will into the world in order to shape justice on behalf of those who had been harmed.

What would Vision be without the Shamans?

Standing back, Danyal watched Zhahar lead Lee into sorrow's room. Was the blindness real? Yes. And recent. Lee didn't move like a man used to making his way through a world he couldn't see. Was the blindness permanent? Locked in his desk he had the medicines Lee had been given. This evening, he would walk the streets and see if he could find the Apothecary's shop that matched the seal on the bottle of eyedrops.

That would tell him some things about this man. This room would tell him more.

Zhahar settled Lee on one of the cushions, gave him a small mallet, then guided his other hand to the gong. "You just strike the gong."

"Why?" Lee asked.

Danyal scuffed his feet as he walked up to them so that Lee would hear him approach. Kneeling next to Lee, he said, "Striking the gong helps you release sorrow."

An odd pause. Then Lee shrugged and tapped the gong—and flinched. "Guardians and Guides."

When the sound faded, he struck the gong again, harder. The third time he struck the gong, tears began rolling down his face and his teeth were clenched.

Lee was full of summer storms that offered a fierce kind of cleansing. Danyal had doubts about the man, but the pain in Lee's heart was real.

When Zhahar picked up a mallet and struck a gong, doubling the sound that lanced heart wounds, Lee let out an anguished cry and collapsed.

Danyal caught him, held him tight, and asked quietly, "Do you know the cause of this sorrow? Can you give it a name?"

"Glorianna," Lee sobbed. "My sister, Glorianna."

"Why does your sister cause you such pain?"

"She's gone. She's gone. I lost her."

Zhahar sucked in a breath and looked stricken.

"You've been angry with her for leaving you," Danyal said, rocking the weeping man. "You've been hurt and angry and grieving, haven't you?"

"Y-yes."

"Perhaps it's time to heal."

The hurt and anger and grief went deep in this man. It wouldn't be healed in a day. But healing the heart was something Danyal could help Lee do.

After that, he would decide how far the man could be trusted.

Chapter Thirteen

Zeela strode down the shadow street, and everything about the way she moved told the men watching her from dark doorways that she had business on this street and wasn't looking for company.

Halfway down the second block, she spotted the Apothecary's sign.

Shaman Danyal had spent two evenings walking this street and the surrounding ones, looking for this shop. When Zhahar suggested letting her sister find the Apothecary, he hadn't been happy about sending a woman but had agreed to let Zeela try.

Of course, the Shaman wasn't aware that Zeela had had dealings with the Apothecary before and wouldn't have any trouble finding the shop.

Don't be smug, Zhahar scolded. *He really is concerned about you being here.*

=I know.= She was also fairly certain that, good man or not, the Shaman wouldn't let Zhahar keep her job another minute if he found out they were Tryad and what that meant. But that was an opinion she took pains to keep from both her sisters.

She opened the shop door and took a swift look around. This wasn't business she wanted to transact when there were other customers present.

When she reached the counter at the back of the shop, the Apothecary pushed aside the thin curtain that separated the shop from his work area.

"What can I do for you today?" he asked pleasantly.

Apothecaries were shadowmen, neither good nor evil. Like the streets where their shops were located, they couldn't be found by everyone, but those who could find them came from the Light as well as the Dark. They made what their customers asked them to make, and it was said that whether they were good or evil depended on the person standing on the other side of the counter.

It was also said that the potion in the bottle could turn against the person buying it if that person lied to the Apothecary.

Zeela pulled the bottle of eyedrops out of her trouser pocket and set it on the counter with the label facing the Apothecary. "I need this refilled."

"Are you sure?" he asked.

She withdrew money from her other pocket, set it on the counter beside the bottle, and fanned the bills enough to show him it was the standard amount he charged for information. Whatever he might put in a bottle to justify the visit was never more than an additional token fee.

"I would like this bottle refilled with information about who first bought it and why." She saw him hesitate, so she added, "I'm asking on behalf of a Shaman."

"Ah." The Apothecary relaxed a bit. "A man who doesn't know enough to mind his own business. Or so I've heard."

"I've heard he doesn't let anyone tell him what should be his business. The man these drops were used on? He's now the Shaman's business."

He nudged the bottle with a fingertip. "First bottle? Pain and cloudy eyes. Blindness. But once the drops are no longer used, sight will gradually return, although it might never be all that it was. Second bottle?" He shook his head. "Destroys the eyes. Permanently."

"Is there anything that can help reverse the damage already done?"

"Perhaps." He studied her, then went behind a curtain. When he returned, he set another bottle on the counter, along with a pair of dark glasses. "Two drops in each eye, morning and evening. After the drops go in, put a cool, damp cloth over the eyes to soothe. Sunlight will be painful while the eyes are healing—might even cause damage, so be careful."

"When this bottle is used up . . ."

"This much will fix whatever can be fixed."

Lee might still be blind, Zhahar said, sounding fretful.

=He might,= Zeela agreed.

::But we'll help him,:: Sholeh said.

"What do I owe you for these?" Zeela asked, waving a hand over the eyedrops and dark glasses.

Another long look. He pocketed the money she'd already placed on the counter. "This is enough."

Giving him a nod of thanks, she slipped the bottle into her trouser pocket. After a moment's thought, she tucked the glasses under her shirt, between her breasts.

"Two other things, because you came on behalf of the Shaman," the Apothecary said. "First, he should not wander the shadow streets for a while. Something has been slithering in the corners lately, and the shadow streets have gotten darker because of it—and I've heard whispers that what slithers would like to silence those who are the voice of the world."

Zeela suppressed a shiver. There was something out there that posed a threat to the Shamans?

"Second," the Apothecary continued, "the men who purchased that first bottle were killed last night."

Zeela felt Zhahar and Sholeh's fear, but she held herself quiet—and ready. "How?"

"They were struck by lightning. Both of them."

She frowned. "There was no storm last night."

"This lightning came out of an alley and burned through them. It wasn't a kind death. They screamed as they burned, but there was nothing anyone could do to help them. I've heard rumors that other men have died that way in the northwestern community—good men who asked too many questions."

"A strange death, to be sure," Zeela murmured.

"Stranger still because the city guards had been around that very afternoon, looking for those men. Made the citizens of our little street wonder if those men had become an inconvenience to someone."

"I'll pass along the information." She turned and walked swiftly to the front of the shop.

As she reached for the door, he said, "Travel lightly."

She looked at him over her shoulder. "Travel lightly."

Slipping out the door, she strode up the street, straining to hear anything, everything. Knives and brass knuckles weren't going to keep them safe against an enemy who controlled lightning.

Whoever killed those men can't connect you to the Asylum, Zhahar said.

=Not yet anyway.=

::What should we do?:: Sholeh asked.

Give the eyedrops and glasses to Shaman Danyal tonight, Zhahar said.

Zeela didn't like feeling so uneasy, but she was their Tryad's defender for a reason. =We aren't going home tonight. Women aren't safe after dark anymore in our part of the city. Zhahar, you need to figure out some excuse to stay at the Asylum tonight.=

We don't have any clean clothes.

=Shaman Danyal will have to give us time to go home and get some in the morning, because we're not going tonight.=

::You're afraid of that lightning,:: Sholeh said. ::I am too.::

Zeela growled and lengthened her stride. Not enough people out, even now when she was away from the shadow streets.

I'll think of a reason, Zhahar said quietly.

Zeela didn't say anything. She didn't breathe easy until they were in Shaman Danyal's office, handing over the eyedrops and glasses—and telling him everything the Apothecary had said.

Chapter Fourteen

Danyal watched Lee from a distance, letting Zhahar and Kobrah deal with the man. They helped him at meals and led him to the toilet and bathing room. They walked him to the temple, where he struck the gongs and released a little more of the sorrow in his heart. The rest of the time he spent on the screened porch, sitting quietly, which gave Zhahar time to tend to the other inmates in her care.

As a Shaman, Danyal walked the grounds of the Asylum, much as he'd walked the streets of Vision in the years before he'd been assigned to the Temple of Sorrow. And he walked around the porch thrice a day, making his presence a balance between the world and the troubled hearts confined to this place, and making himself available to anyone, inmate or staff, who wanted to talk.

This time he stopped when he came abreast of the woven lounge chair Lee occupied.

"You look content," Danyal said quietly. Lee's eyes were closed. Zhahar had been putting the eyedrops in morning and evening, but it was too soon to expect any change in the cloudiness. Still, he would like to see the man's eyes.

And he was curious what Lee might have seen in his own eyes.

"I am content," Lee replied with a smile. "There is shade, a breeze, a comfortable chair, water to drink, and I have nothing to do."

"Would you like something to do?"

Lee laughed. "Daylight, no. Do you know how long it's

been since I've had the luxury of doing nothing for this many days?"

"How long has it been?" Danyal asked, lacing his voice with amusement.

"Since I finished my training at the Bridges' School and started traveling to maintain the bridges needed to connect various landscapes. Even when I stayed over a day somewhere to rest, there was always the weight of duty." Lee's good humor faded. "But a blind man can't wander through the landscapes on his own, so that duty isn't mine anymore."

And that's both a relief and a sorrow for you, Danyal thought. "Come along. On your feet."

Lee tensed. "Why?"

"We're going to take a walk."

"Why would anyone want to take a walk in this heat?"

Not hostile, but definitely the tone of a man who wasn't used to taking orders—and was wary of obeying most of the ones he was given.

Danyal looked at the screened window above the chair where Lee sat.

"Because I would like to understand you better," he said. "Because the room behind you is currently unoccupied and has a window that looks out onto the porch—and it gets the cooler night air. Because I could decide you are rational enough to be given that room and some privileges instead of being returned to an isolation cell after the evening meal."

"Be lazy and stay in isolation or take a walk and get a real room." Lee swung his legs off the lounge chair and got to his feet. "You drive a hard bargain, Shaman. You're an amateur compared to my mother, but still, you drive a hard bargain."

"Put on your glasses, then take my arm," Danyal said. After Lee put on the dark glasses and wrapped a hand around Danyal's upper arm, they headed toward one of the porch doors that opened onto the grounds. Danyal nodded to Nik, who unlocked the door and held it open for them. "Two steps down."

They navigated the steps, then headed off on one of the paths toward the decorative water garden that was shaded by palm trees—a mystery whose sudden appearance had startled the groundskeepers and unsettled him.

"Waterfall?" Lee asked when they paused.

"A created one," Danyal replied. "And a clever one. The cascade of water over a series of stone ledges produces a restful, pleasing sound. A small windmill drives the pump that circulates the water. It has a crank, so when there is no wind, it can be manually turned. There are plants in and around the water that the groundskeepers are not familiar with, as well as several gold and white fish with long, graceful tails."

"Koi."

"What?"

"The fish. They're called koi. There's a koi pond in"—Lee paused—"a place I used to visit. Is there a bench nearby?"

"There is." Danyal studied Lee. "This was a stagnating reflecting pool surrounded by weeds during the tenure of the last Keeper. Despite our groundskeepers' best efforts, the reflecting pool remained unpleasant and unclean. Two days ago, it disappeared, replaced by this waterfall and pond, and these unknown plants and fish. How would you explain that?"

"Either this was here all along and so overgrown no one realized what it was, or Ephemera made a swap in response to someone's heart, and now some country home in some other landscape has a stagnating reflecting pool surrounded by weeds instead of a pretty water garden."

"Or? I did hear the silence of a third possibility."

Lee turned his head in Danyal's direction. "Or you're more than you say you are, and Ephemera made this because you wanted a pretty water garden for the people here." He waited a beat, then added, "But I'd bet on the swap. You might be able to guide the world into shaping the waterfall, pond, and plants, and even bringing in the fish, but it couldn't make the windmill and pump. People made those."

Dumbfounded, Danyal just stared. "Are you saying the city *stole* this water garden for the Asylum?"

"No, I'm saying *Ephemera* stole it for the Asylum. It's getting to be a fairly clever thief," Lee finished in a mutter.

A moment later, Lee stepped away from him. "Daylight! Did you just fart?"

"I did not," Danyal replied coldly. Then he clamped a hand over his mouth and nose.

"Ah, shit." Lee grimaced. "Sorry. That one is on me."

The smell intensified and seemed to be much closer. So close that Danyal's eyes watered. He grabbed Lee's arm and headed away from the water garden.

They went toward the main building, and the smell eased. Didn't completely vanish, but it eased enough that Danyal could take a clean breath.

"What was that?" he asked.

"Stinkweed," Lee replied. "It pops up when a person swears. Never saw the da— stuff until a few months ago, and I haven't smelled it since I arrived in this city."

"Then what . . . ?" Danyal stopped and stared at the two men walking quickly to intercept them. "Could it also be a warning?"

Instead of answering, Lee tensed at the sound of hurried footsteps.

"There you are, nephew!" Styks said heartily. "We were worried when we found your bed empty."

"Do you remember us?" Pugnos said.

"Of course," Lee replied just as heartily. "It's Bonelover and Trapspider. Been chewing up many corpses lately?"

A weird silence surrounded them.

"You know who we are," Pugnos snarled.

Lee gave them a vacant smile and said nothing.

"I think Lee has had enough stimulation today," Danyal said, watching the other men.

"Lee?" Lee's smile faded. His voice sounded confused, almost fearful.

"You are Lee," Styks said solicitously.

"Oh." Lee paused. "Do I know you?"

The two men stared at Lee and looked as if they wanted to beat some sanity into him. Or do something much worse.

"Gentlemen," Danyal said firmly. "Lee needs quiet time now."

"But we came to see him," Pugnos protested.

"And you have," Danyal replied. "And you can see that he is much improved—at least in body."

"Yes," Styks said softly. "We can see that." He reached out, but Lee shrank back enough to avoid being touched. "You are always in our thoughts, nephew. In that way, we are always with you, always aware of you."

Something under the words made them sound like a threat.

Danyal looked past the men and noticed Nik and Denys, another Handler, watching them at a discreet distance. He nodded.

Styks turned. His face tightened when he saw the men. "We'll go now."

Danyal held Lee's arm while he watched Styks and Pugnos walk back to the visitors' gate, feeling the tension and the slight tremble in the muscles. "Do you truly not know who they are?"

"I know what they are." Lee's voice was low and harsh.

Anger bordering on hatred. And fear. Rock slides and quicksand.

Spotting Zhahar, Danyal raised a hand. She quickly joined them and slipped an arm around Lee's to guide him back to the inmates' residence.

Danyal watched them, then focused on the direction the two "uncles" had taken. "I don't know what to think about those men."

A few moments later, he gagged on the smell rising behind him. Turning, he looked at the flower bed. A large half circle of flowering plants was missing, now replaced with squat green plants that *stank*. But it was the other plants, rapidly growing in the center of the stinkweed, that kept him there, despite the smell. Leaves so dark a green they were almost black. Fleshy pods swelled as he watched, and when they split and the flower began to push out . . .

They looked—and smelled—like turds steaming in the hot sun.

Gagging, he retreated and grabbed Teeko, the first groundskeeper he saw.

"There is a vile-smelling weed in the bed by the main pathway," he said, pointing toward the spot. "Get a barrow and a shovel. Dig those things up *and burn them.*"

"Yes, Shaman. Right away." Teeko rushed off.

Danyal hurried to the private washroom connected to his office. He scrubbed his hands and washed his face twice—and still couldn't get rid of all the stink.

As he walked back into his office, Teeko tapped on the open door.

"Shaman? You sure you want us to dig up that plant? It's a pretty little thing. And you didn't say if you wanted that rock dug up with it."

Danyal stood there, not knowing what to say. "Can't you smell it?"

"Oh, there's a foul smell around there, to be sure. I'm thinking we'll find a soiled pair of pants stuffed under a bush nearby. But it's not coming from that plant."

Then you're not looking in the right place, Danyal thought as he went back outside to point out the plants.

Except the stinkweed and the turd plants weren't there. Instead there was a chunk of polished, black-veined white marble beside a delicate little plant covered in buds and one open, rose-colored flower.

Light. Hope.

"I was mistaken," Danyal said. "The smell isn't coming from the plant."

"I'm glad to hear it," Teeko said. "Might have broken my heart to dig up that little plant."

An odd thing to say—and absolutely true.

"The only other thing we found was this." Teeko held out a gold pocket watch. "Thought the visitors might have dropped it, but it's broken and looks like it's been in the ground for a while."

Danyal took the watch and returned to his office. But he couldn't settle at his desk to read the daily reports or take care of all the other things that demanded his attention. Instead he stared out the window.

The Shamans were the voice of the world, but he had never seen the world respond like *this*, had never experienced it responding like *this*. Except at the bridge in his home village when the wind had pushed him back and didn't allow him to cross to the other side.

I don't know what to think about those men.

Moments after he'd said those words, those plants had started growing—and blooming. As if *the world* had expressed its opinion, telling him plainly enough what *it* thought of those men.

And then to have those plants disappear and be replaced with marble and that other little plant?

Was this happening to other Shamans? Or just him? Was he *that* different from the others, or had something changed around him that had, in turn, changed him?

Or was the change here being caused by someone else?

*   *   *

Ephemera flowed through the currents of Light and Dark in this part of itself, listening to all the tangled hearts. But it wasn't supposed to listen to those hearts, wasn't supposed to make what those hearts wanted unless a Guide told it to.

But that one didn't belong in this part of itself. That heart yearned for a different place.

Ephemera flowed away from that heart and went to see if the Voice-guide it had found wanted to play again. The Voices that walked in this part of itself helped it stay balanced, allowing Light and Dark currents to flow in response to the hearts that lived here. But *this* Voice could be a Guide to the world, could *play* with it like the Music did, like *she* did. *She* was like the Old Ones, like the first Guides of the Heart that it had shaped long ago. *She* had known how to be a Guide to the world and played with the world, helping it remake parts of itself. *She* was teaching the Music how to play with the world and shape small makings. *She* and the Music would teach Voice-guide how to play too.

Now the world and the Music were playing the Lee-heart game. The Music met the world at the playground on *her* island and played the song from the Lee-heart. He gave the world all the bits of stolen time to leave where the Lee-heart would find them, so the Lee-heart would know the Music had not forgotten him.

And it had found the Lee-heart in this part of itself that was far from *her* landscapes! And the resonance of the Lee-heart in this part of itself had changed a Voice enough to become Voice-guide for the world!

Then the dark hearts had shivered through the Dark currents of this place, dimming the Light in all the hearts, even the Lee-heart and Voice-guide.

When Voice-guide wanted to know what was in those hearts, it had shaped a small making and *shown* its new Guide.

After Voice-guide went away, it took away the dark making and made the Lee. Stone like *she* used for Sanctuary—light with veins of dark. Heart's hope, full of promise. And a bit of stolen time.

But another heart took the time.

It had many bits of stolen time and could fetch more. The Lee-heart would find one, and the Music would be happy.

Ephemera circled around this part of itself again, listening to the hearts, listening to the yearnings that wanted this part of itself to change just a little, just enough to connect with another piece of itself.

Listened to the heart wish that came from three hearts that were one heart. A heart wish that was also being made in another part of itself.

Hearts that needed the Guide, needed *her*.

It would return to the playground and show the Music what it had found. But first . . .

Ephemera listened to that one yearning heart that didn't belong in this part of itself.

She wouldn't be angry if it reshaped a piece of itself to make that one heart happy. Not if it was a *small* making that would feed the currents of Light.

Pleased, Ephemera remade a piece of itself before traveling through the currents of power and returning to the Island in the Mist, where *she* and the Music waited.

Feeling edgy, Lee sat on a lounge chair in the screened porch, listening to Kobrah and a couple of cleaning people prepare his new room. A big jump from an isolation cell to a room for the almost normal. There was a bolt on the door to keep inmates from wandering when they became agitated, but his impression was that these rooms were similar to spartan accommodations that could be found in many places where travelers couldn't afford luxury. He'd stayed in enough places like that in the years when he'd been a Bridge for Glorianna and Nadia.

He hadn't lied to Danyal when he said he was content to do nothing. Nine years of doing with little time to rest was enough. He'd done enough. His last effort to save his sister and mother and their landscapes had put him in the hands of the enemy and left him blind. Hadn't he given the world enough of himself?

Apparently not, because being in the hands of the enemy had led him straight to Danyal—a Landscaper in desperate need of a Bridge. Some of the inmates were truly mind-sick people, and some were troubled because they were in the wrong place and needed to cross over to the landscapes that resonated with their hearts.

The best he could figure, the Shamans were the Landscapers for this part of the world, keeping the currents of Light and Dark power balanced, tending the landscapes that leaned toward the Dark as well as the Light. He was pretty sure Danyal was one of the rare Guides of the Heart. Like Michael, the Magician. Like Glorianna Belladonna.

He was also pretty sure something that had been dormant in Danyal had woken up—or responded to another resonance. Again, like Michael, who had more of a connection to Ephemera than the other Magicians in Elandar, but that connection had become more direct and immediate after Michael found Glorianna.

Glorianna wasn't here, but he—a Bridge—was. Someone who connected pieces of the world, allowing people to cross over to the landscapes that resonated with their hearts, regardless of the physical distance between those places. Sometimes it was the landscapes that pulled at him, wanting a connection. Sometimes it was a person.

If Shamans were the Landscapers in Vision, who were the Bridges? Who connected the various pieces of this city?

Shouting and the sound of people running brought Lee to his feet. Then he swayed there for a moment before sitting down again.

Nothing he could do.

That wasn't as pleasing a thought as it had been a little while ago.

Danyal stared at the rough stairs leading down to stone walls covered with vines and listened to the inmate down there, just out of sight, laughing and weeping with delight, saying *this* is where he belonged. *This* place.

Several Handlers were crowded behind him, including Zhahar. As his eyes skimmed over them, he realized he was looking for one other person: Lee.

As Danyal took the first step down into this place that hadn't existed an hour ago, he felt a strong hand grab the sleeve of his white robe, felt two heart-cores where a moment ago there had been one.

"You shouldn't go down alone," Zhahar said.

"Come, then," he replied.

She followed him down. It was cool and shady near the stairs. When they rounded the bit of wall that blocked their sight of the rest of the place, they stopped.

Sunlight and heat and air that almost dripped with scents. Vines clung to the stone walls, and he could almost see the bunches of small fruit growing as he watched. Vito, an inmate who had been indifferent to his surroundings, touched the plants and the stones, laughing and weeping with a joy that could have broken Danyal's heart if he hadn't heard Zhahar's choked sob.

"He's so happy," she whispered. "It's as if his heart woke up. But . . . what is this place?"

Not a part of Vision, Danyal thought. There were vineyards in some of the northern communities, but there were no grapes that grew like this. Not in Vision.

And how had this place been made when no man had picked up a shovel to dig or a barrow to haul stone?

"Shaman?" Zhahar pointed to something gold that poked up from the ground near the vines and caught the sunlight.

He walked over to the spot and picked up the broken pocket watch.

"Shaman Danyal, isn't it wonderful?"

Danyal looked at Vito, a man whose heart-core had been mud and stone. Now . . . Dawn. Clean water. Rich earth. The abundance of a good harvest lovingly tended.

"Yes, it's wonderful," he replied, then added gently, "Tend your vines until the evening meal. Then you must come in and rest."

"All right, Shaman. I will."

Danyal went back up the stairs with Zhahar. He tipped his head at Denys. "Stay with him to make sure he comes to no harm. Observe him." He turned to Zhahar. "Escort Lee to the temple."

"What should I tell him?" she asked.

Summer rains, both gentle and fierce. Madman or teacher?

"Tell him the voice of the world wants to talk to him."

"Could you pick a pace and stay with it?" Lee snapped after stumbling for the third time because Zhahar couldn't settle on whether to go step by ponderous step or sprint to the temple.

"The Shaman wants to see you," Zhahar snapped in return. She tightened her grip on his arm and put more muscle into hauling him down the path.

"Hey!" Lee stopped so abruptly, she was pulled around and smacked into his chest.

Two resonances. Two *familiar* resonances where there had been one a moment before. He grabbed her left arm. Even through the jacket he felt the jagged, raised scar before it seemed to withdraw into the skin.

"What happened that's got you bouncing out of your skin?" he asked. He could almost feel her panic at his mention of skin.

"We— I'm not. It's just . . . unsettling."

"Then shouldn't the Shaman and the Handlers be taking care of whatever this is?"

"We don't . . . It's never . . . Places can *shift*, but not like this."

"Places shift?" *What does that mean?* If it meant what he thought it meant, Zhahar knew more about the world than she was saying. And wasn't that interesting?

"Lee."

"Just tell me why the Shaman wants to see me, because I know that calling himself the voice of the world means we aren't going to be having a friendly little chat."

He felt her hesitate, felt her struggle to regain control of herself.

"There's a new place in the Asylum," she finally said. "It wasn't there and now it is, and no one knows why."

"Is *anyone* happy about this?"

"One of the inmates. He thinks he belongs there."

"Then he probably does." Still didn't explain why Danyal wanted to see him, but it explained all the shouting before Zhahar came to fetch him.

She finally settled into a reasonable pace—or *someone* did—and they arrived at the temple. Didn't need to wonder if Danyal was there, because the gongs were sounding. *All* the gongs. Quietly, yes, but Lee would have bet a week's worth of chores that the Shaman hadn't struck any of those gongs with a mallet. Voice of the world, indeed.

Zhahar helped him up the steps and into sorrow's room.

"Leave us," Danyal said.

Lee felt her hesitate before she retreated, closing the door behind her. That was nothing more than a token gesture of privacy, since he could tell by the breeze that all the windows were open, and he didn't think anyone was going to have to strain to eavesdrop on *this* conversation.

"Don't need eyes to know you're pissed off about something," Lee said. "Shouldn't you be dealing with it instead of chatting with me?"

"Maybe chatting with you *is* the only way to deal with it," Danyal replied.

Lee felt the other man come closer, felt the way the song of the gongs seemed to vibrate against his skin. Judging by what he could sense of Danyal's mood and temper, if the Shaman walked across a resonating bridge right now, he'd find himself in a dark landscape that had few, if any, connections to the Light.

"Things are happening in the city of Vision that have never happened before," Danyal said. "I think you know why."

Lee turned his head toward one of the windows, straining to hear. Was there someone out there besides Zhahar? *Had* he heard the scuff of a boot under that window? *Could* he have heard anything beyond the sound of the gongs?

Things were happening in the city of Vision. If he kept his voice low, would anyone outside be able to hear him over the gongs?

He waggled a finger, signaling for Danyal to move closer. When the Shaman was close enough that he could feel the man's heat, he asked quietly, "My uncles told you about my sickness? About my delusions?"

"They told me," Danyal said just as quietly.

"So you know you can't believe any answers a madman gives you in response to your questions." Lee paused. "But that doesn't mean you can't ask the questions."

Did Danyal understand the message in the words?

Lee was fairly certain he wasn't *always* being watched by those who had given their loyalty to the thrice-damned wizards, but he could never be certain that he wasn't being watched. As long as Danyal—and Zhahar?—continued treating him like he was mind-sick insofar as what he *said*, he could tell them anything, *everything*, that might help them understand what was happening to their city.

And in helping Danyal, he might be able to do something for himself.

Danyal walked past him and opened the door. A moment later, Zhahar joined them.

"I've had a special cane made for Lee," Danyal said. "I think, with some help, he can learn to navigate around the Asylum's grounds on his own."

"Oh," Zhahar said.

Did she sound disappointed? Guardians and Guides, he hoped so. He'd like an excuse to be with her when she wasn't taking care of him. And he wanted some independence so he could spend time with the woman instead of the Handler.

"Besides the daily session with the gongs to bring troubling emotions to the surface, where they can be released, Lee will also spend time talking about the events that brought him here," Danyal continued.

"Ah . . ." Lee said.

"These talks can be combined with physical exercise, which will improve the body and promote healthful sleep."

"Aren't we a bundle of suggestions all of a sudden?" Lee muttered. He raised his voice enough to direct the words to Danyal. "If there is going to be talk, there will be a fair exchange."

"Meaning?"

"In the city of Vision, you can find only what you can see. I'd like to know more about this city and how it works. I'd like to know more about this part of the world. So, an exchange. I'll tell you what I know, and you tell me the equivalent. And you shouldn't always be the one having these chats with me."

A pause before Danyal said, "Really?"

"The Keeper can't be spending that much time with one inmate. That won't go unnoticed, and getting noticed right now isn't healthy for any of us. Don't you know anyone who might have an interest in the world beyond Vision who would give you an accurate report?" Lee asked.

"My sister Sholeh," Zhahar said quickly. "She's something of a scholar—or would have been if she'd been able to continue with her studies. She could do this, and she'd be very thorough in her reports."

"Not to mention having her older sister nearby to keep an eye on her?" Lee asked sweetly.

A startled pause.

"Well, it's not like you're going to take her walking in the moonlight," Zhahar said, sounding defensive.

"No, I'm not interested in taking Sholeh for a walk in the moonlight."

Another pause before Danyal harrumphed. "I could arrange my schedule to have these discussions in the evening."

"Wasn't what I had in mind," Lee said. "I don't hear Zhahar offering an opinion."

"Judging by her expression, that's probably for the best," Danyal said. "That will be all. Zhahar, escort Lee back to the porch. And ask your sister if she'd like to participate in these discussions."

"Yes, Shaman."

Lee felt her grab his arm and haul him to the door.

"Step," she snapped.

He managed to get down the steps without falling. His longer legs made it easy enough to keep up with her, but he wasn't sure she wouldn't smack him into a tree. So he dug in his heels and yanked her to a stop.

"What's wrong with you?"

"My sister is a loving, intelligent woman!"

"I'm sure she is," Lee replied mildly.

"Any man would be lucky to take a walk with her in the moonlight."

"I'm sure that's true too—*unless* the man is interested in taking a walk in the moonlight with *you*. Going out walking with two sisters?" Lee shook his head. "That's just asking for trouble—not to mention getting whacked with a spoon."

"*What?*"

"Wooden spoon with a long handle. My mother's preferred disciplinary tool. What does your mother use?"

"*My* mother had *daughters* and didn't need tools."

She released his arm and walked away.

"Zhahar?" Lee called. "Zhahar! Daylight, woman. Are you going to just leave me here?"

He heard footsteps behind him and braced for an attack, until he recognized the resonance he now associated with Danyal.

"Are you usually skilled with women?" Danyal asked.

"Not so much," Lee replied sourly. "Are Shamans celibate?"

"Not so much."

"Then don't sound smug. There's a woman out there at this very moment waiting to tangle up your life." He'd found the woman who was going to tangle up his—at least for the foreseeable future.

Another of those pauses. "Did you leave someone behind, Lee?"

"Not the way you mean."

"Come," Danyal said gently. "I'll escort you back to the porch. We both have much to think about."

"Yes, we do."

After passing Lee over to a frowning Kobrah, Danyal intended to go back to his office and work. But he wasn't used to this heat, and the room had little air at this time of day, so he headed back to the temple to think. Then he changed directions and walked along the main path, stopping when he reached the small plant and the black-veined white marble.

Light. Hope. Inmates and Handlers alike seemed to find their way to this spot at some point in the day in order to look at this plant. Just for a moment. And it seemed that another bud opened in response to that person's presence.

Madman or teacher—which one was Lee?

He had started to turn away when a glint of gold caught his eye.

That pocket watch hadn't been there a moment before. He was sure of it.

Crouching, Danyal pushed his fingers into the dirt and picked up the watch—and would have sworn that, in the moment when his fingers closed over the gold, he heard music.

Michael lowered his tin whistle and shifted on the bench that sat on the safe part of the playground. "Glorianna, come take a look at this."

Glorianna took a step toward him, then clamped both hands over her nose. "I'd rather not."

"Now, don't be getting all prissy. It's just a smell."

"Well, at least . . ." She pointed a finger, then adjusted

direction so she wasn't pointing directly at the house. "Ephemera, shift the wind so it blows that way."

yes yes yes

When the world shifted the wind, she stepped into the gravel side of the playground and sat beside Michael.

"All right, wild child," Michael said. "Show Glorianna what you just showed me."

Palm trees that held the scent of dusty heat. Dark plants whose flowers looked like turds. Stinkweed. A heart's hope. Grapes and a different, earthy smell. Lots of sharp, jagged bits of stone. A piece of granite. A wilted water lily.

And a gold pocket watch.

"You found Lee," Glorianna said as she studied Ephemera's message.

"Don't know what landscape he's in, but, yes, darling Glorianna, the wild child found him." Michael bumped her shoulder with his. "What's Ephemera telling us?"

She felt Belladonna scratching along the threads that connected the Light side of her heart with the Dark. Threads Michael shaped and strengthened each day by playing the music he heard in her—the music that wasn't just Belladonna or just Glorianna but was both. Not who she had been, but who she was now.

"It found Lee," she said grimly. "And it found some wizards in the same landscape."

Michael nodded. "I was thinking the same thing."

And wizards, among a people who didn't know what they were, could twist enough hearts to change the resonance of a landscape before anyone realized the danger. Nothing she could do about them, and nothing she could do to help Lee. Not yet. So she would take care of the things she could do something about.

She gave Michael a sideways look. "That wasn't all you were thinking, Magician."

"It wasn't?"

"You were thinking that parts of that landscape need to be returned to where they belong."

"I was thinking that?" Michael asked innocently.

She sighed and leaned forward, bracing her forearms on her thighs. "Ephemera? Hear me."

???

"Take the parts you shifted to that landscape and put them back where they belong."

???

"Put. Them. Back. Now."

!!!

Michael frowned. "There's no cause to be using that tone, wild child."

!!!

Glorianna looked at her lover and narrowed her eyes.

"Now, don't be giving me that look," Michael said. "I've made some mistakes when I'm talking with the world, and I'm bound to make more, but *this* I didn't do. Whatever it is."

"Well, *someone . . .*" Glorianna studied the offerings in the sandbox. "Is there a Landscaper in that landscape?"

yes yes yes

Everything sank under the sand except the piece of granite.

"Anger makes stone," she said reflectively, "and strength makes stone. That stands for strength."

"If Lee and this Landscaper are in the same place, let's hope they can help each other."

"Let's hope." *I can do more than hope. Ephemera, hear me.*

She sent her heart wish through the currents of power, both Light and Dark.

A whisper of another heart wish came back to her from an unexpected place.

She gripped Michael's hand. "Come with me."

The quick grin and the heat in his smoky blue eyes faded as he studied her face. "I'm guessing we aren't going inside for a nap."

"No." She paused and considered the feel of his mouth and the touch of his hands. A different kind of music that also reached both sides of her heart. "Not yet anyway."

They left the playground and went to her walled garden, the place where she tended all the landscapes in her care. She led him to the part that held the dark landscapes.

Michael studied the triangle of grass. "It's still tugging at you, isn't it?"

"It is. It resonates with me—or some part of it does—but not enough to cross over. The *call* isn't strong enough yet."

She looked at him, her partner in so many ways now. "Do you hear anything, Magician?"

"The music of the place, you mean?" He tipped his head and closed his eyes. "Chords. Three notes played together. Not a tune, as such. Dark tones and light. I'd be careful about going there unless I was sure of my welcome." He opened his eyes and looked at her. "Is that what you wanted to know?"

"It is."

"Why are you asking? Are you thinking it might not be yours?"

"Oh, I know it's mine—or will be."

Glorianna hesitated. She hadn't told Michael, hadn't told anyone that the dark landscape that held the Eater of the World—the landscape that should have been closed to *everyone*—was a place Belladonna could reach simply by taking the step between here and there. And sometimes she craved the power she had wielded there without constraints, without conscience. That was the main reason she felt so wary of that triangle of grass that was almost an access point. Belladonna could cross over to the Eater's dark landscape, but she wasn't sure if Belladonna would be able to leave again—and she *was* sure the part of her that was Glorianna wouldn't survive.

"I felt a heart wish in the currents a few minutes ago," she said. "Faint, but it was there. It felt like it came from the landscape where Lee is, but it also has some connection to that landscape." She tipped her head to indicate the triangle of grass.

"But it's not Lee's heart wish."

"No." *Let your heart travel lightly.* The best thing she could do for Lee—and the rest of the family—was remember the truth of that saying.

She smiled at Michael. "Let's go take that nap."

Guardians of the Light and Guides of the Heart were created by Ephemera long ago to help the world manifest the true wishes of the human heart. The Guardians preferred to be cloistered from the turmoil of daily life, but the Guides walked among the people, lived like the rest of the people, except they could talk to the world. After the war with the Eater of the World, the Guardians disappeared. So did the Guides, but their descendants are still known by many names—Landscapers, Magicians, Heartwalkers, Heart Seers, Shamans. They are the ones who now provide balance between Ephemera and the people who live in the world (although a few Guides still exist and still walk in the world).

Ephemera also made beings called the Dark Guides as a response to the people who embraced the darker aspects of the heart. Most of the Dark Guides were trapped in a place called Wizard City, but there are still some wandering through Ephemera's landscapes. Their descendants are called wizards, and they have the power of persuasion as well as a deadly magic they call wizards' lightning. Many wizards nurture the dark feelings in the heart, but some are called Justice Makers and do, in fact, help maintain order in their part of the world.

There was a brief discussion of men called Bridges and their ability to change an ordinary bridge of wood and stone into something that can link different parts of the world.

I feel confident that Lee believes what he told me about Guardians, Guides, Dark Guides, and wizards. However, his comments about Bridges might have been a test to see if I'm gullible enough to believe everything he says.

—Sholeh's first report to Shaman Danyal

Chapter Fifteen

Danyal put Sholeh's report in a separate file from his notes about Lee. It disturbed him to see Shamans listed so casually, and yet there was an odd relief that Shamans were not as unique as everyone in Vision believed. But the words, so casually spoken and so carefully written down for anyone to see, made it clear that Shamans, like the Landscapers and Magicians that had also been mentioned, did not have their roots in humankind. That was something he wanted to discuss with Farzeen in private before telling the rest of the Shaman Council.

What disturbed him even more was the note about Guides being able *to talk* to the world.

Did the world ever talk back to the beings it had created?

There was someone he could ask, but he wasn't ready for the answer. Because he knew, with absolute certainty, that his life would change into something he couldn't yet imagine once he had the answer.

Tap tap. Tap tap.

"Branch," Sholeh said, grabbing Lee's left arm. When he stopped moving, she released him, and he heard her flipping through the pages of some kind of book. "I'll make a note for Zhahar. She'll have the groundskeepers take care of it."

"Are you sure she'll tell the groundskeepers?" he asked. "She's still not feeling friendly toward me."

"She's my sister. The three of us look out for each other."

A pause. "*I* wasn't insulted that you wanted to walk in the moonlight with Zhahar instead of me."

"She *told* you what I said?" That wouldn't be kind, and he couldn't picture Zhahar being insulted on her sister's behalf and then telling Sholeh.

A hesitation. "I sort of overheard you."

Now, how could you have done that? Lee thought. Unless . . .

He was free of the drugs, he knew he wasn't crazy, and he'd seen his share of unusual races. Not as unusual as what he'd been thinking about Zhahar and her sisters, but he'd had plenty of time to think lately. He just needed some physical information to help that thinking along, and right now, if he could trust the single resonance that was Sholeh, baby sister was on her own during this interview. Since they were out walking the Asylum's grounds and there was no one around them, how fast would her sisters show up if Sholeh was goaded into saying something she shouldn't?

Once he knew what he was dealing with, he'd figure out how he felt about it. Zhahar's compassion for others pulled at him and pulled hard. She could fit in with his family in the same way Lynnea fit, and he wanted a chance to see how well she could fit with him. Her reaction to the moonlight-walk comment made him hopeful the attraction wasn't just on his side. He'd like the chance to know the woman, to *touch* the woman, and . . .

"Ready?" Sholeh asked.

"Ah . . . sure." Maybe a little too ready, and this wouldn't be a good time to let his mind wander through that particular daydream.

He let Sholeh guide him around the branch, then began tapping the long stick again. The paths were made of some kind of stone or brick that sounded different from the ground when he tapped them. By using sound instead of sight, he could keep to the paths and learn how to reach some parts of the Asylum on his own.

This morning he had awakened to a lighter darkness. His window looked out on the part of the porch that received the morning light. Since being given that room, he'd stood at the window in the morning just to breathe in the cooler air, but today there were dark stripes on a lighter gray—porch posts and daylight.

He didn't tell anyone, not even Zhahar, that the eye-drops were helping, that some of his sight was returning. The wizards stopped by the Asylum several times a week to check on him—and to remind him that if he tried to leave, tried to get back home, *someone* would be close enough to go with him, to open a way into Belladonna's landscapes.

He didn't think there was anything in *Belladonna's* land-scapes that couldn't take care of a wizard or two, but there was always the chance of one of the bastards stumbling into Sanctuary, always a chance that the damn Dark Guide could somehow touch the Places of Light.

So he said nothing. As long as his "uncles" thought he was blind and helpless, he was no use to them. As long as he was no use to them, they had no reason to harm the other people in the Asylum.

Except that they were wizards and fed the Dark currents of the world.

"What would you like to talk about?" Sholeh asked.

Oh, they would get to what he wanted to talk about, but first he needed to get her involved enough to speak without thinking. "Lady's choice. Do you want to know about places, people, or demons?"

"Demons?"

He could picture her eyes going wide—excited and a little scared. Talking about Guardians and Guides yesterday had been interesting, but they weren't nearly as interesting as Ephemera's demon races. At least not to someone who was sheltered by two older sisters.

Sometimes the baby in a family should be allowed to scrape her knees and learn about life directly instead of just watching her sisters.

"Demons it is." *Tap tap. Tap tap.* He followed the sound, hoping he was heading away from the buildings and all the potential eyes watching them. "There are the waterhorses. They come from a country called Elandar. They're beautiful black horses that act as tame as a cosseted pet and are more than willing to let you climb on their backs to take a ride."

"That doesn't sound bad." Pencil scratching on paper.

"Up to that point, it's not. But their magic binds you to them. Once you mount, you can't get off until they release you. They'll take you for a ride—and most of the time that ride ends at the bottom of a pond or a lake or a deep river.

Doesn't bother the waterhorse. He stays down until the rider drowns."

Scratch scratch. Hesitation. *Scratch scratch.*

"Then there are the Merry Makers," Lee continued. "They come from Elandar too. They live in the bogs and have a humanlike body but are not human. They *look* like they were made from the bog—moss and twigs. They're strong and they're deadly. Travelers who get lost in their pieces of Ephemera see the light from lanterns and hear music and think they've found some help. What they've really found is an invitation to be the Merry Makers' dinner. Sometimes you can barter for your life, but not often."

The Magician had crossed paths with the Merry Makers twice and walked away. The first time they let him go because of his music; the second time, they took him to Sebastian because Michael had told them he was seeking Belladonna, that her darkness was his fate.

Michael had been right about that. Her darkness *was* his fate.

And mine? Lee thought. Wasn't blindness another way to snuff out light?

The scratching stopped.

"Bull demons," Lee said. He heard Sholeh gulp, and clenched his teeth to stop the grin. Zhahar met the world through a passionate heart but was practical as well as compassionate. Zeela leaned toward the physical and was, he admitted, a bit scary. But Sholeh's passion was knowledge, and she sounded so gleeful about having an opportunity to learn, he almost felt bad about tricking her into revealing something about her own people.

"Bull demons," Sholeh said, her tone a reminder that he'd drifted from the topic.

"We've never seen a female, so I can't tell you what they look like. The males mostly look like large, strong, well-muscled men, but their heads are bovine—like a bull, horns and all. It's said they eat meat—*all* kinds of meat—but they consider vegetable omelets a delicacy and barter olives and olive oil for the treat." He paused. "Now it's your turn."

Scratch scratch. "What are olives?"

"Your turn," he repeated. "Fair exchange, remember?"

Hesitation. "What do you want to know?"

"Tell me about a race of people from this part of the world."

"I don't know about any demons from this part of the world."

That wasn't what he'd asked, but he found it interesting that it was what she'd heard. "Then any demon you've heard about."

The dark glasses wiped out the small distinction he could make between light and dark, and he couldn't have seen her as more than a woman-shaped blob anyway. Still, he wanted to take off the glasses and *see* her face, her expression, because he was suddenly feeling that triple resonance, and he was *certain* Zhahar and Zeela were close by—and were trying to stop Sholeh from saying anything.

Too bad they were up against someone who knew how to play the sibling game.

"It's all right if you don't remember anything from your studies. We can continue this another d—"

"Tryad," Sholeh said, sounding scared and defiant.

"And what are the Tryad?" he asked mildly.

"One who is three. Three who are one."

Lee rocked back on his heels as he absorbed the words. "Three personalities?"

"Three *people*."

That explained the three resonances and the three voices he sometimes heard despite only one voice actually speaking. "One body?"

"A common core, but not the same outer body."

Zeela had that jagged scar on her left arm, but Zhahar didn't. So the outer body changed but they shared the innards?

He thought about men and women and how their parts went together.

Ooookay. If he *was* dealing with a Tryad and only wanted to snuggle with one sister, he was going to have to know more about the race before he and Zhahar put their parts together. And since body and heart were pulling him in the same direction, he was highly motivated to find out more.

"Hypothetically, if you and your sisters were a Tryad, how would you be identified? What would your name be?" he asked.

"I don't know," she stammered.

"If you can't even discuss something hypothetical, how will you ever meet the actual world?" He said it gently, but he meant it. Yes, he had tricked her into starting this, but he sensed this was a fork-in-the-road moment—the kind of moment that could alter a landscape enough to alter a life.

At first he thought a swarm of bees was in front of his face. Then he realized it was the buzz of voices all trying to speak from the same throat.

"Sholeh Zeela a Zhahar," Sholeh said abruptly, clearly stung by his question—or frightened by the truth of it.

The buzzing stopped.

Youngest sister to oldest. That age difference probably was counted in minutes, but he had the feeling those minutes were significant in deciding place within the family. That could explain why, before discovering they were a kind of triplet, he'd thought Sholeh was several years younger than Zeela and Zhahar—really the baby of the family.

"All the same gender?" he asked, still willing to pretend this was an academic conversation. "Or could there be two sisters and a brother, for example?"

"Rarely, but it happens. It's usually three sisters or three brothers."

"Who have different personalities and different skills."

"Sisters in a one-face family wouldn't be expected to be the same," Sholeh said defensively.

"One-face?" Lee whistled. "Darling, I know an insult when I hear one. Although calling me two-faced . . ." He stopped, feeling fragile as he remembered a sister who was no longer whole.

Sholeh sucked in her breath. "That's a *terrible* thing to say."

Why? But she wasn't the sister he wanted to ask.

"So," he said. "The Tryad sound like an interesting people. They'd have some symbol to represent their people, don't you think? Something like a heart inside a triangle?" The tattoo Zeela said she had on her arm.

"I think we should go back now."

Sholeh sounded afraid. Her lack of experience in dealing with the world probably made it easy to trick her into giving too much information about herself and her people—and left her and her sisters vulnerable to discovery. If there wasn't a reason to fear discovery, they wouldn't need to hide what they were.

Something else to discuss with Zhahar.

"If that's what you want," he said.

"Yes. We— I—"

"All right. Answer one last question, and then I'll tell you about another demon race." And he was going to let all of them know he wasn't going to be put off by physical differences unless there was a good reason.

"What's the question?" Wary now.

"When I kiss Zhahar, are you and Zeela going to be watching us?"

A squeaky sound.

"I'll take that as a yes. Not that I mind, you understand. I learned a lot about kissing when I visited my cousin, and in the Den, you get used to people watching you kiss— although being critiqued by a relative as he's walking by isn't appreciated, so you two put aside the idea of being bratty sisters and keep your comments to yourself."

More squeaky sounds. A flutter of pages as a book hit the ground and was retrieved.

"However," Lee continued, smiling, "if your sister and I reach the point of making love, you and Zeela are going to have to leave the room, so to speak. I'm not an incubus. I don't consider sex a performance art. At least, not one that includes an audience." He paused. "Shall we go back?"

He felt the shifting of resonances and wondered what it looked like when one sister changed into another. Then he didn't wonder. He felt friendly toward Sholeh and wary of Zeela. But when he was around Zhahar, he felt a heat spiced with something more than lust.

"Weren't you listening?" Zhahar said fiercely.

Lee pursed his lips. "Am I talking to Zhahar, or is there a little Zeela in the mix?"

Silence.

"I heard what Sholeh said. Knowing you're a Tryad makes you a lot less confusing for someone like me."

"Someone like—" A moment of buzzing. "Sholeh didn't say we were Tryad."

"I'm blind, Zhahar, but I'm not stupid. Everything about you and your sisters fits the race Sholeh described. Or do you want to try to float an explanation about how you and

Zeela could show up so fast without me hearing anyone approach? There is nothing wrong with my hearing, darling. You weren't here, and then you were. That's something we need to talk about. But just so there is no misunderstanding when we get there, what I said about not walking in the moonlight with more than one sister also applies to sex." When she didn't respond, he reached out and touched her arm before she stepped back.

"Incubus," Zhahar said. "You said you aren't an incubus."

"I'm not." Judging by her tone of voice, he figured it was best not to mention—yet—that his cousin Sebastian was. "They were the last demon race I was going to tell Sholeh about today, but it sounds like you, at least, already know about them."

"I don't know much." She sounded upset. "Not enough. I thought they were harmless. When she talked about him, he sounded harmless. What are they?"

Not an idle question if she knew someone who crossed paths with the incubus but didn't realize what he was. "The incubi are sex demons. They travel through the twilight of waking dreams to be dream lovers for women yearning for romance or sex. The succubi are female sex demons."

"Are they dangerous?"

"The purebloods are deadly. They can kill with sex—and they can change their appearance to look like anyone. Others see humans as prey, since the incubi and succubi feed on emotions, and sex provides a banquet. And there are others who provide a service of sorts." He took a step toward her but didn't try to touch her. "You know someone who tangled with an incubus?" Not one of her sisters. He pitied the incubus dumb enough to tangle with Zeela without an invitation. Sholeh? No, if the little sister had crossed paths with a sex demon, even one who was acting harmless, he figured *Zeela* would be the one asking him questions now.

But a pureblood incubus could do plenty of damage even if the woman lived. And he wondered what being two-faced meant to a people who normally had three.

"Who has met an incubus here?" he asked.

Zhahar hesitated, then said, "Kobrah. I think there have been two others—two inmates, a man and woman."

"Are they all right?"

"The woman was getting better for a while. But I didn't know the dream lover she talked about was a *demon*, was something *real* trying to get to her. When I told Shaman Danyal the dreams had *helped* her, I didn't know they came from a demon. And when Kobrah told me about her friend, I didn't know he was *a demon*."

She paced a few steps away from him, then back, her agitation growing. In another minute, she might rush back to Danyal and stir everyone up. And that would have everyone looking too hard for someone who wasn't *completely* human.

Had it occurred to her that he and Danyal were also people in the not-completely-human column?

"Slow down," Lee said. "Zhahar, slow down. Not all dark landscapes are bad places, and not all demons are bad either. They're like any other people. Have the people who connected with the incubi or succubi said anything about them?"

"The man kept insisting that he had to cross over, had to meet his lover in the flesh. He became violent when he ran across one of the footbridges on the grounds and nothing happened. He's been in isolation ever since."

"If she gets as much pleasure in tormenting a man as she does from sex, being in isolation won't help, since the succubus can still reach him. What about the woman?"

"She was improving until the previous Keeper ordered her to be heavily sedated at night so she couldn't dream. She's failing now. The Shaman rescinded the order, but the dreams didn't come back."

"The incubus moved on," Lee said quietly. "He couldn't reach her anymore, so he moved on." He waited a beat. "What about Kobrah? I had the impression she hates men."

"Yes, she hates men. Something happened to her before she came here. I don't know what it was, but a man named Chayne did it."

"And yet she's drawn an incubus to her?"

"Her ... *friend* ... comes to her in dreams. They take walks in the moonlight. Hold hands. That sort of thing. He doesn't push to have sex."

"Wait a minute. Wait." Lee took off the dark glasses. She wasn't more than a dark blob, but he didn't want any kind of barrier between them. "Kobrah is *Teaser*'s friend?"

He saw her body blob jerk. "You know Teaser?"

"I've known him for years. He lives in the Den of Iniquity."

"That place is *real*?"

"Sure. My cousin Sebastian lives there." He hesitated, then decided it was better to tell her now. "You read Sholeh's report, didn't you? Well, Sebastian is an incubus and he's also a wizard, but he's a Justice Maker—the good kind of wizard. So I've grown up knowing some incubi, which is why I'm a good kisser. Just a point of information."

The body blob got shorter.

"You feeling all right?" he asked.

"Dizzy."

Translation: she was bent over, probably with her hands on her knees.

Then he caught a whiff of stinkweed. Someone Ephemera didn't like—or didn't like around him—was approaching.

"You can't believe anything a madman says," Lee said quietly, urgently. "You do remember that?"

Zhahar straightened slowly. "You made all this up?"

"I didn't say that." He kept his voice low. "We need to go now, *Sholeh*. We need to go back to the residence *now*." He slipped the dark glasses on and breathed a sigh of relief when he felt her resonance change from Zhahar to Sholeh. "Are you all right?"

"I'm fine," Sholeh said. "I guess I had too much sun. I need a drink of water and a little time to sit in the shade."

"Sounds like a good idea to me."

"Here." She brushed her arm against his. He cupped his hand around her elbow and let her take them back to the inmates' residence at a pace too brisk for the heat.

She didn't greet anyone, didn't speak to anyone, and the smell of stinkweed faded. Which meant whoever had been approaching had slipped out of sight.

"How different do you and Zhahar look?" he asked quietly.

"She has brown hair and blue eyes. I have auburn hair and green eyes. Zeela has dark brown hair and eyes. We look different."

Based on his physical contact with each of them, he agreed. Sholeh: thinner and nervier. Zeela: more muscle and physical strength—and that scar on her left arm as well as the tattoo that was a sign of her people. Zhahar: between the two, and a figure he suspected had a bit more softness and curve than her sisters. At least, that was his impression from the times when she'd assisted him. He wanted a chance to put his hands on her and find out.

"You think someone was coming?" Sholeh whispered.

"I *know* someone was coming. But I don't think he got close enough to see us."

"That's good," she murmured. "That's good. We've gotten careless. Can't afford . . . Oh!"

"What?" He swayed a little to balance the abrupt halt.

"The waterfall and pond are gone. And the fish. That smelly reflecting pool is back."

Lee sighed. "You're not used to things being so . . . fluid?"

"Are you?"

He sighed again. "Tell Danyal that he and I need to talk."

"All right." She started walking again. He hoped they were heading for shade and water.

"Don't worry about Kobrah. She'll be fine with Teaser."

"Why are you sure of that?"

He laughed softly. "Because if he gets out of line, my mother will whack him with a wooden spoon."

He heard male voices. The Handlers Nik and Denys. Good resonances that belonged in this landscape.

"Thank you for the walk, Sholeh," he said.

"I was glad to help," she replied. "I hope we can talk again."

Lee grinned. "Just ask your sister to arrange it."

She walked away without saying another word.

Nik and Denys let him find his own way up the stairs, but he felt them stand ready to help if he stumbled.

"Sholeh mentioned that the pond changed to a pool?" Lee put enough doubt in his voice to make the statement a question. After all, something like that changing would be unsettling for a man who couldn't see.

"It changed," Nik said grimly. "Not even the Shaman knows how or why."

Not a good answer. "Anything else change?"

"Those stone walls with the vines are gone. Had to wrap

Vito in restraints when he saw the place was gone. He's been wailing ever since."

"Anything else?" Lee asked.

A hesitation, as if they were deciding whether they were answering an inmate or a fellow Handler.

"Nothing significant," Denys finally said. "Just that weird treasure hunt."

"Treasure hunt?"

"Yeah. These old pocket watches keep showing up in the flower beds. And Teeko found a piece of a sundial this morning. Somebody must be slipping out at night and burying them around the plantings."

"I guess it provides a bit of interest," he said. "And like you said, it's weird but harmless."

Counting the steps from the door, Lee tapped his way to the lounge chair that was under the window in his room. Kobrah appeared a few minutes later with a large glass of water.

He sat alone, letting his mind drift as it picked up the pieces of information he'd been given and put them down again, shifting things around until they formed a different pattern.

Message received, Magician.

Was this some kind of heart lesson, that it was *Michael* who had found a way to locate him, to let him know his family was trying to reach him?

Message received. But until I can figure out the risks, I won't be sending a reply.

Danyal waited until dusk to have Lee brought to him at the reflecting pool. Teeko and the other groundskeepers had drained the stagnant water — or most of it. Tomorrow they would clean out the rest. Again. Then what?

A reflecting pool gets replaced by the waterfall and pond. That disappears and the reflecting pool returns. Then that mysterious place Vito was so excited about vanished. If Danyal hadn't seen the place for himself, he would have said it was a delusion of a troubled mind.

In the city of Vision, you can find only what you can see. But nothing like this had happened in the city before.

Ever? some part of him asked. *We've accepted the nature*

of this city without ever asking why it is the way it is. We've accepted it as a reflection of the rest of Ephemera. But if we've accepted for so long without looking, what don't the Shamans see? And why does everything keep pointing to this blind man having some of the answers?

He watched Lee tap his way toward him, with Kobrah keeping pace. When Lee reached him, Danyal thanked Kobrah—a gentle dismissal.

"Is there something I should know about?" Danyal asked quietly.

"Any number of things," Lee replied, sounding distracted. "You asking about anything in particular?"

"I asked Zhahar to escort you to me. Why was Kobrah your guide?"

"If that's your way of asking if I did something inappropriate with Sholeh, I did not. But I suspect Zhahar and her sister are currently engaged in a lively discussion because of a couple of things that were said." Lee wrinkled his nose. "I wonder if this used to be Sorrow's Ground."

Danyal felt a prickle along his spine. "What?"

"Something I've wondered, Shaman. All that sorrow that's released in your little temple. Where does it go? Most villages have a dark place—a piece of land that has sinkholes or that looks fine but won't grow crops. A place where the Dark currents are swollen with all the bad feelings. It's often called Sorrow's Ground. At first I thought it might be the whole Asylum, that this place was a dumping ground for the rest of the city and people were sent here as punishment."

"They're sent here to have a chance to heal," Danyal snapped. Then he caught himself. Was that true because that's what he wanted the Asylum to be—a place for these people to heal? When he raised his voice to the world, wasn't he hoping to bring something that *would* change the emotionally barren earth of this place?

He looked at Lee and the prickle along his spine grew stronger. "Several months ago, something arrived in Vision and . . . stained . . . a piece of the city. Turned a shadow street so dark the Shaman who tended that part of the city could no longer find that street. Then other shadow streets were lost from the Shamans' sight, and some bright places began to have pools of shadow."

And every letter he received from his nephew Kanzi, assuring him that Nalah and the baby were well, eased his heart. So did the assurance that the strangeness he'd felt at that one bridge hadn't crept into the village.

"So this stain happened before any of the inmates—or Kobrah—began having vivid dreams?"

"Erotic dreams, don't you mean?"

"Not in Kobrah's case, if what she told Zhahar is true."

"Yes, the stain was reported first, the streets lost to our sight. I wasn't here when those dreams were first reported by the Handlers, but I've checked the files of all the inmates. Only two of them and Kobrah have had such dreams."

"Any other kinds of dreams?" Lee asked. "Someone whispering in the dark? Whispering inside your own head?"

"Mice in the walls," Danyal replied quietly. "Mice in the walls, scratching to get in. Always scratching. But the walls are strong."

Lee shifted his body closer to Danyal. "You?"

"Yes. Perhaps others, but I've felt what you described. Tell me about your sister."

Lee jerked.

Danyal felt a measure of surprise too. They had been speaking of something of grim importance to the whole city. But now that the words were spoken, they felt right.

"Why?" Lee asked warily.

"You grieve for her. I don't think she is the only sorrow that is released when you are in the temple, but she is the sorrow you named. What happened to her, Lee?"

"Who is asking? You? Or the mice in the walls?"

"I—" Danyal stopped. Thought. Why had he asked about Lee's sister at that moment? "I'm not sure."

Silence. Then Lee said, "The Warrior of Light must drink from the Dark Cup."

The words pulled Danyal into a current that was Light and Dark, hot and cold, that pressed him under before letting him go.

He breathed in deeply, as if to assure himself that it was air he took in. Then he released it slowly. "I don't understand."

"It's a story from the country of Elandar. I'll tell you my version of it.

"Once upon a time," Lee began, "the Dark Guides

shaped a terrible creature called the Eater of the World. It was made from the dark feelings that live in the human heart, and Its purpose was to change the world into a terrible place where fear ruled and hope could not survive. It wanted to snuff out the Light in the world. A war was fought. The Guides of the Heart rallied and broke the world into pieces in their effort to contain the Eater. Broke it more and more until they trapped the Eater in one piece — and caged It and the landscapes It had shaped and the creatures It had made. Unable to return to the places they had called home, the Guides remained in that landscape, hiding the cage from the Dark Guides. They learned how to reconnect some of the pieces of Ephemera, and some of them and the children borne to them became Landscapers who kept the currents of Light and Dark balanced in the pieces of the world that resonated with them. And some of them became Bridges who had the power to connect the broken pieces, allowing people to cross over from one place to another."

Cross over. Danyal sucked in a breath. Wasn't that what the inmate had wanted to do? Cross over to find his dream lover?

"Generations came and went," Lee continued. "One day a special girl was born. Her father was a wizard and her mother was a Landscaper. Because of that, she had a connection to the Dark currents of the world as well as the Light. And because she came from a bloodline that was a secret protected by her mother's family, she was not only a powerful Landscaper; she was also a true Guide of the Heart. She had a special connection to Ephemera, a connection so strong she could *shape* the world, make new places, rearrange pieces."

Danyal stared at the empty reflecting pool that had been a lovely water garden a couple of days ago.

"One day the Eater of the World escaped Its cage. It attacked the school where Landscapers and Bridges were trained. It killed all the people It could find there and opened the school to Its creatures and Its landscapes. It hunted, and where It hunted, the Dark currents swelled and the Light was diminished.

"Because the girl, who was now a grown woman, could control the Dark currents as well as the Light, she was the only one strong enough to stand against the Eater of the World. But she didn't know how to stop it, how to fight it, until a man showed her *his* family's secrets and told her about the Warrior of Light. So she made her plans and prepared for this battle to save the world. She went to the school and built a trap for the Eater. She gathered Its landscapes and Its creatures. She trapped most of the Dark Guides and many of the wizards in their lair. And she stood there as bait, waiting for the Eater of the World to destroy her.

"But the Warrior of Light must drink from the Dark Cup. When the Eater arrived to take back Its landscapes and creatures, she sprang her trap. She gathered up the Light and cast it out of the dark landscape she had made. She—" Lee's voice broke. "In order to close that terrible place so that no one—no friend or family—could reach her and be trapped in that place with her, she cast out the Light in her heart. She ripped the Light out of her heart and threw it away—and the last lock on the trap closed, sealing her in with the Eater of the World. And because there was no Light in her, because she was only the dark feelings that live in the human heart, she was more dangerous and terrifying than the Eater or the Dark Guides. She became the monster that Evil feared.

"Months passed. A Magician, the man who had told her how to defeat the Eater, found a way to reach her in that unreachable place. Because he also had a strong connection to Ephemera, he found a way to touch the Warrior's heart, and he and Ephemera helped her leave that terrible place and come back to the people who loved her.

"But a heart that was torn apart as hers was doesn't mend, can't be healed. Instead of returning as the person she had been, she was now two people, the Light and the Dark. And that is how she remains. The Warrior is all that is good in the human heart, and most of the time, that is who you see. But sometimes, when you look into her eyes, you will see the monster that Evil feared."

Lee let out a shuddering sigh. "That's my version of the story about the Warrior of Light."

Danyal studied Lee. Bitterness. Grief. Sorrow. "That is a powerful story, and a tragic one." He laid a hand lightly on Lee's shoulder. "But you were going to tell me about your sister."

Lee stepped away from Danyal and said, "I just did."

Tap tap. Tap tap.

Danyal let him go, but when he saw Zhahar standing outside the inmates' residence, watching, he signaled her to go with Lee. Then he stared at the reflecting pool.

The Warrior of Light must drink from the Dark Cup.

She became the monster that Evil feared.

Lee being held captive—drugged and blinded—by men posing as his uncles.

Voices whispering in dreams, scratching at his own mind, trying to influence him. *Why?*

Lee's version of a story. Not an evasion but a veiled answer.

Danyal stood still, hardly daring to breathe as particular words resonated in his mind and heart.

A Guide who became a monster. Lee's sister was a Guide who became a monster.

If Lee was the madman and teacher, was his sister the Guide and monster he was supposed to find?

He wouldn't mention Lee's sister to the Council yet, but the Eater of the World and Warrior of Light? Yes, he would write to Farzeen and ask if any such beings were mentioned in the Shamans' myths. He would do it now and send the messenger out at first light.

And he would hope that nothing else changed in the dark hours.

Tap tap. Tap tap.

"Lee, wait!"

He ignored Zhahar, since her tone sounded a bit too much like a command, and he wasn't interested in *anyone* giving him orders. Not right now.

"By the Mother's third eye, will you wait?"

She grabbed his loose-weave shirt and hauled back with enough strength to pop a few stitches in the seams. He would have shoved forward, trying to break a hold he suspected had more than a little Zeela added to it, but a quick stir of air brought the sound of leaves close to his face.

Zhahar got a firm grip on his left arm. "Let me take you back to the residence."

"If I'd wanted to go back to the residence, I would have

gone to the residence," he snapped. "I need to walk. I need to think."

He felt her hesitation. "If we walk, will you talk to me? Or at least think out loud, so I have some idea what's going on?"

"You can't trust anything a madman says." And even though he participated in this particular ruse, he was getting damn tired of it.

"You maneuvered Sholeh into telling you too much, but Zeela and I didn't try that hard to stop her. And it wasn't a madman we trusted with a secret that could destroy our people," she said, her voice low and rough.

That statement startled him enough that he took a step back in response to her tug on his arm. "Destroy your people? How?"

"Do you think we're wanted? Accepted? We're adrift in the world. Our land, our people."

Lee stood perfectly still but felt as if everything was swirling around him.

Whatever you give to the world comes back to you.

Opportunities and choices.

Heart wishes.

He didn't want to see Glorianna, and now he was blind.

He wanted to get away from the places held by his mother and sister, and now he was in a city he'd never heard of.

But the enemy was already here, working to alter the landscapes that made up the city of Vision.

"All right," he said. "I'll talk. You listen. Don't say *anything* about your people. Lead us away from the buildings, but if you smell stinkweed, take the straightest route back to the residence."

"This way."

He wasn't sure where they were going and was certain he wouldn't find his way back by himself.

"Talk," she said quietly.

"In other pieces of Ephemera, if you travel to a place you don't belong, you feel so uneasy you leave. Where I come from, you can't reach a landscape, dark or light, that doesn't resonate with your own heart. How do people reach this city, Zhahar?"

"Reach it? Ships travel upriver from the sea. There are roads, so people come on horseback or in carriages. Although it's been said that not everyone can find the city." She paused, then asked, "Did you see the signs when you arrived?"

"No. What do they say?"

"As you cross the boundary into the city, there is a sign that says 'Ask your heart its destination.' Then you end up crossing a bridge or going under an arch and there is another sign that says 'Welcome to Vision. You can find only what you can see.' Is that what you wanted to know?"

"When the landscape that held Wizard City was taken out of the world, there were Dark Guides and wizards traveling in other parts of Ephemera. If Heart's Justice had exposed all of the Dark Guides for what they are, they can't pass for human anymore. But the wizards, being descended from the Dark Guides but not pureblood, still wear a human face. If someone suddenly takes your stronghold, what do you do? You run fast and far. Get on a ship and hope it takes you somewhere. Cross a resonating bridge and focus on reaching a part of the world your adversary hasn't touched. One way or another, a Dark Guide and some of the wizards ended up here in Vision."

"But the Shamans . . ."

"Can't see an enemy they don't know exists," Lee said. "They didn't even realize something was wrong until bits of the city changed and are now out of their reach. Now they can't see what's happening in those places or what's causing the change."

"This way," Zhahar said, leading him toward the right. "There's a—"

"No bridges," Lee said sharply.

She stopped, and he could feel her eyes on him. "How did you know there was a bridge?"

"I can feel it." He could also feel that it wanted to change into more than simple wood. It wanted to *resonate*. It would pull at him, at his power, if he tried to cross it. Which told him how many hearts didn't belong in this place. "No bridges, Zhahar." Especially with her. What would happen to someone with *three resonances* if she tried to cross a resonating bridge? He didn't want to find out. Not if there was another choice.

"We won't be able to get as far from the buildings as you wanted," she said.

"Fine. Just . . . no bridges."

They walked in silence for a minute or two. Then she said, "Bits of the city are changing?"

He nodded. "Because the Dark Guide and the wizards are nurturing the Dark currents, making it easier for people to get away with doing harm. And they can get into people's minds and influence them or weaken them. They dim the Light." He felt her shiver. "But when you connect with a place, you change its resonance just a little. The Dark Guides and wizards are from my part of the world. When they came here, they left a trail of sorts. Because there is a similarity in their powers, the next ones to cross over were the incubi and succubi, traveling through the twilight of waking dreams. Demons who have never been in this city before. Then I was attacked by wizards and I made a choice: to get the enemy away from my family, especially my mother and sister. I don't think I brought those wizards to Vision. I think they were able to focus their will on the resonating bridges I made and bring me with them because they already had a little piece of the city under their control. I was captured and blinded and drugged to sound and act insane."

"They didn't want anyone to believe what you said about them," Zhahar said.

"That's part of it," he agreed. "But they weren't paying attention to the nature of Ephemera. If they had, they wouldn't have brought their own enemy to the city."

"But what can you do?"

He heard the hesitation in her voice. She didn't want to hurt him or remind him that finding his room, the porch chair, and the toilet were huge accomplishments for him right now.

Guardians of the Light and Guides of the Heart . . . No, Lee thought. He didn't need to ask for help from all the Guardians and Guides. Just one.

"Why are you here, Zhahar? Why did you come to Vision?"

"We can't talk about this," Sholeh Zeela a Zhahar whispered.

"We have to," he insisted. "Did you cross over a border or a bridge at some point and find yourself here, away from your people?"

She shook her head. "When our leader sensed we were close to another piece of Ephemera, she cast out lines of power that provided a connection between Tryadnea and Vision. In order to keep that connection, some Tryad have to live in the city, providing a kind of living anchor that holds Tryadnea in place. Six Tryad came here. I'm the only one left. If I fail, the last connection between Vision and Tryadnea will break, and my homeland will be adrift again."

Maybe not, he thought. *Maybe you need to let go of this connection in order to make a more permanent one.* "All right. Here is something you and your sisters need to think about. Heart wishes are powerful, and Ephemera does listen."

What you give to the world comes back to you.
Opportunities and choices.
Heart's hope lies within Belladonna.
Was that still true?

"Where is Vito?" he asked.

"In isolation. We're afraid . . ." Zhahar's hand clamped on his arm. "There is concern that he'll try to harm himself."

"I need to see him, talk to him. We need to do it now."

"They won't let anyone see him now. That will get him stirred up all evening, and if he's stirred up . . ."

"Tomorrow morning, then. As soon as possible. You can help me slip into the room so I can talk to him before too many people are up and around to notice."

"Why?"

Lee took a deep breath and let it out in a sigh. "Because it's time for me to go back to work."

Chapter Sixteen

Zhahar's hands shook as she rolled up trousers, tunics, and underclothes as tightly as she could, packing as much as she could into the large cloth traveling bag. The bag had shoulder straps, and that would help, but it would be as much as she could carry. Maybe more than she could carry in their present condition.

How are you? she asked. The bruise along her ribs was black and spongy in a way that told her there was blood under the skin. Which meant the knife slash Zeela had taken was still bleeding.

=Hurting,= Zeela replied. Then she added reluctantly, =I'm going to need someone to sew me up.=

::Leave the books,:: Sholeh said when Zhahar reached for them. ::I'm not strong enough to carry what we're taking, and the weight of the clothes is going to hurt both of you.::

We agreed that we could each take something personal, Zhahar said, although, after packing Zeela's weapons, she chose to leave her own trinkets behind. *We don't know if our things will still be here when we're able to come back.* Or if any of them would want to come back for a few possessions. If Zeela was attacked and wounded two doors from their rooms, Sholeh wouldn't be able to come into view at all on this street anymore.

::I'm changing the agreement,:: Sholeh said. ::Books are heavy. We take clothes, shoes, toiletries. Only enough to get us by. Don't argue, Zhahar! If you can't make it back to the Asylum, there's no place we can find help for Zeela.::

Painful truth. But Zhahar's hand hovered over Sholeh's precious books a moment longer before she turned away.

They had bandaged the wound as best they could, but it was serious enough to weaken all of them. Zeela couldn't carry the traveling bag. Neither could Sholeh, who could drag it if she had to, but that would tell the men who had turned into predators that she wasn't strong enough to defend herself against them. And maybe those men *were* only after dark-haired women, which is what they were shouting when they attacked, but if that wasn't true, Sholeh wouldn't stand a chance.

I'm sorry about the books, Sholeh.

::If something happens to us, we lose more than books,:: Sholeh replied. ::There isn't much of Tryadnea left that isn't desert. If we lose this connection, we'll lose more arable land, and our people won't survive long if that happens.::

I know.

Zhahar packed everything she could into the bag, knowing its weight would stagger her for the few blocks between their room and the omnibus stop. Despite that, and ignoring Sholeh's mutters, she took their largest market sack and filled it with as much of their food as possible. Their money she hid in the traveler's pouch around her waist, keeping in her trouser pocket just enough for the omnibus fare.

Zhahar took a last look around. Despite their best efforts to fit in and belong, the connection between Vision and Tryadnea had slipped during the past few months and was now somewhere in the northeastern end of the city. How much longer would it hold?

And what had Lee meant by heart wishes?

She had burned their mother's letters so that no one would know about the Tryad—and so that no one would know where the last connection between the lands was located.

Nothing more to do except leave while she had the strength to reach the Asylum.

Settling the straps on her shoulders, Zhahar tried to stifle the moan as she felt the pull of the bag's weight. If Zeela didn't get help soon, they would be faced with the terrible choice of letting one sister die in order to save the other two.

Clenching her teeth, Zhahar left their rooms and stepped out into the gray light that held the promise of dawn.

"Lee?"

Lee opened his eyes to gray light that held dark shapes. He pushed up and rolled off the narrow bed as someone turned the handle on his door.

"Lee? It's Sholeh."

Swearing softly, he stepped toward the door, hands in front of him to protect his face if she pushed open the door.

"Hold on," he said. He found the edge of the door and pulled it open. "What are you doing here?"

She didn't answer. Probably couldn't, since she was puffing while dragging something into his little room.

"Daylight," he muttered. Finding her shoulder, he held her still while his other hand traveled down her arm to the soft bag. "What have you got in here? A body?"

"Clothes. Shoes. Our things. Zeela was attacked outside our rooms. We were afraid to stay there. She's hurt."

He found a strap and hauled the bag farther into the room—and Sholeh with it. Then he closed the door.

There were too many questions he wanted to ask, but he heard her breathy efforts not to cry. "Where is Zhahar?"

"She needs to rest, so I'm in view now. Sh-she's hurt too. Not cut like Zeela, but the wound is showing through on her too."

Lee's heart jumped. The wound was *showing through*? "How badly is Zeela hurt?"

"Bad. A knife slice along the ribs. It's still bleeding."

Now he swore in earnest. "Why didn't you get to the infirmary and have whoever is on duty summon Meddik Benham?"

"And say what?" she cried. "How can I explain Zeela being here without Zhahar or why I have our things? We trust you to know about us, but . . ."

"I know how to keep family secrets," he said. "Sit in the chair. Zeela needs to . . ." He hesitated, trying to remember her phrasing. "Zeela needs to come into view now."

He didn't wait for her agreement. Feeling his way to the

door, he opened it, winced a little at the soft light, then began moving down the hallway, fingertips brushing the wall on his left, traveling over other doors.

The door at the end of the hallway opened.

"Lee?" Nik's normally friendly voice held a challenge and warning. "You're not supposed to leave your room until first call."

"I need to see the Shaman, and you need to fetch the Meddik. *Now.*"

"Look here—I know Shaman Danyal has been lenient with you, but . . ."

"A woman is hurt and needs Meddik Benham. *Fetch him now!*"

The hallway lit up so bright that Lee ducked his head to protect his eyes. A heartbeat later, thunder rattled the building.

He braced a hand on the wall. "Guardians and Guides, *that's* never happened before." At least, not in response to *his* temper.

"You go back to your room," Nik said, sounding shaken. "I'll fetch— Shaman!"

"What happened?" Danyal asked, huffing a bit as if he'd run to the building from wherever he'd been.

"I'll explain," Lee said. "Nik is going for the Meddik. Zeela is in my room. She's been hurt."

"Tell Benham he's needed here," Danyal said.

A moment after Nik dashed off, Lee felt Danyal approach—and wondered if he or the Shaman had caused that flash of lightning and the thunder that followed.

"What's Zeela doing in your room, Lee?" Danyal asked softly.

"I won't betray a trust," Lee replied just as softly, "so I won't tell you all you want to know. I understand some things about Zhahar and her sisters. I think that's why they came to my room. Or that was as far as they could get."

"Zhahar and Sholeh are here too?"

"Yes." *Would I trust this man enough to gamble with my own family? Would I tell him enough to help him guess the rest?* "Their full name is Sholeh Zeela a Zhahar."

Danyal jerked, then said, "Brooks full of bright water. Storms. A summer lake."

So Danyal *had* felt something when he was around the sisters.

"Some of the spiritual practices of Zhahar's people would be compromised if she were to stay in the infirmary," Lee said. He wasn't sure calling them spiritual practices was accurate, but that explanation would receive the least resistance when it came to changing the rules. "She can stay in my room."

"No, she cannot."

Lee huffed out a breath. "I'm not going to see anything I shouldn't see, but I can offer some muscle, because I think they'll need it. Kobrah can help. And I can sit on the porch under my window so I can hear if she needs help without being in the room all the time." He could feel Danyal's resistance. "Daylight, man! If Zeela can strip me down and bathe me, I can sit by the bed and watch over her."

"Zeela?"

Lee shrugged. "It's amazing how much people let you see when you can't see."

Silence when they heard two people running.

"She's down in Lee's room," Danyal said.

"Why didn't someone have sense enough to bring her to the infirmary?" Benham growled as he trotted past them.

Lee assumed the door he heard opening was his, especially when the Meddik's footsteps stopped.

"Get a stretcher!" Benham shouted. "Get it now!"

Nik ran.

Danyal's hand closed on Lee's arm, guiding him as they hurried back to his room.

Based on the arrangements of dark blobs and gray light, Lee figured they were standing in the doorway of his room.

"How is she?" Danyal asked.

"She has a deep knife wound between two ribs," Benham snapped. "How do you think she is? As soon as Nik returns with that stretcher, she's going to the infirmary."

"Just need a little sewing up," Zeela said, her voice slurred.

"A couple of hours ago, you *might* have needed just a little sewing up," Benham said. "Now . . ."

"Benham," Danyal said.

"If you have something to say to me that you don't want shouted to everyone within hearing, come in. I've got to keep pressure on this wound. And who is this anyway? And why is she in a male inmate's room?"

"She's Handler Zhahar's sister. She had reasons to seek help from Lee."

Picturing the dark look he was getting from Benham, Lee said, "I'm not having sex with Zeela."

"Tch," Zeela slurred. "Wouldn't have him anyway, since he wants to rub skin with Zhahar."

"Which we haven't done," Lee said firmly. Rub skin? He'd been fantasizing about a bit more than that lately, but he didn't know the Tryad's customs when it came to having sex. Maybe touching skin, which was unique to each sister, was considered more intimate than touching body parts that were shared?

Nik returned with a stretcher and Denys. A protesting and no doubt frightened Zeela was moved from chair to stretcher and hurried to the infirmary.

Lee wanted to go with them but figured a blind man would be in the way. Besides, hearing the door close and Danyal quietly turning, he didn't think leaving the room was an option right now.

"What's that?" Danyal asked.

"If you're referring to the pack, it's what they could bring. They ran, Danyal. Something turned sour where they live, and they ran after Zeela was hurt. Took what they could and most likely left the rest."

"Should I understand that I won't be able to talk to Zhahar until Zeela is out of the infirmary?"

"Yes, you should understand that."

Silence. Then, "Where did you come from, Lee?"

"I come from a village called Aurora. I don't know where that is in relation to this city except the air has less heat there even on a muggy day, and I'm pretty sure the plants look different based on the leaves I've felt. But we don't measure distance the way you do. We don't travel the way you do."

"Why not?"

"Because I grew up in the part of the world that was a broken battlefield. I can walk down the road and never be able to reach the neighboring village if it's not a place that resonates with my heart, but I can cross a bridge and be in another part of the world. That's the Ephemera I know."

Lee cocked his head. "Does it bother you that she told me some things about her people that she didn't tell you?"

"Yes. The Shamans protect this city and its people."

"Zhahar has the skills that earn the wages that allow them to stay in the city. If you couldn't accept some of her ..."

"Spiritual practices?"

Lee nodded. "Their lives would get a lot harder. Me? Not as much risk having me figure it out."

"Unless the wound is so severe that Zeela must stay in the infirmary, I'll convince Benham to let her return here. You and Kobrah—and Zhahar—will take turns watching over her. I'll let you figure out what to tell Kobrah about Zhahar's *spiritual practices*."

"And Sholeh will help," Lee reminded him. "She's here too."

"All right. In the meantime, the morning routine has been disrupted enough."

"I had arranged with Zhahar to visit Vito this morning."

Weight to this silence. "Why?"

"I think I can help him," Lee said. "I think it would be better if you didn't ask how. At least, not yet."

Another silence. "Have you put in your eyedrops this morning?"

"No."

"I'll have Kobrah come and assist you, and escort you to the isolation cell where Vito is being held."

"Thank you, Shaman."

The door opened and closed and Lee was alone in his room.

The wound was showing through. Were they all feeling weak from blood loss? How badly was Zhahar hurt? Until she was able to come into view, there was no way for anyone to see the damage or help her.

A rap on his door, a token courtesy, since Handlers and Helpers could enter whenever they wanted to.

Kobrah entered. "Shaman said I was to help with the eyedrops and then take you to see Vito."

"Yes."

"Zhahar's sister is in the infirmary. Knife wound."

He heard something dangerous in Kobrah's voice. "What happened to you, Kobrah?"

"The first Chayne hurt me, made something go wrong inside my head."

Damn.

"Zhahar says you're a good man, says you're not a Chayne and I can trust you."

"She's right." And he hoped with all that was in him that Kobrah believed it.

She stepped over to the dresser.

"The eyedrops are in the top right-hand drawer," he said.

"I know." She paused. "Can't sit on the chair. There's blood on the floor."

Not good. If Zeela was still bleeding that much, it was not good.

"Sit on the bed. It's just behind you."

He felt for the bed and sat. She put in the eyedrops, as quick and gentle as Zhahar. While he sat with a damp, cool cloth over his eyes, she replaced the bottle in the dresser, and, based on what he was hearing, must have done a little tidying up while she waited. Then she led him to Vito.

They weren't going to leave him alone with a restrained man—and he didn't want them to. But he leaned over the bed and said quietly, "That place you saw the other day. Is that where you belong?"

"Yes," Vito sobbed. "I found home. But it's *gone.*"

"It wasn't supposed to stay," Lee said. "It was meant to be a chance for you to look, to let your heart feel."

"I found *home.*"

"I don't know if you'll find that exact piece of the world, but I can help you find the place it came from."

The sobs trailed off and finally stopped.

"You can find it?" Vito asked.

"I can give *you* a chance to find it. But the first thing you have to do is get well enough to be released from this room. There are steps you'll have to take, things you'll need to do. If you can do them, I'll help you."

Lee stepped back from the bed. "Could you take me to the temple? I'd like to spend some time there while we wait for news about Zeela."

A pause. Then Kobrah said, "Yes, I'll take you there."

* * *

Ephemera flowed through the currents of power in this part of itself, waiting for the Lee-heart to find the new access point and cross over to the Music, waiting for Voice-guide to listen to another heart and help it shape a little making. *She* did not want it bringing other pieces of itself to this place, but *she* wouldn't be unhappy with it if *another* Guide helped it make something new.

But the Lee-heart passed by the access point, not even looking when it pushed the stolen time above the ground. So it added violets to the access point. *She* always smiled when it made violets from the Music's song.

Then Voice-guide approached the access point and picked up the stolen time, but didn't take the step between here and there. So the world flowed through the currents of itself, both Light and Dark, changing little pieces of itself to match the resonance of the strongest hearts. And it waited.

Danyal and Benham watched Kobrah and Nik settle Zeela into Lee's bed.

Benham turned away from the door and pitched his voice low. "You're leaving a wounded woman in the hands of an inmate. Do you think that's wise?"

"Maybe not, but it's the choice I'm making," Danyal replied absently, his mind preoccupied with the new planting in the flower bed between the inmates' residence and the temple. Slipping his hand in the pocket of his white robe, he fingered the pocket watch that had pushed itself out of the ground as he studied the plants. He was still waiting for some response to his last report to the Council, but in all the years he'd been a working Shaman, and even during the years when he'd been training, he'd never heard of the world being this responsive, this *active*.

"I've overheard enough whispers lately to know many of the Handlers are wondering the same thing I am about Lee."

"And what is that?"

"If he's someone from The Temples. Not a Shaman, but someone who might be strongly connected."

Danyal looked at Benham in surprise. "What makes you think that? Have you forgotten his uncles or how he came to the Asylum?"

"Oh, no one has forgotten that, especially since those men used to come by often to check on him but have suddenly stopped visiting. You treat him more like an injured colleague than an inmate, and after you dismissed those false Handlers and got him clean of the drugs they were giving him, he has acted more like someone who is used to being in charge. So there is speculation among the Handlers about who he really is. I thought you should know."

"I appreciate that." *And it's still a question I would like answered myself. Especially after seeing the latest change in the flower bed.*

Tap tap. Tap tap.

They both turned as Lee tapped his way down the hallway.

"Lee," Danyal said, giving him time to stop.

"Shaman." Lee tipped his head. "Meddik Benham?"

"It seems your hearing has sharpened," Benham said.

"And you wear a distinctive cologne," Lee replied, smiling.

Kobrah and Nik stepped out of the room.

"See to your other duties now," Danyal told them.

"And I'll see to my other patients," Benham said. "I left a dose of pain medicine on the dresser. If Zeela needs it, Handler Zhahar can give it to her." He hesitated, then gave Danyal a nod—and gave Lee a searching look.

"Benham and others are speculating that we're colleagues," Danyal said.

Lee's smile didn't look easy or amused. "That's true, since Landscapers and Bridges have complementary skills that help keep the world balanced."

"I found another pocket watch on the ground beside some little purple flowers and a nightshade plant." He had felt the power of tidal waves and avalanches when he'd looked at that plant. Noting the sudden tightness in Lee's face, he asked, "Do you know it by another name?"

"Where I come from, we call it belladonna."

"What does it mean, Lee?"

"That depends. Was there a heart's hope plant in the same bed or nearby?"

Light. Hope. "I don't know a plant by that name, but one I've never seen before appeared a few days ago. It seems to lift the spirits of everyone who walks by."

Lee sighed. "Message received."

"Lee?" Danyal's voice sharpened.

"Let it go, Danyal. For now, let it go. Zeela needs care."

"I'd like to speak to Zhahar."

Lee felt his way to the door and into the room. "I'll tell her. Wait here a few minutes."

The door closed. A couple minutes later, Zhahar opened the door and slipped out of the room. She had dark circles under her eyes and moved like she was in pain.

"Shaman?"

"You're relieved of all duties for today and tomorrow. Get some rest and tend your sister. There is pain medicine on the dresser."

"Yes, Lee mentioned it."

"Your sister Sholeh can take her meals in the Handlers' dining hall." When she nodded, he added, "I'll take a cart and a couple of men back to your rooms and clear out the rest of your things before they're stolen."

She paled, and he wondered what she'd left behind.

"That isn't necessary."

"No, it's not, but it will be done."

"Thank you."

Bright water. Summer lake. But the storm, the strength he usually felt in her was dimmed—but not, he hoped, failing. "Get some rest."

She slipped back into the room.

Perhaps it was foolish to go back to a street that was clearly changing into something troubled, but . . .

Kindness is a gift to yourself as well as to another.

One of the basic lessons.

Thinking about the plants in the garden—the heart's hope and the plant Lee called belladonna—Danyal had a feeling that when it truly mattered, every bit of kindness he gave was going to be counted.

Lee's fingers brushed against Zhahar's arm. "Sit down before you fall down." He waited until she sat on the bed, then sat beside her. "How bad is it?"

"Lots of stitches. More than we'd thought there would be. Sholeh has withdrawn. She doesn't deal well with the sight of blood."

Must be interesting with the two of you as sisters, Lee thought. "Sholeh said you're hurt too. How bad?"

"Oh, I'm not—"

"She said the wound was showing through. You can tell me what that means, or I can haul you to the infirmary."

"You wouldn't!"

"You're in no shape to stop me."

Two voices said some very bad words—and he was sure that, being a one-face, he couldn't do a lot of what they were suggesting he do.

"That's it." He took a firm grip on her arm.

"No!" Zhahar slumped. Then she sucked in a breath. "I have a bruise in the same place as the knife wound. A bad bruise. People would ask too many questions if they saw it. But it's not a cut or anything. Just a bruise." She hesitated. "And I'm staying close enough to Zeela to support her, so right now someone could feel her stitches under my skin."

"I see," he said. He wasn't sure if she was talking about supplying her sister with physical energy, life energy, or something else, but he wondered if Zeela would have survived this long if Zhahar hadn't been taking on some of the effects of the wound.

"I put our money belt in the dresser under your other set of clothes," Zhahar said. "I put the key to our rooms there too. You should give it to Shaman Danyal if he's really going to fetch the rest of our things."

"I'll see that he gets the key. And the dresser is as good a place as any for the money belt right now." Releasing her arm, he began rubbing her back, an easy motion meant to soothe and comfort. "What's the best thing for you to do now? I think Zeela needs to be in view, since different people are going to be taking watch and Benham is bound to check on her. But we can slide around that if we need to."

"If she wasn't so hurt, it would be better for Zeela to stay submerged and rest, but if there was trouble, she might not be able to come back into view and get help in time."

Which meant every minute she and Sholeh had been in view in the effort to get them to safety had put Zeela at risk. Had Zhahar and Sholeh also been at risk? Those kinds of questions would have to wait until he could get Sholeh alone—or as alone as any of them could be. The little sister could be coaxed into giving him more information than the other two.

"So except for meals, which Sholeh can eat for you . . ." He frowned. "*Can* she eat for all of you?"

"Yes, but don't let her eat any spicy foods. Zeela and I aren't up to dealing with the result when it reaches the other end."

He opened his mouth, but no words came out. Finally, "Got it. No spicy food for Sholeh. Anything else?"

"I can't think of anything."

He heard her voice slur from exhaustion. He continued to rub her back and felt her relax. She was still a dark blob in a room filled with gray light, but that showed him enough. Tipping her face toward his, he kissed her. Warmth and comfort. A physical reminder that she wasn't alone.

"You can see me?" she asked when he eased back.

"A little," he said, giving her the truth. "Dark shapes in gray light. But I've been kissing girls in the dark since I was fifteen, so I've had a bit of practice." He kissed her again, adding a little heat. Not enough to stir her, but enough to give her something to think about.

That kiss stirred him plenty, though.

He stood up. "Get yourself settled in bed so Zeela can come into view."

She did as she was told while he positioned the wooden chair near the end of the bed.

"Lee."

Zeela's voice was slurred. He didn't know if it was from the wound and loss of blood, or the pain, or the medicine they had given her for the pain.

His fingertips followed the edge of the bed until he found her hand. Her fingers closed around his, but there was no strength in her grip, and that worried him.

"Rest, Zeela. You can rest now."

"Shaman. Going to our rooms. He'll find things. About us. He'll . . ."

"I don't think he'll find anything he can't understand or accept. No matter what he finds, he won't ask you to leave before you're well enough to travel. And if he asks then, well, I know some people who could take a Tryad pretty much in stride. Although I can't promise you won't be pestered with questions."

Zeela made an effort to smile. "If they offer fair exchange, Sholeh will answer questions every minute she's in view."

That was exactly what he was counting on. He had information about all kinds of landscapes he could put on the table in exchange for information about the Tryad.

"Well, then. There's nothing to worry about."

Her hand went lax. He listened to her breathing even out into what he hoped would be a healing sleep. Then he sat back and thought about the people he was growing to care about here—and the people he'd left behind.

Danyal walked down the street where Zhahar lived. Thin ice. Black slush. Dead trees. Spring flowers withering as they tried to grow.

He hoped it hadn't felt that way all the time Zhahar had lived here.

His white robe told everyone watching from the street or doorways what he was. Some made a sign of blessing. An equal number saw him and, shrinking back, made a sign against evil.

What else had walked this street recently, hiding what it was? Or pretending to be something that it wasn't?

In a few more days, he wasn't sure any Shaman would be able to see this street anymore. Something else he needed to report to the Council.

When he reached the building where Zhahar had her rooms, he left Denys to watch the pony and cart while he and Nik took traveling bags and carry sacks up the stairs to Zhahar's rooms.

Their rooms? She had, after all, lived here with her sisters.

Not much left behind, he thought as he scanned the front room and the little cooking area. But enough.

"Start with the books," he told Nik. "I'll pack up the other room."

When he opened the dresser drawers and saw the underclothes, he wished he had brought Kobrah. Not because women's underclothes were unfamiliar—as he'd told Lee, Shamans weren't celibate—but because he could picture Zhahar's embarrassment that he'd seen what was intimate.

Then he picked up a carving and knew she wouldn't fear him seeing her underclothes, but this.

A triangle of wood as high as his forefinger. On each side, a woman's face. The faces were similar to each other, enough that one would call them sisters, but different enough not to be the same woman with different expressions. No, this . . .

Body, heart, and mind, he thought, turning the wood as he studied each face and decided what the expression represented. *Or body, heart, and spirit?* Pushing aside the underclothes, he found a flat piece of wood with a picture burned into it. Another woman's face, but she had a third eye in her forehead.

That represented spirit. Maybe wisdom as well?

He wrapped them in underclothes and tucked them into the travel bag.

Why wood? Was that the usual medium for the sacred symbols of Zhahar's people? Or were these made of wood because they could be burned if someone got too close to suspecting the truth? Whatever that was.

Lee said her name was Sholeh Zeela a Zhahar. One person with the name of all three sisters?

She hadn't been honest with him, and that scratched. He was chosen for difficult assignments because he *could* be trusted, *was* trusted.

It all came down to trust, didn't it?

The Shaman Council had made him the Asylum Keeper here because they'd said he was needed, that the city of Vision was going to need a bridge to span the distance between people.

As he checked every drawer and packed everything he could find, Danyal wondered if the council had sent him to the Asylum to be that bridge, or if they had sent him there because he would be trusted by the man who *could* span the distance between people.

Chapter Seventeen

Zhahar slowly came into view, careful not to disturb the bandages. The stitches were only in Zeela's body, although she could feel them under her own skin, a sign that Zeela was still borrowing strength from her aspect. But the bandages, like clothes, had to be worn by all of them, or they wouldn't be there for Zeela when she came into view.

Soft light came through the screened window, but not a breath of air. The heat in the small room was a weight against Zhahar's skin, and she desperately wanted to slip away to the bathing room and soak in a tub of cool water for a while.

A shape stirred in the chair, drew in a breath.

"Hey-a," Lee said, sounding sleepy. He leaned forward, reaching until his fingers brushed against her hand. "How are you feeling?"

"It's Zhahar."

"I know."

"You can tell just by touching my hand?"

"You feel different from your sisters. You smell different."

Feeling self-conscious because she was pretty sure she stank right now, she pushed herself up and eased her legs over the side of the bed—and was glad Lee couldn't see her wince from the effort. "We all use the same soap." And had argued for an hour in the shop while trying to find a scent all three of them liked because they could afford only one.

"It smells a little different on each of you." Lee sat back and smiled. "A bit tart on Zeela; sweeter on Sholeh. Just right on you."

She didn't know what to say.

"Would you like some broth?"

Now she knew what to say. "Sholeh had beans and rice with chicken. And she had *two* servings of the sweet." Unfortunately, even to her own ears, she sounded pouty when she said it.

"Sholeh doesn't have a wound that's showing through," Lee replied with enough bite to make her wary. "However, Kobrah said you liked those dishes, so she set some aside for you. But I'm not sure you want them for breakfast."

"I'm hungry. I wouldn't mind." She looked at the window and frowned. She remembered Sholeh telling her about the meal—and the odd wobble that was close to panic in her youngest sister's voice. She remembered keeping her aspect close enough to Zeela's to feel someone wiping down arms and legs to ease the fever, and wished she could feel that cool cloth on her own skin. She remembered hearing Lee and Danyal talking but couldn't recall what they had said. Hearing Kobrah. Hearing Benham.

"Yesterday morning," Lee said.

"What?"

"I can see you well enough to know you're looking at the window, so you're probably wondering how much time has passed since Sholeh knocked on my door. That was yesterday morning. You've hardly been in view, and when you have been, you sounded punch-drunk."

His voice had that bite again that she finally realized was caused by an effort to control his temper.

"Sholeh did pretty well for the first few hours, but when it became apparent that you and Zeela were so removed you weren't responding to anyone, even her . . ." He huffed out a sigh. "The last time Zeela came into view, her fever broke. Benham checked the stitches and put on a clean dressing. You came into view about an hour after that, long enough to drink a glass of water. We haven't seen you since. Sholeh surfaced a few times to use the toilet or drink some water, but she disappeared after Benham suggested a sedative. She probably needed one, but she was afraid it might harm Zeela."

"You don't understand about us."

"And that's going to change," Lee snapped. "Living in this city is too dangerous if *no one* knows how to help you when you're in trouble."

"What would you have me do?" Her voice was low but fierce. "My homeland is at stake. My *people* are at stake."

"Right now, your *sisters* are at stake."

A hazy awareness from Zeela. Sholeh coming close enough to the surface to listen.

"You don't understand," she said.

"Two-faced."

She and Sholeh gasped from the pain those words caused. Zeela moaned.

Lee braced his forearms on his thighs.

"Two-faced," he said again, his voice so full of understanding her eyes stung with tears. "It means one member of a Tryad is lost, doesn't it? It means someone made a hard choice. I've had a lot of time to think while I've been sitting here, Sholeh Zeela a Zhahar. One who is three. Three who are one. I'm guessing if one of you gets a knife in the heart, all of you die. I'm not sure about other things that would kill a different kind of person, but you might be able to survive a lot of injuries if you let the injured sibling die—or, more likely, if the injured sibling chooses to die to save the other two. Catastrophic damage. That's what it would take, wouldn't it? Something that would threaten the welfare of the other two to the point of death or permanent injury. It has happened often enough that your people have a word for it."

"Stop," she whispered as tears ran down her face.

Instead he took her hands in his, giving her someone to hold on to who didn't need her to be strong.

"I don't understand how you can be physically different in some ways and the same in others, but I'd say you've been supporting Zeela since she got you back to your rooms after the fight. That's why the wound is showing through on you. That's why you've sounded so dazed."

She heard Sholeh crying and wondered if Lee heard it too.

"If something happens . . ." She hesitated, but it had to be said. "Sholeh can't handle the one-face world on her own. She's smart, she really is, but she's more fragile than Zeela and me." *And if we don't make it . . .*

"Yes, she's smart. Yes, she's more fragile. And there are places where she would do just fine."

That bite in his voice again.

"But that's a discussion for another day," Lee continued, "because Zeela's wound is healing, and you don't have to hold on so tight it makes you ill. The best thing you can do for Zeela now is help yourself."

=He's right,= Zeela whispered.

::Please listen to him, Zhahar,:: Sholeh pleaded.

She slipped her hands out of his and rubbed the tears off her face.

"Why do you understand so much about us when you don't know us?" she asked.

"Like I said, I've had a lot of time to think while I've been watching over you," he replied. "I realized I know a few things about being in a triad."

Sweat trickled between her breasts and the heat in the air made it hard to breathe, but she wouldn't have moved for any reason. Not then. "How?"

"I've been one side of two triads," Lee said. "My father disappeared when I was very young, so it's been my mother, my sister, and me. There were secrets about our lineage that had to be kept for Glorianna's safety. Mine too, but mostly hers. My mother and sister are Landscapers; I'm a Bridge. Besides being family, I had a working partnership with both of them. While other Bridges traveled through my mother's landscapes, I was the *only* Bridge who worked with Glorianna."

"Because of the secrets?"

He nodded. "The other triad was Glorianna, our cousin Sebastian, and me. Sebastian is a few months younger than Glorianna and two years older than me. He wasn't accepted by other children in the daylight landscapes because he's an incubus, and while Glorianna and I had friends in the village where we lived, there was no one we could completely trust except Sebastian."

She had never considered that people who were not one could form such bonds.

"Then Glorianna met Michael, and everything changed," Lee continued. "It didn't change when Sebastian met Lynnea, but it changed when the Magician came into our lives."

"Your triad changed," Zhahar said, trying to understand how that would feel.

"For a little while, when Glorianna, Michael, and I were traveling, we were . . . connected. But in the end, the triad that formed was Glorianna, Michael, and Sebastian, and I became an outsider. Or, at least, I felt like one."

The pain of that truth showed in his face.

He sighed. "I understand the choice, Zhahar. I do. The wizards still want to destroy my sister, and they wouldn't hesitate to kill my mother too. When I stumbled across them and some of their men, they were in one of my mother's landscapes and less than a mile from a bridge that might have provided some of them with access to one of my sister's landscapes. So I used my abilities as a Bridge to get those men away from my family. I got them far away from my sister. I didn't expect to end up like this"— he raised a hand to indicate his eyes—"but I chose to sacrifice myself in order to save them."

She studied his face. Something more. Some deep hurt that was still inside him, despite his daily visits to the temple.

"What happened to your sister, Lee?"

He drew in a shaky breath. "She was a . . . The only word you have for it is meant as an insult."

No, they just hadn't shared the respectful alternative with him.

"She had a single aspect," Zhahar said gently.

"Yes. She had a single aspect. And now she is split into two."

Zhahar gasped. So did Sholeh. Even Zeela, who was drifting in and out, sucked in a pained breath.

"Who did such a thing to her?" they asked.

Lee's smile was regretful and bitter. "She did it to herself. To save the world, she did it to herself." Tears filled his eyes. "And as much as I love my sister, I haven't been able to accept what she's become."

"If you can accept us, why can't you accept her?" Zhahar asked.

"Because one part of what she's become frightens me," he whispered.

But that part of her doesn't frighten Michael and Sebas-

tian, she thought, understanding why the new triad formed. *Or even if it does, they can still accept.*

Lee let out a shaky sigh. "Enough. You need to get some food."

"And take a cool bath."

"Danyal brought the rest of your things from your rooms. He's given you a room in the Handlers' residence, once you're all well enough to be alone, but your private items are here in the dresser's top left drawer."

"Thank you. Both of you." She hesitated. "We haven't dared trust anyone. It has never been safe for us to reveal what we are."

"This is what my sister calls opportunities and choices. You have an opportunity to allow some people to learn about the Tryad. That knowledge might open up possibilities for your people that don't exist now. Whether you take that opportunity is your choice—and Ephemera will help you fulfill that choice."

There was a weight—and a warning—to his words. "And if I choose not to trust?"

"You could miss the chance of meeting the one person who could help you save your people." Lee rose and stretched, then moved to the door, a clear hint that he wanted to leave the room.

Moments after he opened the door, Kobrah and Nik were there—Nik to go along with Lee to the men's bathing room, while Kobrah assisted Zhahar.

Kobrah carefully removed the dressing, never asking why it was on Zhahar when she'd last seen it on Zeela, never asking about the bruise that now had yellow and sickly green added to the deep purple center that was as long as Zeela's knife wound.

As she lay in a cool bath, Zhahar thought about what Lee had said about opportunities and choices.

Do we trust him? she asked her sisters. She wanted to, but that had nothing to do with using her head and everything to do with her heart and how she felt when she was around him.

=We have to,= Zeela said.

::We don't have to, but I think we should,:: Sholeh said.

Why?

::Because I think he already knows who can save the

Tryad, but he won't be able to help us find that person unless we do trust him.::

Danyal walked the Asylum grounds, the wind chime singing with every step. Peace. Harmony. Light. Hope. Those feelings were carried in the air with the sound.

His own heart didn't feel those things. The dreams scratched at him, evasive and persistent, making his sleep sour and restless. Whispers in the dark, but in the dreams the wind chimes and the gongs drowned out the words so he felt their marks but not the full wounds.

Even those marks left him feeling raw and uncertain.

Because he suspected that was exactly how he was supposed to feel, he fought against it with the rituals the Shamans had used for generations to guard the city. But he wasn't sure how much longer he could hold out against a relentless enemy.

He stopped walking when he noticed Vito moving toward him, clearly wanting to speak to him, and just as clearly not wanting to disturb the morning ritual.

"Shaman?"

Danyal smiled. "How are you today, Vito?"

"Better." Vito bobbed his head. "I'm better." Then he said nothing more.

"Is there something I can do for you?" Danyal asked.

Another head bob. "Lee says I need to find some stones. Tumbled stones that would easily fit in a hand." Vito put two fingers of his left hand into the palm of his right and closed his fingers over them to demonstrate. "He said that you, being the Shaman here, should ask the world to make the stones and leave them where they'll be easy to find."

He was supposed to *make the stones*? How? Was he supposed to purchase stones somewhere and seed them through the grounds like a treasure hunt? Or did Lee actually believe Shamans could *make stone*?

But there *were* those plants that appeared and disappeared, not to mention the waterfall and that place of stones and vines.

A shiver went through Danyal as he remembered what Pugnos and Styks had said about Lee believing he could send people to other places using stones. Pugnos and Styks weren't good men, but perhaps all their words hadn't been lies. Maybe Lee's form of madness made him *sound* exotically rational.

And maybe what whispers in your dreams doesn't want you to learn from the man who can be your teacher, and floats these doubts about him into your mind.

"Shaman?"

"A moment." Danyal closed his eyes. Vito's heart-core had steadied since Lee talked to the man yesterday. So much so that Vito had been released from isolation. Now that heart-core felt like bright sun, cool stone, rich earth—all the things that had been in that strange piece of the garden.

He pictured tumbled stones the size Vito had specified. Let the colors and shapes fill him until he could almost feel them in his own hand. "A dozen stones. Six banded agates, three quartzes, and three jades. You will have to look carefully to find them, but if you are meant to find them, they will be in sight."

He opened his eyes to see Vito's head bobbing.

"Lee said it might take a day or two to find them because the heart has to come into alignment with the eyes."

"Yes," Danyal said. "That is exactly what must happen." *And exactly the way I, or any other Shaman, would have explained the need for patience when someone came to The Temples searching for answers.*

"I was assigned to the weeding detail, so I'll be watchful while I do my work," Vito said.

"Yes."

Vito trotted away. Danyal turned and walked back to the temple. After putting the wind chime in its place, he stripped off his white robe, hung it on a peg by the door, and knelt on a mat behind one of the gongs.

The sound of the gong flowed over him, went through him. As he lifted his voice, he felt the poison left in him by the dreams drain away. Again. He didn't count the cycles of sound, but when the sound of the gong faded, he heard *tap tap, tap tap,* and knew he was done.

Sitting back on his heels, he waited for Lee to enter the temple.

Lee removed the dark glasses, squinted in the soft light, then put the glasses back on.

"This much light is too strong?" Danyal asked.

Lee nodded. "Even with the glasses it's hard to be outside in the brightest part of the day. But I'm starting to see again. Not just dark blobs against a lighter background, but real shapes. It's like seeing the world as rough charcoal sketches. Not much detail, but enough that I can see where I'm going and identify objects—and I can see faces again. The cane still helps though."

"And conceals the fact that some of your sight has been restored."

"That too." Lee paused. "Who sits at the gong—the Shaman or the man?"

Danyal set the mallet beside the gong. "Is there a difference?"

"Not always. Probably not often. But sometimes there is."

"I don't know. Shaman or man, today my heart is equally troubled."

"My uncles haven't been around lately. I've been focused on Zhahar and her sisters, so that didn't occur to me until I was walking over here."

Danyal hesitated. "I thought it best that they were no longer able to see the Asylum."

"And in the city of Vision, you can find only what you can see," Lee said softly. "Is that how it works here? Even if the eyes are in alignment with the heart, if the Shamans decide something shouldn't be found it won't be?"

"We aren't petty tyrants who play with people's lives," Danyal snapped as he rose. "We have a saying: let your heart travel lightly."

"Because what you bring with you becomes part of the landscape," Lee finished. "I know the Heart's Blessing."

He walked over to the peg where his robe hung. He reached for the robe, then let his hand drop. "You're not a Shaman, but you sound as if you had studied at The Temples."

"Different school, but some of the teachings seem to be common among those who help the world maintain its balance."

"And the stones? What are they supposed to do?"

"Two things. One, a holy man I know uses stones as receptacles of sorrow. You carry the stone with you for a day, telling it all your sorrows, then it's cleansed with water to wash the sorrow away. Basically the same thing you do with the gongs, but since Vito is focused on working with the land, I thought that might be a good tool for him."

It would be, Danyal thought. He could think of a couple of other inmates who might benefit from that kind of cleansing. "What's the second thing?"

"I wanted to confirm that you had the kind of connection to the world that could make the stones," Lee replied.

Danyal stared at Lee. "You were *testing me*? Me? A Shaman?"

Lee shrugged. "Where I come from, there are seven levels of Landscapers. Most of them, even the ones at the seventh level, don't have the kind of connection that can reshape the world in specific ways, or make something new. My sister can. So can the Magician. I don't know how you compare with other Shamans, but I wondered if you might also be a Guide."

Danyal snatched his robe off the peg and shoved his arms into it. "And what happens when Vito finds no stones?"

"Were you sincere when you asked Ephemera to make them?"

The question unnerved him enough to snap, "Let's go." He took a firm grip on Lee's arm and led him out of the temple.

"Where?"

He didn't know. Before he could decide, Vito ran up to them.

"Shaman, look! I found these while I was weeding!"

An agate, a quartz, and a jade.

His grip on Lee's arm tightened to help him maintain his own balance.

"Let's see those." After tucking his cane under his arm, Lee held out a hand. He rubbed his thumb over the stones Vito dropped in his hand and nodded. "Yes, these are good. Take one back. Put it in your pocket. Whenever you feel doubtful or sad, hold the stone for a few moments and let the stone absorb those feelings."

"All right," Vito said. "I will."

"Well done," Danyal said, smiling.

"Thank you, Shaman. Thank you." Vito bobbed his head. "I'd best get back to my work."

Lee slipped the other two stones into his pocket. "Guess that answers the question about you being a Guide." He turned his head to look at Danyal. "Which means you need to be more careful than the other Shamans from now on, because you're the enemy the Dark Guide has to destroy if he's going to take control of the city."

"Because I spoke the names of some common stones and Vito happened to find them while weeding?" Danyal snorted. "What does that prove?"

"Besides the fact that you're getting stubborn about accepting the possibility because you're afraid it's true?" Lee replied. "All right. If the stones could have been in the garden already, how about trying for something more exotic? Like a precious gemstone you wouldn't find in the garden."

???

The ground felt . . . strange, and he had the odd sensation that a large, friendly cat was rubbing against his legs—and that made Danyal reckless. "What should I ask for? A ruby the size of my thumbnail?"

Phhhhhtttt

Dirt shot up like a tiny geyser next to his foot. Moments later, in the small crater formed by the shifted dirt . . .

"Is it pretty?" Lee asked.

Danyal picked up the stone. Rough, to be sure, but still recognizable as a ruby. His hand shook. "I began my formal training as a Shaman twenty-five years ago, when I was sixteen. This has never happened before."

"A dormant ability that woke up because you need it now," Lee said. "Or it's something you've always had and used, but it's more apparent now."

Always different from the other youngsters who were training at The Temples. Always different from the other Shamans. And always restless because of the difference that both intrigued and worried his teachers.

Danyal slipped the ruby into his trouser pocket. "I'll have to be more careful with my words."

Lee nodded. "You've become one of Ephemera's Guides. You'll have to learn how to tell it when it's not supposed to listen."

!!!

Another geyser of dirt, this one lasting a bit longer. When the world finished expressing its opinion, Danyal picked up the gold pocket watch and handed it to Lee. "I think this is yours."

Lee rubbed a thumb over the watch and sighed. But he slipped it into his pocket.

"Pocket watches have been showing up in the gardens since you arrived," Danyal said. "What do they mean?"

Lee shook his head, then said, "You never told me what happens to the sorrow. Your gongs draw it out of people's hearts, but you never said where it goes."

As Lee spoke the words, the first fat drops of rain began to fall.

Finally something in this day made Danyal smile. "Sorrow is drawn up into the sky and is transformed into the world's tears, which cleanse as well as nourish."

It was late afternoon the next day when Vito pressed the last piece of jade into Lee's hand.

"That's all of them the Shaman said I would find," Vito said anxiously.

"That's fine." They were standing at the edge of the open space where inmates were allowed to wander on their own. "Vito, be sure you want to do this. I can't promise that you'll find what you seek. I can't tell you that the place you're going to will have people who speak a language you understand. I can't tell you there won't be demons there unlike anything you've seen before. I can't tell you what you'll find. I can tell you only that what you find, for good or ill, will be a place that resonates with your heart."

"I know. That's why you wanted me to do the heart cleansing with the stone. And I did do it, Lee, and I threw the stone in the creek just as you said to do."

"All right. You'll need to bring some water with you and a little food, in case you don't meet up with anyone right away."

"And my other change of clothes. I've already got it, Lee. Can't you see— Oh. Guess you can't."

Nothing more I can do for him except what I'd promised.

Lee closed his hand over the jade, letting his power flow into the stone. A one-shot resonating bridge. One chance for a man who didn't know about such things to find a piece of the world he'd seen for a few hours.

When the resonating bridge was ready, he wrapped the

stone in one of the squares of cloth he'd wheedled out of Kobrah—with Zhahar's help.

"Slip away," Lee said. "Get out of sight. When you're alone, unwrap this stone and hold it in your hand. The magic in it might tingle or feel warm."

"Then what do I do?"

He handed the wrapped stone to Vito. "Walk forward. The magic will take you, and between one step and the next, you'll find yourself in another place." He hesitated, wondering if there was anything more he could say. "Let your heart travel lightly. May it guide you home."

"Travel lightly," Vito replied.

The wind shifted, and Lee caught a whiff of stinkweed. "Get moving."

Vito darted away.

He turned and began tap-tapping his way back to the inmates' residence. He hadn't gone far when Teeko called to him.

"Was that Vito?" Teeko asked.

"Where? I didn't see anyone."

Teeko didn't reply for a moment, and Lee wondered if the man was still pondering his answer.

"There's been some talk about these stones Vito was finding for you," Teeko finally said. "There's a rumor that there's some kind of dark magic in them that makes people disappear."

"Dark magic that makes people disappear?" Lee pulled one of the stones out of his pocket and tossed it to Teeko. "See for yourself."

Teeko let out a fearful cry and jumped back.

Ah, Teeko. Danyal may have shut the wizards out of the Asylum, but they still had eyes and ears inside. Nothing he could prove to anyone else, of course. But that whiff of stinkweed was proof enough for him.

That and Teeko's belief that the stones held dark magic, letting fear turn something that could help some of the people here into something terrible.

Danyal was already feeling unsettled, so Lee decided to wait for a better time to broach the possibility that Teeko was spying on them all for the wizards and, in turn, the Dark Guide. And, in truth, what he'd just done wasn't going to help things settle down anytime soon.

"It's just a stone," Lee said. "In another part of the world, people use them like the Shaman uses the gongs—as a way to release unhappy thoughts and feelings. The only magic it has is the belief that the stone can hold a person's sorrows, and the magic is only as strong as the belief. I'm sorry I scared you just now. I hadn't realized you actually believed the rumors."

"I don't," Teeko said hurriedly. "Just caught me by surprise is all." He paused. "You heading back to the residence?"

"Yes." Lee shaded his voice with uncertainty. "This is the right path, isn't it?"

"Sure it is. Sure. You're fine."

"Thanks, Teeko."

He tapped his way past the groundskeeper and walked steadily to the residence. He stopped at the men's personal area to use the toilet and splash some cool water on his face. Then he settled on the porch in the chair that was under his window.

"Lee?" Zhahar's voice at the window.

"Are you all right?"

"We're fine. Kobrah is going to help us move our things to the room Shaman Danyal gave us, so you'll have your room to yourself again."

He sighed dramatically. "Just when you were feeling well enough to snuggle." The startled silence made him smile. "Are you going to dream about me tonight, Zhahar?"

"Don't you want Sholeh and Zeela to dream about you too?"

That pulled a laugh out of him. "No. At least not *those* kinds of dreams."

"Oh." Another silence. *"Oh."*

He heard a rap on the door, followed by Kobrah's voice.

It wouldn't have been a good night for a snuggle—still too damn hot, despite yesterday's rain—but it would give her something else to think about.

When Vito didn't show up for the evening meal, the Handlers and Helpers spread out and searched the grounds. The Asylum covered acres of land, including its own small farm, but the area available to the inmates was fenced in and not that large.

They searched carefully, thoroughly, until full dark, and the only thing they found was a scrap of cloth on one of the paths leading to the more secluded areas where inmates weren't supposed to go without a Handler being present.

Lee remained on the porch until last call, then made his way to his room—where he found Danyal waiting for him.

Danyal followed him into the room and closed the door. "Where is Vito?"

Lee removed his dark glasses and set them on top of the dresser. Then he turned and looked at the Shaman. There was no light in the room except from the lamps on the porch, so he figured they could see each other equally well. And he figured it was equally important not to hide his eyes right now.

"Where is Vito?" Danyal asked again.

"He went home," Lee replied softly.

During the next few days, inmates were allowed free movement only on the porch and in their rooms. No one was permitted to visit the temple or walk around the grounds without a Handler or Helper as escort. At night, all inmates were locked in their rooms as a precaution.

Despite that diligence, three more inmates—people whose troubled hearts had brought them to the Asylum—disappeared from their locked rooms. Since none of them had friends or family listed in their records, Danyal made a notation in their files and said nothing.

Lee sat on the porch chair day after day with one of the Handlers always nearby, and also said nothing.

Danyal,

My heart is heavy with sorrow as I send you this news. The darkness has spread to the center of Vision. Two Shamans were killed—murdered—in the bazaar yesterday. Within hours of the deaths, storms savaged the heart of our city, flooding the streets. Lightning struck some houses and set them on fire. They burned out of control, despite the rain. Crops in the central community are ruined, and all the wells are fouled. By morning the storm was over, but the turmoil in people's hearts has not diminished as they struggle to take care of their families. The people need us, and some of us will go out to give what help we can. But the council has decided to remove The Temples from sight until we find a way to face this enemy who is changing the city and its people.

The bazaar is closing for a week as a mourning period for the dead—both the Shamans and the people who died in the storm. There is speculation that the bazaar will not open again. As one of Vision's gems, it brings ships from other lands to our ports. It is rumored that those ships, and their contact with distant places, are the reason this plague walks among us. Our city is vast, but it is also finite. If people begin to fear outsiders so much that we lose our connection with others now, I'm afraid we might not be seen again.

Travel lightly, Danyal, but please travel with speed to find an answer.

Farzeen

Chapter Eighteen

Danyal folded the letter, set it in the desk drawer with his other private papers, and locked the drawer. Then he closed his eyes and let the pain flow through him.

Shamans murdered. The bazaar closed. Crops ruined.

Had he done too little to find the answers the Shamans needed to deal with this enemy that was creeping through the city? Lee hadn't been as much help as he'd hoped. Oh, the man answered any question he asked, but had he been asking the right questions? Or was Lee acting like a Shaman and waiting for Danyal's heart to come into alignment so that he could see?

"I see well enough," he muttered as he left his office.

He spotted Lee coming out of the Handlers' dining hall with Sholeh, who seemed happy and animated—and then cringed at whatever she saw in his face. Even Nik and Denys took a step back as he approached.

"What . . . ?" Lee began.

Danyal grabbed his arm. "Walk with me."

"I promised to tell Sholeh about demon cycles before Zhahar started work."

"Walk with me."

After a couple of stumbling steps, Lee found his stride. Danyal took them outside and kept moving swiftly until they were halfway to the temple. Then he slowed and released Lee's arm.

"If you were trying to prove that Shamans aren't always

patient and kind, I'd say you made your point," Lee grumbled. "And since I'm pretty sure you scared Sholeh, you should count yourself lucky that Zeela is still recovering from that knife wound."

"Your banter isn't appreciated today," Danyal snapped.

Lee stopped walking. "What's different about today?"

Danyal turned to face him. "Two Shamans were murdered at the bazaar that borders The Temples."

"I'm sorry," Lee said. "Were they friends of yours?"

Grief burned in his chest. "They were two of the people who provide voice and balance to this part of the world. Does it matter if I knew them?"

"No, it doesn't. After I completed my training, I didn't have much contact with other Bridges, but when the Eater of the World attacked the school and killed so many, I felt the loss."

"These carriers of darkness came from your part of the world," Danyal said, striving to make a statement but hearing the accusation.

"The wizards or the Dark Guide found a way to this city before I got here," Lee replied hotly. "You will not lay that blame on me."

"You know how to defeat them."

"Daylight, man! We didn't even know what they really were until a year ago. Do I know how to defeat them? Yes. Raise an army, hunt them down, and kill them before they kill all of you—if you can."

Danyal's voice rose to a shout. *"We can't find them!"*

Lee drew in a breath as if he was going to return the shout. Then he breathed out and looked away. "You really have no one who can walk in the dark places?"

"In the shadow places, yes, but the nature of Vision applies to the Shamans as well as other folk. These dark places the wizards have made are like nothing we've seen, so we can't find them. And there is only so much of the city we can keep from their sight."

Lee sighed. "I'm not a Landscaper, Danyal. I can't assess the power you have well enough to know if you could remake parts of this city and take them beyond the reach of the rest of the world."

"If ships stop finding our ports, if travelers no longer find any of the roads, we'll disappear from the world. The Shaman Council sent me here because they believed I was their best hope of finding help or at least an answer to how we can help ourselves."

"What you give to the world comes back to you," Lee said quietly.

He laughed bitterly. "And I haven't given enough?"

"I didn't say that." Lee hesitated. "Here is the question your heart needs to answer: In order to save this city from the wizards, are you willing to deal with the monster that Evil fears?"

Danyal stared at Lee, unable to speak. Finally: "Would you?"

There was love—and pain—in Lee's smile. "That's a question I've been trying to answer these past few days. Excuse me, Shaman. Even with the glasses, the sun is bothering my eyes."

"Yes. Of course."

Danyal watched Lee walk back to the inmates' residence.

Are you willing to deal with the monster that Evil fears? That's a question I've been trying to answer these past few days.

His breath caught as he remembered the story Lee had told him about the Guide who became a monster in order to save the world.

Are you willing to deal with the monster that Evil fears?

In order to save Vision, *was* he willing to deal with Lee's sister?

"Light duty," Kobrah said.

Since her back was to the other woman, Zhahar rolled her eyes as she put on the Handler's jacket. "I know. No lifting, no pulling, no dealing with any but the almost-normal inmates. Sit and rest ten minutes out of every hour. *I know.*"

Kobrah sniffed. "You didn't mention eating a light meal every few hours to keep up your strength, or drinking enough water."

Zhahar turned and looked at her Helper. She couldn't tell if Kobrah was serious or teasing. "Anything else?"

::Could you ask Lee about the demon cycles?:: Sholeh

said, sounding a little plaintive. ::I didn't have a chance when I was in view earlier.::

Not now, Zhahar sighed.

::But . . . ::

=Leave it be,= Zeela said. =Didn't you hear the Shaman shouting when he took Lee for that walk? Give them both time to cool down.=

Sholeh withdrew, sulking.

=I'm not sure having Lee help her make up a journal of demons is the best idea.=

It gives her something to do.

::I heard that.::

"Zhahar?"

Forgot about you. She smiled at Kobrah. "Let's get some work done." Despite how much time they'd spent together in the past few days, she hadn't really talked with the other woman. They were being very careful not to discuss anything Kobrah had seen while helping care for Zeela. "Is your friend still coming to visit?" she asked as they left her room.

"Yes, but he doesn't stay long. He's worried about a friend who went missing."

Zhahar stutter-stepped. She'd forgotten that Kobrah's dream friend knew Lee—and that Lee knew the dream friend. She hadn't told Kobrah, hadn't told anyone.

Should she?

She considered asking Lee, but when she found him sitting in his chair on the porch, he was brooding about something and clearly not in the mood for conversation. So after saying hello and wondering a bit wistfully if a man of single aspect really would consider doing more than flirting with a Tryad, she got on with her work and forgot about Kobrah's friend.

Lee sat on the porch and felt the air suck the moisture from his skin. Guardians and Guides! If this place didn't have the big screened porch, it would be unbearable. Too bad they weren't allowed to sleep out here. If you had to endure this kind of heat at least part of the year, a big, screened room at the back of the house with woven chairs and a couple of cots for sleeping could be a comfortable way to live.

Maybe he could add on a screened porch to his cabin in Aurora. Jeb would help him build it, so it shouldn't cost too much. Something to think about.

Something *else* to think about.

In the city of Vision, you can find only what you can see. From what he'd been able to piece together, that worked pretty well for these people and was just another way of living in the landscapes that resonated with your own heart. Yes, it worked pretty well for the people whose lives could be fulfilled by the landscapes held within the city. But what about the people whose hearts yearned for something beyond Vision? Sure, they could buy passage on a ship or one of the passenger coaches that made a circuit to other cities, but that method of finding a heart wish left too much to chance. Sholeh had been studying everything she could find about Vision, and nothing she'd told him indicated the city had the equivalent of resonating bridges like the ones that existed back home or the Sentinel Stones in Elandar that took a person to the place that matched his heart.

There was nothing here for people like Vito, who had become heart weary to the point of becoming mind-sick because he had no way of finding what his heart needed.

He hadn't done anything that he wouldn't have done back home. Of course, the timing could have been better. Having four inmates disappear—especially the ones who vanished from locked rooms—hadn't done anything good for Danyal's emotional balance. With a little more time, he was certain he could have convinced the Shaman of the value of giving people another way to find their place in the world. But now two of the Shamans had been murdered, and those deaths would feed the Dark currents in the city.

He didn't have time. None of them had time to wait and see if all the problems would cross over a bridge or take a wrong turn and simply go away.

He had a stone in his pocket that he could make into a one-shot bridge that would take him back to the Den of Iniquity. He could be home in a minute. Or maybe, since Michael was the person looking for him, he could go to Dunberry or Foggy Downs, just in case Glorianna's landscapes were out of reach. Or he could go to Darling's Harbor, where Caitlin Marie now lived. There was a stationary bridge connecting Darling's Harbor to Aurora. Caitlin could cross over and ask the family to meet him in Darling's Harbor. He had options, and the "come home" messages Ephemera was leaving on the Magician's behalf told him clear enough he didn't have to leave his family behind, no matter where he'd gone.

If he made a one-shot bridge to Sanctuary and gave it to Danyal, it was likely the Shaman would reach that Place of Light. He was sure Danyal would benefit from talking with Yoshani.

The problem wasn't leaving; the problem was how to get back. If two landscapes didn't resonate with each other, a bridge couldn't be made to connect them. Finding help wouldn't matter if no one could get back here. He'd thought about it for days now and came to the same conclusion every time: he couldn't count on returning.

The other thing he'd thought about was whether a Tryad could use any kind of bridge. Would the aspect in view be the deciding factor of where they could go, or would a place have to resonate with all three of them for them to safely cross over? What would happen to them on a resonating bridge that determined a person's destination by matching what was held in that person's heart?

Zhahar. So much passion waiting to be touched. He hadn't forgotten Zeela's comment about Zhahar wanting to rub skin with him. Oh, he hadn't forgotten that at all. And he hadn't dismissed that this woman had come into an unknown city, alone, to find help for her people. He understood that kind of commitment too.

He wanted to know her better, wanted to know her in ways an inmate couldn't know a Handler. He might be given extra privileges—or had been until those four men disappeared—but he was still an inmate, and being intimate with him would cost Zhahar her job.

He wanted to see her and wasn't sure he ever would. Not well enough. Not for all the fine details he'd like to know. But he would settle for not seeing her well over not seeing her at all.

If the island still answered to him, he could have brought Zhahar and Danyal with him. Even if they couldn't step onto the landscape he'd chosen, his family could have gathered on the island to talk to them.

There *was* a possibility for Zhahar and her people: that

triangle of grass that had appeared in Glorianna's garden. A dark landscape that wasn't quite dark, that almost had a border that connected it with the Den, but wouldn't truly be connected until it became one of Glorianna's—or Belladonna's—landscapes.

A year ago, he wouldn't have hesitated to bring these people and these lands to the attention of Glorianna Belladonna and ask her for help. But Glorianna Belladonna didn't exist in the same way anymore. While he didn't know which side of his sister would be drawn to Vision, he *knew* Zhahar's homeland called to Belladonna, the monster. So it came down to one question: would bringing Vision and Zhahar's homeland to Belladonna's attention give these people the help they needed or destroy them?

Danyal left the Asylum and walked for hours, stopping every so often at a shop or a house to ask for a drink of water. Except for that brief contact, he spoke to no one.

He didn't know how long he'd been walking or even quite where he was when he stopped to rest beneath a palm tree and realized he'd let grief lead him to physical imprudence.

Heat sick. He knew the symptoms. The day after he'd arrived at the Asylum, Benham had made sure he knew what to look for, in him and in Handlers, Helpers, and inmates.

"Shaman?"

He turned toward the voice, but it still took him a moment to see the man standing a few paces away from him.

Shadowman.

"Do you need help, Shaman?"

Yes, he needed help and . . .

Danyal looked in the opposite direction and spotted the bridge arching over a channel of water.

Cross the bridge, a voice whispered. *You'll find the answers you seek on the other side of the bridge.*

Did he recognize that voice? Had it scratched at him in dreams?

When he turned back, the shadowman was standing right in front of him, holding a jug.

"Water?" the man asked.

"Who . . . ?"

"I'm an Apothecary."

"I don't remember a bridge near the shadow streets," Danyal said as he accepted the jug. He took some water, letting it ease the dryness in his mouth before swallowing.

"There isn't one," the Apothecary replied. "I closed up my shop. Decided it was time to do some traveling. My wagon is right over there."

"Where are you going?" Danyal asked.

The Apothecary smiled grimly. "I don't know. I just know I can't be on that street anymore. Will you give me your blessing, Shaman?"

"May your heart travel lightly," Danyal said, letting the words flow through his own heart to make them the voice of the world.

The Apothecary hesitated. "I'm not heading in any particular direction. Can I give you a ride back to the Asylum?"

What you seek is on the other side of the bridge, the whispering voice insisted. *Hurry, before it's gone.*

Something in Danyal shivered. "How did you know I'm from the Asylum?"

"Saw you on the street a while back, but you didn't see me. A couple of days after that, a woman came into my shop. Has a long scar on her left arm. Said she was there for the Shaman who was the Asylum's Keeper."

Danyal looked toward the bridge again and frowned. Was the land on the other side of the bridge *fading*? He handed the jug back to the Apothecary. "I would like a ride, but there is something I need to look at first. This will take only a few minutes." Some instinct made him add, "The woman you saw is named Zeela. Her sister Zhahar works as a Handler."

"I'll get my horse and wagon and wait for you," the Apothecary said.

A little breeze suddenly played with the hem of Danyal's white robe. "Wait." He said nothing more until he was sure he had the man's full attention. "If anything . . . odd . . . happens around that bridge, I need you to go to the Asylum and report what you saw to a man named Lee. He has knowledge that is not common to our city, and everyone should listen to whatever he says."

"You expecting trouble?" the Apothecary asked sharply.

What you seek is on the other side of the bridge, the whispering voice insisted again.

"I don't know," Danyal replied. He walked toward the arched bridge. Walked across the bridge. Stopped before taking that last step.

The land looked . . . strange. Barren. Sticky.

Sticky webs and treacherous bogs.

Hurry, the voice whispered.

He was heat sick. What was he really hearing?

???

A puff of air in his face, bringing the scent of stinkweed and turd plants. Combined with the heat, the smell was enough to make him gag.

If he took the last step, was there someone on the other side of the bridge who had the answers to what was happening in Vision?

!!!

One foot on the ground now while the other remained on the bridge.

Seeing the glint of something poking out of the dirt at the edge of the bridge, Danyal took that last step, bent down, and picked up the gold pocket watch. When he straightened up . . .

Five of them. Two burly men holding clubs. The two wizards, Pugnos and Styks, who claimed to be Lee's uncles.

The last one wasn't human. Danyal couldn't hold on to the details of the face to *see* it, except to know it was dark-skinned, had two eyes, a nose, and a mouth.

Mouth full of worms. Sweets filled with poison. The slow death of a city.

Dark Guide.

"You shouldn't have interfered, *Shaman*," the Dark Guide said. "You shouldn't have hidden the Bridge from us by hiding the Asylum. You have become more than an inconvenience, so you will disappear."

The voice sounded like claws slicing through his flesh.

Danyal swallowed hard and eased one foot back until his heel rested on the bridge. He needed help. He needed a way to escape.

this way

The pocket watch began to tingle. His hand tightened over it as he eased his foot back a little farther.

Pugnos and Styks rubbed their right thumbs over the pads of their first two fingers—and smiled viciously.

The Shamans had no understanding of these wizards, no way to fight this *thing*. He had to get back to the Asylum so that Lee could help him find the people who *did* understand.

Before all the Shamans died.

Before Vision disappeared.

this way

The pocket watch felt warmer.

"Do you think you can outrun wizards' lightning?" the Dark Guide asked, laughing. "Try."

Let my heart guide me to what I seek. Danyal sent that wish into the world with all the strength he had.

The pocket watch tingled so hard it buzzed against his palm.

Danyal spun around and ran back across the bridge.

He saw the Apothecary standing next to the horse and traveling wagon. As his foot touched the apex of the bridge, something struck his right shoulder and hip, burning through his robe and clothes, burning through skin and into muscle.

He stumbled, staggered, and almost fell as he adjusted to the footing of the cobblestone street in front of him.

Night instead of afternoon sun, and a refreshing crispness in the air that heralded a change of seasons. Cobblestone street instead of packed earth. Colored lights on poles gave the place a festive look, but . . .

Something out of nightmare stepped out of one of the buildings—a cross between a man and a bull. Danyal lurched away from it and gasped at the pain in his shoulder and hip.

He kept moving down the street, and with every step the tingling in the pocket watch faded a little more.

He reached a place that had a courtyard with tables and erotic statues. Suddenly a dark-haired man stepped out into the street a few paces in front of Danyal. Another man, this one with light brown hair, stepped out beside the first. A third, a blond, moved in front of a woman.

The dark-haired man rubbed his right thumb against finger pads. "Who are you? Where did you come from?"

"I seek . . . help," Danyal said.

"There's some grand music in him," the brown-haired man said quietly.

"That doesn't explain what he's doing here," the dark-haired man replied.

"Bridge," Danyal gasped. Hard to think past the pain. Hard to breathe past the pain. "And . . . this." He opened his hand.

"Lady's mercy," the brown-haired man said. "I asked the wild child to take the pocket watches to Lee."

The dark-haired man moved close enough for Danyal to see the sharp green eyes. "You know Lee?"

"Y-yes. As . . . y . . . lum." His legs began to buckle. If he asked, would they give him water? "H-heat sick."

Another male voice, probably the blond, said, "Daylight, Sebastian! He's been hit by lightning!"

Sounds. Voices. Movement. Everything coated in thick syrup. Hands taking away his clothes. Hands gently touching him. The relief of cool water drawing the heat from his skin. Feeling ice-cold and shivering uncontrollably while he burned.

Sounds. Voices. Movement. Then music, so familiar and nothing he'd heard before, wrapped around him, and everything else went away.

Chapter Nineteen

Zhahar hurried to the visitor's gate with Kobrah and Nik on her heels. A man who had news about Shaman Danyal. A man who wouldn't speak to anyone except Zeela's sister and Lee.

=Apothecary,= Zeela said as soon as they saw the man standing next to a horse and traveling wagon.

"Good day to you," Zhahar said, relaxing a little now that Zeela identified the man.

The Apothecary tipped his head in a slight bow.

She glanced at the horse and wagon. "You wanted to—"

"Zhahar!"

Lee ran toward her, followed by Denys, who didn't have the speed to catch him.

"The drops have helped his eyes," the Apothecary murmured. "That is good."

How did he know the eyedrops were for Lee? Zhahar asked.

=Probably figured that out because of the dark glasses,= Zeela replied dryly.

Then Lee was beside her, then a little in front of her, pushing her back a step. His right hand remained in a tight fist, as if he were holding something.

The Apothecary studied Lee. "I bring news, nothing more. If you are Lee, the Shaman told me to report to you."

"Then why ask for Zhahar?" Lee said, making it clear with posture and voice that he wasn't accepting anything on faith—and if a person wanted to stay safe, the answers had better be to his liking.

She hadn't thought Lee could be dangerous—until now.

"Her sister Zeela has dealt with me," the Apothecary said. "I thought if I was acknowledged by someone here, you would be more inclined to listen."

Lee nodded. "All right. We're listening."

"He asked for me," Zhahar muttered.

"In order to report to *me*," Lee replied.

=Don't argue with him,= Zeela whispered. =Right now he is more our mothers' equal than ours.=

Since she understood what *that* meant, Zhahar clenched her teeth and kept quiet.

"The Shaman disappeared," the Apothecary said. "When I came across him, he was heat sick. I offered him a ride back to the Asylum, and he accepted, but there was something on the other side of a bridge that he wanted to see. I fetched my horse and wagon and stood in the shade of a palm tree, unseen by watchful eyes." He gave Lee a strange smile. "A gift given to us by the world for being shadowmen. So the Shaman crossed the bridge and picked up something. When he straightened, I saw five men. I couldn't see them clearly, but after what I saw moments later, I knew they were the reason the shadow streets were turning dark, even for people like me. They were the reason I decided to pack my wagon and leave."

"Those men took Danyal?" Zhahar asked. "They took a *Shaman*?"

"No. Whatever was said . . . The Shaman turned and ran. Halfway across the bridge, lightning shot out of the fingers of two of the men. As it struck him, the Shaman disappeared." The Apothecary studied Lee. "You understand this? The Shaman said we should all listen to you."

Kobrah stood tense and trembling beside her. Nik and Denys were behind her, muttering to each other. But she knew all three of them were eyeing Lee, especially after he slipped his fist in his trouser pocket and then withdrew an open hand.

What had he been holding?

"You know what this is," the Apothecary said, watching Lee. "You have seen these kinds of shadows."

"I've seen more than shadows," Lee replied. "And, yes, I know what this is."

Those dark glasses hid too much, and Zhahar wished she could see his eyes.

=Be careful,= Zeela warned. =He's changed.=

No, Zhahar replied slowly. *We're just seeing who he really is.*

"How could lightning come from a man's fingers?" Nik asked.

"Two men were killed on a shadow street by such lightning," the Apothecary replied. "I assure you it exists."

"Wizards' lightning," Lee said. "It exists, Nik, and it's deadly. You said Danyal picked up something on the other side of the bridge. Did you see what it was?"

It took Zhahar a moment to realize the last part was directed at the Apothecary, who shook his head.

"His hand was closed over it when he was running across the bridge. But I did see something bright dangling from his fist."

"Like a gold chain?"

"Perhaps."

Lee drew in a breath and huffed it out. He looked toward her but turned enough to include Nik and Denys. "If the Shaman is gone, who's in charge of the Asylum?"

"Meddik Benham would have the most authority after the Keeper," Nik replied.

Now Lee turned his head toward the Apothecary. "You have any room to spare in that wagon?"

"It's designed to be both shop and home for a traveling Apothecary, but if someone sat on the driving seat with me, there would be room for two or three more to hide inside."

"Will you help us?"

The Apothecary gave Lee a strange smile. "A voice of the world told me to listen to you, so I will give you whatever help I can."

"Lee?" Zhahar placed a hand on his arm. "What are you thinking?"

"Danyal's gone. I know how he disappeared but not where he's gone—or if he'll ever find his way back. Whatever he did to hide this place from the wizards and the Dark Guide probably will fade without him. I need to be gone before that happens, and you need to go with me. You and Kobrah. Nik? Denys? The men who claimed to be my uncles are actually wizards who have that deadly lightning. If they show up, you tell them one of the Handlers thought she was in love with an inmate, helped him escape, and ran off with him. Zhahar, where is your homeland's connection to Vision?"

She stared at him, shocked. "Lee . . ."

"We don't have time for secrets." There was a hardness in Lee's voice she'd never heard before. "There might be a way to save this city from the wizards and Dark Guide. There might be a way to save your people. Both of those things depend on me getting to your homeland before the wizards catch me."

"But . . . you have those stones, that magic. You can get away without the wagon."

"Yeah, I can go anytime. I could make one-shot bridges that would get Nik, Denys, Kobrah, Benham, even the Apothecary here away from the Asylum. There's no telling where they would end up, but most likely it would be away from this part of the city—maybe even away from this part of the world." Lee pressed his lips together for a moment. "But I don't know what crossing a bridge would do to you and your sisters, Zhahar. I don't know if you could survive crossing over. I do know that if you want to save your people, we have to run *now,* because I'm not leaving without you, and every minute we delay is a minute the wizards have to get closer to stopping us."

Zhahar stared at him. Zeela's major strength was the body. Sholeh drank in knowledge. Her strength was the heart, and her heart had been drawn to this man from the first time she saw him.

"We'll go with you," she said.

A fleeting smile. A lessening of tension in his shoulders, telling her how relieved he was by her answer. Then his hand closed around her wrist for a moment, warm contact before he let her go.

"I'm sorry," Lee said. "We're going to have to travel light."

She nodded, then wasn't sure he truly saw the movement. "I know. Come on, Kobrah."

::You didn't tell him that as soon as we return home, the last link holding Tryadnea to Vision will break,:: Sholeh said as they ran to their room. ::We'll be adrift again.::

We can't stay, Zhahar said as she hauled out the big traveling bag and began stuffing it with clothes and whatever else came to her hand.

=Don't forget the Three Faces and the Third Eye,= Zeela said.

Zhahar pulled open the top drawer of the dresser and wrapped the two wooden objects in underclothes before putting them in the bag.

::We could stay,:: Sholeh insisted. ::We've made some friends here. I like Lee, but he doesn't understand why we have to stay.::

=Zhahar is the reason the wizards lost control of Lee,= Zeela snapped. =They'll want to hurt her for that, and that lightning they wield most likely would kill all of us. And then Tryadnea *will* be adrift, and whatever connection Lee thinks he can help us make will be lost.=

Sholeh began to cry and withdrew from them.

She's scared, Zhahar said as she continued to pack. *We all are.*

=It's not just the wizards we should fear.=

You mean that Dark Guide?

=No. You know who I mean. But he stayed for you, Zhahar. He can see well enough now to get around without help. He could have disappeared like Vito and the others. But he stayed. For you. No matter what happens in the days ahead, that's something all of us have to remember.=

"We could use more food, more water," the Apothecary said. "If we want to stay ahead of the wizards and their master, we'll need to travel through part of the night. The longer we can delay stopping for provisions, the harder we'll be to track."

"I'll get the food and water," Denys said.

"I'd best find Meddik Benham and tell him what's happened," Nik said.

"But keep it quiet," Lee told them. "The fewer people who know about this, the safer we'll all be. And tell Meddik Benham I'll need to talk with him too."

They both nodded and hurried off.

"Do you need help to reach your room?" the Apothecary asked.

"No, I can see well enough. The drops that are healing my eyes. Those are from you?"

"Yes. The things that did you harm also came from my shop."

Lee almost reconsidered traveling with this man. Almost. What helped him decide was the feeling that the Dark and Light in the man were almost equally balanced, and maybe like the Shamans, the shadowmen would benefit from a larger view of the world—and the people who touched Ephemera.

And maybe, in that moment before he decided, he recognized a truth about himself and his own connection to the Dark currents.

"You said you can remain unseen," he said.

"In stillness and in shadow," the Apothecary replied. "Not while in motion. I can't hide the wagon while we travel."

"But you could hide it now?"

"For what purpose?"

"To avoid someone tampering with a wheel or the harness."

"You think the lightning men have allies in the Asylum?"

"I know they have one."

"Then I'll stay here."

"I won't be long."

Lee strode toward the residence, squinting despite the dark glasses. He should pick up a hat somewhere. The brim would give his eyes extra protection.

"Lee!" Teeko called. "What's going on?"

Lee just raised a hand and kept going. When he reached his room, he stripped the pillowcase off the pillow and stuffed his spare set of clothes into it. The eyedrops went into the middle of the clothes, protected on all sides. He wasn't sure how much of his eyesight would be restored, but he didn't want to lose whatever chance he had of regaining as much as possible.

Something to ask the Apothecary once they were on the road.

He slipped four of the smooth stones into his pocket and put the rest in the pillowcase. Finally, he picked up his long cane and left the room, meeting up with Nik on his way to the wagon.

"Denys has the food and water," Nik said. "Meddik Benham is waiting for you by the wagon."

"Kobrah and Zhahar?"

"They brought their bags to the wagon. Zhahar dashed back into the building to use the toilet." Nik shrugged. "She didn't say that, but ..."

After hiding the truth about herself and her sisters, living in such close quarters with other people wasn't going to be easy for Zhahar. He understood her wanting to empty herself as much as possible before getting into the wagon.

"You have your eyedrops?" Nik asked as they reached the wagon.

Lee lifted the pillowcase. "Tucked in here. The bottle should be all right as long as nothing is dropped on the case."

"Give it to me. I'll stow it while you talk to Meddik Benham."

He handed the pillowcase to Nik.

"You have any idea where Danyal might be?" Benham asked.

He shook his head. "It sounds like Ephemera turned a pocket watch into a bridge that connects to another place. If he survived the lightning, Danyal will end up in a landscape that resonates with his heart—or a place that would provide the potential for him to find what he wanted the most at that moment. But where that might be isn't something anyone else can know."

"You think these wizards are going to come here?"

"I'm sure they'll come, so this is what you need to do: contact the city guards. Tell them some threats have been made against the Asylum and you need their help guarding the inmates from harm. Will they respond to that?"

"They will," Benham confirmed.

"Send a message to the Shamans. Whoever is in charge. Tell them Danyal is missing and that a witness saw him being attacked before he disappeared. Tell them an inmate escaped with the help of a Handler, and that you have informed Pugnos and Styks of my disappearance. Be sure to name them. Send the same message to whoever oversees all the Asylums in the city. Get those messages out as fast as you can. When the wizards come—and they will—tell my 'uncles' everything, including the part about mentioning them in the letters."

"You think that will stop them from hurting anyone?" Nik asked, sounding doubtful.

"In my part of the world, the wizards hid in plain sight

for generations, using their ability to influence people's minds to help them eliminate the Landscapers who would have been their strongest adversaries. They aren't going to want too many people in Vision to know what they are. Not yet. So if Meddik Benham jumps in as soon as they arrive and tells them about Danyal's disappearance and my escape, I think they'll play their role of concerned relatives and leave the rest of you alone." Lee hesitated. "I *can* make people disappear by using a stone filled with my particular kind of magic. The stone becomes what we call a resonating bridge. I can give a stone to each of you to use as a way to escape if the wizards do attack."

All three men shook their heads, which didn't surprise him.

"We're not leaving the people who need us," Benham said quietly.

"I didn't think you would," Lee replied.

"So you are a colleague of Danyal's? We've all wondered."

"I come from a distant land, so I don't have the same abilities as the Shamans, but there is a lot of common ground between Danyal's training and mine."

"Thought so."

Lee frowned as he looked back at the building. What was keeping Zhahar? If one of them needed to pee, did *all* of them need to pee separately? But if they shared the innards, wouldn't one be able to do it for all of them? He'd had that impression when Zhahar had told him to stop Shóleh from eating spicy food while she and Zeela were recuperating.

He'd barely finished the thought when he heard a woman screaming his name.

"Let me go! Lee! *Lee!*"

This time Nik and Denys were ahead of him. The sun was too bright, making his eyes burn and tear—making it hard to see who was struggling.

Then Nik snapped, "Damn it, Teeko. What are you doing?"

"What I have to," Teeko said, sounding frantic. "You think I want to work in this place forever? I've got plans, and there's a big reward for keeping *him* here until *they* come to fetch him. Sent one of the boys off with a message. They'll be here soon. Hand over Lee, and you can have this freak."

"He hit Zhahar," Sholeh screamed as she struggled futilely in Teeko's grasp. "She's not answering!"

Guardians and Guides. Teeko had seen Zhahar shift into Sholeh. No wonder the man sounded frantic.

Lee pulled a stone from his pocket, then shoved between Nik and Denys, moving far enough ahead of them that he wouldn't hit them. Teeko's plan had been simple: knock out Zhahar to delay their leaving until the wizards arrived and scooped up their troublesome "nephew." Would have worked if Zhahar hadn't been a Tryad.

Zhahar was hurt and Sholeh was scared past thinking. And Zeela? Had Sholeh come into view because she was the only one who wasn't injured?

Zhahar's pain. Sholeh's fear.

Anger filled him, swelling the Dark currents that flowed through the Asylum. Then those Dark currents filled him in turn as his power flowed into the stone to create a resonating bridge.

"Let her go, Teeko," Lee said, his voice rough with the swelling rage.

"As soon as Nik and Denys put you in a jacket, I'll let the freak go."

"We're not a freak," Sholeh sobbed.

"He's only holding her by one wrist," Nik said out of the corner of his mouth. "We could take him."

That's when Teeko yanked Sholeh closer and revealed the short-bladed knife in his other hand. "You come at me, I'll cut her. I'll cut her bad!"

"Let her go, Teeko," Lee said. The stone throbbed in his hand, all power and anger. *Ephemera, give him what he deserves.*

Problem was, if Teeko was still holding Sholeh when Lee hit him with the stone, she'd be pulled into that landscape with him.

"She's got a scar on her left arm," Denys whispered. "What's going on?"

Was Zeela starting to come into view?

"Is that what they offered you, Teeko? Gold and precious jewels in exchange for someone's life?" Lee asked.

"I'll be a rich man!" Teeko yelled.

"If that's all it takes to buy you, I can match that and more. Here's a lump of gold as down payment." As he cocked his arm, he yelled, "Zeela!" and threw the one-shot bridge at Teeko.

He couldn't see well enough to be sure it was Zeela in view until she punched Teeko. Not a hard blow, but enough to startle him into releasing her.

Zeela twisted away from Teeko and fell on her hands and knees.

Teeko caught the stone—and disappeared.

Silence, except for Nik's and Denys's rough breathing.

Lee rushed over to the fallen woman and yelled, "Get Benham over here!"

"Already here," Benham said. He stopped several paces away, then approached warily.

"Zeela?" Lee asked, resting a hand between her shoulder blades.

"I'm all right," Zeela said, not sounding all right.

"Need to check those stitches," Benham said. "Make sure she didn't pull anything."

"Zhahar needs to come into view," Zeela said. "He hit her on the head. Don't know how bad."

"We'll check you first," Lee said firmly. When Benham did nothing, Lee looked at the man. What did the people here see now when they looked at him? "I have no quarrel with you."

"What about them?"

"They come from a race called the Tryad. Short version is, three siblings share a body but are still individuals."

"I could have done more for them if Danyal had been a little more forthcoming about their 'spiritual practices,'" Benham grumbled as he knelt beside Zeela and pulled up her tunic enough to look at her ribs. "No fresh blood on the dressing. I don't think she took any damage from that fall."

"Didn't," Zeela said. "If I'm going to be seeing my mothers in a couple of days, I wouldn't lie about how a wound is healing. Now . . ."

Lee felt the difference, the slight change in muscle tone, the scent of a different woman.

Benham sucked in a breath. "That's the damnedest thing." He gave Lee a sour look before gently examining Zhahar's head. "Got a good-size bump there, but I'm not feeling more than that. Didn't hit her hard enough to crack her skull. She was probably dazed by the blow and disoriented enough to scare someone."

"Can she travel?"

"I'm right here," Zhahar grumbled.

"Getting rattled in a wagon won't make her feel good, but I can't see it doing her—them?—harm," Benham said. "And you're traveling with an Apothecary. Next best thing to a Meddik."

"Then we've got to go." Lee picked up Zhahar, grunting at the weight. From the physical contact he'd had with her, he hadn't expected her to be this heavy.

As he walked back to the wagon, he only half listened to Benham's telling Nik to get some ice, aware that Denys kept pace with him.

"I'm not going to drop her," Lee panted.

"Didn't say you would," Denys replied. "But you should let me get her into the wagon. I'm used to handling bodies, and if you bang her head against the doorframe, you'll have Kobrah chewing on you."

Couldn't argue with the truth of that, so he handed Zhahar to Denys when they reached the wagon.

"Looks like we don't have as much time as we'd hoped," the Apothecary said as he watched Nik hand Kobrah a filled ice bag.

"Not much time at all," Lee agreed. "We need to go north, but Zhahar will have to tell us exactly where we're headed."

"Plenty of roads lead to the heart of Vision, and it's not odd to see an Apothecary's wagon headed that way. I come this way at least once each season to buy ingredients at the bazaar I can't find anywhere else in the city." The Apothecary huffed out a breath. "You should stay in the wagon with the sisters. The other one can sit on the driving seat with me."

"All right." He thought for a moment. "You're not disturbed about them being a Tryad?"

"You and the Shaman knew they came from a different race of people. It didn't bother either of you, so there's no reason to let it bother me." The Apothecary gave him a long look. "The one who threatened the sisters. Where did he go?"

"To a place that resonates with the darkest part of his heart," Lee replied.

"To the darkest part of his heart? Or the darkest part of yours?"

Denys stepped out of the wagon. Lee started to step up, then stopped, tilting his head to catch the sound.

Wind chimes and gongs.

Would they be enough to create an access point? Maybe not for most Landscapers, but Glorianna had created access points to landscapes from a single brick or a stone that held the resonance of the place. If he brought gongs and chimes that carried the Dark and Light resonances of the Asylum, would that be enough for Glorianna to get them back here?

"Fetch three of the wind chimes and three of the gongs," he said. "Doesn't matter which ones."

Kobrah poked her head out of the wagon and started to protest, then looked at him and said nothing while Nik and Denys hurried to the temple and returned with the gongs and wind chimes. They handed them up to Kobrah, who began fussing about where to put them.

"Guardians and Guides," Lee snapped. "Just store the damn things and get down from there. You're riding on the seat with the Apothecary."

A silence. Then a flurry of sound before Kobrah rushed out of the wagon and muttered, "Maybe you're a Chayne after all."

Lee looked at Benham, Denys, and Nik. "Travel lightly." Then he stepped inside the wagon, closed the door, and sat on the floor beside the narrow bunk where Zhahar lay.

The wagon began moving. Not with the speed Lee would have liked, but the window behind the driver's seat was open partway for air, and he could hear all the other carts and carriages around them as soon as they left the Asylum. No one would be moving quickly during the busiest time of the day, but another wagon plodding along with the rest would be less noticed than a wagon in a hurry.

As he kept watch over Zhahar and coaxed Sholeh and Zeela to come into view for a few minutes, just to be sure they were all right, he thought about the Apothecary's question. *The one who threatened the sisters. Where did he go? To the darkest part of his heart or the darkest part of yours?*

They were good questions. Too bad he didn't have answers.

Chapter Twenty

A fire burned beneath his skin. A vicious, terrible fire that tried to burrow deeper, reaching for heart and lungs. But raging water battled against the fire, drawing it up and up and, finally, drawing it out through skin so charred it flaked away.

At least, that's how it seemed.

As Danyal gave himself to that battle between fire and water, he dreamed of Kanzi, Nalah, and the baby struggling to survive, trying to scratch out a little food from the barren, cracked earth that had once been the beautiful city of Vision.

A wall of water thundering over the edge of the world. Thorn trees with sinuous limbs, their fruit the rotting corpses of their prey. And a voice that was and wasn't Ephemera, saying, *Despair made the deserts, and hope the oases.*

Heat lightning and the quiet of a simple garden. And the fire burning beneath his skin.

Danyal opened his eyes and looked into the dark eyes of the man sitting in a chair beside the bed.

The man gave Danyal a gentle smile as he closed a book and set it on the bedside table. "So," he said. "You're awake. That is good."

"Am I a prisoner?"

Humor—and understanding—in those eyes. "No. When

you arrived here, you were injured and asked for help. We've given what help we can."

Danyal shifted, then gasped at the pain the movement caused in his shoulder and hip.

"Easy. Your injuries should not be taken lightly."

"Could I have some water?"

"Of course. Let me help you sit on the side of the bed. I think that will cause you the least discomfort."

As the man helped him shift from lying on his left side to sitting on the edge of the bed, Danyal got a better sense of his companion.

About his own age, with hair as dark as the eyes. A cadence in the voice that he didn't recognize. And Light—with a hint of shadows. That was the heart-core of this man. Under other circumstances, he wouldn't hesitate to trust that heart, but now that hint of shadows made him uneasy.

After going into an adjoining room, the man returned with a glass of water. He handed it to Danyal, then sat in the chair and said, "I am Yoshani. You are in the Den of Iniquity. This room belongs to the Den's Justice Maker." He smiled, genuinely amused, as he made a graceful gesture that took in the decor. "Not a typical place one might expect to find men such as us—at least according to the Den's residents." The amusement faded. "But you needed help swiftly, and this was the closest place they could bring you."

The bridge. The pocket watch. The wizards and—

Danyal sucked in a breath, then moaned when even that much movement brought pain. "Wizards and a Dark Guide have come to the city of Vision. We need help."

"I am not familiar with your city," Yoshani said, "but if there is anyone in the world who can help you find answers, it is the people here."

"I need—"

"To *rest*. Your sudden arrival has raised many questions and concerns. The people you need to talk to are making sure their pieces of Ephemera aren't in danger. They will be back in a few hours. The physician from Aurora will be back in an hour to look at your injuries. He will decide what you can and can't do."

Danyal stared at Yoshani. "No one decides what I can do."

Yoshani stared back. Then he laughed softly. "You aren't used to living around strong-minded women, are you?"

Before Danyal could decide what that had to do with anything, someone tapped on a door. The brown-haired man who talked about music and a wild child walked into the room.

"How are you?" the man asked Danyal.

"He is awake and alive—and not yet understanding why he should be grateful to be both," Yoshani replied. He tipped his head to indicate the man. "This is Michael. He is a Magician from a country called Elandar." Then he looked up at Michael. "Our guest has not yet gifted us with his name."

"I am Danyal. I am a Shaman in the city of Vision." Unless one of them had visited the city, they might not understand what a Shaman was.

Michael studied him too long for comfort. "I thought Shamans were holy men like Yoshani here. But the music in you has dark notes under the bright, so I'm thinking Shamans are another kind of Landscaper—more like the Magicians."

"What is a Magician?" Danyal asked stiffly.

"Ill-wisher. Luck-bringer." The look in Michael's eyes was now sharp-edged but still friendly. "So I have dark notes in me too."

A warning.

"Shamans are the voice of the world," Danyal said.

Michael nodded but didn't look impressed. "Just so you know, the Den is one of Belladonna's landscapes. You may be a voice in your part of the world, but here Ephemera answers to *her*."

Danyal shivered.

Belladonna. Lee's sister. The monster that Evil feared. She was *here*?

"I have to leave," he said.

"To go where?" Yoshani asked gently. "How will you get back to your part of the world?"

"You came here looking for help," Michael said. "You're going to walk away without talking to anyone?"

Good questions. Too bad he didn't have answers to Yoshani's questions and knew the answer to Michael's. "When can I talk to the people who might be able to help?"

"If the physician says you're well enough, we can take you down to Philo's for something to eat. Or we can ask the others to gather here if you don't feel strong enough to be up and about."

Danyal turned his head to look at his heavily bandaged right shoulder. When Yoshani had helped him sit up, he'd noticed the bandages on his right hip and outer thigh. "What's wrong with me?"

Yoshani hesitated. "You were burned. At least, that's the closest way to explain what happened. The physician has prescribed the best treatment based on other experience, but we weren't sure how effective it would be in your case. However, your body seems to respond best to the things that help draw out the heat, like cool water and a plant extract that is used on sunburned skin. We think, given time and rest, that you will heal completely."

He looked at Michael, then at Yoshani. "But you're not sure. Why aren't you sure?"

"Because," Yoshani said, "you are the first person to survive being struck by wizards' lightning."

The physician arrived, expressed his opinion that the shoulder and hip were healing well, prescribed cool baths and the generous application of the plant extract, and said the skin would now benefit from being open to the air. He also told Danyal not to be alarmed when the skin blistered and peeled—and admitted that there was no way to know yet how much damage the lightning had done to the underlying muscle. But with work, it was hopeful that Danyal would regain full range of motion in both shoulder and hip.

Lucky to be alive.

A glancing strike.

His robe had provided some protection.

Exhausted from the examination and the cool bath that followed, Danyal fell asleep for a few hours—and dreamed of an oasis guarded by erotic statues.

When he woke the next time, Yoshani was gone, and the door to the bathroom was open. After making his way to that side of the room, Danyal noticed the other door into the bathroom was also open.

"Hello?" he called softly.

The blond-haired man appeared in the other doorway, gave Danyal a quick, appraising look, and grinned.

"Glad to see you're not a prude. Although having holy men staying at a bordello is going to give the Den a bad reputation."

Danyal hoped his embarrassment at being caught naked didn't show. "A *bad* reputation?"

"The Den is a carnival of vices—gambling, whoring, drinking. You know." The blond paused. "Well, maybe you don't. Anyway, get any more of your kind showing up, and the next thing you know, the most potent stuff Hastings will be serving at his tavern is some fancy tea, and Philo will stop making Phallic Delights because the 'ladies' who come visiting have never seen a real penis, let alone put their mouths around one. I'm Teaser, by the way."

For a moment, Danyal thought—hoped—the man had said he was teasing; then he realized that was his name.

"I'm Danyal. I'm a Shaman."

"Shaman Danyal." Teaser gave him an assessing look. "I might have heard about you."

Was that good or bad? And where had he heard Teaser's name before?

Teaser disappeared, then returned with a set of clothes. "Yours were crisped by the lightning, so we got you these. Mr. Finch has your old robe. He's using it as a pattern to make a new one for you. You should have heard the discussion Mr. Finch, Lynnea, and Sebastian's auntie had over a fine tailor being asked to make something as ordinary as a plain white robe. Not even a line of embroidery on the sleeves or hem!" He grinned. "They had to get a bolt of cloth from a tailor in Aurora because Mr. Finch doesn't waste shelf space on such pedestrian fabrics, and he tried to insist that, given the choice, surely you would prefer something in leather, since you have the coloring for it."

A tip of the head and an expression in Teaser's eyes made Danyal wish he could cover himself without looking like a fool.

"Mr. Finch does have a point," Teaser said. "You *would* look like a badass if you were wearing a long leather coat instead of that robe."

Not sure if he should be appalled or pleased, Danyal extended his left hand. "May I have the clothes?"

"Sure." Teaser crossed the bathroom and draped the clothes over Danyal's left arm. "Your shoes are in front of the wardrobe. We can walk over to Philo's when you're ready. Or I can see if a demon cycle will give you a ride. Not sure about swinging a leg over one with a bad hip, though."

"I think walking would do my hip some good." And he wasn't about to swing a leg over any kind of demon.

He retreated to the other room and sorted out the clothes. Shirt and trousers. A pair of socks. No under—

Danyal picked up the remaining bit of material and wondered why anyone would bother with something that was such a brief step away from nothing. Then he considered the trousers and decided something was better than nothing. Shamans weren't celibate, but they weren't . . .

He looked toward the bathroom door. Putting on the underwear and trousers, he walked back to the doorway. "Teaser?"

Teaser appeared in the other doorway, buttoning a fresh shirt. "Need some help?"

"No. I don't mean to give offense, but I just wondered . . . What are you?"

"Incubus." Teaser flashed him a grin. "You're not my type. There are a few succubi in the Den who'd be willing to nibble on you if you're interested."

Incubus. Succubi. He knew what those words meant: sex demons. "Not right now."

"What made you wonder?"

Was he hearing suspicion in the question? "The underwear."

The laugh was boyish and naughty. "We gave you a modest pair."

Having no response to that, Danyal retreated and finished dressing. A few minutes later, Teaser joined him, locked up the room, and gave him a supporting hand down the three flights of stairs. That care surprised him, especially since he didn't see what Teaser had to gain from it.

When they walked out of the bordello and reached the main street, Danyal stopped. The colored lights and cobblestone streets and the edgy feel in the air hadn't been caused by heat sickness. It was as if the bazaar at the center of Vision had blended with some of the shadow streets. Not a safe place for anyone looking for trouble, but not a deadly place at its core.

Although it could be.

Shaken by that certainty, Danyal followed Teaser the couple of blocks to Philo's Place. This was the courtyard he had reached before he collapsed. And there was . . .

"Bull demons," Teaser said. "They come here for the vegetable omelets. We're using the inside room." He opened a door, letting Danyal go in first.

Several square tables had been pushed together to create a long table. More people than he'd expected, coming to hear what he had to say.

He wasn't sure if Teaser had sent a message ahead of their arrival or if their appearance was the signal, but people began entering the room. Yoshani was the first and stood on the other side of Danyal, providing introductions.

Nadia came in next. She was an attractive, middle-aged woman who, Yoshani explained, was a Fifth-Level Landscaper—which meant she had a significant connection to Ephemera, since there were only seven levels. With her was her husband, Jeb, who was a carpenter and woodworker. Right behind them were Caitlin Marie, a Landscaper-in-training who was Michael's younger sister, and Lynnea, a young woman who worked at Philo's and was Sebastian's wife.

The simple garden, Danyal thought when he saw Lynnea. As bountiful as it was restful—but not without its prickles.

The door opened again, and Danyal tensed as the dark-haired man with the sharp green eyes walked in.

Heat lightning. Danger. *And wizard,* Danyal realized when he saw the way the man rubbed thumb and fingers together. The wizards at the bridge had done the same thing before the attack.

"Would you like something to drink, Sebastian?" Lynnea asked.

Those sharp eyes never left his when Sebastian shook his head. "Nothing just yet. You should get off your feet."

"I'm fine. Nadia, tell him I'm fine. Women get pregnant every day."

"You are fine," Nadia replied. "Women do get pregnant every day, but it's your first time and *his* first time, so do us all a favor and humor him."

His eyes never leaving Danyal's, Sebastian pulled out a chair for his wife. Lynnea sat down, looked at the empty table, and huffed. "I was going to get some food."

"I'll get it," Teaser said quickly. "What kind do you want?" He looked at Sebastian. "What kind does she want?"

"Just food," Lynnea said. "And why are you asking him?"

"Because he's the other person who gets to listen to you throw up in the morning," Teaser muttered. When Nadia smacked his arm, he hurried out of the room.

Family, Danyal thought. Related by blood or not, all the people in the room were family.

His hip began to ache and he wanted to sit down, but Sebastian hadn't taken a seat yet—and still stared at him. He didn't think he could escape another attack, but he had a better chance of surviving a few seconds longer if he was on his feet.

Then Michael walked into the room, and the woman who came in with him . . .

All the Dark currents of the world given female form. Every cruelty the human heart could conceive was in her green eyes. She was the thorn tree with the sinuous limbs. Then Michael touched her hand, and the Dark shifted and became a thunderous, breathtaking Light.

"I am Belladonna," she said. "We'll hear your story and then decide if we can help."

You'll decide, Danyal thought as they all took their seats around the table. *Because of what you are, you'll be the one who decides.*

???

Sebastian sat on Belladonna's right, his arm resting along the back of her chair, his fingers drifting through her long black hair. Michael sat on her left and kept his hand linked with hers.

Contact. Connection. Balance.

Seeing those three together, he had a better understanding of the story Lee told him about the Warrior of Light. Michael and Sebastian's physical contact helped her maintain the balance between her two halves—and kept the rest of them safe in her presence.

Then Danyal felt currents of power flow around him, saw Michael's look of surprise, and saw Belladonna tip her head as if listening to a child whisper in her ear.

Then she looked at him, and the amusement in her eyes was almost as chilling as the cruelty of a moment before.

"Voice-guide?" she asked.

yes yes yes

He wasn't sure if they all felt Ephemera's response, but he was certain Michael and Belladonna had.

"All right, voice of the world," Belladonna said. "Tell us your story—and remember to include the part about how you know my brother."

Teaser and a young man came through the swinging doors at that moment, carrying trays filled with dishes of food. "We brought enough for everyone. I think."

Caitlin Marie jumped up and started unloading Teaser's tray, putting a selection of food in front of Lynnea before distributing the rest of the dishes along the table, while Nadia helped the young man. Bottles of wine were opened, and glasses of water were poured.

Grateful for the momentary reprieve, Danyal drank some water and watched everyone else at the table trying to help Lynnea fill a plate without appearing to be *too* helpful. It reminded him of Kanzi and Nalah, and it would have been amusing if he hadn't been so aware that his escape from the wizards might not have been an escape after all.

"Phallic Delight?" Teaser asked, holding up a basket half full of penis-shaped rolls.

"No, thank you," Danyal replied.

"Not turning into a prissy prig, are you?"

"No, but—"

"I'll take one," Yoshani said.

Teaser sighed and passed the basket. "I'm not sure Danyal here qualifies as a holy man—"

Danyal choked.

"—but *your* being so comfortable here is just not right."

"I like to think of my presence as a way to help you expand your view of the world," Yoshani said calmly as he swirled a Delight in the bowl of melted cheese.

"My view is expanding just fine," Teaser muttered.

No one ate much, but the talk remained general until Lynnea pushed her plate away and sat back. Then everyone focused on Danyal again.

Taking a last sip of water, he set the glass aside and told them about the darkness that had come to Vision and the Shaman Council's decision to send him south to be the Asylum Keeper, because that was where they hoped he would find the answers that would help them save their city. He told them about the arrival of a blind madman named Lee who, once free of the drugs that made him act insane, was providing some of those answers about the enemy who had come to Vision. He told them about the plants that appeared and disappeared, and the pocket watches that kept showing up in the gardens. He told them about the place of stone and vines that had appeared and then vanished—and how Vito had vanished a few days after that. He told them that Lee had been befriended by one of the Handlers at the Asylum, but he didn't tell them what he knew about Zhahar. Last, he told them about the death of the two Shamans and the walk that had led him to a bridge where he found another pocket watch—and also saw the Dark Guide with the wizards who had posed as Lee's uncles.

Silence. Then Nadia said, "He's still blind?"

"The eyedrops we were given to reverse the damage are helping," Danyal replied. "Some sight has been restored. But there is no way to tell how much of his sight Lee will regain. I'm sorry."

Nadia blinked away tears and leaned against Jeb when he scooted his chair closer to hers and put an arm around her shoulders.

"Does he want to stay away from us so much that he wouldn't come home even after he was hurt?" Lynnea asked. "Why didn't he come home?"

"He wanted to stay away from me," Belladonna said.

Danyal heard pain in her voice—but the cruelty she struggled to control still flickered in her eyes.

Sebastian and Teaser made a rude noise.

"Blind or not, surrounded by enemies or not, he didn't stay to avoid *you*, Glorianna," Sebastian said. "He stayed for the girl."

"Sebastian wins the pot," Teaser said as he broke a Delight in half and scraped the remaining cheese out of the bowl.

"The Shaman was being careful about what he said about . . ." Sebastian gave Danyal a sharp look. "Zhahar, wasn't it?"

Wary, Danyal nodded.

"If Lee is still pretending to be mad in order to stay clear of the wizards, a Handler couldn't afford to be seen romancing with an inmate," Sebastian continued. "That would raise questions that could get her dismissed from her job—or even put her in danger. But that doesn't mean Lee isn't feeling a pull."

Teaser snorted out a laugh and got another smack in the arm from Nadia.

"A one-shot bridge could get them both to safety," Michael said. "I'm not making light of the danger to your people, Danyal, but Lee would have known he wasn't able to fight against them on his own. If he didn't want to leave the girl, she could have come with him."

"There was . . . concern . . . about Zhahar's sisters," Danyal said.

"Ah." The sound was made by every person around the table.

"Yes," Yoshani said. "His heart may be somewhat conflicted right now, but Lee understands and respects loyalty to family."

A thoughtful—and aching—silence filled the room. When Nadia finally broke the moment by reaching for her wineglass, Danyal asked, "Is there a way you can help us?"

"Can people travel anywhere in your city?" Belladonna asked.

Or had Glorianna asked the question?

Thorn trees. Thunderous Light.

Or had both sides of this woman spoken the words? He sensed two distinct heart-cores in her, the same way he'd sensed three in Zhahar.

"In the city of Vision, you can find only what you can see," he replied.

"So if your heart doesn't resonate with a part of the city, you'll do what?" Sebastian asked. "Walk past the street without seeing it? Head out for a particular part of the city and never quite get there?"

"Something like that," Danyal agreed.

"Not quite as noticeable as it is here, but more apparent than in Michael's part of the world," Nadia said. "What about people who don't belong in your city?"

"There are coaches that travel to cities and towns beyond ours. There are ships that bring passengers as well as cargo. A person could buy passage on one of those to reach another part of the world."

"Reaching another part of the world doesn't mean they would reach the right part," Michael said. "You can travel as far as you can afford to reach and still not find the place your heart needs."

Caitlin Marie's breath caught. Lynnea reached across the table to clasp her hand.

An old grief in Michael and his sister that was just beginning to heal. Who had they lost—and how?

"You have no stories about a special place in your city where a person could go to begin the journey to find what his heart desires?" Yoshani asked.

Unsettled by the question, Danyal shifted too quickly and then had to wait for the pain to settle back to a dull ache.

"In this part of Ephemera, a person can't reach a place that doesn't resonate with his heart," Sebastian said. "It sounds like our stationary bridges, which provide limited possible landscapes, act more like the pieces of your city. But the resonating bridges—"

"Are like the Sentinel Stones in Elandar," Michael said. "They take you to a place that resonates with your heart. Maybe your will can exert some influence on the destination, but when you walk through the Sentinel Stones, it's a fair certainty that you're leaving behind everything you know."

"Lee must have created resonating bridges for the people who disappeared," Nadia said, looking at Glorianna Belladonna.

Glorianna nodded. "I probably muddled things when I made Ephemera put back the pieces that it had taken from other parts of itself."

!!!

"Pushy little world," she muttered.

"Can't you . . ." Danyal stopped, not sure what to ask.

"Do what, Shaman?" Her voice was sharp with frustration. "You survived an attack because Ephemera turned a pocket watch into a resonating bridge that brought you here. Maybe it did that because your heart and will were focused on escape, and because of your association with Lee, it brought you to a place he knew. Maybe there was some residual power flowing in the currents from your contact with him. Maybe Ephemera is changing. I don't know.

Here, the Bridges are the ones who connect the pieces of the world, but other parts of Ephemera aren't broken and have shaped other ways for hearts to find the place they call home. The point is, even Landscapers can reach only the places in Ephemera that resonate with their own hearts. Nadia, Michael, Caitlin, and I don't know your city, which means none of our landscapes are in your city." She hesitated, and there was sadness in those green eyes. "Which is one of the reasons why Lee is there. It wasn't a place we—I—could reach."

Danyal started to sit back, but Yoshani touched his left shoulder, stopping him before his injured shoulder brushed against the chair.

"Can I get back?" he asked.

Glorianna looked at Nadia before answering. "We don't know. Ephemera and I can create a pair of Sentinel Stones that will act as a resonating bridge, but whether it will take you back to Vision . . ."

No way back? He had wanted to see the world beyond the city, but he had never considered that he would find himself unable to return home.

Teaser shifted in his chair and cleared his throat. "I don't have any suggestions for getting the Shaman home, but we might be able to send a message, let his people know where he is—if Zhahar has a friend named Kobrah."

Sebastian and Michael snapped to attention. Danyal stared at Teaser. *That* was where he'd heard the name—when Kobrah had told him about her dream friend.

"The girl you go out walking with?" Sebastian asked.

Teaser nodded. "She's never said much about *where* she is. Doesn't say much about anything, really. But she did mention a friend once or twice. Kobrah and Zhahar aren't names from around here. That's why I remembered them."

"Kobrah is a Helper at the Asylum," Danyal said. "She mostly works with Zhahar."

"So we can get a message to Lee," Sebastian said. "Let him know what happened to Danyal and find out what he knows. Or at least what Kobrah knows."

"Can't always reach her," Teaser said. "It's usually easier after I've prowled the Den for a while, but I'll go back to my room and give it a try."

"Is there anything else we can do?" Nadia asked.

Glorianna stared at Danyal. A few years ago, he had faced down a grief-crazed man who had come to the Temple of Sorrow, still holding the bloody knife that had been used to kill the man's wife. He hadn't felt this vulnerable.

"Glorianna?" Michael asked softly.

A slow release of breath as she said, "Perhaps the Shaman should sit out in the courtyard, where he can get a feel for the Den."

"Good idea," Sebastian said, giving her a smile that warmed the room by a couple degrees. "The Magician can keep him company, and you can prowl with me."

Lynnea leaned forward. "While you're here, Glorianna, I wanted to talk to you about making a little garden in that one corner of the courtyard."

Sebastian and Teaser groaned.

"Some of the flagstones are all broken and loose back there."

"It's behind a statue," Teaser said. "No one sees it."

"I do." Her look dared them to say anything more.

???

"Did you have something in mind?" Glorianna asked, smiling.

Lynnea caught her lower lip between her teeth, then said, "Philo wouldn't want something that would dig into the walls, but maybe a plant that is sturdy enough to grow upward to cover the space—and will flower?"

"You need a trellis?" Jeb asked. "It would be easy enough to put one together."

"Oh," Lynnea said. "A trellis would be wonderful."

"Ephemera," Glorianna said at the same time Michael said, "Wild child."

They sounded like parents who had just stopped a child before it could do some mischief.

Danyal's eyes widened as the currents of power suddenly swirled around him.

"If you can't get candy from your parents, try your uncle," Nadia said, watching him.

"Uncle Voice-guide knows better than to give out candy without permission," Glorianna said. "Doesn't he?"

He could have sworn he felt the world sulk for a moment before the currents drifted away.

Remembering how quickly Ephemera had responded to

his flippant remark about a ruby, Danyal reached for his water glass and drained it—and said nothing.

"Fine," Sebastian said, pushing his chair back. "You two rearrange Philo's Place to your liking. And then, Glorianna, we'll prowl. Just try to remember it *is* Philo's place, and he should have the final say."

"Of course," Lynnea said sweetly. Then she turned to Glorianna. "Maybe we could add a couple of pots for autumn-blooming plants to give that spot a bit of color now."

The four women and Jeb left the table and went outside.

"I'll try to contact Kobrah and let you know what I can," Teaser said. Then he left too.

Danyal wanted to sit out in the courtyard, wanted the chance to see something unlike anything he'd seen before, wanted to talk to these men whose understanding of the world was so different from his own. But remembering Teaser's comments about holy men visiting the Den made him hesitant. "I don't want to make your people uncomfortable," he said to Sebastian. "Perhaps I should go back to the room."

Sebastian studied him and then smiled. "Even a Shaman's heart has no secrets from Glorianna Belladonna. Not much scandalizes the Den's residents, so your presence will just add spice."

"Come," Yoshani said.

They settled at a table near the street, where they could watch the carnival called the Den of Iniquity. Sebastian, Michael, and Yoshani pointed out the incubi and succubi. Not that they had to point out the succubi. His body did that all on its own, making him glad he was wearing underwear, no matter how brief.

Then there were the bull demons and the demon cycles—machines that looked like engorged bicycles without wheels and had a demon living inside them. The cycles could be persuaded to give you a ride, but were just as willing to have you for dinner.

After a while, Michael pulled a tin whistle out of the inner pocket of his jacket and began to play. The first song was beautiful and haunting, so full of despair and hope it made Danyal's heart ache. The second song . . . He knew that tune but couldn't say why it was so familiar.

Michael finished the song, put his whistle away, and asked Philo for a glass of ale.

"Those songs are beautiful," Danyal said. "Did you write them?"

"I play what I hear," Michael replied, murmuring his thanks when Philo brought a pitcher of ale and glasses for all of them. "The first song is Glorianna Belladonna. It helps her to hear both sides of herself while she works to fit the pieces back together."

Michael didn't explain what that meant, and Danyal didn't ask. The story Lee had told him was explanation enough. "And the second song?"

Michael gave him an odd smile. "That's the music I hear in *your* heart."

Chapter Twenty-one

"Any sign of the Apothecary?" Lee asked.

"Nothing has changed since you asked me a minute ago," Zeela replied. "Nothing is going to change a minute from now either. Thought I'd save us both the annoyance of you asking again."

"No need to get snippy about it."

"You think this is snippy? I can show you—"

A *hummm* of sound. Not knowing what was private and what Zhahar would be willing to share with everyone in their party about the Tryad, he didn't ask about that *hummm*. He had decided for himself that when the sisters who weren't in view were close enough to the surface for him to sense their presence, he translated their proximity as voices speaking in unison. When they were submerged to rest or allow a sister some privacy, the voice he heard became singular. This *hummm* was new—probably them discussing something with each other.

Lee waited. When it became clear that the sisters weren't going to include him in a conversation, he said, "What did Zhahar say?"

"She said you didn't have a bowel movement this morning and that's why you're cranky," Zeela snapped.

Kobrah, who was sitting farther back in the wagon, snorted out a laugh but said, "If you have to fart, aim it out the window. No reason I have to smell it in here."

"It would scare the horse," Zeela replied in a prim tone

that was more suited to Sholeh. "And we wouldn't want that, would we?"

Lee sighed and wished Zhahar would come into view, but Zeela could handle the horse and wagon, which was why she was on the driving seat while he and Kobrah hid inside. A man wearing dark glasses would be noticed. And a man with limited sight wouldn't be able to spot danger until it was on top of him.

So he and Kobrah stayed hidden, and Zeela sat outside and waited for the Apothecary to return from the bazaar with some supplies.

"Watching the pot doesn't make the water boil faster," Zeela said. "But when you don't pester the grown-ups, things do happen."

It was tempting to reach through the window behind the driving seat and slug her in the arm, but he was pretty sure Zeela lived by the "hit back and hit harder" rule of physical discussion, and he would be the one who ended up bruised.

"What's happened?" he asked.

"Apothecary is coming." She sounded wary, despite her voice being barely loud enough to be heard. "And it doesn't look like he found much at the bazaar. Close the window and stay quiet. Tell Kobrah to latch the top half of the door and open the bottom half a handspan so he knows which part to use."

Lee relayed the instructions to Kobrah, then secured one shutter and closed the other until there was a two-finger strip of light. Holding the shutter in place, he waited.

A minute later, the Apothecary pushed open the bottom half of the door, set the carry sacks inside, and muttered, "Lock this up," as he pulled the door closed.

Lee heard Kobrah's quiet movements as she worked all the bolts that secured the two halves of the door to the wagon and to each other.

"Let's get out of here," the Apothecary said quietly. "Go up to the end of the street and turn right. Follow that road until I say different."

"What happ—" Lee began.

"Not now." The words were quiet but sharp. "Once we have some distance between us and the bazaar, we'll talk."

They drove for an hour. No one spoke except when the

Apothecary gave Zeela directions. Eventually they reached a travelers' well—a resting place off the road that provided water and a place for people to stretch their legs.

"No one else here," the Apothecary said. "You two should come out and get some air."

Lee pulled open one shutter to give Kobrah some light to work the latches on the door. Zeela secured the horse while the Apothecary took the bucket from its place on the outside of the wagon, filled it at the well, and set it down for the horse.

Kobrah hopped out of the wagon. Lee squinted at the rectangle of light, put on his glasses, then felt his way to the door.

"Mind the step," Zhahar said.

Glad to hear her voice, Lee stepped down and reached for her hand. She stiffened for the moment it took her to remember that the rules governing the conduct of Handlers and inmates no longer applied. Then she relaxed and moved with him to the wide bench set under a tree where the Apothecary and Kobrah waited.

"Two Shamans were killed in the bazaar a few days ago," the Apothecary said. "The bazaar is closed for a week of mourning. Other people have been hurt; visitors have been robbed and beaten. The bazaar is right next to The Temples, which are the Shamans' home and the community at the heart of the city. Oh, there might be a cheating merchant running a booth or a pickpocket lifting his wages from visitors' pockets, but this violence and killing Shamans? *Nothing* like this has ever happened there. And while Shamans are still walking among the people, no one has seen The Temples since the deaths. We're talking about acres of land and the temples people went to for guidance and comfort no longer being visible *to anyone.*"

"How can that be?" Zhahar asked. "The Temples are surrounded by a wall, and Zeela says one side of that wall forms a boundary for the bazaar. People have to be able to see it."

"They see it and they don't. I wasn't able to talk to any Shamans, but the shadowmen say this is strange even for *this* city."

Lee scrubbed the fingers of one hand over his head. "I've seen this before—or something close enough. Landscapes that are visible from a distance but fade as you get closer. If The Temples are a Place of Light, or have a Place of Light within them, then the Shamans are right to get them out of the reach of the wizards and Dark Guide. But the longer no one can reach them, the harder it will be on the people."

A thoughtful pause. Then the Apothecary said, "There is talk among the merchants of packing up their booths and moving their families to another part of the city."

"But you found some supplies," Zhahar said. "So not all the merchant booths were closed."

"Yes and no. There is nothing for visitors to buy, and the merchants who were loitering in the bazaar weren't looking to sell anything to outsiders. They were there to quietly trade among themselves to keep their own families fed."

"What about the rest of the people who depend on those booths to stock their larders?" Lee asked.

The Apothecary shrugged. "It may not be as plentiful or have much variety, but food will find its way to people."

"Where did you get our supplies?" Zhahar asked.

"There are a few booths run by shadowmen near the entrance to the bazaar, where you waited for me. Those booths were still open, since they aren't seen by many. My brethren gave me what they could spare, and they told me about a riddle the bone readers were given right after the Shamans were killed that seemed to fit a curious message the fortune tellers read in their cards: a shadowman, a three-sided heart, and a blind man hold the answer to the riddle."

Lee wasn't sure if the ground had gone soft under him or if his knees had suddenly gone weak. "What is the riddle?"

"The hope for the city will be found in nightshade."

Which was another name for belladonna.

Heart's hope lies within Belladonna, Lee thought. Sebastian had sent that message through the twilight of waking dreams when he'd been captured by the wizards and did what he could to find allies for Glorianna. Were the ripples of that sending still being felt more than a year later?

The Apothecary paused. "I said nothing about my traveling companions, but if you *do* have the answer to that riddle, we need to keep moving, because the people behind the darkness that has stained Vision will not want you to reveal the answer or reach your destination."

Lee considered what the Apothecary said. Did the wizards *still* want him to reach one of Belladonna's landscapes? If the wizards and Dark Guides who hadn't been locked away from the world managed to gather in Vision, they could change the resonance of the city enough to take it from the Shamans' control. They could turn Vision into another Wizard City and manipulate people's hearts to feed the Dark currents of the world.

Unless he reached the one person who could stop them.

"Beyond general directions to keep me heading the right way, I haven't asked where we're going or what you hope to find there," the Apothecary said. "I think it's time for me to know."

"We're going to find Zhahar's people," Lee said. "What happens after that is someone else's choice."

Zhahar dunked the rag in the bucket of water, bent at the waist to avoid dripping on her clothes, and wiped her arms. Dunking the rag again, she wrung out the excess water and wiped her neck.

Your turn, she told Zeela.

A glance at Kobrah, who looked away. Ignoring each other was the only privacy they could give each other right now. Because of that, and because Kobrah had kept silent about what she'd seen while caring for Zeela, Zhahar had told the other woman enough about the nature of a Tryad to explain the emergence and submergence of her sisters—which simply confirmed what Kobrah had already witnessed while helping care for Zeela.

Zeela's aspect came into view and gave her arms and neck a quick wash.

Do you think the Apothecary is having second thoughts about Lee? Zhahar asked.

=Not second thoughts,= Zeela replied, =but I think he's seeing something he didn't expect, and it's making him uneasy.=

*Does Lee make *you* uneasy?*

Zeela dunked the rag and washed her arms again. =He's attracted to you, and you're attracted to him. But you have to be careful, Zhahar. We're going back to Tryadnea, and Lee is a man of single aspect. It would be dangerous for you to feel too much for him. It would be dangerous for all of us.=

I know. But I can have this little bit of time with him, can't I?

=You're risking a bitter future to have a little sweetness now,= Zeela said darkly. =Sholeh, it's your turn.=

::I don't want to.::

=Take your turn,= Zeela snapped.

Don't yell at her, Zhahar snapped back.

"What's wrong?" Kobrah asked.

"Sholeh is feeling shy about coming into view," Zeela replied.

"The Chaynes aren't looking," Kobrah said quietly. "And I'll turn my back if it helps."

Come on, Sholeh, Zhahar coaxed. *A quick wash. Then we have to go.*

::I don't want to!::

Zeela swore silently. When Sholeh began sounding like a whiny young girl instead of a sister of an age equal to hers and Zhahar's, it meant it had been too long since they'd eaten, and Sholeh was becoming disoriented. If they didn't eat soon, she'd start feeling disoriented too, leaving Zhahar to fend for all of them.

She looked at Kobrah and mouthed, *Ask a question about food.*

Kobrah nodded. "How does this work for the three of you? One of you can eat for all of you. Sholeh did that when you and Zhahar weren't well. But you have to wash separately?"

"It's hard to explain—" Zeela began, but Sholeh, responding to a request for information, suddenly pushed into view. Her lips quivered with the effort not to cry as she dunked the rag in the water and washed up.

"The food one of us consumes benefits all of us, although only the aspect who is actually eating enjoys the tastes and the experience," Sholeh said, her voice slurring a little. "And the aspect who is eating or drinking feels the effects of whatever is ingested before the others do, since the parts of the aspects that aren't shared need water and nutrition too."

"So if you're thirsty, you all benefit from one of you drinking water, but the one who drank the water will *feel* the thirst being quenched while the other two *know* the thirst was quenched?"

Sholeh thought for a moment and nodded. "That's close to how it works for what is shared. But the surface body is individual, so each of us has to bathe. Otherwise only one smells nice and the other two stink."

Kobrah studied her. "You feeling all right?"

"A little dizzy. It's nothing."

As soon as Sholeh finished washing, Kobrah took the bucket and poured the water on the plants at the edge of the resting place. She wrung out the rags and headed back to the wagon.

Zhahar came into view and followed Kobrah. Sholeh being dizzy wasn't nothing, but seeing the restless way the men were moving around close to the wagon, she wondered what her companions would say about a necessary delay.

Lee turned as she approached and gave her an odd smile.

"I'll have to remember that when you get ready for something, it's woman time in triplicate."

"Woman time?" Zhahar said, while Kobrah sputtered and the Apothecary choked on a laugh.

Lee grinned at her.

"We'd best be . . . on our . . . way," the Apothecary said, his voice changing from amused to wary as he watched a man ride into the resting place.

"Sholeh needs to eat," Zhahar said.

"That will have to wait," the Apothecary said.

Lee dipped a hand in a trouser pocket. As he withdrew his hand, she saw one of the tumbled stones before his fingers curled around it. "Someone you know?" he asked.

"I know of him," the Apothecary replied. "There are all shades of shadowmen. He's one of the darkest."

"Can he see the dark places the wizards have made in the city?"

"No."

=If I have to come into view and help fight, do you have my knife tucked in the boot?= Zeela asked.

Yes, Zhahar replied.

The man rode over to them at a slow walk, then stopped when he was close enough to talk quietly.

"Apothecary," he said.

The Apothecary tipped his head in an informal bow. "Knife."

=Knife? By the triple stars, that means he's an assassin,= Zeela said. =Or an escort for hire who permanently eliminates any problems a person may encounter on the road.=

The Knife scanned the surrounding trees. "You should have been gone by now."

"Woman time," Lee said.

The Knife nodded. "You need to pick up the pace and get out of this part of the city. You've got a pair of Clubs following your trail. I'm between you and them, but your still being here means they're too close."

"Thank you for the warning," the Apothecary said. "We'll be on our way."

"You'll have shadows on the journey," the Knife said.

The Apothecary gave Zhahar a little push. "Ride in the wagon. There are dates, flatbread, and a bowl of soft cheese in the supplies I obtained at the bazaar. You and Lee eat now."

"Come on." Zhahar gripped Lee's arm and tried to lead him to the back of the wagon, but he braced himself and didn't move.

"Why are you helping us?" he asked, looking at the Knife.

"The shadow places in Vision are my people's home. We've found out enough to know it's not the nature of Vision but a flesh-and-blood adversary that is taking the shadow places away from us, so we're not going to give up one more street to these outsiders without a fight. But until we find someone who can see the streets that have already been taken, the enemy is nothing but a wrongness in the air. Some of my brethren and I heard some Clubs asking about an Apothecary's wagon that had come up from the south. Made us think the shadowman or his companions might be able to find the answer to the bone readers' riddle. Isn't that reason enough?"

"It is," Lee replied. Now he moved with Zhahar to the back of the wagon and climbed inside. Kobrah joined them.

The Apothecary climbed onto the driving seat and urged his horse to walk on.

Lee sat on the bench behind the driving seat, his back against the closed shutter so that he wouldn't block the light coming from the open shutter. Kobrah found the bags of supplies and made simple meals for all of them.

"Sholeh, you should come into view and eat," Lee said quietly.

He's right, Zhahar said. *Remember what you told Kobrah? The food will help you faster when you're the one eating it.*

When she came into view, Sholeh took a bite of the cheese and flatbread, eating slowly while Kobrah handed a folded bread to the Apothecary.

Halfway through her meal, Sholeh, sounding adult again, asked, "What did he mean about us having shadows?"

"Protectors," Lee said. "People who will make sure we reach your homeland."

=This isn't a good time to ask questions,= Zeela whispered. =Just eat your food, all right?=

::But I want to learn.::

=Not now, Sholeh.=

Not now, Zhahar agreed.

Kobrah put away the rest of the food, storing it all carefully, since it was all they had for the evening meal. Then she brushed her hands against her tunic and said, "Maybe I should try to sleep."

"That sounds like a good idea," Lee said. "Hopefully, you'll have a chance to deliver my message to Teaser."

Zhahar wasn't sure what giving a message to a dream friend would accomplish. According to Lee, Teaser wasn't near enough to help them physically, but he had insisted that Kobrah try to reach the incubus—or be receptive to Teaser trying to reach her through the twilight of waking dreams.

The bunk in the wagon was meant for one person—or two people who were very friendly—so Zhahar came back into view and moved over to the bench next to Lee, leaving the bunk for Kobrah.

She turned partway on the bench so that she could talk to both men. "I'm sorry we took so much time."

Lee took her hand. "Wasn't something any of us considered. And it hadn't occurred to me that the wizards would be able to track us *this* fast."

"If there are other wizards near the bazaar—and it seems likely—then the ones in the south could have used a message rider to send orders here ahead of us," the Apothecary said. "I don't think the ones who attacked Shaman Danyal saw me, but maybe they did. However they've figured out what to look for, you have to do your magic before we're caught, so we'll keep moving."

"Northeast," Zhahar said. "I'll be able to tell you more when we get closer."

"You don't remember the name of the village that was closest to your homeland?" Lee asked.

Zhahar hesitated, then thought, *We can't afford to worry about secrets.* "When I left home, my connection between Vision and Tryadnea was near the Asylum. As each of the Tryad fled the city and their connections faded, that connection slipped. Now it's somewhere in the northeast. That's all I know."

"We'll find the connection in time," Lee said. "Your homeland may not end up being connected to Vision, but it won't be adrift."

"How can you be sure?"

He gave her hand a comforting squeeze and didn't answer.

Chapter Twenty-two

S tanding outside the bordello, Danyal eyed the demon cycle. Then he turned back to Sebastian and said in a low voice he hoped wouldn't carry, "I can walk to wherever we're going. Shamans are used to walking."

"Your hip is still healing, and even though it's a stationary bridge, it will be better if you travel with one of us this time." Sebastian gave him a sharp-edged smile. "You faced down wizards and a Dark Guide, and you're afraid of a demon cycle?"

"The wizards didn't have talons or that many teeth." And he hadn't known about the wizards' lightning, so he hadn't been aware of how deadly those men could be.

He glanced at the demon cycle again. The way it had cavorted when it saw Lynnea, it reminded him of the puppies with the pushed-in faces—cute in an ugly sort of way. Add to that the big red eyes and tufted ears, and it looked rather comical—until you took into account all the razor-like teeth, the muscular arms and torso, and the talons that Teaser had assured him could gut a man with one swipe. The cycles, also according to Teaser, had once had wheels and badass riders who had come to the Den to prove they were the biggest, baddest badasses around.

The demons those riders met up with discarded the wheels, ate the riders, and turned the cycles into traveling homes.

Sebastian gave him a friendly slap on the arm. "It already promised Lynnea and Glorianna that it wouldn't eat you. What more do you want?"

He wanted a gentle horse pulling a cart, but, according to Teaser, the black horses most willing to give him a ride would also want to kill him—and maybe eat him. Teaser wasn't sure about the last part.

"Isn't anyone else coming for this . . . test?" Danyal asked.

"They're already at the cottage," Sebastian replied. "Except Teaser, but I think he's still asleep or traveling in dreams, so I don't want to disturb him."

Danyal breathed in slowly and breathed out slowly. He thought about the wind chimes and the quiet morning rituals the Shamans performed to prepare themselves for the tasks of the day.

"All right," he said.

Sebastian studied him. "Every part of Ephemera seems to work a bit different, but the world does the same thing in every piece of itself. It manifests the heart. So if it turns out that Glorianna can't figure out a way to get you back to your city, maybe you should consider that you're not meant to go back."

Danyal stared at him. "Not go back? But my people are there. My *family* is there."

"Yeah. But if the need to go is stronger than the need to stay . . ."

Is that what they had thought happened to Lee? That he'd needed to be away from the places his family controlled? "You still tried to find him." He spoke the thought aloud, not expecting Sebastian to follow his thinking.

But the incubus-wizard followed his thinking quite well. "We found signs of an attack, warnings that something had happened to him. We searched so he would know he wasn't alone, especially if he was hurt or held prisoner and was trying to get back."

Lee had been both, because wasn't the Asylum a kind of prison?

"Come on," Sebastian said. "We can't figure out what we can do to help you until you take this test for Glorianna." He walked over to the demon cycle and mounted, setting his feet on the footrests. Then he looked at Danyal, who gingerly mounted behind him.

The demon cycle moved sedately to the corner, then turned onto the Den's main street.

As they approached a shop, a little man with glasses stepped outside and frowned at them. Sebastian raised a hand in greeting.

"It will be ready this evening," the little man chirped. Then he went back inside and closed the door.

"Your robe," Sebastian said. "He's less annoyed with you about making something so plain because Lynnea asked him to design a strut outfit that was appropriate for a pregnant woman but would still remind her incubus husband of how he got her pregnant in the first place. Mr. Finch has never had a pregnant customer before, and the challenge Lynnea provided has made up for your lack of adventure."

"The white robe is a symbol of the Shamans," Danyal said. "Something easily seen in the bazaar or in a village—and understood by everyone in the city."

"You don't have to convince me. Hold on," Sebastian added as they reached the end of the main street and glided over a span of grass to a dirt lane.

Hold on? Danyal wondered. *Why? And to what?* Then he grabbed Sebastian's waist as the demon cycle leaped forward and flew over the lane.

A minute later, it slowed and finally stopped in front of an odd bit of road. Straight ahead of them, the lane continued. But there was also a curve with two stones set far enough apart to allow a wagon to pass between them.

"We're going to Aurora," Sebastian said.

The demon cycle headed for the curve. As they passed between the stones, night instantly turned to daylight.

Danyal squinted as he looked around. On their right were tall trees. A break in the trees showed him the horizon and the rolling blue of water. On their left was a two-story cottage.

It looked different, smelled different, *felt* different.

"Where . . . ?"

"This is Aurora, my aunt's home village," Sebastian replied. "That's the cottage where Lynnea and I live most of the time. If we'd continued down the lane on that side of the bridge, we would have reached the border between the Den and the waterhorses' landscape. On this side, the lane turns into the main street of the village."

Danyal frowned. "How far away is the Den from Aurora?"

"It's a step away. That curve in the road is a stationary bridge."

"I meant—"

"I know what you meant, but that's the only answer I have. We'll get off here." After Danyal dismounted, Sebastian swung off the demon cycle, thanked it, waited until it disappeared between the two stones, then headed around the cottage. "We don't measure distance or location like that. We can't. According to Michael, Elandar is an island, and it would take days of sea travel to reach it—assuming ships that dock at any ports within reach of us *could* reach Elandar. But we can go a couple of miles down a lane, step between two cairns, and be in that part of the world. This part of the world was broken a long time ago during the battle between the Guides of the Heart and the Eater of the World. They put it back together as best they could with the pieces they could find. It's still a puzzle with bits disconnecting and connecting. A year ago, it wasn't easy getting from the Den to Aurora. Now there's a bridge that connects the two."

"What changed?" Danyal asked.

Sebastian smiled. "I did." Reaching the back of the cottage, he whistled. "Glorianna?"

Her face appeared on the other side of a screened window. "I'll be out as soon as—" Her face disappeared, and they heard Lynnea say, "No toast until you go back to your house."

Danyal's eyebrows rose. Lynnea didn't strike him as a rude woman. Quite the opposite. But pregnant women could be moody. Or so he'd been told.

Then he heard a noise that was, for lack of a better description, a bitching scold. He looked at Sebastian, who sighed.

"It's Bop, the keet. Apparently, he's not happy with his humans wanting to do something besides play with him. Featherheaded tyrant."

"Is he dangerous?" What sort of pet would an incubus-wizard have?

Sebastian snorted. "Don't let the sound fool you." He held up thumb and forefinger spread almost their full distance. "He's that big, plus a tail. Doesn't make him less of a tyrant."

The back door opened, and Glorianna slipped outside with Michael, who was grinning.

"You do this every morning?" Michael asked Sebastian.

"I have sense enough not to open his cage until *after* breakfast. Damn bird tries to steal koffea beans. Besides being expensive, they aren't good for him. But if a person has it, he wants it."

"Which is why he gets toast and bits of fruit in the morning to distract him from what he's not getting." Michael winked at Danyal.

"Why don't you two have a keet?" Sebastian asked. "After all, Aunt Nadia raises them."

"We travel too much," Glorianna replied. She headed for the back of the lawn, then crooked a finger at Danyal. "Lynnea said we could do this here if you have no objections, Sebastian."

He shook his head as he joined her. "I have no objections. *Can* you do it here?"

Michael tsked. "Having grown up with her, you ask that?"

Danyal struggled to hold back impatience. They were playing with birds and teasing each other while a part of the world was under attack?

He looked into the faces of the men and felt a jolt of understanding, a realization of just how innocent and protected the Shamans had been for all these years. The wizards weren't new to Sebastian and Michael. This battle wasn't new. They were always aware of the danger and had already stood against the enemy. They worked and lived and laughed and loved on a battleground, while his people had tended a distant city that hadn't been touched by that ancient war—until now.

"Ephemera, hear me," Glorianna said as she pointed to the ground in front of her. "Shift the playground from the Island in the Mist to this spot."

A rectangle of grass disappeared. In its place was a long wooden box. Part of the box was filled with sand. The other part held gravel and a bench.

"Sit on the bench," Glorianna told Danyal. "Don't touch the sand."

"What will this do?" Danyal stepped into the box and sat on the bench.

"It will tell me about you, and tell me what skills you have."

Before he could ask what that meant, she said, "Ephemera, show me this heart."

He watched the world swiftly reveal his heart to this woman. Rough granite, like the stone that made up the mountains that formed the northern boundary of Vision. Wildflowers that grew in the northern community where he'd grown up—and where his nephew still lived. Mist. One corner changed to hard-packed earth that reminded him of the Asylum's grounds and was filled with thorny vines. Beside it was a pile of stones with water trickling down into a pool surrounded by plants. In front of the mist, a pile of pocket watches wiggled out of the sand. The last thing that appeared was one of his favorite flowers. He used to grow them in his private courtyard when he served the Temple of Sorrow. As it appeared, he thought he heard wind chimes.

When nothing happened for a full minute, Sebastian said, "What does it mean?"

"Strength makes stone," Glorianna replied. "Bright feelings—love, laughter—make flowers. Mist hides. Combined with the watches, it could mean there are times when you would like to put aside being a Shaman—hide that aspect of yourself—and be among friends who see the man."

Danyal jolted. How could she know that?

The heart has no secrets from Glorianna Belladonna.

"But this?" She pointed to the barren, hard-packed earth. "That resonates with the Dark currents, which means you do have a connection to the Dark as well as the Light, Shaman. Despair made the deserts and hope the oases." Then she looked at him.

Thorn trees with sinuous limbs.

Michael reached for her, but she shifted away from him while those cold green eyes stayed fixed on Danyal.

"Do you help make the deserts, Shaman?" Belladonna asked. "Or are you trying to shape an oasis for hearts in turmoil?"

I could do that? Can those hearts truly heal enough to return to the world?

He wanted to do more as the Asylum Keeper than keep the people there docile and caged, but he hadn't been sure anything he might do would make enough of a difference.

The sand stirred. They all watched one more plant appear in front of the granite.

"Heart's hope," Glorianna murmured. She took a deep breath and blew it out on a sigh. "All right, let's—"

"Hey-a!" Teaser rounded the corner and jogged over to them. "I connected with Kobrah, and she gave me a message from Lee."

Danyal followed Yoshani to a bench in front of a koi pond. After a polite minute, he asked, "What are we doing here?"

"We are watching the koi," Yoshani replied calmly.

"Why?"

"Why not?"

The answer was so like something he would have said to someone seeking his counsel, he smiled.

Sanctuary. A Place of Light where people could come to renew the spirit. And according to Yoshani, many Places of Light in the world were connected to this one.

He had crossed over a bridge and ended up here with Yoshani, Glorianna, Michael, and Sebastian. Glorianna took Michael and Sebastian to her Island in the Mist, leaving him to explore Sanctuary with Yoshani.

"You're not from this place," Danyal said.

"Originally? No. I come from a country that I think is in a different part of the world. Much like you." Yoshani smiled. "I still cross the bridge to my homeland and visit the Place of Light where I trained, but mostly I am here now to welcome visitors—and to listen. Brighid, Michael's aunt, is another who has found a home here. She is a true Guardian of the Light, but even so, her heart was troubled until she came here and realized this Place of Light could give her what she needed for herself."

Danyal hesitated. "Did you show me Sanctuary to occupy me while we wait or to let me know there is another place besides The Temples where I might do some good?"

"Both." Yoshani watched the koi. "Do the Shamans run all the places in your city that contain the sick hearts and minds?"

"No, I was the first to be assigned as a Keeper."

"Why?"

Danyal watched a flash of gold disappear beneath the floating plants, then turned to Yoshani. "I was needed."

"Why?"

"Because . . ." Danyal turned back to watch the fish. "I had served as the leader at the Temple of Sorrow for several years. That work demands much from the Shamans who serve there, and it was time for me to leave. I was supposed to be free of duties for a year to rest and explore the restlessness in my own heart. But a wrongness came to Vision, and the Shaman Council felt my presence at the Asylum would draw a madman and a teacher, and they would help me see where help could be found."

Yoshani laughed softly. "Heart wishes are powerful things to send out into the currents of the world."

Anger surged in Danyal, and for a moment, the Dark currents in Sanctuary rippled. Then those currents were gone, a reminder that here he was only a visitor and not the voice for this part of the world.

"You think I wanted this to happen to my city?" he asked.

Yoshani shook his head. "I think you and Lee would have had an opportunity to meet, and what you chose to do with that acquaintance would resonate through your lives. But, Danyal? I'm not sure it was your heart wish that drew Lee to your city."

Glorianna studied the triangle of grass in the part of her garden that contained the dark landscapes.

"Still not resonating with me enough," she muttered.

"You couldn't reach that landscape?" Michael asked.

"I could, yes. But I'm not sure going there now would do the place or the people any good. They aren't *mine* yet."

"What about you, Magician?" Sebastian asked. "I know that patch of grass is in Glorianna's garden, but could it be resonating with you, but fit in better with her dark landscapes?"

She watched her lover and partner, the man who had used the music in his and Sebastian's hearts to bring her out of that terrible landscape she'd created for the Eater of the World.

Michael stared at the grass triangle, his eyes softly focused. After a minute, he shook his head, but he looked puzzled.

"It's an odd thing," he said. "The music I hear doesn't fit

a dark landscape—or at least doesn't fit what I've seen and felt in the darker places. Maybe that's why you're having so much trouble pinning it down, Glorianna. It's dark and light and something in between, and I'm thinking Ephemera is nudging it toward the Den because whatever lives there wouldn't find much welcome in the daylight landscapes."

"Like an incubus?" Sebastian asked.

"Maybe." Michael tipped his head. "Not one song, but three that harmonize back into one."

"So I'm only resonating with one or two but not all three?" Glorianna asked.

"Not yet anyway," Michael replied. "I'm thinking it's going to be like Lighthaven. These people are going to have to choose you before you and Ephemera can make that final connection."

Lee's message kept circling through her mind. They were running from the wizards and the Dark Guide and going to the landscape that belonged to Zhahar's people. Those people needed her help. The access point was probably a triangle of grass.

He'd seen this triangle the last time he came to the island.

A triangle of grass. Three songs. A landscape that wasn't dark but wanted to connect with a dark landscape—specifically the Den, a place that didn't automatically pass judgment on demon races.

"The Shaman didn't tell us much about Zhahar, did he?" Glorianna said.

"I had the impression it wasn't his secret to tell," Michael said.

"Are you worried because Lee stayed for the sake of a girl?" Sebastian asked.

Glorianna huffed. "He's twenty-nine. I hope the girl is old enough to be considered a woman."

Silence. Then Sebastian said, "Lynnea is younger than me."

"That's different." But she looked at her cousin and considered Sebastian and Lynnea—two people who shouldn't have met but were drawn together by each other's heart wish.

Was it Lee's heart or someone else's that had drawn him to the city of Vision?

"From what Kobrah told Teaser, they've got another

day's traveling ahead of them before they reach Zhahar's homeland," Sebastian said. "I think we should spend that time getting ready. A daypack with a change of clothes. Water. Some food that's ready to grab. We'll get some rest. Can Ephemera give us some warning if the access point becomes strong enough to cross over?"

"I'll know. If I'm anywhere on the island, I'll know," Glorianna said.

"You keep saying 'we,' Justice Maker," Michael said.

Sebastian looked at Michael. "I'm going with Glorianna."

"Why you and not me?"

"Because if we run into trouble, you have the music that will guide us home."

"He's right, Michael," Glorianna said. "Besides, Sebastian should have a say in whether this unknown landscape connects with the Den."

Nothing more to be done, she thought as the three of them went back to the house. *Not yet.*

A few months ago, all Lee wanted was to get away from her and everything connected to her. She had felt that truth in his heart the last time she saw him. So what did it mean that he was asking for her help now?

Chapter Twenty-three

"We're being followed," the Knife said as he came abreast of the driving seat.

"The same Clubs who were behind us at the traveler's well yesterday?" Lee asked. They'd found him a hat with a soft brim that helped conceal the dark glasses as well as provide the extra protection he needed to ride on the driving seat during daylight hours.

When the Apothecary made an odd sound, Lee wondered if he'd asked a question that shouldn't have been asked.

"Some of my brethren have made sure those Clubs are well behind you and will stay that way," the Knife said. A moment's silence, then he added, "Hiring this many Clubs to chase you down takes a hefty bag of coins."

"Are you wondering if it would be worth switching sides?" Lee asked. He heard the Apothecary suck in a breath, and figured he'd deeply insulted the Knife.

"I've chosen my side, and I told you my reasons," the Knife replied calmly. "But I'm wondering what makes you so valuable—or dangerous—to whoever is changing the city."

When the Knife said nothing more, Lee thought, *Whatever you give to the world comes back to you—and that includes trust.* "I'm a Bridge. I have the ability to connect pieces of the world, even pieces that are distant from one another. The men who are changing the shadow streets are called wizards. They're dangerous men who came from my part of the world."

"Is that why they're after you?" the Knife asked. "To force you to make this magic so they can travel to and from Vision?"

Lee shook his head. "At first they wanted to use me to reach my sister, who is their most dangerous enemy and lives in a place that they can't find by themselves. Now I think they want to stop me from reaching her. Without my . . . magic . . . I think the journey to your city would be a long one. And I don't think anyone in my part of the world knows about Vision, including my sister." Well, there was Teaser, but this wasn't the time to tell the Knife about the incubi and the way they could travel through the twilight of waking dreams.

"So the wizards' enemy won't be able to find Vision unless you get back to your part of the world and tell her," the Knife said, nodding.

"Yes." Lee sighed. "And even if I can get back, whether help can reach Vision will depend on Ephemera."

"Then let's hope the world is looking kindly toward us. I'm going to drop back a bit to stay between the Clubs and you, but not so far I'll lose sight of the wagon. You need to get where you're going before dark. My brethren will delay some of the Clubs permanently, but there aren't enough of us who can see the northern community up ahead to keep you safe if enough Clubs have a chance to catch up."

"If there are that many of the bastards after us, you should stay close," the Apothecary said. "We can't afford to lose your skills if there's a fight." When the Knife dropped back, he added quietly to Lee, "And I'm not sure he'll still be able to see the road we're traveling if he's too far back. This isn't a part of the city his guild usually visits. Clubs are dangerous, but they're hired muscle and don't stand in the shadows as deep as the Knife Guild."

"So he could lose sight of us and the Clubs won't," Lee said grimly.

The second shutter behind the driving seat opened, and Zhahar muttered at Lee's left shoulder, "Zeela says she can fight."

Lee wasn't sure Zeela was fit enough, but having two people with fighting skills gave both of them a better chance of surviving—and gave all of them a better chance to reach the spot where Vision was connected to Tryadnea. "How much farther?" he asked Zhahar. "Can you tell?"

"I don't know exactly where the connection is. But it's that way." Reaching between Lee and the Apothecary, she pointed.

Thankfully, the road was still going in the right direction.

"We're close," she said, withdrawing her arm so that she was no longer immediately visible to anyone they might meet on the road.

"How long will the connection remain once you're back in your homeland?" Lee asked.

"Since we're the last Tryad in the city, not long," Zhahar replied. "Less than an hour, I think. Then Tryadnea will be adrift again."

Less than an hour is still too long, he thought. If the enemy was close behind them, having that connection last even a few minutes after they crossed it might be too long. So he would need to break that connection and change it into something else as soon as they were on Tryadnea ground.

A sound came from behind him. Not the *hummm* he associated with Zhahar talking with her sisters. *This* sounded more like annoyed buzzing. And judging by the way the Apothecary suddenly hunched his shoulders, Lee wasn't the only one hearing it.

"If you all keep trying to come into view and talk at the same time, at least one of you is going to end up with a sore throat," he said.

The buzzing stopped.

"You usually whack a hornet's nest to see what happens?" the Apothecary asked quietly.

"I'm usually smarter than that," Lee replied.

"Could you try being smarter when I'm close enough to you to get stung?"

Lee huffed out a soft laugh. Then he sobered.

No way to tell if this was going to work. No way to tell if his presence would negate the effort of the others to send out a call for help through the currents of the world. No way to tell anything, but he had to believe that, if Glorianna received the message he'd sent through Kobrah and Teaser, she would help him.

Glorianna would help him. He was sure of that. He believed it with all his heart. But would Belladonna help him?

He twisted on the seat to look toward the window. "Can I ask you something?"

Zhahar's face appeared in the window. "Sholeh says the community up ahead is an artisan community. When she was researching other parts of Vision, she didn't find mention of any shadow streets or dark places."

"Every community has a shadow street of sorts," the Apothecary said. "But it might not be dark enough to have shadowmen."

"Why was Sholeh looking for a street like that?" Lee asked.

"In case we needed to try again in a different part of the city."

"But Sholeh . . ." Lee paused. Thought. Sholeh definitely belonged to the daylight landscapes. Zeela? Yes, *that* sister would like the things that weren't so proper—and might even need to spend time in shadowy places to feel comfortable with her surroundings. "Must be a challenge to find a place that suits all of you."

No answer.

"Was that what you wanted to know?" Zhahar asked.

Distracted by thoughts of Zhahar and her sisters and where they could live, he'd forgotten what he'd wanted to ask. Something about sisters. Ah yes. "If one of you was upset with someone, would all of you be upset with that person? Could one of you stop the others from helping that person?"

"Damn fool," the Apothecary muttered as he hunched his shoulders and told the horse to giddyup.

The horse made an effort, probably because it could hear the angry buzzing too.

"Why do you ask?" Zeela growled.

"My sister," Lee replied quietly.

A pause. Then Zhahar said, "Oh." She reached through the window and rested her hand on his arm for a moment before withdrawing again. "We might not help with a small thing if we were upset with someone, but we wouldn't walk away from someone in real trouble. Not if we cared about him."

Not the same. There was Light and Dark in each aspect of Sholeh Zeela a Zhahar, and that wasn't the same as Belladonna. Not the same at all.

Heart's hope lies within Belladonna.
He was going to hope—to *believe*—that was still true.

Hurry, Zhahar thought. *Hurry hurry hurry.*

Kobrah, keeping watch out the wagon's door, gave them constant reports now of four riders—still following from a distance, but closing on them. The village itself was up ahead, and the Apothecary was aiming for it in the hope the Clubs wouldn't attack them with other people around. But the connection to Tryadnea wasn't *in* the village, and once they were out of sight of other people . . .

Maybe if we take Lee, those Clubs will leave the others alone, Zhahar said.

=Not anymore,= Zeela said. =At this point, everyone with us knows more than those wizards want anyone to know. Maybe the Clubs have orders to capture Lee instead of killing him, but the wizards have no reason to think the rest of us are anything but trouble if we're left alive.=

Shaken by her sister's assessment, Zhahar leaned out the window and pointed west. "We have to go that way."

"Let's see if we can get into the village itself before heading in that direction," Lee said. "Being the only wagon on the road makes us conspicuous."

Saying nothing, the Apothecary coaxed the horse into a trot. A short while later, they slowed to a walk as they joined the other conveyances on the main street. Being on horseback and more able to maneuver, the Knife rode up ahead, then returned in a few minutes to ride beside the wagon and report.

"The market fills the center of the village," he said. "I don't think wagons or carts are allowed in there once the merchants set up their booths, but even if we did go in there, we'd never get through with all the people on the street. I saw what looks like a western road just before the market begins. When I inquired, a young man confirmed the road headed west, but he said there is nothing but woodland and fields that way because the bridge doesn't work. He said his uncle, who's a Shaman, was up here visiting and warned the village not to use that bridge—that it didn't lead to the fields beyond it that the eye could see."

"That must be the connection," Zhahar said.

Lee nodded. "Makes sense. It sounds like the connection turned an ordinary bridge into a stationary bridge that links the two landscapes. It's not surprising that a Shaman trying to walk across that bridge would sense the other landscape, but I think most of the villagers would have crossed that bridge and ended up on the road they'd always traveled." But a few of them would have crossed that bridge and gotten lost in Ephemera's landscapes.

"What about us?" the Apothecary asked.

"Zhahar resonates with her homeland. Her presence should be enough to get us there."

"Then let's move," the Knife said at the same time Kobrah said, "Four riders. Almost on us."

They turned onto the narrow western road, still moving at a walk while they were in sight of houses and workshops. As soon as the fields were the only thing in front of them, the Apothecary whipped the horse into a gallop.

Zhahar grabbed the window ledge and Lee's arm. Behind her, she heard Kobrah yelp as the wagon rocked enough to make standing precarious.

"You need to pull up on the other side of the bridge as soon as you can," Lee said.

"We should keep going as long as the horse can," the Apothecary argued.

"Unless there are armed Tryad waiting right on the other side, we can't outrun the Clubs long enough to find help if all of us cross that bridge," Lee argued. "But I can stop them from reaching Tryadnea."

=Can he do what he did to Teeko?= Zeela asked.

Zhahar relayed the question and saw the Apothecary tense when Lee replied, "Something like that."

The Knife shouted. Zhahar didn't catch the words, only the urgency.

"You sure this is the place?" the Apothecary asked.

"Doesn't matter," Lee said before Zhahar could reply. "Just get us over that bridge."

"The Knife is behind us," Kobrah shouted. "The Clubs!"

"Bridge is up ahead," the Apothecary said.

Zhahar wasn't sure if he said that in case Lee couldn't see it or to make sure *she* was aware of it.

A few lengths from the bridge, the Apothecary eased the horse back to a less reckless speed.

Hurry, Zhahar thought. *Hurry hurry hurry.*

::I can feel Tryadnea,:: Sholeh said.

"Give the Knife room to get off the bridge, then pull up," Lee said.

Horse and wagon clattered over the bridge, followed by the Knife, who turned and pulled out a long blade from a sheath on his saddle.

Lee scrambled off the driving seat and ran for the bridge.

Zhahar climbed through the window to the driving seat, jumped down, and ran after him.

Lee dropped to his knees and grabbed the post on one side of the bridge.

"Lee!" she yelled as two of the Clubs rode onto the bridge, with the other pair a length behind.

"Stay back!" Lee snapped. He flattened on the ground, but his hands still held the post.

One of the Clubs was focused on Lee; the other on the Knife. Zeela came into view, ran the few steps between her and Lee, and pulled the knife from her boot.

The Clubs came over the bridge, weapons raised—and disappeared in the moment their horses' feet would have touched land.

The men coming behind the first pair vanished too, but Zeela could hear them.

"What happened? Where did they go? Where's the wagon?"

A clatter of hooves, as if the second pair of horses was being turned around. Then no sound from the riders. Too quickly, there was no sound.

Releasing the post, Lee rolled onto his back. "Guardians and Guides, that was close."

Zeela watched the Knife dismount. She didn't think a man like him was used to feeling so wary of another man, and she didn't know how he would respond to a man who could do . . . What *had* Lee done?

As Kobrah and the Apothecary joined them, both looking around with dazed expressions, Lee sat up, pulled off the hat, and scrubbed his fingers over his short hair.

The Knife took a step toward them. Zeela stepped in front of Lee, who didn't seem to notice.

"What happened?" the Knife asked.

"There was a tree on this side of the bridge," the Apothecary said. "I saw it. Now it's gone."

"It's not gone," Lee said. "It's just not in this landscape."

The Knife shook his head. "What happened to the Clubs?"

"For the moment, this is a resonating bridge. It can send a person to any landscape that resonates with that person's heart. The Clubs who crossed over the bridge are now in a landscape that matches who they are."

"Where is this landscape?"

"Don't know. The other two are still in the northern community—unless they tried to cross the bridge. In which case, they've also crossed over to somewhere else."

"You don't seem too concerned about that."

"Why should I be?"

The question seemed to shock everyone—even the Knife.

Chilled by the casual way Lee had just sent two men into the unknown, Zeela sheathed her knife, and Zhahar came back into view.

"What do we do now?" she asked.

"Finish this," Lee replied. "This bridge no longer connects your homeland to Vision. I don't know how long it will take for Tryadnea to start drifting, so we need to talk to your people's leaders, and we need to do it fast."

"This leads to our mothers' village," Zhahar said, pointing to the cart track. "At least, it did when I left here."

"No reason why it wouldn't still lead to the village," Lee said.

Isn't there? she wondered.

He looked around, picked up his hat, and headed for the wagon.

The Knife and the Apothecary stared at her.

"*Is* he going to help us?" the Knife asked.

"Yes," she replied with all the conviction she could put into her voice. "He said he would, so he will."

Nodding, the Knife returned to his horse and mounted while the Apothecary and Kobrah returned to the wagon.

=Lee's sister isn't the only one who has a dark side,= Zeela said.

I know that, Zhahar replied. *But I wonder if it's occurred to him?*

*   *   *

He had frightened a Knife. He knew plenty of demons who wouldn't hesitate to kill a human—or kill anything else, for that matter—but in the landscapes he'd called home, he hadn't heard of anything like a guild of assassins.

Shadowmen.

If he understood the neutral morality and position the shadowmen held in Vision, would his ability as a Bridge make him a shadowman?

He had always considered his power as something neutral. He made a bridge, and what happened to the people who crossed that bridge was none of his concern. People were drawn to the landscapes that resonated with their own hearts. Nothing to do with him.

When he'd been in Elandar and tossed a one-shot bridge at a man who was about to start a brawl, he'd known the man would end up in a rough landscape and might not live to find a gentler one. But the Dark currents in Raven's Hill had been swollen by the Eater of the World, and *that* had turned his heart toward darker feelings.

Hadn't it?

He and Glorianna had the same mother, and through Nadia's bloodlines, they had a strong connection to the Light. But they also had the same father. A wizard. Whose power had come from the Dark.

Glorianna could command the Light *and* the Dark landscapes in Ephemera. That's why she'd been more of a danger to the wizards than other Landscapers. Because her father was a wizard.

Their father was a wizard.

It hadn't occurred to him until now that he shouldn't have been able to travel through all of Glorianna's landscapes. All the daylight ones, sure, but not the dark landscapes. Not *all* of them. But where she led, he could follow.

Because the power he'd inherited from his father had come from the Dark. Which meant that some of *his* power as a Bridge also came from the Dark.

Compared to other Bridges, that made him something other than neutral.

When he threw the stone that held a one-shot bridge at

Teeko, he'd *wanted* the man to end up in a dark landscape, and he knew with a bone-deep certainty that Teeko had crossed over to a dark place. He'd known when he turned the bridge that connected Tryadnea to Vision into a resonating bridge that the Clubs who were riding over it to kill him and the others would cross over into a landscape that held dangers they couldn't begin to imagine. And because they would have killed Zhahar, he had no regrets that those men had little chance of surviving.

What did that say about him?

What did that say?

Zhahar sat on the window seat, her view restricted to the strip of space between the Apothecary's body and Lee's. The Knife was riding beside the wagon instead of scouting ahead, because she'd warned the men that people of single aspect usually thought of her people as demons and, therefore, something to destroy, so an armed man riding toward a village would be seen as an enemy.

=We'd get there faster if we walked,= Zeela growled.

::The horse is tired,:: Sholeh said.

We're all tired, Zhahar said.

::Yes, but we didn't have to pull the wagon, so the horse is more tired.::

Zeela swore.

"Is there any food left?" Zhahar asked Kobrah. She was usually more vigilant about how long they went between meals.

Kneeling on the floor, Kobrah checked the food box. "A couple of dates and a piece of flatbread." After wiping her hands on her trousers, which weren't all that clean either, she handed the food to Zhahar.

"Do you want some of the bread?" Zhahar asked.

Kobrah shook her head.

Zhahar ate one of the dates, then bit into the bread, chewing slowly. Zeela came into view and took a bite of bread. Then they insisted that Sholeh eat the rest.

::Will we be home soon?:: Sholeh asked.

=I don't know,= Zeela said gently. =The village lookouts will spot us soon, I think.=

Unless things drifted on this side too and we're no longer close to our mothers' village, Zhahar thought, being careful to keep that thought private.

"Zhahar?" Lee said. "We're close to some structures. Is that your village?"

While she hurriedly chewed the last bite of bread, Sholeh made noises so he would know they had heard him. As soon as Zhahar came into view, she twisted on the seat to look out.

"Sorry," she said. "Sholeh needed some food. I can't see. Can you . . . ?"

Lee leaned to his right, giving her more of a view.

Her heart sank. Did he think she came from such a rough place?

"It's a camp," she said, then added silently, *Where our village used to be.*

"Would your leaders be there?" he asked.

=They would have set up the camp near the connection, hoping we'd get back before Tryadnea went adrift again,= Zeela said. =But the camp and the connection must have drifted apart.=

"They'll be there," Zhahar told Lee. She touched the Apothecary's arm, then pointed toward the right. "Those ropes and posts are pickets for horses. You should tie up there."

"They know we're here," the Knife said quietly, "and I guess they really don't like company."

"They'll have to cope with more," Lee said as he climbed down.

Zhahar scrambled to get the wagon's door open. As she came around the side, she saw Lee, the Knife, and the Apothecary standing next to the wagon, their hands at their sides, holding no weapons. Facing them were a dozen Tryad, all armed. And standing slightly in front of her warriors, dressed in fighting leathers, was Morragen Medusah a Zephyra, leader of the Tryad people—and their mothers.

Zhahar rushed over and wrapped her arms around one of Lee's. As her mothers' faces kept shifting, she saw the desperate fury and despair over what would happen to the Tryad when the last connection broke completely—and also saw a painful joy that the daughters had returned.

When Morragen came into view and stayed, Zhahar said, "We ask our mothers and our leader to accept the presence of our friends, and to listen to this man. He comes from a different part of the world, and he can help us."

Morragen stared at Zhahar, then focused all her formidable presence on Lee.

"The connection between Tryadnea and Vision has broken," he said.

"I know that," Morragen said.

Under that voice, Zhahar heard Medusah speaking the same words with the same controlled fury—and realized, when Lee stiffened, that he heard that second voice too.

"Yes, you know that." Lee nodded. "But one—or more— of you have also sent a heart wish through the currents of the world, and that heart wish was strong enough to create a tentative connection to another part of Ephemera. If you act now, I think you can send a message to the person who can connect your homeland to another landscape. But if you do this and she answers, you have to accept that her heart will be the bedrock of your homeland."

"Do you think we haven't heard such promises before?" Morragen snarled. "'Give us your gold, your jewels, your livestock, your crops, your bodies, or whatever else is wanted in order to be accepted.' The one-faces take and take and *never* accept, *never* give anything in return. And now you want the rest?"

"I don't want anything," Lee said quietly.

"Nothing?" Morragen sneered.

"Well, yes, there is something. But, frankly, it's none of your business, even if you are Zhahar's mother."

=By the triple stars! Did he *really* say that? To *Morragen*?= Zeela sounded shocked, but not anywhere near as shocked as Zhahar felt. Of course, she hadn't told him about the taboos surrounding any involvement with a man of single aspect, so he had no way of knowing how badly he had rocked the Tryad just now.

::Could have been worse,:: Sholeh said. ::He could have said it to Medusah.::

For the first time in memory, none of her mothers' aspects seemed able to respond.

"I can assist you in sending a call for help through the currents of the world," Lee said. "The rest you'll have to discuss with her."

"With who?" Morragen and Medusah asked.

Zhahar felt a shiver run through her a moment before Lee said, "With Belladonna."

Silence. Then Morragen looked at Zhahar. "Do you trust him? Do all of you trust his words?"

"Yes," they replied. "We trust him."

Morragen gave the at-rest signal, and all her warriors lowered their weapons. Then she looked at Lee. "What do we do?"

"Want this with everything in you, and say these words: 'heart's hope lies within Belladonna.'"

"Should Morragen be the only one saying these words?" Zhahar asked.

Lee shook his head. "The more voices, the more hearts, the stronger the wish will flow in the currents and the faster it will be heard."

"If we do this, how soon before we have an answer?" Morragen asked.

"I think there is already an access point to Tryadnea in her garden." Lee waved off questions before they could be asked. "What is important to you right now is that if you truly want her to help, Belladonna can reach us simply by taking a step from her garden to here."

Morragen studied him for a moment, then nodded. "We will try this."

::What if Belladonna doesn't answer?:: Sholeh said.

She's his sister, Zhahar replied. *She'll answer.*

Turning slightly, Lee looked at the Apothecary, the Knife, and Kobrah. "Since you aren't from this land, I think it's best if you three don't participate. Might tangle things up in the currents."

The two men nodded. Kobrah said nothing.

"Heart's hope lies within Belladonna," Lee said, raising his voice.

Morragen Medusah a Zephyra raised their voices. "Heart's hope lies within Belladonna."

The next time, Sholeh Zeela a Zhahar added their voices. After that, one by one, the Tryad warriors joined the chant.

Two people appeared out of nowhere—a black-haired woman with green eyes so cold and deadly even Morragen flinched, and a dark-haired man with sharp green eyes who rubbed his thumb against his finger pads in a way that made

Zhahar think of someone striking flint against stone to start a fire.

Was that what he was doing?

"I am Belladonna," the woman said. Her eyes were focused on Morragen, who had turned to face her.

"I am Morragen Medusah a Zephyra."

The man's eyes roamed over the rest of them, assessing them in a way that had Zeela pushing to come into view. Then those eyes passed over her and settled on Lee.

"Hey-a," he said.

Belladonna looked away from Morragen.

"Lee?" She pushed past Morragen and the warriors as Zhahar released Lee's arm and stepped aside. *"Lee!"*

Belladonna let her pack slide to the ground as she threw herself into Lee's arms. He grabbed her and swung her around. "Glorianna!"

Zhahar sucked in a breath. So did Morragen. The face hadn't changed the way it did with the Tryad, but the *difference* between the woman who had appeared out of nowhere and the woman Lee now held in his arms was like seeing another aspect come into view. Everything about her *felt* as if she were someone else.

Glorianna cupped her hands around her brother's face. "Oh, Lee. Your eyes."

"It's all right," he said, wrapping his hands loosely around her wrists. "They're getting better."

"Let me see." She reached up to remove his dark glasses, but he pulled his head back. "I need to see."

Lee let her take the glasses. Reaching behind her, she said, "Hold these."

Her companion took the dark glasses and tucked them into his shirt pocket.

Glorianna stared at Lee's still-cloudy eyes—and her face changed as she gave him a hard shove that knocked him back a couple of steps.

"You ass!" she screamed.

"I could say the same about you," Lee growled. "And if you want to have this out here and now, I'll oblige you."

"Oblige me? *Oblige me?*"

"But first you need to anchor this landscape to one of yours. Tryadnea is adrift in the world and won't survive long without a connection."

"It's connected to the Den," Glorianna shouted. "A border formed as soon as Sebastian and I crossed over. Which you would have realized if you were using your brain these days to do more than try to look up your ass!"

Lee took the two steps that separated them, his hands clenching into fists. "At least I haven't been acting like some pouty, prissy prig *girl*!"

"Idiot!"

"Moron!"

"I'm not the one who let wizards take me to an unknown landscape!"

"And I'm not the one who locked myself into a landscape with the Eater of the World!"

Glorianna balled her hand and looked like she was going for a roundhouse punch.

Zhahar leaped forward to help Lee but was hauled back by the man who had come with Glorianna.

"No no no no no," he said, pulling her away. "This fight is long overdue, and you do not want to get in the middle of it. Trust me."

As Glorianna threw the punch, the ground all around her and Lee changed into knee-deep mud. She slipped and landed face-first. Lee, who had jerked back out of reach, fell on his ass. Snarling at each other, they made it upright as far as their knees before they started slinging mud.

"In one of the landscapes, mud slinging is a time-honored tradition for settling some kinds of disputes," the dark-haired man said as he released Zhahar. "Give them a few minutes. We'll all be better off for it." He gave her a smile that said he *really* enjoyed women. "I'm Sebastian. Are you Zhahar?"

"Yes."

He looked around, puzzled. "Where are your sisters?"

It was petty to want to unnerve this man because he stopped her from helping Lee, especially since Lee didn't look like he needed help, but she did it anyway. One by one, the aspects of Sholeh Zeela a Zhahar came into view.

"We," Sholeh said.

"Are," Zeela said.

"Here," Zhahar finished.

Sebastian stared at her. "Guardians and Guides." Then he let out a wickedly delighted laugh. "Oh, do I have questions, but—" He glanced at Morragen. "I think they should wait for a more appropriate time."

"Like when my mothers aren't close enough to hear them?" Zhahar asked sweetly.

Another glance at Morragen. "That too," Sebastian agreed.

"Did not!" Glorianna shouted.

"Did too!" Lee shouted back as he slung a handful of mud at his sister.

Sebastian gave them a considering look, then shook his head. "They're still in the 'nyah, nyah' stage of the fight, but that usually doesn't last long."

"How can you tell?" Zhahar asked.

"I've been watching them do this since we were children," Sebastian replied. "They don't fight with each other very often, so when they do it's always the same pattern. Although the mud wallow is new—and wasn't, I think, something either of them asked Ephemera to make." Turning away from the mud wallow, he looked Morragen in the eye—something very few people would dare to do. "So. Being the Den's Justice Maker, I have to ask: why do you think Ephemera wanted to connect your land to a dark landscape like the Den of Iniquity?"

"Perhaps because we're demons," Morragen replied coldly.

Sebastian tipped his head. "Nope. I can see why the prissy prigs in the human landscapes would slap that label on you, but while you may be unusual, you're not a demon race."

Morragen looked surprised—and curious. "How would you know?"

"First, I've seen my share of demons. And second, being an incubus, I *am* from a demon race." Sebastian smiled. "Having three lovely faces makes you interesting, but it doesn't make you a demon."

"You're a sex demon?" Zhahar's voice had a bit of a squeal from Sholeh.

"Yes. No. Sort of. I *am* an incubus, so I am a sex demon, but I retired from that line of work when I got married. Now I'm the Den's Justice Maker." He gave Morragen a "women are *wonderful*" smile. "You have questions, but"—he listened for a moment to the voices behind him—"all the intriguing questions will have to wait."

"I didn't want this for you!" Glorianna's voice broke. "Not this, Lee. Never *this.*"

"I never thought you did." Lee's voice broke too.

They knelt there, covered in mud, barely moving to avoid falling down.

"You didn't want to see, but that doesn't mean I wanted you to be *blind*," she cried.

"What are you talking about?"

"You! That last time in the garden. Y-you didn't want to see me, couldn't accept what I am now, and I was angry and hurt, but I also knew . . ." She slipped in the mud.

Lee grabbed for her—and went down with her.

"Knew what, Glorianna?" he asked when they got to their knees again.

"It was time for you to go." She began to cry. "The heart has no secrets, Lee, and yours was telling me it was time for you to go, to cross over to someplace that wasn't mine because you needed to be away from what was mine. So that day, when you left the garden, I asked Ephemera to give you the opportunity to find a place that resonated with your heart but not mine. So that you could go and make your own life. Without me. But I didn't want you hurt. I didn't want that. Neither part of me wanted that."

He gathered her in his arms and held her tight. "This wasn't your doing. It was my choice. Another Bridge got a couple of wizards into one of Mother's landscapes. They were a mile from a bridge that could have taken them to you. I couldn't risk that. And not just for you, Glorianna. I couldn't risk them finding a way to reach the Places of Light. I didn't expect this to happen either when I threw those resonating bridges into a pileup of bodies. I didn't expect to end up in a city unlike anything I'd seen before, and I didn't expect to be held captive. But neither of those things was your fault!"

"You hate me." Her voice cracked with the pain in those words.

"I don't hate you. I—" Lee released her and moved back, putting a little distance between them. His voice rang with anger. "I could have reached you, Glorianna. I could have gotten my island into that landscape and reached you, except the damn Magician started that fight and broke my arm, and then it was too late. But I could have reached you, and I've only just realized in the past few hours why I could have gotten into a landscape that dark."

"You could have reached me in that landscape," she agreed. "Because you're my brother, you could have reached me. But even using your island to get in, you couldn't have gotten out—and you wouldn't have survived. So Michael did what I asked him to do. He kept you safe. The others as well, but mostly you because you could have reached Belladonna, but you wouldn't have survived. Not with her. Not in that landscape."

Crying, they hugged each other.

Zhahar felt tears well up and spill over. She looked at Morragen and was surprised by the tears in *those* eyes. Just as Zeela was the warrior of the a Zhahar Tryad, Morragen was the warrior of the a Zephyra Tryad—and like Zeela, Morragen rarely cried.

"She was a single aspect?" Morragen whispered.

"Yes," Zhahar replied.

Sebastian cleared his throat. "She split her heart between the Light and the Dark in order to save the world. Right now she's Glorianna and Belladonna—and she's trying to learn how to be Glorianna Belladonna again."

Zephyra came into view. "Perhaps we have some knowledge that would help—at least in terms of learning how to live with two aspects."

"I guess you would know all about being separate and together." Sebastian lifted his chin toward the mud wallow as Glorianna and Lee climbed out. "You have a couple of big washtubs or an outdoor trough?"

"Why?" Zephyra asked.

He looked scandalized. "Do you want to let those two into your house to get cleaned up?"

Morragen Medusah a Zephyra stared at Lee and Glorianna. "By the triple stars. I—"

"Don't feel obliged because of some misguided sense of hospitality," Sebastian said cheerfully. "Even my auntie, who is their mother, wouldn't let those two, looking like that, anywhere near the house."

::Let me ask,:: Sholeh said.

Giving in, Zhahar's aspect waned so that Sholeh could come into view.

"If the world made the mud, couldn't it make water for them to wash in?" Sholeh asked Sebastian.

He studied her. "Which one are you?"

"I'm Sholeh."

Now he grinned. "That's not a bad idea." Turning toward his cousins, he said, "Hey-a, Glorianna. If you don't want to be chiseling mud out of your hair, Sholeh thinks you and Ephemera should call up some fast-moving water that will clean you off before you start to harden."

"Sholeh thinks that, does she?" Glorianna asked.

"I didn't say that!" Sholeh squealed. "I didn't!"

"Not in those words, but that's what she meant," Sebastian said.

Zeela pushed her way into view—and noticed Medusah had done the same.

"What do you think you're doing?" Zeela snarled.

"Priming the pump," Sebastian replied. His eyes gave her a fast—and thorough—look. "You're Zeela?"

She held out her left arm, drawing his attention to the scar. "I won that fight."

"Good for you." He looked at his cousins. "You two still thinking about this?" He turned back to Zeela. "If your sister Zhahar is . . . whatever she's doing . . . with Lee, you and Sholeh will have to get used to the rest of us. Might as well start now, when the odds are even."

What did *that* mean?

"Ephemera, hear me," Glorianna said.

A moment later, they all stumbled back a few steps as the mud wallow changed into a part of a river.

Sebastian pursed his lips as Glorianna and Lee turned to look at him. "I said fast-moving water. I didn't say anything about rapids. Neither did Sholeh. I'm not going to guess what Zeela's thinking."

"*Nobody* has to guess what Zeela's thinking, since she looks ready to punch you," Glorianna said. "Lucky for you, you're so damn charming."

"He's not *that* charming," Zeela muttered.

Zeela! Zhahar shouted.

Sebastian burst out laughing. Then he looked at Medusah. "Do you have any rope?"

Following Glorianna's instructions, Ephemera obligingly made some adjustments to produce a waist-high pool up against the bank and below a short waterfall, a spot of relative calm compared to the rapids roaring around it. With ropes tied securely around their waists, Glorianna and Lee slipped into the pool, while Morragen and Zeela secured the ropes to stone pillars that had risen on the bank.

While Glorianna and Lee let the water pound the mud off them, Zeela assessed the people around her. For all his light words and distractions, Sebastian watched everything that concerned his cousins, as aware of the people around them as she was. The Knife, the Apothecary, and Kobrah, as well as her mother's warriors, were hanging back enough to be considered spectators rather than participants. As for her mother's Tryad . . .

What do you think? Zhahar asked.

=I can't tell if they're stunned or angry,= Zeela replied.

::Are we safe now?:: Sholeh asked.

Good question. One she thought the Tryad's leader would like answered very soon.

"Could someone give us a hand?" Lee asked tartly.

Sebastian helped Zeela haul Lee out of the pool and up the bank while the Knife stepped forward to help Morragen pull up Glorianna.

After freeing them from the ropes, everyone stepped back while Glorianna bent to one side and wrung water out of her long hair.

Lee scrubbed his fingers over his head. "Well, that was invigorating."

Holding out the dark glasses, Sebastian said, "What did you do to your hair? You look like a sheared sheep."

"It was hot." Lee took the glasses and put them on. "Short hair was practical. And what do you know about sheep anyway?"

"They rattle less than cows when the demon cycles eat them."

"That's because they're smaller than cows," Glorianna said, straightening up and pushing her hair back. "And the Den does owe that farmer for three sheep."

"Yeah, yeah, I'll fix it with Dalton."

"So now that we've got . . . that . . . settled," Lee said, as he and Glorianna turned and pointed to two adolescent boys who were standing with the warriors.

"What is it?" Morragen asked sharply. "What's wrong?"

"Nothing's wrong," Glorianna replied absently. Then, tipping her head toward Lee: "You felt it?"

"I felt it." He wagged his finger and raised his voice. "You two. Over here."

The boys came forward slowly, their eyes flicking between Morragen and Lee.

Zhahar, you take this, Zeela said. *I think the incubus cousin will be more inclined to talk to you than me right now.*

Zhahar came into view and whispered to Sebastian, "What's going on?"

He shook his head. "Landscaper and Bridge, darling. They'll tell the rest of us once they have it sorted out."

"Not here," Glorianna said when the boys stood in front of them. "But it *was* here."

Lee nodded. "We need each of your aspects to come into view and hold for a few seconds."

The boys glanced at Morragen, whose aspects were continually shifting because it was unclear which of them was best suited to deal with whatever was happening now.

=Mother has never dealt with anyone like them,= Zeela said.

*I don't think any Tryad has even *seen* anyone like them,* Zhahar replied.

::There is so much we could learn,:: Sholeh said wistfully.

"Go ahead," Zephyra said, apparently having decided the heart aspect was the one who should be in view.

The boys' aspects changed and held for a few seconds before the next set of brothers came into view.

"There!" Glorianna and Lee shouted, pointing to one boy. "Hold right there."

The boy looked scared but seemed to find reassurance in Zephyra's presence.

"What are you two sensing?" Sebastian asked.

Glorianna smiled. "He's a Bridge."

Lee nodded. "His brothers aren't, but *he* is a Bridge."

"What does that mean?" Zephyra asked.

Lee gave her a brilliant smile. "It means that, with proper training, he can help you keep Tryadnea connected to other parts of the world."

"Parts of the world that are compatible with your people," Glorianna added.

Zhahar sucked in air and swallowed hard. Heart's hope. Heart wishes. In a few words, Glorianna and Lee had said what the Tryad had yearned to hear for generations.

"Well," Glorianna said. "That will have to wait until we deal with what's in front of us."

"Agreed," Lee said. "You're sure the border is solid?"

"I'm sure," she replied with no hint of temper.

"Then the first thing I need to do is break the resonating bridge I made."

"You think the Clubs can find their way into this land?" the Knife asked.

Lee shook his head. "It's unlikely anyone from the city will reach Tryadnea. But the people in Vision don't know about these kinds of bridges, so I'm concerned with someone from that northern community accidentally crossing over and getting lost in the landscapes. They were told not to cross the bridge. . . ."

"But boys of a certain age might not be able to resist a game of 'dare you; double dare you,'" Glorianna finished. "All right. While you do that, Ephemera and I will make the cairns to mark the border." She looked at the camp, then at Morragen, who had come into view again. "Temporary lodgings?"

Morragen nodded. "Our village is an hour's ride from here."

"Being a few miles away from a border isn't unusual," Glorianna said thoughtfully.

"I'll go with Lee," Sebastian said.

"So will I," the Knife said. "There could be trouble there. A weapon could come in handy."

Sebastian held up his right hand and rubbed thumb and forefingers together. "I have a weapon, but yours would be more easily understood."

Zhahar stepped away from him. "You said you were a sex demon."

"He's also a wizard, so he does control the wizards' lightning," Lee said absently as he turned in the direction of the bridge. "His wife is still working out how much lightning is needed to properly broil a steak."

"I wouldn't mind the experiments so much if we didn't have to eat the failures," Sebastian muttered, lowering his hand.

::Do you think he's teasing?:: Sholeh asked.

=Yes,= Zeela replied.

I don't know, Zhahar said. *They're strange enough that he might mean it.*

Lee turned back to Morragen. "Could we borrow a couple of horses?"

"Horses?" Sebastian sounded pained. "We'll have to ride horses?" He sighed.

"The man doesn't blink about riding demon cycles, but he whines about horses," Lee muttered.

Morragen gave the orders, and three horses were saddled. Kobrah handed Lee his hat. As the men mounted, Glorianna said, "Travel lightly."

Lee looked at her, standing between Morragen and Zhahar. He smiled. "We won't be long."

They rode off, the Knife in the lead.

Glorianna watched them ride away, and when they were distant enough to hide details, Belladonna came into view.

Zhahar stared at the face so alike and yet so different from Glorianna's. So cold and deadly. She glanced at her mother and saw how intensely Morragen watched the woman who now controlled their homeland.

Belladonna closed her eyes, and Zhahar felt shocked when she heard the faint notes of a tune instead of a third aspect coming into view.

"I hear the music, Magician," Glorianna and Belladonna whispered. "I hear it." Then she opened her eyes and said briskly, "Let's define the border in a way your people will recognize."

She walked away from them.

Medusah came into view and studied Zhahar. "Who have you brought among us?"

"I don't know," Zhahar replied. "Lee was in danger. He could have gotten away alone, but he wouldn't save himself until he got me home. I did what I thought best."

"They have powers and magics unlike anything we've ever seen, but they recognized that same magic in one of us." Medusah hesitated. "Zephyra says she felt music when the woman's core aspect tried to come into view. You felt it too?"

Zhahar nodded.

"A core aspect being remade with music," Medusah said

thoughtfully. "That too is unknown to us. But even if the core can be remade to some degree, I don't think she will ever be a single aspect again."

"Do you think you can help her accept what she is now?"

Will Lee listen to me when I tell him how I see his sister?

Morragen Medusah a Zephyra looked at her daughter. "I will try."

Lee reached for the end of the bridge, swore quietly, and stepped back. He turned to look at his two companions.

"Problem?" Sebastian asked.

"Besides having the two of you ready to stab or sizzle anyone who comes over the bridge? No problem at all," Lee replied.

"Then the sooner you take care of this, the sooner we can step back," Sebastian said.

The Knife didn't indicate in any way that he would step back or lower his guard.

Not that Lee blamed the man for being wary of having an enemy reach them from the bridge, but having a wizard and an assassin standing behind him made his shoulder blades twitch. He figured it was a waste of breath to talk to either of them right now, so he focused on the task of changing a resonating bridge back into an ordinary bridge.

Within moments of his breaking the power he had put into it, the physical bridge disappeared.

"Where . . . ?" the Knife asked, looking around.

"It was never part of this landscape," Lee replied, turning toward the men. "Now it's completely back in Vision and connects nothing but the road on either side of that creek, just like it used to."

"Can you give us a minute?" Sebastian asked the Knife.

"I'll wait by the horses."

Stepping in front of Lee, Sebastian said, "Glorianna won't feel easy about asking, and Aunt Nadia and Lynnea won't feel comfortable asking either. So I will. Your eyes. How bad are they?"

Lee shifted so his back was to the sun. Then he removed the dark glasses, keeping the hat on to provide some protection.

"I can see you well enough to know who you are. This

close, I can see your expressions. I know your hair is dark, but if I didn't already know they're green, I wouldn't be able to tell the color of your eyes. Sunlight hurts. Colors are mostly light or dark. Can't see well enough to read. The eyedrops the Apothecary supplied are reversing the damage the wizards did, but there's no way to know until the treatment is complete how much of my sight I'll regain. I can get around on my own in a familiar place, but I'm not sure my eyes will ever be good enough to travel alone the way I used to."

"How far along in the treatment are you?"

"About two-thirds. Yesterday Zhahar said there was a third of the bottle of eyedrops left."

"Can't the Apothecary make more of the eyedrops?"

"I'll ask, but he told Zeela that what can be restored of my sight will happen in the time it takes to use up that bottle."

Sebastian sighed. "Then we'll hope for the best." He gave Lee a strained smile. "And I hope you and Glorianna work things out so you can spend time in her landscapes again. Lynnea and I would like the baby to know Uncle Lee."

"What . . . ? *Baby?*" He gave Sebastian a bruising hug and laughed. Then he released his cousin and slipped the dark glasses back on—and felt awkward, almost shy. "We'll work things out. Maybe not having one kind of sight has helped me see a few things."

"Then let's get back to it."

They joined the Knife, mounted the horses, and rode back to the camp.

I think Sholeh should handle this, Zhahar said as she followed Glorianna to a piece of ground that didn't look any different from the rest. Medusah also followed, but stayed back far enough to indicate that the a Zhahar Tryad was expected to take the lead.

::Me? Why?:: Sholeh sounded surprised—and thrilled.

You're the one who was learning about Vision and different races in Ephemera, so you have a better chance of understanding what Glorianna is doing.

=And you're more likely to know what questions to ask,= Zeela added.

Sholeh came into view and watched Glorianna walk back and forth. She wanted to learn, to know about so many things, but it wasn't easy to ask questions anymore when the asking felt so formal. Before she had been dismissed from the school in Vision, some of the instructors had implied—or said outright—that her lack of intellect wasted time they could spend on more deserving students. Even the ones who didn't think her stupid were curt because she missed classes. Those things hadn't diminished her desire to learn, but they had made it harder to approach people—something neither Zeela nor Zhahar would understand.

Before Zeela and Zhahar realized something was wrong—or worse, before the a Zephyra Tryad realized something was wrong—Sholeh blurted out, "What are you doing?"

"Waiting for you to ask me what I'm doing," Glorianna replied with a smile.

Stunned, Sholeh looked into Glorianna's eyes.

The heart has no secrets. She'd heard those words when Lee and Glorianna were fighting in the mud, but she hadn't considered the significance of those words.

Glorianna knew. Sholeh wasn't sure *how* she knew, but Glorianna knew why she was hesitant to ask questions.

"Borders and boundaries," Glorianna said. "A boundary is a place that connects two landscapes that belong to the same Landscaper or connects landscapes that resonate with each other but belong to different Landscapers. Those require a bridge in order to cross between one part of Ephemera to the other. Borders are places that connect two landscapes that belong to one Landscaper and that resonate with each other. No bridge is needed." She gave Sholeh a considering look. "Until we have a chance to discuss what challenges your people may face when crossing a bridge, having a border is the safer choice. Limits where you can go, but my sense is what you need first is a solid connection to another part of Ephemera."

Sholeh nodded, struggling to sort through all the words. "Borders," "boundaries," "landscapes," "bridges." Common words that had uncommon meanings. Lee had talked about these things, but talking about them wasn't the same as seeing physical things appear and disappear just because someone spoke a few words.

"Give it time," Glorianna said. "It will make sense. Right now, some decisions need to be made."

"I—" Sholeh looked back at Medusah, who didn't step forward. "What kind of decisions?"

Glorianna wagged a finger in a "come here" movement. When Sholeh stood beside her, she pointed at the ground. "This is one end of the border. You stay there." She took several long steps, then pointed again. "This is the other end. Which means this one is wide enough to accommodate a wagon."

"Aren't all of them?" Sholeh asked.

Glorianna shook her head. "Some are narrow enough that only a person on foot or horseback could use them. Even some bridges are nothing more than a couple of planks over a stream—sturdy enough for a person and maybe a horse or cow. How two landscapes connect depends on a lot of things. This"—she moved her finger to indicate the space between herself and Sholeh—"needs to be identified in some way so that people who want to find it can, and people who aren't intending to cross over don't find themselves in a strange place."

Sholeh looked at the ground. "How?"

"At some borders, we use cairns to indicate the spot without calling too much attention to it. The border between the Merry Makers and the Den uses Sentinel Stones because those are common in Elandar, even if they usually indicate a resonating bridge. What we want here is something that would have significance to your people."

"A triangle of stone," Sholeh said without thinking. Then she winced. The Tryad had needed to be careful about how much one-faced people knew about them, and they used the triangle for so many kinds of secret communications.

Glorianna thought for a moment, then nodded and said quietly, "Ephemera."

Two triangles of rough-hewn stone rose out of the ground. The base of the one next to Glorianna faced them. The one next to Sholeh showed the point.

"Coming and going," Glorianna said, sounding pleased as she examined her triangle. "Walk around to this side and take a look. *Around,* not between."

Sholeh jerked to a stop. Or, more accurately, Zeela

jerked to a stop, preventing them from darting between the triangles.

"Between is the border," Glorianna said sternly. "And no one walks through it until I do."

Blinking back tears, and self-conscious because she'd been reprimanded in front of Medusah, Sholeh scurried around the triangle.

"Do you see?" Glorianna pointed as if nothing had happened. "The triangles point in opposite directions. That's good."

"We're still in Tryadnea," Sholeh said, noticing how Medusah warily came around the stone to join them.

"And that's how it should be," Glorianna said. "You'll remain in your own land unless you walk between the stones." Now she looked at Medusah. "You should come with us, since there are decisions that will have to be made for your people. You may want to leave some guards here until you have time to explain what this is and what it does."

"We're still not sure what it does," Medusah said.

"The first time you cross over, you'll understand." Glorianna walked around the stones and raised a hand to the three riders. "And it looks like it's time to confirm what's on the other side of the border."

Chapter Twenty-four

Lee itched to cross that border and find out what was taking Glorianna and Sebastian so long to confirm that Ephemera had connected Tryadnea to the Den, but he waited with the others.

He wanted to go home, was ready to go home. He yearned for the familiar landscapes he'd wanted to leave a few months ago. He wanted to spend time with his mother, even wanted to talk to that ripe bastard Michael. And he wanted to talk to Yoshani about the truths he'd seen about himself in the past few days.

He wanted those things. At least for a while. And all that separated him from those things were a couple of steps across a border.

The Knife and the Apothecary stepped up to him.

"Does it usually take this long to make a connection?" the Knife asked quietly, glancing over to where Zhahar was talking with Morragen.

Lee shook his head. "A border was made the instant two landscapes connected with each other." *And what is made in an instant can be broken just as quickly,* he added silently. "None of us have dealt with a race like the Tryad, so Glorianna is taking extra care to be sure people won't be harmed when they cross over." He didn't mention that this was the first landscape she'd brought into her garden since she tore her heart in half, and he suspected that was a good part of the reason she was taking so long to do something she'd been doing since she was fifteen. "And since this is the only place where Tryadnea is connected to the world, no one is going to be cavalier about securing it to the Den."

"What about us?" The Apothecary wagged a thumb to indicate himself and the Knife. "Will we be able to get back to Vision?"

"I don't know. But if it can be done, my family can do it." He hadn't considered how much skill that extended family had now, between Sebastian's recently awakened power as a wizard and Michael's different way of connecting with Ephemera, not to mention his mother's and Caitlin Marie's talents as Landscapers. And Glorianna Belladonna, Guide of the Heart.

"Lee?"

He turned to find Zhahar standing nearby. He smiled and held out a hand to her. She took his hand but didn't return the smile.

"If you'll excuse us?" Zhahar said, looking at the other men.

"Problem?" Lee asked when the Knife and the Apothecary stepped out of hearing.

"Maybe. How . . . carnal . . . is this Den?"

"Very. It's a dark landscape that welcomes the incubi and succubi. Sex is a commodity, so it isn't hidden, if that's what you're asking." She was troubled, but he wasn't sure why. Working as a Handler, she'd seen her share of naked men. Then he glanced toward her mother. Mothers. Which did the Tryad use? "Are you worried about Sholeh? Lynnea and Caitlin Marie don't have a problem being in the Den, so I don't think Sholeh will have trouble being there." Of course, he was assuming that having Zeela for a sister had broadened Sholeh's intellectual experience with regard to sex—and her physical experience as well? Not a discussion he wanted to have with Zhahar while Morragen Medusah a Zephyra watched them.

"Not Sholeh," Zhahar said. "Kobrah. Something happened to her before she came to Vision. Something bad. She hates men and reacts badly to seeing male parts."

"Guardians and Guides," Lee muttered. The Den of Iniquity was what it was. A quick chat with Philo would keep his specialties off the table, but there was nothing they could do about the erotic statues that decorated Philo's courtyard. And that was a quick brush of what she might see. "Kobrah?" He waved her over to them.

"Lee," Zhahar warned. Or maybe that was Zeela, since he was suddenly hearing two voices.

Kobrah looked at the space between the stone triangles. "Did something happen?"

"No," Lee said, "but I need to know if you can handle being in the Den. It's an edgy place with a lot of sex." He still had trouble seeing subtle expressions, but he had no trouble seeing the loathing on Kobrah's face. "The rest of us need to go, but maybe you could stay here with Zhahar's people."

"Of course you could," Zhahar said quickly.

Kobrah shook her head. "I'll go. You might need my help. I can stand it as long as I don't have to touch any Chaynes."

"You don't have to touch anyone or anything you don't want to," Lee said. Then he added, "Teaser lives there." *And Yoshani likely will be present.*

"Teaser?" The loathing faded from Kobrah's face. "I like Teaser. He's not a Chayne, even if he is a sex demon."

Good to know. "Then you already have a friend you can look forward to seeing." Lee added finding out what a Chayne was to the list of things he wanted to discuss with Zhahar.

Sebastian suddenly reappeared, startling everyone. He nodded at Lee. "The border is solid. Tryadnea fits like it's always been there." He waited until Morragen joined them. "We're ready for you to cross over, but I'd like to limit the number of Tryad coming to the Den this first time."

Lee thought he could see Morragen's temper rising—and the way Zhahar clamped her hand around his fingers confirmed it.

"Why?" Morragen and Medusah asked coldly.

Sebastian gave her a sharp-edged smile. "Because we get enough crap from the daylight landscapes about corrupting their youngsters. I don't need that in triplicate from parents in your landscape."

Lee huffed out a sigh. "Yep. I'm home. Morragen, until you've seen the Den, it would be prudent to restrict the visitors to adults." He paused. Thought. "Experienced adults." Then he tightened his hold on Zhahar's hand, since it occurred to him that he might have just excluded two-thirds of her Tryad and he didn't know how many toes he'd just stepped on—or how many women were annoyed with him.

Glorianna returned and stared at them. "Problem?"

"Sebastian is sounding like a prissy prig, and Morragen is still deciding if she should feel insulted on behalf of her people," Lee replied.

"I am *not* a prissy prig," Sebastian growled.

"And I am not insulted," Morragen snarled.

"Then it's settled," Glorianna said. "Only the people involved in the discussions about Tryadnea and what do to for the city of Vision are coming to the Den. Everyone else stays on their respective sides of the border. Sebastian, did you tell these men to bring the wagon and their horses?"

"We didn't get that far," Sebastian replied.

"Then get that far." She pointed at Zhahar and Kobrah. "You two. Come with me."

"Glorianna," Lee protested as Zhahar released his hand.

She turned to him, but it wasn't Glorianna who looked at him.

"You know better than to create dissonance this close to a border, Bridge," Belladonna said. "Or have you forgotten Lighthaven and the White Isle?"

An island that held a Place of Light. A land that had been whole until two women passionately rejected each other—and by doing so, split Lighthaven from the rest of the White Isle so completely the two pieces *couldn't* be connected anymore.

Lee's heart leaped into his throat. Fool to forget something so basic—especially when Morragen's will and heart seemed to guide Tryadnea like a tiller provided direction for a boat, and Sebastian was the Den's anchor, the heart that kept the Den protected and kept it from turning dark in ways that would make it too dangerous.

"I'm sorry," he said. "You're right. I shouldn't have needed the reminder."

"Neither should I." Sebastian sounded embarrassed.

"Now that we have that settled . . ." Belladonna turned and walked between the stone triangles—and disappeared.

"You and Kobrah should go," Lee told Zhahar. "We'll catch up to you."

"Is your sister upset with you?" Zhahar asked.

"Us," Sebastian said, looking at Lee. "She's upset with us."

"And she's right to be," Lee acknowledged. "We come from this part of Ephemera. We know better than to let emotions run without considering consequences."

"Don't keep her waiting, Zhahar," Morragen said. "We'll gather what we need and be along."

Zhahar took Kobrah's hand, and the two of them walked across the border.

"Do we need supplies?" Morragen asked.

"Not food and water, unless you need something special," Sebastian replied. "A change of clothes and toiletries should be sufficient."

She walked away, followed by the Knife and the Apothecary.

"Are you uneasy about coming back?" Sebastian asked.

Lee shook his head. "A moment's stupidity. We've been running for the past two days, and getting away from the men the wizards sent after us. . . . It was too close. And if we don't find a way to help the Shamans defend Vision, the surviving wizards and Dark Guides will be able to turn at least some of it into another Wizard City—a stronghold from which they'll feed the Dark currents in a way that will change a piece of the world."

Sebastian laid a hand on Lee's shoulder. "You all need to rest. We all need time to talk and think and consider what can be done."

"They need us. The Tryad. The Shamans. They need us."

Sebastian took a step closer to him. "We need each other. I've missed you, cousin."

Lee hugged Sebastian. "I missed you too."

Holding Kobrah's hand to offer encouragement and contact, Zhahar trailed behind Glorianna, watching the world playfully change. Glorianna walked a dozen steps, then pointed at the ground. Moments later, a boulder pushed out of the earth. The result was a string of markers from the stone triangles to a dirt lane that began in the middle of a field.

"That's enough," Glorianna said as a boulder pushed up a long step away from the lane. She looked at Zhahar. "This lane leads to the Den. When your people cross over to visit, you keep the markers on your right on the way to the Den, and on your left when you go home. That will keep you from stumbling someplace you shouldn't be."

Because you don't want us to explore? Zhahar wondered. Before she could think of how to phrase the question without causing offense that might make Glorianna change her mind about helping them, Kobrah pointed in the opposite direction and asked, "What's over that way?"

"The border to the Merry Makers' landscape," Glorianna replied.

"They sound festive," Zhahar said, trying not to jump when Sholeh yelled ::No!::

"They're not," Glorianna said. "They respect the Den's rules when they visit the Den, but very few people who go into the bogs the Merry Makers call home survive long enough to walk out again."

"Oh," Kobrah said.

::Lee told me a little about the Merry Makers and the waterhorses,:: Sholeh said. ::They're *dangerous.*:: Then she added wistfully, ::But I'd still like to see them.::

Zhahar sighed, which had Glorianna raising an eyebrow in question.

"My sister Sholeh was exchanging information with Lee about some of the races found in Ephemera, and she's curious."

"How old are you?"

"Twenty-four."

"Not so young, then."

"I beg your pardon?"

Glorianna laughed. "Never mind. The others are coming." She looked down the lane and laughed again. "Tell your sister she's about to have an opportunity to meet a demon." She sounded as concerned as if the family dog was heading toward them—a dog large enough to be scary, but usually friendly.

Zhahar looked at the swiftly moving lights and felt weak-kneed relief when she turned and saw Sebastian and Lee walking ahead of the Apothecary's wagon. Her mother shared the driving seat with the shadowman while the Knife rode alongside.

"Why are we stopping here?" Sebastian asked.

"We were waiting for you," Glorianna replied.

"How did you set the markers so quickly?" Morragen asked, pointing to a boulder.

Glorianna smiled. "Ephemera helped. Shall we—"

"Wait," Zhahar said, her voice so sharp everyone looked at her. But all she saw was a boulder that hadn't been there a few minutes ago. All she remembered was a mud wallow changing into rushing, *fresh* water.

She changes the world. Glorianna can change the world.

"If you can make boulders, can you repair farmland?" Zahar asked. "Can you restore streams? Turn sparse grass into rich grazing?" She looked at Glorianna and heard Morragen suck in a breath. Her mothers understood the reason for the questions. "Can you?"

"This isn't the place to discuss this," Glorianna said at the same time Lee said, "Zhahar," and touched her arm.

She pulled away from Lee. *"Can you?"*

"Despair made the deserts, and hope the oases," Glorianna replied. "Ephemera manifests the heart."

Zhahar stared at her in disbelief. "You think we did this to our homeland? You think we wanted this?"

"Wanted it? No. Did your people do it? Yes. Heart's Blessing, Sholeh Zeela a Zhahar," Glorianna Belladonna said in a cold voice that was oddly laced with compassion. "May your heart travel lightly, because what you bring with you becomes part of the landscape." She turned and started walking down the lane toward the Den.

Lee grabbed Zhahar's arm. "That's enough. You don't make demands of a Landscaper. It isn't done."

"Well, maybe it should be!" Zhahar tried to jerk her arm out of his grip. When she couldn't, she appealed to Zeela.

=No,= Zeela said, sounding troubled.

Why not? Zhahar continued to try to pull away from Lee, ignoring the fact that the harder she struggled, the tighter he held her arm.

=Because our mothers didn't agree with you.=

::And because what Glorianna said is true,:: Sholeh added.

She looked at Morragen Medusah a Zephyra and realized Zeela was right. Their mothers were angry—at *her.* If Sholeh knew why Glorianna had spoken the truth, then so did Medusah.

She stopped struggling. Lee released her arm and stepped back to stand beside Sebastian, who no longer looked friendly.

"We ask you to overlook our daughter's unconsidered, and inconsiderate, words," Medusah said, coming into view. "She needs rest, so Zeela should continue this journey."

"Not Zeela," Lee said. "Not yet. I think Sholeh should finish the trip to the Den."

Medusah tipped her head, considering. "Why?"

Lee's smile looked forced, but it was still a smile. "Because there's someone she should meet."

Sebastian glanced at the lights heading toward them, then at Lee. "You sure?"

"Lynnea did all right with them."

"Oh, daylight. Then you'd better ride with her, or she'll never get to Philo's."

Ashamed for being reprimanded before the others and angry enough not to want to be around Lee, Zhahar's aspect waned and Sholeh's came into view.

Sebastian pointed to the Apothecary and the Knife. "Wait there so the horses don't spook."

"Come on, Sholeh." Lee walked over to the lane.

"What about Kobrah?" Sholeh asked, hurrying to catch up.

"She can take a look and make her own choice," Sebastian said.

That's when Sholeh saw two *somethings* racing toward them. Big eyes, long arms, and . . .

"Blaaarrrrgh!" one of them roared, waving those long arms and displaying too many sharp teeth. It stopped within touching distance of them. "Blaaarrrrgh!"

She had never seen anything like them. Not even in the pictures she had found in the books she'd studied in Vision.

"Demon cycles," she breathed, smiling so widely her cheeks hurt. "Are you a demon cycle?"

It seemed to ponder her reaction. "Wanna ride?"

The voice like gravel in a metal barrel thrilled Sholeh.

"This is Sholeh, who is Lee's friend," Sebastian said. "They could use a ride to Philo's Place. Belladonna will be waiting for them there."

One demon cycle turned its odd metal body as an invitation to mount while the other drifted above the road until it was looking right at Kobrah.

Sebastian smiled at Kobrah. She swallowed hard but nodded.

"Kobrah will ride with me." Sebastian walked up to the cycle and swung a leg over the leather seat. "Come on. You can ride behind me."

"Take the front position," Lee said, guiding Sholeh over to the cycle that was waiting for them.

"But I don't know how to steer!"

He laughed. "You don't steer. You just hold on."

She mounted. He got on behind her and rested his hands lightly on her waist. A friendly touch that warmed her and made her wish he could remain their friend after he learned about the taboos. It wasn't likely, but she still wished it.

"The lane will take you to the Den," Sebastian told the shadowmen. "You should be fine on your own, but I'll send Addison or Henley to guide you."

"Appreciate it," the Knife said.

Sholeh turned her head and spoke over her shoulder. "The horses weren't afraid."

"The horses were upwind and don't understand what they're seeing," Lee replied.

They headed down the lane.

After a minute, Sholeh sighed. Now that she was used to how the demon cycles looked and how they floated over the road, they weren't very exciting.

"Daylight," Sebastian muttered. "All right. You two go ahead. We'll catch up."

Suddenly the ground was a *blur*.

"Hang on!" Lee shouted.

She whooped in answer. Zeela did exciting things, but even her warrior sister hadn't done anything like *this*.

It seemed like they'd barely started when she saw lights coming up fast. Lots of lights.

"We're here already?" She didn't say it loudly, but she didn't take those big, tufted ears into account. As they reached the place where dirt lane changed to cobblestone street, the demon cycle made a tight turn and went speeding back the way they'd come.

"Hey!" Lee shouted.

"Yay!" Sholeh shouted.

"Blaaarrrrrgh!" the demon cycle shouted.

They passed Sebastian and Kobrah, then made another tight turn to race alongside the other cycle, which sped up, responding to the competitive spirit—or something—until Sebastian made a sharp sound that caused both cycles to slow the pace to halfway between amble and blur.

She wanted to tell him it was all right for the cycle to go

faster, but a glance at Kobrah made it clear that the other woman had never ridden anything that went this fast and was, according to Lee, very dangerous, even if it was acting friendly. So she contented herself with the more sedate return to the Den.

When they reached the cobblestones, the demon cycles slowed to the pace of a fast walk and finally stopped in front of a courtyard that had tables and statues.

"That was wonderful!" Sholeh said as she dismounted. "Can we do it again?"

"Later," Lee replied, grinning.

She noticed the blond-haired man who stared at them a moment before hurrying toward them. And she noticed the way Kobrah stood frozen, staring at the statues.

Oh no, Zhahar said. *Sholeh, you'd better let me—*

=It's my turn,= Zeela said.

Kobrah needs help.

::I want to stay a bit longer!::

Zhahar withdrew from them in a way that told her sisters she was hurt and upset.

"Lee!" The man bounced up to Lee and hugged him. "Welcome back, you fool." Then he gave Kobrah a delighted grin—and put himself between Kobrah and her view of the statues. "Hey-a, Kobbi. Welcome to the Den."

Kobrah blinked. "Teaser?"

"All the way."

Teaser cocked a thumb over his shoulder. "Nothing but statues tonight. No live performance. But if they bother you, we could go down the street and listen to some music."

"I think it would be best for us all to stay together for a bit," Sebastian said. "But we can use the inside room if the statues bother Kobrah."

"No," Kobrah said. "I can—" Her mouth fell open. *"Shaman Danyal?"*

It *was* Danyal heading for them with a dark-eyed, dark-haired man.

"I'm happy to see you all," Danyal said. He looked at Lee. "And I'm glad you found your way home."

"Me too," Lee replied.

"Lee!"

He'd barely had a chance to turn toward the voice when a woman leaped into his arms.

"Lynnea!"

Sebastian leaned over Sholeh's shoulder. "Let's find some seats for you two. People are going to be pouncing on him for a while."

"Is that his lover?" Sholeh asked, worried because jealousy was seeping through despite Zhahar's withdrawal from her and Zeela.

Sebastian choked on a laugh. "No, that's my wife, which makes her family."

The hug might have been from a lover. The punch in the shoulder that followed it? That was family.

Sholeh relaxed, determined to enjoy as much as she could before Zeela demanded some time to explore this place.

A round man with dark, receding hair hurried up to them.

"Sit. Sit. I'm closing off this half of the courtyard for you," Philo said.

Before Lee could take his seat at the table, a male voice said, "Lee, you ripe bastard. It's about time you stopped ignoring a helping hand and got yourself back home."

She saw pleasure in Lee's face as he turned toward the man, but there was shame mixed with that pleasure.

"Magician," Lee said. A hesitation. Then he grabbed the man in a hard hug.

More people. So many people, Sholeh had trouble keeping track. There was Yoshani, the holy man with Shaman Danyal. There were Nadia and Jeb, Lee's mother and stepfather. There was Caitlin Marie, Michael the Magician's sister.

And there, at the edge of the courtyard, part of the group and still apart from it, was Glorianna Belladonna.

"Come on, Kobbi. Have a seat," Teaser said, pulling out a chair across from Sholeh and Lee. As he pulled out a chair for himself, he looked at her. "So you and your sisters are together all the time?"

"We are Tryad. We are three who are one, one who is three," Sholeh replied, noticing how sharply Medusah watched Teaser—and how sharply *Nadia* also watched Teaser.

He gave her a smile that was naughty and boyishly good-natured. "How does that work when one of you has sex?"

"Teaser," Lee warned.

"If one of you is romping, do you all feel the *fizz-bang* at the end, or is it each to herself? And if one of you has a lover, do the other two have to do without cuddles?"

"Teaser!" a chorus of voices shouted.

"What?" He looked around. "I'm just asking. It's not like I'm inviting myself to the party. Although . . ." He gave Sholeh a considering look. "*Would* it be cheating if the other lover was just a dream? *Ow ow ow!*" That last because Nadia grabbed his ear and pulled him toward another table.

Sholeh hunched down in her chair, hoping to look smaller as she tried to interpret the look on her mother's face. She was certain that *no one* had *ever* said such things in front of Medusah before now.

=By the triple stars,= Zeela whispered.

::Are you appalled or amused?:: Sholeh asked.

=I don't know.=

Sebastian gave Medusah a smile that had *heat* and said, "It's a valid question. Especially when asked by an incubus."

"Oh, daylight," Lee groaned. "Don't say things like that to Zhahar's mother. Mothers." He put his hands over his face. "Why did I miss any of you?"

"I'm thinking the man now knows what it's like to be dealing with the rest of you for the first time," Michael said, giving Lee a friendly clap on the shoulder.

"Yeah," Sebastian said. "I haven't seen him this embarrassed since the first time I walked in on him and a girl and he had his hands—"

Lee grabbed for his cousin at the same time Nadia said, "Sebastian Justicemaker! If you don't want to be telling that story to *me*, you won't be telling it to anyone tonight."

"Yes, Auntie," Sebastian replied. But he winked at Sholeh. "So where's the other sister?"

She didn't want to give up the chance to experience this place for herself, but she yielded to Zeela as everyone sorted themselves out among the tables, leaving them the lone female at a table that included Sebastian, Lee, the Apothecary, and the Knife.

Morragen Medusah a Zephyra, Zeela noted with relief, was at a table with Nadia, Jeb, and Danyal. Glorianna was sharing a table with Michael and Yoshani.

What about Kobrah? Zhahar whispered.

=She's with Teaser and . . . Caitlin?= Hard to remember all those faces when they moved about separately. Especially when she wanted to pair Lynnea with Caitlin as siblings, but it was *Michael* and Caitlin who had that connection.

Philo and an adolescent boy returned with two large trays. "Lynnea modified some of the specialties for Teaser's table," Philo said, "but the consensus was that adjustments weren't needed for you." Saying that, he set down a large basket and two bowls of melted cheese, a platter of mushrooms stuffed with breading, and various other bowls, while the boy gave them plates and silverware. "Drinks?"

"Bottle of wine and a pitcher of ale," Sebastian said.

Zeela picked up an object from the basket and considered its length and diameter.

"This is a Phallic Delight," Sebastian said.

"This is wishful thinking," she replied. But after Lee finished choking, she followed Sebastian's example and swirled the tip of the penis-shaped bread in the melted cheese. Giving the cheese a moment to cool, she took a big bite.

Sebastian looked at the men around the table and laughed. "Daylight. Shadowmen blush and the holy men don't even blink when these are set on the table. What does that tell you?"

"That holy men don't understand why they should blush?" the Knife asked.

Lee shook his head as he filled his plate. "Nope. Neither Yoshani nor Danyal is required to be celibate, so they've had experience enough to be thinking all kinds of things."

::Could you try one of those round black things?:: Sholeh asked. ::They look interesting::

"What are these?" Zeela asked as she picked up the bowl.

"Olives," Sebastian replied. "Bite carefully. They have a pit in the center."

"Bite carefully" was good advice for pretty much everything on the table, but the flavors were unlike anything she'd tasted. She wanted to eat until she was full, but she stopped when she had half of everything left on her plate. She leaned toward Lee and said quietly, "Would the other people here be offended if Sholeh came back into view to eat?"

Lee smiled. "This is the Den, Zeela. It takes a lot more than a Tryad to offend anyone here."

::I like this place,:: Sholeh said a minute later as she took a dainty bite of a Delight.

=So do I.=

Zhahar, they both noticed, said nothing.

Michael walked down the Den's main street with Lee, heading for the lane that would lead to Sebastian and Lynnea's cottage.

"I don't know how many times I ended up sleeping on that couch," Lee said, huffing out a laugh. "And here I am again."

"Since they're staying at your cottage, Danyal did offer to let you have your room back," Michael said. "We weren't sure if you'd be coming back, so it seemed practical to let him and Yoshani stay there."

"It was practical, and I'm not complaining." Lee slowed his steps.

"We can keep walking as long as you need to," Michael said quietly. Yoshani and Danyal were waiting at Sebastian's cottage to help Lee put in the eyedrops, but when Lee asked *him* for help getting back to the cottage instead of going with them, it was clear the man had something on his mind.

"There are shadows in every garden," Lee said when they reached the end of the cobblestone street and headed down the lane.

Michael nodded. "One of the lessons the Landscapers learned at the school, yes?"

"Yes. But not a lesson that was taught at the Bridges' School, because the bridges that are made are neutral. Someone who has that ability just connects the pieces Ephemera wants to connect. Dark, Light—doesn't matter. Those things are the Landscapers' responsibility. But I have shadows in me, Michael. Last year, my mother was touched by a wizard and influenced just enough to begin to wonder about the dark side of Glorianna's heart. She wondered about it because Glorianna's father was a wizard."

"He was your father too."

"That didn't seem to occur to anyone—that I would have a stronger connection to the Dark currents because of it."

"Are you making a point?"

Lee stopped walking and stared straight ahead. "I blamed you when Glorianna locked herself in that landscape with the Eater of the World. I blamed you for stopping me while there was still time to get into that place. I blamed you because I thought you stopped me so that the Warrior of Light would drink from the Dark Cup, that you'd convinced her to sacrifice herself in order to accomplish your own plan."

"I told her the story," Michael replied. "The heart has no secrets, Lee. Not from her. She knew I had the answer to saving Ephemera. Denying it would have betrayed her trust. Just like . . ." No. That wasn't his to say.

"Just like you broke my arm because she asked you to keep me safe? To keep all of us safe?" Lee's smile held sadness as well as understanding. "By stopping me, you protected everyone who was there that day."

"Yes." Michael touched Lee's arm. "I'm sorry for the broken bone."

Lee shook his head and started walking again. "Funny how losing one kind of sight made other things so clear."

"You'll get your sight back."

"I hope so. But I seem to be hoping for a lot of things lately." Lee hesitated. "Can I ask you something?"

"Which side are you asking?" Michael countered. "Man or Magician?"

"I'm not sure. The day I tangled with the wizards and ended up in Vision, I was checking a stationary bridge. Should have connected landscapes that belonged just to Glorianna and Nadia, but the resonance for Glorianna included the possibility of someone crossing over to Foggy Downs. Wasn't the first bridge that had connected landscapes that belonged to them and now also connected to you. I heard faint music. It made me angry that it was never just my sister anymore. You were always there."

"You were still adjusting to the idea of Glorianna having a man in her life who wasn't passing through," Michael said. "Part of being a brother, I'm thinking. Caitlin Marie goes to a dance in Darling's Harbor—and she's as safe and snug in that village as a baby in its cradle—and I still feel twitchy about the boys."

"Could be worse," Lee said in a singsong voice. "Could be Teaser."

At another time, he would have felt obliged to respond to that reminder of Caitlin's friendship with the incubus, but not tonight. "Glorianna hears the music in my heart. It's what Ephemera used to guide her home. And I hear the music in her heart. All of it. Dark and Light. Every day I play the music that is Glorianna Belladonna. I play both the tunes I hear, and then I blend them to be one song again. Hearing who she is provides a kind of bridge between the two sides of her heart, and some days she stays in that in-between place for hours—the place where she is both, as she used to be. She can travel with me to most of my landscapes, but out of those, Foggy Downs is her favorite. So . . ." Michael shrugged. No one thought Glorianna would be completely whole again, but the music *was* connecting the two halves of her heart bit by bit.

They walked for a few minutes in silence before Lee asked, "What kind of music do you hear in Zhahar's heart?"

"You're asking about something that's very private. If you want to know her heart, you should ask her."

"The part of the question that's personal is private," Lee agreed. "But I'm asking Bridge to Magician. She doesn't belong in the Den, does she?"

"No. Zhahar's music is out of tune with the Den. Zeela, on the other hand, is *very* in tune with the carnal carnival. So is Sholeh." Which had surprised everyone except, perhaps, Glorianna Belladonna.

Lee laughed softly. "Sholeh wants to interview the bull demons."

"Lady of Light," Michael muttered. Then he sighed. "Not fitting in with one place that you do doesn't mean she won't fit in with the rest. And because her sisters are easy with the place, she *can* reach the Den."

"I know. I'm just not sure she wants to fit in—and I'm not just talking about the Den."

"And you'd like her to fit in?"

"Yes, I would. But as we got closer to Tryadnea, I had the feeling there were things she hadn't told me about her people. It's made me wonder if a Tryad would—or could—care about—" Lee stopped walking abruptly. "Who's that?"

"It's Yoshani." Michael raised a hand in greeting. "It appears he's been waiting for you at the bridge."

"In that case, why don't you go back? Glorianna is waiting for you, and we'll all have a great deal to discuss tomorrow."

"Yes, we will. Good night, Lee. Welcome home."

Lee hesitated. "I'm not sure I'm back to stay."

Michael smiled. "I'm not sure anyone expects you to stay. Yoshani? We'll see you and Danyal tomorrow?"

"Yes," Yoshani replied. "We are to meet at Nadia's house."

Michael nodded and headed back down the lane to the buildings and colored lights that made up the Den.

Travel lightly. Lee's heart had not been traveling lightly when he tangled with the wizards, but . . .

Come on, wild child, Michael thought. *Let's bring a bit of luck into Lee's life.*

Currents of power flowed around him, and he sent out the Magician's gift of luck-bringing so that some good would balance whatever Lee had suffered in the past weeks.

As he reached the edge of the Den, he spotted Morragen Medusah a Zephyra sitting on a bench near one of the garden islands that ran down the length of the main street and contained dwarf trees and flowers that drew sustenance from moonlight instead of sunlight.

She's dangerous, Magician, Belladonna had warned. *Don't push her.*

I won't push, Michael thought as he sat on the other end of the bench and smiled at the Tryad leader. *But there's no harm in telling a story.*

"Nice night," he said, smiling. "Then again, the sun never shines in the Den."

"So it's always a nice night," Medusah said.

"Ah no. The Den doesn't see the sun, but it does follow the seasons. A cold, rainy night is just as uncomfortable here as anywhere else. The only difference is how people pass the time once they get indoors."

"I'm not sure this is a good match for the Tryad."

"More often than not, what a person needs doesn't always match what you imagine. And maybe you shouldn't be looking at just the surface."

She gave him a look that chilled him. But she didn't understand what it meant when a man was an ill-wisher as well as a luck-bringer.

"One of the things we do for entertainment on a stormy night is tell stories. Something Sholeh would enjoy, I'm thinking. Anyway, there are enough of us from different parts of Ephemera to compare what Yoshani calls story-truths. Well, one thing led to another this evening, and a few of us were reminded of an old story. Don't know where it began, since plenty of landscapes have some variation."

"I'm not interested in stories tonight."

"Oh, I think you'll be interested in this one. You see, a long time ago, there were three sisters. Some of the stories mention two sisters, but we'll go with a version that has three. So there were these three sisters who lived together and worked together and were as close as kin can be. Then one day, a man came by, passing through or looking for work—your choice. Anyway, some of the versions say he was a charmer with a shallow heart; others say he was an honorable man who enjoyed the flirtations of the eldest sister but found himself falling in love with the youngest sister. The day came when the sisters realized they wanted the same man. Now, these sisters had some power or magic, and their anger with each other grew to a fearsome thing. They turned against each other, each determined to destroy the other in order to have the man to herself.

"The middle girl ran to her sisters, wanting nothing more than to stop the fight. But she got caught in it. Some stories say a knife found her heart; others say it was the magic the sisters were flinging at each other that found her instead. It came to the same end. The remaining sisters, seeing what they had done, lost all interest in the man, and he lost interest in them and continued on his way. But the sisters still blamed each other for the death of the third sister—and they blamed the man. Wrapped in that blame, they gathered their power and made a terrible wish and turned love into a weapon. They wished to be kept apart from the world as punishment for wanting an outsider. And because they truly wanted to be set adrift, the world answered. And even to this day, the sisters drift through the world, never connecting to another place long enough to touch another heart."

Michael watched the careful way Medusah swallowed.

"That's an interesting story," she finally said.

He nodded. "More interesting to those of us who were on the White Isle the day a young Landscaper and a Sister of Light spoke hard and heartfelt words that split an island into two places that now can't touch. Story-truths, Medusah. The wrong words said in the wrong place by the right people, and a piece of the world is torn from the rest."

She said nothing, so he added the last thing. "If the Tryad have some taboo about loving a person of single aspect, now is the time to mention it. Lee is falling in love with Zhahar, and I'm thinking he's been given enough encouragement to believe those feelings can be returned."

"She is Tryad."

Three voices. Three tunes. All of them held sharp notes of fear.

"Yes, she is. I'm guessing love isn't an easy thing, even among your own people."

"No, it isn't," they whispered. "Is it easy among your people?"

He shook his head and smiled. "Not always easy, even when you're with the right person. But maybe that story needs to have a different ending, one that gives love a chance to heal what magic cursed."

"We can't ignore our laws and taboos for one heart," Medusah said. "Not when others paid so dear a price for wanting the same thing. If we allow our daughter to have what has been forbidden, it will tear the Tryad people apart." Zephyra came into view and looked at him, her eyes bright with tears. "If the Triple Goddess could find a way to give a Tryad a chance at that kind of love without destroying our people, we would wish for it with all our hearts."

???

Wild child, no!

Too late. Michael remained completely still while the currents of Light and Dark swirled around him and Morragen Medusah a Zephyra—and faded.

Lady of Light, have mercy. He'd have to check with Glorianna, since the Den was her landscape, but he was certain Ephemera had just responded to a heart wish. He just hoped Glorianna would have an idea of *how* the wild child had responded.

"Well." Michael rose on shaky legs. "Teaser said he'd

meet you at Philo's and make sure you got settled in your room all right."

Leaving her, he headed for Philo's. Halfway there, he found the Apothecary kneeling in another of the garden islands while the Knife stood uneasy watch.

"Problem?" Michael asked.

"This plant," the Apothecary said, lightly touching the leaves. "Does it grow here?"

Michael crouched beside the Apothecary and sighed. "I rake what I'm told to rake, dig where I'm told to dig, and wheel the barrow to the compost bins. If you want to know about plants here, you need to ask Glorianna."

"Ask me what?"

He looked over his shoulder as Glorianna and Sebastian came up to them. Some sharp notes in both their tunes, which told him that Glorianna had felt that heart wish, and whatever she told Sebastian had the Justice Maker on edge.

"He's wondering about this plant," Michael said. Best to talk to Glorianna in private.

???

Glorianna cocked her head, then looked at him. He nodded, indicating he felt the wild child too.

"I don't remember seeing that plant before," Sebastian said, sounding cautious.

"I don't think it was here before. Not in the garden islands anyway. Maybe it usually grows freely in some of the open land around the Den," Glorianna said.

yes yes yes

Easier to find a plant in a flower bed than by wandering around in the dark on unfamiliar land. "Why are you interested in this plant?" Michael asked.

"It's similar to one of the ingredients I use in the drops that help eyes heal," the Apothecary replied. "But this is much more vibrant than the plants we're able to obtain. Those plants need full shade, but still tend to be spindly."

"Probably they need moonlight instead of sunlight in order to grow," Glorianna said. Then she gave the Apothecary a sharp look. "You think this plant could help Lee? He said whatever was left in the bottle he had would give him the best sight he could have now."

"That was true with the plant extracts I had to work

with," the Apothecary replied. "But with this? More of his sight might return."

"What about the other ingredients?" Glorianna asked. "Do you have them with you?"

The Apothecary nodded. "I brought everything I could in the wagon."

"Then bring a sample of each with you to the meeting tomorrow, and we'll see what else can be found."

Thank you, wild child, Michael thought as he rose and reached for Glorianna's hand.

Sebastian escorted the two shadowmen to the bordello, where he'd arranged for them to stay. Then he caught a ride with a demon cycle to make a last check around the Den and see if the guards, Addison and Henley, had anything to report.

Michael and Glorianna stopped by Philo's, but the only person left at the tables was Zhahar, so they bid her good night, accepted a ride on another demon cycle, and crossed over the stationary bridge that would take them to Nadia's house.

In the privacy of Glorianna's old room, Michael told her about his talk with Morragen Medusah a Zephyra—and about the heart wish that even now might be manifesting changes throughout pieces of Ephemera.

Zhahar sat at one of the tables, drinking a glass of wine and nibbling on the food Philo had brought for her.

=You don't feel easy here, do you?= Zeela asked.

No, I don't. I want to get away from here. She hesitated long enough to be sure Sholeh was preoccupied with her own thoughts. These weren't fears she wanted to share with her youngest sister. *I think I love him, Zeela. And that scares me.*

=Scares me too,= Zeela replied. =A man of single aspect has never stayed with a Tryad for long—even when the aspect who loved him gave up everything else.=

I know. She took a deep breath, then let it out in a sigh. *When I was private, I would fantasize how it might be between him and me and all of us.*

=I hope that fantasy didn't include me rubbing skin with him too,= Zeela said.

Zhahar choked on the wine she'd just swallowed. *No, it didn't.* She looked around to make sure no one had noticed her. *It's just . . . Everyone Lee cares about feels easy here, but I don't. Maybe it's a sign.* And hadn't she seen another sign that it would be dangerous to be near Lee while they were here?

A long silence.

Zeela?

=What did you see, Zhahar?=

What?

=I'm the warrior of our Tryad. You're the heart. But I know you. You came into view once earlier, and you've been hiding until now. What did you see that scared you so much?=

I thought I saw Allone, Zhahar whispered.

Zeela swore viciously. =You have to tell our mothers.=

They're upset with me. Maybe you could—

=I didn't see her. She shouldn't be here.= A pause. =By the triple stars, no wonder you want to get away from here. If she suspects that you and Lee have feelings for each other, if *she* accuses you . . . =

I know.

=Talk to our mothers. Tell Zephyra if you can't face Morragen or Medusah. Zhahar, if Allone has touched this land, Glorianna Belladonna needs to know.=

A wave of exhaustion made her body unbearably heavy. Before she could push to her feet, her mothers sat down at the table, with Medusah in view.

"We apologized for your behavior and your words," Medusah said. "When Glorianna Belladonna returns in the morning, you should make your own apology for speaking before understanding."

"I will," Zhahar said hurriedly. "And I do want to understand why I was mistaken. So do Sholeh and Zeela. Mother . . ."

"We know what it's like," Medusah said. "When we were your age, we went out into a one-face land to provide an anchor for Tryadnea. Even after we were discovered and were being hunted as a demon, we stayed to the end to give the others a chance to escape. We barely made it back before the last connection broke. We were not pursued by an enemy as terrible as you faced, but we know what it's like to live in fear day after day, interpreting every look, every tone of voice, and wondering if that was the day we would forget for just a moment and betray ourselves. Morragen told you about the risks, but you still wanted to go. You wanted to help the Tryad."

"And I failed." If she had been able to keep the connection to Vision, maybe she could have stayed with Lee without losing her sisters.

Medusah looked surprised. "No, you didn't. You protected Lee when he needed someone, and he helped you to return home. By doing that, his presence brought a person able to forge a link that connects Tryadnea with another piece of the world—a link far stronger than anything I could have created."

Zhahar looked around, searching for a face that shouldn't be there. "This place?"

Medusah also looked around. "My sisters and I all came into view in front of people of single aspect, and there was no disgust, no fear." She laughed softly. "There *was* a candid desire among some of the residents to discuss the Tryad's sexual practices, but the directness was refreshing. Some of their directness and ability to see the heart so clearly disturbs us, and their acceptance is, in its own way, just as unsettling." She sighed. "This isn't what I envisioned when I sent my will questing through the world, but I think this might be what our people need. At least for now." Her eyes held Zhahar's. "Which is why you must mend the break caused by your words."

She was too tired to be prudent, so she was honest. "If Glorianna can make boulders, why can't she restore Tryadnea?"

"These Landscapers say despair made the deserts, and hope the oases," Medusah said.

"So you agree with her that what happened to Tryadnea is our people's fault?"

"Yes, we do. If there is any truth in the story her lover told us tonight, then, yes, the Tryad did this to ourselves, and we're the only ones who can truly fix it."

Zhahar sat back, stunned.

"When we became leader, I searched the official records, the stories, consulted with those who serve as our people's Memory. There was nothing left that explained why Tryadnea broke away from the rest of the world, no mention of first becoming adrift. I thought then, and feel more strongly now, that something happened—an act so shameful that it was expunged from our history. Or maybe the act itself wasn't that shameful, wasn't meant to be harmful, but the result was catastrophic. Considering the nature of our taboos and the penalty for breaking them, it's easy enough to guess how it started.

"I listened to these people tonight, listened to the Landscapers among them. What happened to Tryadnea is not strange to them, and they all agree on one point: somewhere in the Tryad's history, a heart cried out with such conviction, the world responded. And Tryadnea was torn away from the rest of Ephemera so that our contact with other peoples would be fleeting.

"Tryadnea has been adrift for generations, but I think this time, in her own way, the Triple Goddess heard our hopes and prayers. Zhahar, was it happenchance that the man you helped has a sister who began as a single aspect and is now two?"

She'd forgotten that. In the blinding moment when she thought Glorianna could make Tryadnea's land viable again, she'd forgotten what the woman had already done to protect the world.

Medusah's aspect waned, and Zephyra, the core and heart of her mothers' Tryad, came into view.

"It wasn't what you said that offended Sebastian and Lee so much as the way you said it," Zephyra said gently. "That's why their friend Yoshani made a point of explaining to me that Glorianna Belladonna isn't just a Landscaper; she's a Guide of the Heart, and *that* is how she can help us." She tapped her fingers against her chest. "If we want Tryadnea to flourish again, we're going to have to enrich the ground here first."

::Don't cry, Zhahar,:: Sholeh said.

She hadn't realized she was. But she knew she was trembling.

"Mother, I think I saw Allone tonight."

A stunned silence. Then Morragen came into view, her face cold and hard. "Here? Are you sure?"

She shook her head. "I saw someone standing at the mouth of an alley across the street from me. A woman. That

I'm sure of, despite the cloak. When I saw her, I stopped. She stepped back into the alley, out of sight. I was afraid of what she might claim to see if I stayed in view."

"So that's why you avoided Lee and his family." Morragen nodded. "A wise decision, if Allone did slip past the guards and come to this place."

"I don't know what to do," Zhahar whispered.

Zephyra came into view and placed a hand over hers. "You're sharing a room with Kobrah, and I've been given a room in the same building. Much has happened today, and we all need some sleep. Tomorrow I will tell Glorianna Belladonna and Sebastian about Allone and the harm she can do to the Tryad people. Come, daughter. We need to rest."

Wiping the tears off her face, Zhahar left the courtyard with Zephyra. Halfway to the bordello, they met up with Teaser, who went back with them. He escorted Zephyra to her room first, then showed Zhahar to the room that belonged to Sebastian and Lynnea and shared a bathroom with his.

The travel pack that held her clothing had been brought up. Kobrah was already there, looking sleepy as she combed out her freshly washed hair.

Unwilling to get into a clean bed when they felt gritty from the day's travel and exertion, they took a quick bath before joining Kobrah and settling on their side of the bed.

How many lives had Allone destroyed in the years since making the choice that had destroyed her own?

Dreaming of what it would be like if Lee was willing to join hearts with her as well as bodies had been safe enough when they had been in Vision—especially since being at the Asylum helped her resist temptation. But now? If accused, she would have to make a choice before witnesses—and her choice would hurt Lee's heart.

Better to bruise his heart now than risk her sisters. She just hoped that he would understand someday.

Chapter Twenty-five

Keeping his eyes closed, Lee shifted onto his back, put one hand behind his head, and listened to familiar sounds that seemed new: the querying chirps and mutters of a keet who was interested in breakfast, followed by a woman's voice saying quietly but firmly, "Shh. Lee's still sleeping." Added to that, the murmurs of a male voice; Sebastian, talking to Lynnea in the kitchen. Probably discussing if they were going to have breakfast here or go over to Nadia's house early enough to eat there.

When Sebastian's cottage had been in the Den's landscape, Lee had bunked on the couch anytime he came to visit, as at home in his cousin's cottage as he was in his mother's house. But everything was different now. Sebastian's cottage was in the daylight landscape of Aurora and just a few minutes' walk from his own cottage and Nadia's house. Sebastian was married, was the Den's Justice Maker, and was going to be a father in a few months. Those were significant changes for an incubus who had thought he was the Den's best badass.

Everything began changing when Lynnea stumbled into the Den, altering Sebastian's life. So maybe it hadn't been Michael coming into their lives that had started the restless itch that had grown inside him over the past few months. Maybe it had been Sebastian changing that had tilted everything just enough that he'd looked at his own life and had wanted more. He just hadn't known what the *more* might be. Now he had seen a different kind of life, different possibilities.

But would it be possible to bridge his old life with those new possibilities? Or would the old prove too strong and smother the new? Only one way to find out.

Pushing back the sheet and summer blanket, Lee stood up and scrubbed his fingers over his hair. Then he put on the dark glasses to protect his eyes from the day's light and made his way to the kitchen to join Sebastian and Lynnea.

Danyal sat at the big wooden table in Nadia's kitchen, watching her cook a mound of food for breakfast. He *had* offered to help, but apparently she had her own system when it came to preparing a big meal for an extended family, and he wasn't part of that system.

It hadn't escaped his notice that Caitlin had been expected to help. He wasn't sure if that was a comment about gender or an expectation of family versus guest.

It made him curious about whether Yoshani was considered family or guest.

Grumbling male voices approached the outer screen door. Then Sebastian entered the kitchen, followed by Lee.

Nadia glanced over her shoulder. "Have you had breakfast?"

"He did and caused a ruckus," Sebastian growled. "Lynnea will be along as soon as things quiet down at home."

"You're turning this into a drama," Lee snapped. "And I *didn't* have breakfast."

Sebastian turned, standing toe-to-toe with his cousin. "Damn it, Lee! You ate the bird's toast."

Danyal stared at the two men, sure he'd misheard.

"He gets a corner of a piece. I ate the rest of it. So what?"

"He didn't know he just got a corner!" Sebastian replied hotly. "And he still wouldn't know if you hadn't *torn off the corner in front of him* instead of cutting it at the counter. And he wouldn't have known he doesn't get what the other people get on their toast if you hadn't stood there slathering butter and jelly on your part of it and *talking about it while you did it.*"

"Daylight, Sebastian! He's just a keet. He's not that smart."

"He's smart enough to have figured out the thing he hasn't been getting is called butter, which is a word he didn't know yesterday and was trying to say by the time we left."

Danyal considered the absurdity of two grown men arguing about the diet of a small bird, and had every intention of inserting himself into the argument. Then he saw Nadia turn away from the stove at the same moment Sparky, one of Nadia's keets, flew over to the inner screened door that separated the kitchen from the keets' room.

Sparky chirped and whistled and said, "Pazzeh bacon. Gimme kiss!"

Danyal choked, trying not to laugh.

Lee and Sebastian turned toward that door and said, "Not now, Sparky!"

Jeb walked into the kitchen and sniffed. "Is something burning?"

"Cunchy!" Sparky said.

"Their breakfast," Nadia said darkly.

Jeb looked at Sebastian and Lee. Then he shook his head and sighed. Nadia turned back to the stove, removing the overcrisped bacon from the pan and setting it on a plate to drain.

Glorianna and Michael entered the kitchen.

"What's going on?" Glorianna asked.

"Glorianna, keep an eye on the stove and the timer," Nadia said. "The sweet rolls are almost done, and *they* won't be edible at all if they burn."

Lee and Sebastian flinched when Nadia walked past them and out of the kitchen. She returned a few moments later and handed each of them a large pail.

"Stones and weeds," she said. "When those pails are full, you can come in and have breakfast with the rest of us."

"Mother," Lee began, "I don't think I can—"

"*Try.*"

Lee and Sebastian trudged out the kitchen door, passing Lynnea and Yoshani on their way in.

Michael leaned over Danyal's shoulder and whispered, "What started this?"

"Lee ate the bird's toast," Danyal whispered back.

"Tch." Michael shook his head. "He should know better."

*   *   *

Zhahar, Medusah, Kobrah, and the two shadowmen followed Teaser up the Den's main street.

"Teaser?" Zhahar raised her voice enough to be heard.

The incubus turned around to face her.

How did he manage that cocky swagger while walking backward? "I thought it was dangerous for the Tryad to go over these bridges."

"Not crossing over on a bridge," Teaser replied. "Glorianna's figured out how to get you all to Aurora without using one. That's why we're meeting her in the field beyond the street."

"What's she going to do?"

"Don't know." He turned and kept walking.

"He seems unconcerned," Medusah said, her eyes scanning the street and the alleyways.

You should be the one in view, Zhahar told Zeela.

=Right now, you make better bait,= Zeela replied.

Kobrah bristled and gave Medusah a hard look. "Teaser's nice."

"I didn't say he wasn't," Medusah replied. "But he has no stake in what happens to any of us or our lands."

"Maybe he has that much confidence in Glorianna's abilities," Zhahar said. If thoughts and words truly carried so much weight in this part of the world, she was determined to send out positive thoughts about Glorianna.

She felt her mothers' gaze, knew each of them had taken a look at her to reach their own conclusions.

::Mother won't let anything happen to us,:: Sholeh said.

She wouldn't want to let anything happen to them, but Morragen Medusah a Zephyra was the leader of the Tryad and had to uphold the laws and taboos their people lived by when it came to dealing with people of single aspect.

Allone was a reminder of why she didn't want to go back to Tryadnea, but it was no longer safe to be around Lee. Having a man of single aspect as a lover was considered distasteful, but satisfying physical needs while on assignment in a one-face land was understood to some extent. Having *feelings* for such a man? *That* was taboo, and she was afraid her feelings were too apparent.

"Hey-a," Teaser called as he hurried toward Michael.

"A good morning to you all," Michael said, smiling. The smile dimmed for a moment when he looked at Zhahar and Medusah, then returned to its previous brightness.

Teaser stopped and cocked his head. "Isn't that Lee's island?"

"It's the island that used to resonate with him," Michael said. "Now it resonates with Glorianna, if not in quite the same way."

::Island?:: Sholeh said. ::Shouldn't it be called a grove, since those are the only trees in this field?::

Glorianna appeared at the edge of a path between two trees. A path, Zhahar noticed, that didn't extend past those trees.

"There is a temporary border between the island and the field so you can cross from one to the other," Glorianna said.

When the shadowmen gave Teaser a questioning look, he stepped up beside Glorianna, then walked past. The Apothecary and the Knife followed him.

Kobrah grabbed Zhahar's hand, so they stepped up to the path together. As soon as both her feet were on the path, Zhahar heard the patter of raindrops on leaves—and squinted at the sudden daylight.

"Make room for your mother and Michael," Glorianna said. "Hurry up, Magician. It's starting to rain."

Confused, Zhahar moved up the path a few steps.

=How can it be raining here when it wasn't raining a few steps away?= Zeela asked.

::Glorianna said this was a border, so we must be someplace that isn't the Den,:: Sholeh said, sounding excited. ::Zhahar, can I take a look?::

At what? Zhahar wondered as Sholeh came into view for a minute and looked up at the branches that formed an openwork canopy.

As soon as Medusah and Michael walked onto the island, Glorianna said, "Ephemera."

Still looking up at the trees, Zhahar came back into view and didn't think anything had changed until Medusah asked sharply, "Why is there water where the field used to be?"

"This island is located in the middle of a stream," Glorianna replied. "We're in Sanctuary for the moment."

"This place," Zephyra whispered, coming into view. "This is a heart-healing place."

Glorianna gave her a curious look. "Yes, it is. Does your land have a place like this? A Place of Light?"

A great sadness filled Zephyra's face before her aspect waned. Medusah came back into view and said, "Not anymore."

Nodding, Glorianna closed her eyes. A moment later, the stream was gone. Beyond the path was a different daylight and another field—and no rain.

"Teaser, you and Michael go first, since I know you resonate with Aurora," Glorianna said.

Teaser winked at Kobrah and stepped off the island.

"Is something on your mind, Zhahar?" Medusah asked as Glorianna had Kobrah come to the edge of the path.

Lee. Finding a place where love isn't paid for by death. Getting away from the Tryad and Tryadnea before it's too late. "No," she lied. "Nothing."

Lee walked beside Yoshani, self-conscious about the dark glasses and hat, and more aware of what he *wasn't* seeing because he knew his mother's land so well.

"Daylight," he muttered when they crossed the footbridge that separated Nadia's personal gardens from open land and the walled garden that held her landscapes. "Why did Glorianna set the island so far from the house?"

"I don't know," Yoshani said mildly. "Perhaps she and Nadia felt that was the best place."

"It's not like . . ." Lee trailed off as he paid attention to the resonances of two landscapes. He lengthened his stride as much as he dared, reaching Glorianna just as Zhahar stepped up between two trees.

"I'd like each of you to come into view and hold until I tell you to change," Glorianna said.

Lee clamped his teeth to hold back the questions he wanted to ask. Now wasn't the time to interrupt Glorianna's attention.

He couldn't tell colors as colors yet, but the difference between Zeela's dark hair and Zhahar's light brown was something he could distinguish, and he could make out a little more detail in their faces.

"Interesting," Glorianna said quietly.

"What?" he asked.

"Zhahar and Sholeh resonate with Aurora. Zeela does not."

"Does that mean Zeela shouldn't come into view while we're here?"

Glorianna shook her head. "I don't think Sholeh Zeela a Zhahar could cross a stationary bridge and reach Aurora if Zeela's aspect was in view, but once they reached this landscape, any of the sisters could be here. It just wouldn't hold the same interest for each of them. Same as in the Den last night. Sholeh or Zeela could cross over using a bridge, but Zhahar wouldn't be able to reach the Den that way." She wagged her fingers. "Zhahar, you can step off the island so I can see the aspects of Morragen Medusah a Zephyra."

Zhahar stepped off the island and went over to join Kobrah instead of moving to stand by Lee.

Was she self-conscious because her mothers were here, or did that choice signal something more?

He expected Zephyra to resonate with his mother's landscape. It surprised him that Morragen was the other aspect that resonated with Aurora, since she reminded him more of Zeela. But that could mean Medusah was the darkest aspect of that Tryad—and, most likely, the most dangerous.

Morragen stepped off the island. A moment later, he heard all their visitors gasp as the island disappeared and they were standing in open land near a walled garden.

In the silence that followed, while they absorbed what they had seen, he absorbed what he had just felt. He was close enough to see his sister's face. Close enough to make out her expression.

"You swapped land in order to shift the island to Aurora?" he asked, sure he had to be wrong.

"Yes," Glorianna replied. "Doing that created a temporary border."

"Guardians and Guides! Why didn't you impose the island *over* the landscape? If you're exchanging equal ground, you're risking something crossing into Sanctuary that shouldn't be there!"

"*You* could impose the island over other landscapes. It doesn't respond that way for me."

"Daylight, Glorianna! What were you thinking?"

"I was thinking this was a practical way of moving several people without losing one of them. Besides," she added sharply, "I was exchanging ground with one of my landscapes and one of Mother's. Very little risk."

"But a lot of risk if you're shifting to someplace unknown," he shot back.

"Which I didn't do."

No, she hadn't. He felt a little foolish for arguing about it, and wasn't sure *why* he was arguing, except that the island had been his and he felt a deep affection for it.

And yet he had let it go, along with so many other things that had held a piece of his heart.

"Is there any breakfast left?" Teaser asked.

"Aye, there is," Michael replied. "Shall we go up to the house?"

Lee walked over to Zhahar. "Want to give me a hand up to the house?"

An odd hesitation before she said, "Of course."

She offered her arm. Instead, he took her hand and started walking, not pretending that he needed any help.

"Did you sleep all right?" he asked. "When you spend enough time in the Den, you learn to sleep through all the ordinary noises—or don't try to sleep until the Den settles down for a few hours. After Sebastian's cottage shifted to Aurora, we finally realized the businesses in the Den closed down when most of the guests left, which was around dawn in the daylight landscapes that were in the same part of the world." He laughed softly. "Whatever part that is."

"It was fine," she said stiffly. "I appreciate your cousin letting Kobrah and me use his room."

"Huh." Keeping a firm grip on her hand, he led her away from the kitchen door so they wouldn't be underfoot of the people wanting to go inside and get some breakfast. "The words say one thing; the tone says something else. Why don't you tell me what's wrong?"

"Nothing is wrong."

He bent his head, intending to give her a light kiss to remind her that she wasn't alone here. She had acted as his guide when he was fumbling his way around the Asylum; now he could help her adjust to the landscapes that were Tryadnea's neighbors. But when she turned her head to avoid his kiss, he released her hand and took a step back.

"Yeah," he said with some bite in his voice. "Not a damn thing is wrong."

She looked past him, and he wondered who was supposed to be the audience for this little show.

"It's not appropriate for us to be intimate," she said, sounding too much like a Handler for his liking.

"Excuse me?"

"It's not appropriate," she insisted.

"Why?" His chest muscles tightened, squeezing his heart. He stared at her until his eyes burned from the effort to see her more clearly. Except he didn't think it was his eyes that needed clarity.

"It wasn't appropriate when we were at the Asylum," he said slowly. "Any kind of physical relationship with an inmate could have been viewed as a misuse of your authority. I understood that. But I'm not an inmate anymore, Zhahar, and I'm not going to be again." When she didn't say anything, he looked toward the people going into the house. A group was still at the back of the lawn, looking at something, but among those watching them while heading into the house for breakfast was Morragen Medusah a Zephyra.

"Being a Handler wasn't the reason you retreated as much as you encouraged, was it?" he asked softly, his heart getting squeezed a little harder. "That was the excuse. Something kept pulling us toward each other, maybe even before we actually met. And now there's something in the way. What is it? Your mothers? Or just the prejudice your people feel for anyone who isn't Tryad?"

"It's more than prejudice," she said, not trying to hide her own bitterness. "It's taboo to get involved with a man of single aspect. The penalties are harsh, Lee, and I can't take the chance of being accused of having feelings for you."

He stepped away from her. "If you knew you couldn't love me, if you knew there were reasons why you *wouldn't* allow this to ripen past a few kisses, you should have told me. You should have given me a choice about whether I wanted those kisses when there couldn't be anything more."

"Would you have wanted them?" she asked, challenging.

"Not from you." She looked shocked, so he added, "I would, and have, accepted those restrictions from other women because I couldn't give them anything more than a passing affection. But I feel more than passing affection for you, so I would have preferred to have nothing than just a taste of what I can't have." Heading for the gate in the stone wall that separated his mother's personal land from the woodland that they all considered a joint concern, he said over his shoulder, "You should get something to eat. It's going to be a long day."

He'd gotten through the gate and had taken a dozen steps down the path when Teaser caught up to him.

"Where are you going?" Teaser asked.

"Don't know." Not far, since he had no intention of straying off the path that ran between his cottage and Nadia's house.

"Why are you going?"

"Because I got my heart bruised just now, and I don't want to face Zhahar *and* her mothers while I sit at *my* mother's table. I'm not feeling that polite."

"Ah." They walked in silence for a minute. Then Teaser asked, "What about Sholeh and Zeela? You could ask one of them to come into view during the meal if you don't want to deal with Zhahar. They like you."

"I like them too, but I don't want to have sex with them."

"Well, daylight, Lee. I wasn't talking about having sex with them—or anyone else—in front of everyone. Especially at your mother's table. Or on the table. Because it's Nadia's, and that wouldn't be proper." A pause. "Would it be proper? Do you think she and—"

"No," Lee snapped, refusing to think about Nadia and Jeb doing anything that intimate. "I wasn't talking about having sex in front of anyone. But I *was* interested in having sex with Zhahar, until she made it clear just now that her interest in me *never* ran that deep." Couldn't run that deep, which wasn't the same thing. What kind of penalties was she talking about?

"So you want to have sex with Zhahar but not with Sholeh and Zeela."

"That's right." Or was last night.

"*Can* you have sex with one of them and not the others?" Teaser asked thoughtfully.

Lee stopped walking. It figured that an incubus would be too curious about Tryad sexuality not to keep circling around the question. "I don't know. Maybe not. I had the impression they can give each other some measure of privacy, but since they share a physical core . . ." The idea of finding himself in bed with Zeela didn't have any appeal, but waking up and finding himself beside Sholeh? *That* would feel too much like finding himself with Caitlin Marie, who was Michael's younger sister and family now. "Maybe it is a case of all or none. But if that's true, Zhahar should have told me."

Teaser cocked his head. "Could she? We had the impression her being Tryad was a big secret."

"It was," Lee conceded. "Talking about the details of intimacy would be hard enough under any circumstances, and it isn't something she would have done when she was still trying to hide what she was. But after I knew she was Tryad, she should have told me if we couldn't be lovers instead of letting me believe it was possible. Somehow. I would have been disappointed, but I would have respected her choice."

"Even if she wasn't the one making the choice?"

Lee sighed. "You're spending too much time with Yoshani. Or Danyal. Or both."

Teaser grinned. "Or maybe, since we're talking about sex, I'm the best-qualified person to talk to."

A rather terrifying thought—which made it oddly comforting.

"How would you feel about going back to the house and slipping a plate of food out to me?" Lee asked.

"Where are you going to be?"

He turned and started walking back to Nadia's house. "In the garden. It's a good place to brood."

Carrying a full plate and two mugs, Danyal walked to the bench in the garden. Lee looked up, then huffed out a breath and smiled.

"I wondered who would bring the plate," Lee said. "Didn't expect it to be you."

"You don't think I would have that much compassion?" Danyal asked as he handed over the plate.

"I figured you were the only man in the house besides Teaser who wouldn't be looking for an excuse to come out here and yell at me."

"Ah." Danyal sat down and put one mug on the bench between them. "Well, you're half right. I welcomed the excuse to come out here. But I didn't come to yell; I came to listen."

Lee ate some scrambled eggs and swore mildly when the bacon crumbled.

"Problem?" Danyal asked.

"Mother saved the overcooked bacon for me because I don't like it this way. She's a firm believer in letting people live with the consequences of their actions as a way of learning life's lessons." He was hungry, so he ate the bacon anyway. "You heard about this morning?"

"You, Sebastian, and the bird? I saw the second half of that drama—and have an itching regret that I missed the first half, which is *not* an appropriate feeling for a Shaman to have."

"I stirred things up. I can claim I didn't know what would happen, but I grew up in my mother's house. I knew what would happen. I just don't know why I did it."

"You know," Danyal replied, smiling.

"Shaman, I'm not sure I know much of anything right now."

"Then I'll tell you," Danyal said. "The bird and the toast are symbols of the new life Sebastian is building. In order to have those things, he had to see the world differently, and that changed his life. So he values the bird, the toast, and the morning ritual. For you, they are symbols of what you left behind. Because you have a warm, generous family, it would be easy to go back to the life you had, fall back into the patterns and routines. You need something different, and you're afraid you'll go back to those patterns. So you pushed away the symbols and caused disruption so that you don't fit quite so easily into the life you left behind."

More than a spat with his cousin about a bird was causing the storm building in Lee's heart-core. Wondering if the turbulence he felt in Zhahar had the same root, Danyal decided to probe gently.

Before he could shape his question, Lee set his fork on the plate, then lifted the mug of koffee.

"What about you?" Lee asked. "Will you fit back into the life you had in Vision before you crossed the bridge that brought you here?"

"No, I won't." Danyal saw Lee's concern and smiled. "I don't regret that. I hope there is a way to return to Vision and help the other Shamans deal with the wizards and the Dark Guide, but I have much to learn from the people I've met here, and, in learning it, I hope to discover the new shape of my own life."

Lee set down the mug and resumed eating.

Danyal looked out at the garden, since it seemed rude to watch Lee eat. He regretted the darkness that now touched Vision, and he regretted the wounds on his shoulder and hip that were still healing, but he didn't regret stumbling over that bridge and finding himself among these people. He was a Shaman, would always be a Shaman, but he had looked at Yoshani and the choices that holy man had made and had seen a truth about himself: he no longer wanted to be the kind of Shaman he had been. He wasn't certain he *could* be the kind of Shaman he had been, even if he'd wanted to stay within those boundaries. His heart had been ready for change, had craved it. And here it was. Now he had to figure out how to make the most of it.

"By the way, the Apothecary thinks he'll be able to make another mixture that will improve your sight more than the eyedrops you have now," Danyal said.

Lee's hand trembled, shaking the scrambled eggs off the fork. "I'm glad to hear it, but I thought there was a limit to what could be restored."

"Before going up to the house, Glorianna had the world bring the sandbox to Nadia's garden."

"Ah." Lee nodded. "I saw the gathering and wondered, but I was embroiled in my own concerns."

"The Apothecary had found one of the plants last night in the Den. All the ingredients for this healing mixture are brought into the city by ships from other places, and many of the plants lose much of their potency by the time they are sold in the bazaar."

Lee smiled. "The plants are here, aren't they?"

"Nadia recognized some; Glorianna recognized others. I thought the Apothecary was going to weep when Caitlin Marie, pointing out a plant whose dried leaves are so expensive several shadowmen buy a bundle and split it, said the plant grew wild in the field behind her house. He thinks brewing the potion for the eyedrops from fresh-picked plants will double the healing power. If this potion does what he thinks it will, you might regain most of your sight."

Lee set the plate on the bench. "May your heart travel lightly, because what you bring with you becomes part of the landscape." He paused. "Why did I end up being blinded in a city called Vision, Danyal? Why did you end up in the Den of Iniquity? As Sebastian is fond of saying, no one comes to the Den by mistake. By accident, yes, but not by mistake."

He'd been wondering the same thing. "Isn't it our task to find out?" He sighed. "Along with finding a way of returning to Vision."

Lee straightened up slowly. "Heart music."

Danyal frowned. "I don't understand."

"Sorrow and joy." Lee stood up. "I have to talk to Glorianna."

No hesitation in Lee's movements as he skirted the end of the bench and strode toward the house. No indication that anything interfered with his sight.

What interferes with my sight? Danyal wondered. *And what has changed Zhahar from a calm summer lake to swift rapids?*

Gathering the plate and mugs, he returned to the house.

"Glorianna," Medusah said. "We need to speak with you about a potential danger."

Glorianna led the a Zephyra Tryad into Nadia's parlor. "A danger to the Den? From Tryadnea?" The darkness that was Belladonna pushed at her. Who better to deal with danger than the monster that Evil feared? But she held on to the Light in order to listen.

"Not a danger to your people," Medusah said. "But a potential danger to Zhahar, and a reason for your people to think ill of us."

"I'm listening."

"It's possible that someone else from my homeland slipped across the border. Zhahar thought she'd seen Allone in the Den last night."

A jagged song, Michael had said. She had sensed it as a heart that held too much darkness. A corrupt heart linked to a strong mind—a presence strong enough that even Sebastian had felt its sourness in the Den's Dark currents.

"Allone is an aspect of a Tryad?" Glorianna asked.

Medusah shook her head. "She is what is left of a Tryad after the three were merged into one."

Everything in Glorianna went still. "What exactly does that mean?"

"She chose the man who claimed to love her over her sisters, and by our customs, her sisters' lives were the payment for that love."

Glorianna held Michael's hand as they followed Lee and Sebastian to the stable in the Den, where they had left the Apothecary's wagon. At first Lee had insisted that he needed to talk to her; then he changed his mind and said there was something he had to show her.

Medusah hadn't told her much about this merging that was the punishment for breaking Tryad taboos, but the woman had said enough for her to listen very carefully to the hearts around her—especially Lee's and Zhahar's.

"There are some grating notes in his music now," Michael said quietly, lifting his chin to indicate Lee.

That wasn't surprising. "Do you know why?" she asked.

The music Michael heard in people's hearts was the way he recognized when someone didn't fit into a place anymore. Whatever he could tell her would add to her own sense of what was building around them since last night.

"The music doesn't tell me the *why*, but Lee puts me in mind of a man who's pulling both ends of a rope. No matter which side wins, he still loses."

He studied her, but she doubted he saw much. There wasn't much moonlight, and Sebastian and Lee had the lanterns.

"What's on your mind, darling?" Michael finally asked.

"The Wish River and what it looks like in the places where heart wishes are in conflict." Wild. Raging. Water smashing against itself and breaking anything that it could pound against the rocks. Early last night—before the appearance of Allone?—several heart wishes had been flowing in the same direction. This morning? Wild, raging water with fierce undercurrents.

Glorianna stopped as soon as they drew even with the Den's cobblestone main street.

Heart wishes in conflict, smashing against each other. Ephemera's currents of power swirling around her. Enough fury to *glut* the Dark currents *in the Den*.

hurry hurry hurry

And a suspicion about the bloodlines of a Tryad who was no longer three.

"I need to check the border between the Den and Tryadnea, and I need Sebastian to go with me," she said. "Can you stay here with Lee and find out what he wanted to show me?"

"I can. But shouldn't I go with you?"

She shook her head. "I need you with Lee, and I need the wizard with me."

Michael stared at her. Then he whistled sharply. Sebastian turned and headed back to them. Lee walked on a few more steps before he stopped and, after a noticeable pause, turned back to join them.

His heart is more sensitive to the Dark currents than it used to be, she thought. *More sensitive—and more responsive to the darkness in other hearts. Like mine is.*

When she explained that she needed to check the border, Lee said testily, "Can't it wait a few minutes? Can't you even give me that much time?"

They looked at him, and even he seemed confused by the words.

"Glorianna," Lee began.

"You need to get away from the Den," she said with the quiet conviction he had never questioned. "You need to get back to Aurora *now*."

"Is someone whispering to you, Lee?" Sebastian asked.

Lee swayed. Michael grabbed his arm.

"Guardians and Guides," Lee whispered.

"Nothing that invasive," Glorianna said firmly. "But definitely something that doesn't belong here." She felt herself start to slide toward Belladonna's darker state of mind. "Lee, please."

She walked away from all of them. Had to.

Thorn trees with the succulent fruit of rotting bodies. Death rollers hiding in the only fresh water available. Trapspiders as big as dogs, waiting for the unwary. Vines that took root under the skin, spreading fast to anchor around bone so that they couldn't be torn out. Growing out of the skin and spreading until they covered their prey—until their weight was too much to carry, and even a grown man finally buckled while the vines fed on him.

She would not bring those things to the Den. She *wouldn't*. But there were times when she struggled from one minute to the next to make a choice that belonged to the Light.

Love, not sex, was the taboo between a Tryad and a one-faced man. If a Tryad could have an aspect that was a Bridge, there could be some among them who were sired by a wizard—or even a Dark Guide. Someone who fed the Dark currents and had some of the wizards' ability to persuade others into making a truth out of lies could drain hope from a people—especially if there was another explanation for her bitterness and anger.

Everything is in motion, she thought. *But I—and Belladonna—can help Zhahar choose which darkness is her fate.*

When Glorianna paid attention to her surroundings again, she was almost to the other end of the Den's main street, and Sebastian was walking beside her.

"You want to tell me what we're walking toward?" he asked when they stepped from the cobblestone street to the dirt lane that led to the Merry Makers' landscape as well as Tryadnea.

"A possible confrontation with a wizard's offspring."

He swore. "Does this person have the lightning?"

"I don't know, but I doubt it. I think at least one aspect of the Morragen Medusah a Zephyra Tryad would have died by now if their enemy could command wizards' lightning."

"Guardians and Guides," he muttered.

"Come on," she said. "We need to check that border."

They broke into a run, slowing down when they reached the stone markers. Those stones were unchanged, and, Glorianna noted with relief, the large triangles of stone that marked the actual border were in place. But the border itself didn't feel quite right.

Sebastian caught her arm and pulled her back before she stepped between the stone triangles.

"Let me cross over," he said. "Just in case there's trouble in Tryadnea."

"I'm not sure the trouble *is* in Tryadnea," she replied. "But I do know that border doesn't feel right. If you cross over, you may not be able to get back."

"I have a one-shot bridge that will take me back to the Den, so I'll get back here one way or another."

"All right." She didn't like watching him walk up to that border, didn't like watching him cross over to Tryadnea.

Except Sebastian didn't cross over. He *should* have disappeared from sight, *should* have been standing in Tryadnea the moment he passed between the stones. But she could still see him, and that proved something wasn't right.

Resonances. Tryadnea had *wanted* to belong to her, but now it was pulling away, resisting the connection. Why? Because the Den was a dark landscape? Or because the Den wasn't dark enough? All right, the carnal carnival wasn't the most convenient connection, but it *was* a connection to other parts of Ephemera. And what other people would be so accepting of a three-faced bitch who looked down at *her* brother and cousin?

The Tryad thought the Den wasn't dark enough? She knew a place that would welcome the Tryad. That landscape was still within reach, was always within reach. It would be so easy to add Tryadnea to the landscapes in the Eater of the World's domain. Bonelovers and trapspiders wouldn't care how many faces the prey wore as long as the flesh was juicy. And the Eater would welcome the diversion of taking a few Tryad apart to learn how to become one and use their own shape to hunt them.

They didn't want this little piece of her darkness? Then they could have . . .

Sebastian.

The cousin whose heart had saved her stood between the border stones, and even though he was little more than a dark shape, she knew he waited for her to decide if she was going to struggle back to the Light. He understood that struggle, which is why he didn't take a sunrise for granted. And because he understood, she made the exhausting effort to be Glorianna instead of Belladonna.

She was about to tell him she was in control of herself when he pressed a finger to his lips, warning her to be quiet.

He took a few steps away from the border, then moved off to his right. She followed him on her side. He moved cautiously, and she wondered what he sensed that she couldn't.

Still moving cautiously, he retraced his steps and returned to her side of the border. Before she could ask any questions, he shook his head, took her arm, and walked halfway back to the lane that led to the Den.

"Why are you having so much trouble staying in balance?" he asked. "That's the second time you slipped since we crossed over from Aurora. Do you need to go back to the Island in the Mist—or stay away from the dark landscapes?"

She considered the question, then shook her head. "I'll be all right. What happened when you crossed the border?"

Sebastian studied her as best he could in starlight. "I could hear some of the men talking. Couldn't see them, couldn't see a fire or their camp, but I could hear them."

"How did they sound?"

"Excited. Impressed by the way you came to their land. Hopeful that this time the connection will hold and they can be a part of the world again. And a couple of them were scared about what Morragen would say when they told her a woman slipped past them and went to the Den."

"A woman called Allone?"

Sebastian nodded. "She returned before dawn and seemed pleased about something. Maybe an incubus gave her a tumble."

I doubt that would have pleased her. But destroying someone else's life certainly would.

"Is this because of me and Morragen snapping at each other yesterday when we were waiting for you?"

"You're not the dissonance that disrupted the border," she said.

"But someone is?"

"Oh yes. Someone is." She studied the stone triangles. "Conflicting heart wishes, not only between separate people but within Morragen Medusah a Zephyra." *How much courage do you have? Will you sacrifice your daughter for your people?*

Nothing she wanted to do about that border, since the Den was safer if Tryad couldn't cross over, so she started walking back to the lane.

"What is your impression of our guests?" she asked.

"Which ones?" Sebastian countered. "Danyal is solid. He's intrigued by the Den, but he could have just as easily ended up stumbling into Aurora, and the result would be the same—he's looking to change, and you, Aunt Nadia, and Michael are the ones who can show him different possibilities. Probably you and Michael. I gather Danyal is more like you two than like Auntie."

"I agree with that. Go on."

"Kobrah has seen some dark places. She wouldn't find the Den on her own, though. Too carnal for her."

"She wouldn't find Aurora on her own either," Glorianna said. "The currents of Light are too strong to resonate with her as she is now. The fact that she's working at the Asylum is a measure of where her heart is."

"Didn't get much of a feel for Morragen Medusah a Zephyra, except that I'd like all her visits to be short ones," Sebastian said. "But her daughters?" He blew out a breath. "Zeela could settle into the Den without a second thought. She's tough and physical—and probably knows more about men and sex than the other two combined. Sholeh reminds me of Lynnea when she first came to the Den—a little stunned, but determined to grab at a chance to have an adventure before someone takes away that chance."

"She's also physically more fragile than the other two," Glorianna said. "Which makes me wonder if all the Tryad have one weaker sibling."

"You think there's truth in that story Yoshani and Michael patched together last night?"

"Something to think about. So we're down to Zhahar."

"Doesn't fit in the Den."

"Where else doesn't she fit?" Glorianna asked softly. But that wasn't a question either of them could answer. At least, not yet.

A demon cycle gave them a ride to the stationary bridge that led to Aurora. When they crossed over, they found Lee and Michael waiting for them outside Sebastian's cottage.

Glorianna glanced at the rolled blanket at Michael's feet but didn't ask about it.

"Lee might have an access point to Vision," Michael said, "but we weren't sure where to set it up to test that possibility."

"Vision will have to wait," Glorianna said as she stepped in front of Lee. "What were you and Zhahar arguing about at Mother's house?"

"It's private," he replied.

There was a snap of temper in his voice, but under that snap was hurt.

"It may be personal," she countered, "but it's no longer private. Lee, the border between the Den and Tryadnea has faded to the point where no one can cross over."

He reached up and pulled off the dark glasses. "What are you talking about? That border was solid."

"Yes, it *was* solid. Now it's acting like the White Isle did when we first tried to approach. Sebastian could hear the men talking but couldn't see them, couldn't actually cross over."

"But Tryadnea is your landscape," Lee protested.

"I think there's a power struggle going on in Tryadnea that we aren't privy to, so maybe not everyone wants Tryadnea to be one of my landscapes," Glorianna said. "Maybe there are some who want that land to remain barren. What I do know is that Zhahar is at the center of this."

"Zhahar wouldn't want anything bad to happen to her homeland," Lee said. "And she certainly wouldn't want to strip her people of the first chance they've had in years of making a solid connection to another part of the world."

"She's the tool, Lee," she said softly.

He swore quietly but with considerable heat. Then he removed the soft-brimmed hat and scrubbed one hand over his head. "Zhahar has decided that she doesn't have feelings for me, isn't going to have feelings for me, that it was all a moment's madness between a Handler and an inmate, with the romantic notions all on my side." He shrugged.

She didn't need to see the hurt in his eyes; she felt it in his heart.

"Do you believe that?" Michael asked.

"Lee, what would happen if Tryadnea broke away from the Den and went adrift again?" Glorianna asked. "What would happen if you made a one-shot bridge that got Morragen back home and Zhahar didn't go back?"

He shook his head. "I'd make a one-shot bridge for her too. I wouldn't leave her stranded here, Glorianna. I'm churned up right now, but I'm not that selfish."

"No," she said with a smile. "You're not. But if Zhahar didn't go back?"

"She doesn't like it here."

"This isn't the only place, Lee."

"When you're cut off from your own people, you can pick and choose the customs you want to keep." Michael said. "Is that what you're thinking?"

Glorianna nodded. "And you can get away from a kind of heart poison that lives inside too many of your people." She looked at her brother. "The heart has no secrets, Bridge. Zhahar can lie to her mother. She can lie to you. She can even lie to herself. But she can't lie to a Guide of the Heart, not when she's standing in my landscapes. The romantic notions aren't all on your side. I don't know if that helps or hurts, but I can tell you that much." *And Zhahar will have to tell you the rest—if she chooses.*

"What am I supposed to do?" Lee asked.

"Same thing we've always done—fix what we can and hope it's enough."

Michael picked up the rolled blanket. "Then let's see what we can do with these."

Opportunities and choices, Glorianna thought as the four of them walked back to Nadia's house. It took courage to follow the heart.

It was time to find out who had that courage.

Chapter Twenty-six

As they walked to Nadia's house, Lee's thoughts were racing fast and hard. He understood the danger of conflicting heart wishes. Ephemera manifested the heart, for good or ill. It didn't distinguish between a wish that would benefit people from a wish that would do harm. And while the Landscapers could keep the world from manifesting *every* idle wish that came from the hearts of all the people, even they couldn't stop a true heart wish—or prevent all the changes that heart wish would create.

If there was anyone who could minimize the damage being done right now, it was Glorianna Belladonna. But first, he had his own fences to mend. Since he was walking beside Sebastian, that was a good place to start.

"I'm sorry about the bird."

Sebastian shook his head and smiled. "Bop would have learned about butter sooner or later."

Maybe. "It will give you practice spelling out words."

Sebastian rolled his eyes. "Just what I need. The bird teaching the baby to spell."

Lee grinned, but the grin faded when they reached the gate in the wall. He lengthened his stride to reach Glorianna before she walked into the house. "Can we talk before we all talk?"

She studied him, then looked at Michael. Nodding, the Magician carried the blanket into the house.

"I know you have to tell them the border is unstable," he said.

"Yes, I do," she agreed.

"Could you brush over why it's unstable?" He wished he could see better, wished he could read whatever was in her face.

Finally, she asked, "Why?"

He didn't try to dissemble or evade. Not with her. "Opportunities and choices. Zhahar and her sisters were one of six Tryad who went into the city of Vision to anchor Tryadnea to another place. The other five failed, and I think the discovery of what they were was a big reason they failed."

"And gave Vision's citizens someone to blame for the bad things that were happening," Glorianna said. Then she tipped her head. "Lee? How did anyone know the Tryad were Tryad? I had the impression they were very careful to keep their nature a secret."

"Zhahar was revealed fairly quickly."

"By a Shaman and a Bridge. Unless they changed aspects in front of someone, who else besides someone like you or Danyal would sense the difference?"

He thought about that and understood where she was going. "Someone told on them. Someone pointed out the stranger and whispered in the right ear."

"Someone with enough bitterness in her heart to want the rest of the Tryad to suffer."

Lee pulled off the hat. "Guardians and Guides, Glorianna. How are we supposed to prove that to anyone?"

"We can't. And it's not our place to try. The Tryad have to choose whom to follow. We can't make that choice for them."

No, they couldn't make that choice. But that didn't mean there weren't choices they *could* make.

He brushed his fingertips down Glorianna's arm. "One heart can change a landscape. As a Guide, you know that."

"Yes, I do. So be careful what opportunities you create and what choices you make, brother." She tugged him toward the kitchen door.

"What does that mean?"

"That means you would be smart to get as much help as you can."

"With what?"

"How do the Tryad have sex?"

Lee groaned. "Not really something I can ask."

"I agree. But the answer will have a significant impact on the choices that are made. So let Teaser ask. He's bursting to find out, so let him do it."

"You think Zhahar is going to talk to Teaser?"

"No, I think Sholeh will talk to Teaser and tell him a whole lot about Tryad customs and traditions and history that will be helpful in understanding these people. All things Teaser wants to know about, since he looks at the Tryad and sees lots of potential new lovers."

"Daylight," Lee muttered.

"*Zeela*, on the other hand, will tell him the mechanics of Tryad sex, either for her own self-interest or because she'll realize he's going to pass the information on to you. Either way, you'll know if that door is closed to you."

He huffed out a breath. A year ago, Sebastian would have been a better choice to find out about the Tryad. Now he would still listen intently, but not to be a lover in dreams or flesh. Now he would consider whether Tryad sexual preferences would cause any trouble in the Den.

"How did Sebastian go from being the hot badass women drool over to being the prissy prig who enforces the rules?" he asked.

"Sebastian is still hot, women still drool when he walks by, and enforcing his own rules is hardly being a prissy prig," Glorianna said primly as she opened the kitchen door. "And since you look enough alike, if you wore your pants tighter, women would drool over you too."

He choked. She laughed and walked into the house, leaving him sputtering.

Danyal watched everyone gather around the kitchen table. Storms and bright water. Heat lightning. Thorn trees and breathtaking Light. He couldn't get a feel for the other people crowding into the room. Their hearts were all submerged by the intensity of feeling in Sholeh Zeela a Zhahar, Sebastian, and Glorianna Belladonna.

Tension tightened his muscles, making his burned shoulder and hip ache as he began to understand that only specific people were being given a place at the table. Zhahar and Morragen sat beside each other, with Nadia on Zhahar's left. Sebastian and Glorianna sat across from them, with Lee on Glorianna's right. Michael sat at one end of the table, and he had been given the seat at the other end. Yoshani, Teaser, Kobrah, Caitlin Marie, Lynnea, Jeb, the Apothecary, and the Knife filled up the kitchen.

"There's a problem," Glorianna said. "The border between Tryadnea and the Den has faded to the point where no one can cross over."

"You said it was stable," Morragen said. "I'm here, away from my people, because you said it was stable."

"It was. Tryadnea is still connected to the Den, but it can't be reached by using that border. At least one person made a heart wish so powerful it broke down a border between two compatible landscapes held by the same Landscaper. Held by *me.*"

Morragen stared at Zhahar. "You would condemn our people in order to be *with a man*?"

"My son isn't just some man," Nadia warned, leaning on the table to see past Zhahar, who stared back at her mother, looking shocked and pale.

"I didn't!" Zhahar said. "How could you think I would do that? I didn't wish . . ." She glanced at Lee and didn't continue.

Yes, you did, Danyal thought. *But you had no reason to think your wishing could change anything.* And yet Zhahar sounded sincere. Then he looked at Michael, who was watching her closely. Whatever the Magician was hearing in the heart music surprised him.

"Zhahar," Lee said gently, "heart wishes can change a landscape, but this disruption of the border isn't permanent. It can be fixed."

"I didn't do anything!" Zhahar cried.

A moment later, Zeela came into view, pushing the chair back as she stood up and glared at Morragen. "Zhahar didn't make the heart wish to break Tryadnea away from the Den. I did."

Morragen also stood. "Why would you condemn our people?"

"Why not?" Zeela snapped. "It's not going to make any difference. No matter what we do or how hard we try, the connection will break in a few months, and *nothing* will have changed. We'll be adrift again, feeling more bitter because we failed again, and you won't be able to stop it any more than your mothers could."

"That's enough!" Morragen shouted.

"Our connection to the Den is going to break sooner or later, so why not let it break now? Then Zhahar will have a chance to love someone, which is more than you ever had. Do you think we were too young to understand the fights between you and the grandmothers? 'Give him your body if you must do the base act, but never give him your heart.'"

Zephyra came into view for a moment, tears in her eyes. "Stop this. Zeela, please stop this." She faded as Morragen appeared again.

"No, I won't stop this!" Zeela shouted. Her hands clenched into fists as she faced her mother's warrior aspect. "You three have already decided you don't like the connection to the Den. You're never going to like any of *them* because they're one-faced. We could see it in your eyes last night. The disappointment that this place isn't whatever it is you search for."

Wondering what he had missed last night, Danyal glanced at the other people around the table, then at Yoshani—and realized he hadn't missed anything. Which meant Zeela's accusations might have been valid in the past but had no basis in the current truth. But he saw the way Glorianna, Lee, and Michael were studying her so intently, so he focused on her heart-core—and sat back, shocked.

Coating Zeela's stormy core was a bog full of poisoned air.

Michael gave him a "Do you feel it?" look. When he tipped his head in a subtle nod, the Magician returned his attention back to Zeela.

"We want to build a life here, so we're staying," Zeela shouted. "*You* can go back to Tryadnea and drift away again."

Morragen again. "How dare you!"

Zeela bared her teeth. "I dare because I'm a warrior, my sisters' protector. Like you, Morragen."

"And your own heart will break when you understand that it's the part of your sisters you *can't* protect."

"At least one of us will try!"

"That's enough," Morragen and Medusah said coldly.

"The two of you can still silence Zhahar and Sholeh and bend them to your will," Zeela said just as coldly. "But not me. Not anymore. I wish—"

Glorianna, Nadia, Michael, Lee, and Sebastian jumped to their feet and shouted, *"No!"*

Shaken, Danyal watched the other people in the room. Even the people who hadn't reacted so vigorously seemed to be holding their breaths.

Glorianna stared at Morragen and Zeela, her green eyes filled with fury. "Ephemera, hear me. This storm is fierce but *changes nothing.*"

Within moments, the sky darkened and thunder rumbled loud enough to rattle the windows. Moments after that, rain pounded the ground.

"I left the cottage's windows open!" Lynnea wailed before she, Caitlin, and Jeb hurried to shut the windows in the rest of the house, while Teaser and the Knife shut the kitchen's windows and door.

"This storm changes nothing," Belladonna said, extending her hand toward Nadia.

Nadia gripped her daughter's hand and repeated, "This storm changes nothing."

Belladonna held out her other hand. Sebastian gripped it. Looking at Morragen, he said, "As the Den's anchor, I want the border between Tryadnea and the Den to hold. I want the chance to get to know my new neighbors."

The rain stopped just as Jeb, Lynnea, and Caitlin returned to the kitchen.

Teaser opened the kitchen door, stared out the screen for a moment, then muttered, "Daylight. Can flowers swim?"

"Best we deal with what's outside later," Jeb said.

"Sit down," Belladonna said, her eyes still fixed on Morragen and Zeela.

Don't do it, Danyal thought, watching Zeela while trying to get a sense of the depth of Belladonna's anger. What he felt in that divided heart frightened him. *If you bring this storm down on your people, you will never forgive yourself.*

Morragen sat.

Lee said, "Please, Zeela. Do as she asks."

Zeela sat.

Belladonna released Nadia's hand. She tried to release Sebastian's too, but he held on until she looked at him.

Heat lightning and thorn trees. But that connection was enough to add the thunder of clean water to the thorn trees.

When Glorianna sat down, the others did too.

"You don't have to condemn your people to have something for yourself," Glorianna told Zeela.

Danyal considered the little he knew about Sholeh Zeela a Zhahar—the private things he'd seen when he'd packed up her possessions after Zeela had been knifed, and the story Yoshani and Michael had put together that could explain what had happened to the Tryad long ago.

"It's about heart, isn't it?" he asked gently. "That's why what you want you also fear. Because it's about heart."

"It usually is," Sebastian replied, looking at Lynnea.

Medusah came into view. She stared at each of them in turn but said nothing.

"Then I was right about the missing piece of the story," Michael said. "It's not just about us being able to accept you. It's about you having enough heart—enough courage—to accept us. If enough of you want a connection, *hope* for a connection to another piece of Ephemera, there are some of you who can take that hope and wind it into an anchor that will hold for a while. But that's an anchor attached to a rope that frays a little more every day. In order to build a solid bridge between your people and another, you need heart."

"Yes," Glorianna said softly, thoughtfully. "It's not enough to be physically present in a place; you have to *live* in the place. Interact with people. Build a life."

"You don't know what it's like to be an outsider," Medusah said bitterly.

Caitlin let out a pained laugh. "Oh, some of us do. Some of us know all too well what it's like to be different from everyone else around you."

I wish I could bring her to the Temple of Sorrow, Danyal thought. *I wish I could help her release some of that old pain.*

But she surprised him by smiling at Glorianna. "Now I'm learning that it takes time for the heart to embrace being accepted. And it takes time to learn that something doesn't have to be the way it's been." She ducked her head, as if shying away.

"What is it, Caitlin?" Nadia asked.

"It was just a thought," she mumbled.

When she didn't say anything else, Teaser gave her an elbow bump. "They're waiting for the thought."

She's someone he likes but doesn't think of sexually, which must be strange for him, Danyal thought. *Someone he pesters and teases — and wouldn't hesitate to defend. And that has changed him.*

"Well, Sholeh and I were talking last night," Caitlin said hesitantly.

Sholeh appeared long enough to frantically shake her head, but it was Zhahar who came into view, looking pale and sick.

"She explained about the connections Tryad made to hold Tryadnea to other landscapes, and that got me thinking about the journeys," Caitlin continued. "Every person who lives in Darling's Harbor takes a walk between the Sentinel Stones when they reach their majority. They spend weeks preparing for it, putting their gear together and making up a pack much like Michael used to carry for his wandering. Families celebrate, and there are both laughter and tears because no one knows if that person will ever come back. And then the people making the journey walk between the Stones to find out where they belong in the world."

Lee almost bounced out of his chair.

"So I was thinking that maybe some of the Tryad's troubles were caused because they weren't connected with places that had people interested in meeting them. Lots of the people in Ephemera don't meet many beyond their own."

"There's truth in that," Michael said.

Caitlin looked at Glorianna. "Maybe you could come back to Darling's Harbor with me, and we could talk to Peg and some of the others about having a few of the Tryad living and working in the village." She glanced nervously at Medusah. "Do any of your people have experience sailing or fishing? We have a lot of sailing and fishing."

"We have lakes and rivers, but not big water," Medusah replied.

"Doesn't mean some youngsters wouldn't be interested in learning a different skill," Jeb said. "Have to figure out how to fairly divide the work time."

Glorianna nodded. "Something that could be discussed, especially since it's reasonable to assume that each sibling in a Tryad would have different interests."

"Hate to say it, Auntie Nadia," Sebastian said, "but the people in Aurora might be a bit too prissy prig to welcome people as unique as the Tryad."

"They weren't nice to me the last time I went shopping in the village," Teaser said. Then he looked thoughtful. "But that might have been because the shopkeeper noticed the way his wife was smiling, and I'm pretty sure *he'd* never put that kind of smile on her face."

Lee groaned. "Teaser."

"What? I'm just saying."

"Aurora isn't the only possibility," Glorianna said.

"I don't think Dunberry has recovered enough from the deaths the Eater caused to be receptive, but Foggy Downs might be open to a few new residents," Michael said.

"What is the point of this?" Medusah asked. "Your border is breaking, and we'll be adrift again."

"It has faded, which isn't the same as breaking. Is breaking what you want?" Glorianna countered. "If Danyal is right and it's about heart, our accepting you will never be enough. You also have to accept us, have to be willing to look at someone who isn't like you and see more than someone who is a one-face. You have one young man who is a Bridge. With training, he would be able to connect Tryadnea with other parts of Ephemera. If there is one Tryad with that gift, there may be more. You may even have the equivalent of Landscapers among you—Tryad who maintain the balance of Light and Dark in Tryadnea. And you may have darker powers swimming in your bloodlines as well."

"I don't know what you mean," Medusah said.

"Yes," Belladonna replied, "you do know."

Medusah's face tightened but she didn't argue.

Silence. Danyal heard the ticking of a clock somewhere in the house.

"That's it, then?" the Knife finally asked. "The border gets fixed and everything is the way it was?"

Danyal saw gentle sadness and understanding in Yoshani's face when the holy man said, "The border will be fixed, but everything has changed. Hasn't it, Glorianna Dark and Wise?"

"One heart can change a landscape," Glorianna said softly. "And a heart can change and grow to the point where it no longer fits in a landscape. Sebastian and I will go back and repair the border when we're finished here. But despite how well it's marked, I don't think you'll find that border, Sholeh Zeela a Zhahar. I don't know if you'll ever find your way back to Tryadnea. So I'll remind you of Heart's Blessing. Let your heart travel lightly, because what you bring with you becomes part of the landscape."

"W-what does that mean?" Zhahar asked.

"It means Ephemera has responded to all the conflicting heart wishes—including yours," Glorianna said gently. "You didn't want to go back to your homeland. Now you can't."

Zephyra came into view, her eyes full of tears. "Why couldn't you give us a chance to understand?"

Danyal wasn't sure whom the question was meant for. He wasn't sure Zephyra knew either.

Choking on a sob, Zhahar ran out of the room.

"I'll go," Lynnea said before hurrying after the other woman.

"What is Zhahar supposed to do, Glorianna?" Lee asked.

"Her life, her journey, her choice," Glorianna replied.

"I got back." Lee removed his glasses and carefully rubbed his eyes. "When I needed to, I was able to get back home."

"But you don't quite belong here anymore. And you're not staying." Glorianna squeezed his hand. "So let's consider how to get you back to where you need to be."

"What about me?" Danyal asked.

"Your life, your journey, your choice," she said, looking into his eyes.

She was the guide and the monster the Shaman Council had hoped he would find—and it was time to make a choice. "What color are my eyes?"

Glorianna gave him a puzzled smile, but there was no hesitation before she said, "They're blue, with a ring of gray, but whether they look more blue or gray depends on your mood. They're like Michael's eyes in that way."

She saw the man as well as the Shaman, and the wonder of that opened a part of his heart he hadn't known was closed.

"I would like to return here, because you all have so much to teach me," Danyal said. "I would like to walk in Sanctuary again and spend time in the Den." He laughed softly at the dismayed sounds coming from Teaser. "But I need to return to Vision. I need to tell the other Shamans what I've learned about the enemy who has come among us. And I . . ." He looked at Glorianna Belladonna, Guide of the Heart. "And I would like to talk to you. Privately."

Glorianna shifted in her chair until she could see the Apothecary and the Knife. "And you?"

"If the shadowmen don't find a way to eliminate this enemy, we'll be pushed out of our own city," the Knife said. "So I want to go back."

The Apothecary nodded. "I could do some good with fresh-picked plants, but I need to be able to get home to do that good."

Glorianna nodded, then turned to Lee. "What did you bring?"

Standing up, Lee opened the blanket. "You've been able to make access points out of a stone bowl or a brick, so I thought these might work as an access point to Vision."

Nadia, Michael, and Caitlin looked at the gongs and chimes and shook their heads.

Glorianna stared at the gongs, then pushed her chair away from the table. "No. They're not an access point. Not for me."

"Lee, where did you get those?" Danyal asked.

"Glorianna?" Yoshani said with a hint of alarm that brought Michael to his feet.

Lee set one of the gongs upright and reached for its mallet. "Maybe you need to hear it in order to—"

"No!" Danyal shouted. Springing to his feet, he rushed around the table, sucking in a breath at the sudden pain in his hip. He grabbed Lee's wrist so hard the other man dropped the mallet. "Where did you get these?"

"From the temple at the Asylum," Lee replied. "They were the only things I could think of that were easy to carry and might resonate with Vision."

Danyal released Lee's wrist. Then he laid the gong down on the blanket, careful to prevent it from making any sound. "My fault. I've been trying to understand you, Lee, and understand how you connect with the world. It's not our way to share Shaman training with someone who isn't a Shaman."

All the color drained out of Lee's face. "What would have happened if I struck the gong here?"

"These gongs release sorrow," Danyal said quietly. "And there are people in this room who carry a great deal of sorrow. You could have opened a door in some hearts that I don't have enough skill to close. In a temple meant for such things, I could do it. But not here."

Sebastian swore. Michael looked grim.

Lee immediately looked at his sister. "Glorianna."

She reached out, almost touching the gong. "Even the Eater of the World had no secrets from Belladonna," she whispered. "At the end, just before I followed the music and found my way back to the Island in the Mist, I left a heart's hope plant for It. A tiny thread of Light." She looked up at Lee. "That landscape isn't closed anymore. Hard to find, even harder to reach, but it isn't closed."

"Lady of Light, have mercy on us," Michael said as he went to Glorianna and placed his hands on her shoulders.

Danyal felt the thorn trees wrapping around the house, felt the teasing prick of thorns against his skin. Not really there. Not yet.

He waved a hand over the gongs. "These are not a good choice for you." Ignoring the hot ache in shoulder and hip, he leaned over the table and held a hand over each wind chime. He picked up the largest of the three, the one that would have the deepest tones. "But this . . ." He moved his hand to make the chime ring. "This is joy."

He felt a change in the rest of the people in the room, but he kept his eyes on Glorianna. The Light within her made her skin glow.

"Where did this come from?" she asked.

"Until they are brought to The Temples, the chimes, like the gongs, are ordinary," Danyal replied. "But the Shamans breathe a measure of their gift into them in order to serve a specific purpose."

"Temples," she said, staring at the wind chime. "But there is also a Place of Light."

"A portion of The Temples is—or was—open to all who sought comfort or guidance. The rest is the Shamans' piece of the city. Within that is the piece where the masters live. It is removed from the rest of the city, but not unaware of it."

"A Place of Light," Yoshani said.

"And the access point for you, Danyal," Glorianna said.

"What about the others?" he asked.

She shook her head. "Do you agree, Magician?"

Michael hesitated. "If you're saying the sound of that chime is your way of reaching Vision, then you, Danyal, and Yoshani are the only ones whose music is in tune with the place."

"Does that mean the Shaman can get back but we can't?" the Knife asked.

"It means we found one connection between here and there," Glorianna replied. "It's more than we had an hour ago." She stood up and stepped away from the table. "I need some air. Shaman? Come find me in an hour." She pushed the screen door open and walked out.

"With all that rain, she'll be ankle deep in mud before she takes three steps," the Apothecary said.

A beat of silence. Then Lee said, "No, she won't."

Lee found Glorianna working in the flower beds farthest from the house.

"By rights, Zeela should be the one out here pulling weeds," he said.

"Would Zeela know which plants are weeds?" Glorianna asked.

After a moment's thought, he shook his head. "I don't think any of that Tryad knows much about plants, except what they think is pretty." He knelt beside his sister, immediately soaking the knees of his trousers. "Give me the other pail. I can't see well enough to tell the weeds from Mother's plantings, but I can clean up the stones."

Glorianna handed him the pail, then went back to pulling weeds.

"I've been acting like an ass since I got back," he said.

"A bit. Sebastian and Teaser figure it's because of the girl. Since they're incubi, it isn't surprising they would focus on the female. Mother thinks it's because you're scared."

"What about you? What do you think?"

"I've been thinking of Michael's mother and how, because the boundaries between landscapes aren't clearly defined in Elandar, she could be in a place where she didn't really belong. I've been thinking of how that must feel." She stopped working, studied him for a moment, then returned to the weeding. "If you were certain you were just visiting, that being here was temporary, you wouldn't need to push to make sure you didn't belong."

"I'm not trying to get away from all of you," Lee said.

She laughed quietly. "Yes, you are. And you should."

"Are those words coming from my sister or a Guide of the Heart?"

She hesitated, then said, "Not your sister."

Not his sister. Nothing he said right now would surprise her, so he spoke the truth. "I can't do what I used to do. I can't travel to check on the bridges connecting landscapes the way I used to. I can't see well enough to travel alone — and even if I could, I'm tired of that life."

"I agree," Glorianna said. "You should be traveling with a companion whenever you need or want to travel."

"What kind of companion are we talking about?" Would Zhahar be interested in traveling through the parts of Ephemera he knew? Would her sisters object to traveling?

Glorianna made a humming sound and bumped his arm. "Shift over."

"You didn't answer the question."

"A Guide *wouldn't* answer such a question, and as your sister, I'm disappointed that you can't figure that one out for yourself."

"You're starting to sound like Sebastian and Teaser."

"Then you don't want to know how much speculation Caitlin and Lynnea have indulged in about you and Zhahar."

Lee sighed. If he had a choice, he'd take incubi curiosity over inquisitive female relatives any day. Except Glorianna.

"I wasn't trying to hurt you," he said after they'd worked in silence for a few minutes. "Using the gongs in the temple helped me, so I didn't think they would hurt you."

"I know."

"Do you?" He gathered up a few more stones, then shifted slightly to reach another part of the bed.

"Yes, Lee, I do." She hesitated. "The gong. It *was* an access point, but you wouldn't have wanted to see the landscape I would have found."

A dark landscape, no doubt. Maybe even a piece of the landscape that trapped the Eater of the World? No, that wasn't likely unless a piece of Vision had already been part of that landscape. But if there *was* a dark landscape in Vision now that could resonate with Belladonna ...

"Has Michael said anything about me?" Lee asked abruptly. "About what he hears in me?"

"You're a bit out of tune with the Den and Aurora. Have some sharp notes you didn't have before. You've been to a part of Ephemera the rest of us haven't seen, so that's not a surprise to us and shouldn't be a surprise to you."

"But what he's hearing is me? He's sure of that?"

"What else would he be hearing?"

"Wizards. A Dark Guide."

She eased back to sit on her heels, so he did the same.

"They hurt me, Glorianna. They got inside my head and ... hurt me. They wanted to use me to get to you, and when the words and whispers didn't work, they used the drugs and eyedrops." He swallowed hard. "They kept saying that if I tried to get back, they would be close by and would come back with me. To get to you, the person who had revealed what they are. What if all of this was a way to reach your landscapes, to reach you?"

"They let you heal, let a Shaman keep them away from you, in the hope you might lead them back here?"

"Listen to me. It worked, didn't it? I'm here."

"You're here because the Shaman who was protecting you disappeared and was almost killed, and you had the good sense not to stay where the wizards could find you. You got back here because you met Zhahar and realized the significance of that triangle of grass that had appeared in my garden. You brought people with you who have made me wonder some things about the city of Vision, but what you didn't bring were any wizards. And I would know if there was a Dark Guide in my landscapes."

The relief produced by her words made him dizzy, but he had to push. "How would you know?"

"Ephemera?" Glorianna said sweetly. "How would you tell me if a wizard besides Sebastian was nearby?"

Moments later, Lee scrambled away from the flower bed and landed on his ass. "Daylight!"

"How easily do you think wizards and Dark Guides are going to be able to hide if stinkweed and turd plants announce their presence?" Glorianna asked.

"Make those things go away," he gasped. He waited. "Did you make them go away?"

"Yes, but that odor certainly lingers. We should work in another part of the garden."

They picked up their pails, dumped them in the barrows Nadia was using as holding places, and moved upwind.

"That stink isn't going to blow in the house, is it?" Lee asked. He didn't want to think about how his mother would respond to *that*.

"Give me some credit," Glorianna muttered.

Not too many stones or weeds in that part of the garden. Of course, he and Sebastian had cleared this patch a few hours ago.

"That young Bridge needs a teacher," she said.

"Maybe some of the instructors at the school survived." Not likely, but there *were* some fully trained Bridges who hadn't been at the school when the Eater attacked.

"Do you think any of those instructors would work with a Tryad?"

"Why wouldn't . . ." He stopped. Considered. "They would see a demon and not a unique species of human."

"Opportunities and choices," she said quietly. "What opportunities and choices are you considering, Lee?"

He stopped working and said just as quietly, "At the Asylum, I was a different kind of Bridge. Some of those people weren't mentally ill; they were just in the wrong place. As much as crossing a bridge in our part of Ephemera can be a risk, as much as we don't always like the landscape where we end up, we know our hearts brought us to that place. I helped a few people in the Asylum cross over to another landscape. I'd like to help more and work more directly with the people crossing over. And, yes, I would like to help that young Bridge learn to use his gift. And I'd like to do it in a place that wasn't so damn hot."

"Something to think about," Glorianna said. She stood up. "It's time to talk to Danyal. If Zhahar wanders this way, have her help you with the stones."

Alone, Lee continued clearing out the stones made from anger—and wondered if he was also clearing out the ground inside himself.

Danyal took a dozen long, slow steps down the path leading away from Nadia's house. The ground was damp, but it hadn't rained enough to turn the path muddy. A very confined storm.

He turned and walked back toward the house, feeling the muscles in his burned hip stretch and slowly warm up with the movement. He stopped, rolled his shoulders to warm and stretch those muscles, then turned and repeated the steps—and tried to ignore the fierce itching that had started this morning beneath the skin that was peeling.

The third time he turned back toward the house, Glorianna stood at the end of the path, watching him.

Beautiful woman. Powerful woman. Dangerous woman.

"I'm trying to decide what you're doing," Glorianna said.

"I can walk only for so long before the hip hurts and I need to sit," he replied. "I can sit for only so long before the muscles need to work. I've already walked from Lee's cottage to your mother's house today, so I didn't want to walk far." And he'd thought the paths in the woods would be too muddy for him to walk far.

"You could have paced the length of the yard."

"I mean no offense, Glorianna, but your mother's house felt too crowded."

She laughed. "Shaman, right now, my mother's house *is* too crowded." Her green eyes studied him. "Let's walk while you tell me about Vision."

She fell into step beside him, walked the dozen steps, stopping exactly where he had, and turned.

"In the city of Vision, you can find only what you can see," he said.

"Does that also mean you can see only what you want to find?"

He stumbled. There was no obstacle on the path, but he stumbled. "It's the same thing."

"Is it?"

"Are you saying the Shamans don't want to find this evil that has come to our city?"

"Maybe you shouldn't be the ones looking." She waved a hand dismissively. "That's a conversation for another time. Tell me about *your* city. The Vision *you* know."

"I wasn't expecting the heat in the southern part of the city. Can't say I like it much. I grew up in one of the northern communities, close to the mountains. Summers were hot there too, but there was also snow and crisp, invigorating air."

???

"But not in the summertime," Glorianna said.

"When I first arrived at the Asylum, there were days when the heat was so stifling, so oppressive, I'd wish—"

"Not. In the. Summertime," she repeated firmly.

He blinked at her, a little hurt by her tone. Then he thought about what he'd said—and what he'd been about to say—and could guess what Nadia would say if it began snowing over her house.

"In the summertime, we cooled off by going to the swimming hole or sitting on a flat rock with our feet dangling in a stream. We enjoyed snow *in the wintertime.*"

!!!

He felt Ephemera's currents of power swirl around him a moment longer before the world wandered off.

"Is it going to be like this from now on?" he asked as they resumed walking.

"Shamans are the voice of the world, are they not?" she replied. "But like most Landscapers in this part of Ephemera or Magicians in Elandar, most Shamans provide balance between the currents of Light and Dark—and it sounds like you have some of the ill-wishing and luck-bringing ability mixed in. But you, Danyal, are Voice-guide. Something in you was willing to be more, to be a true voice for the world. So, yes, it's always going to be like this now."

"I don't have any training for this."

"Neither did Michael. He knew about the wild child, felt its presence, knew he could make things happen. But the response wasn't as . . . direct . . . as it is now. So he's learning too."

"But he has you to teach him." Feeling her hesitation, he added, "That's not a way of asking if your commitment to Michael is as strong as it seems. I know it is. But I can't help feeling a little envy that he doesn't have to figure this out on his own."

"And you do because ... ?"

"I have to go back." Danyal sighed and stopped walking. "I don't want to. I've found something here among your pieces of the world that my heart has been searching for. But I have to go back."

"Doing one doesn't mean you can't have the other."

"How do we destroy the Dark Guides, Glorianna?"

"How do you cleanse all dark feelings from the human heart?"

"We can't."

She nodded. "You can't. Ephemera manifests what is in the heart. So it shaped the Guides in response to the cries of many hearts that recognized they needed someone to stand between them and the world. The Dark Guides were also shaped in response to a need. They have walked in the world for a very long time, Danyal. When I took a chance and performed Heart's Justice outside the walls of Wizard City, I did it to save Sebastian. And I did it to take Wizard City out of the world. But in doing so, I stripped away the human mask from *all* the Dark Guides."

"So it's possible one of them arrived in Vision years ago?"

"It's possible one crossed over a resonating bridge and found your city. Alone, he could have influenced hearts, helped those who fed the Dark currents. But his efforts were always balanced by the Shamans."

"How do you know this Dark Guide is male?"

"Their females have no ability to wear a human mask. They're feral breeders who had to be hidden from people," she replied. "Wizards are always male, and the Dark Guides are the elite among the wizards."

"I see," he said softly.

"Now, with the Dark Guides exposed and the remaining wizards cut off from their stronghold—"

"They found a bit of rot within the city that matched their own. Because they wanted to find that rot, they found the city."

"Most likely." Glorianna sighed. "Danyal, your city has already changed. The Shamans have to change with it. You have to learn to see the enemy, because they can see you. You can hide pieces of your city, but you can't hide the city. Another part of Ephemera is aware of you—a part that has people who understand how to connect two pieces of the world with a bridge. The wizards have found you. Now you have to decide what to do."

Danyal shook his head, not in denial but in weary frustration. "I was sent to the Asylum because the Shaman Council consulted bone readers and fortune tellers and concluded that I had the best chance of finding what we needed. A madman and a teacher. A guide . . ." He hesitated. "And a monster. I found them, but I don't see how that has changed anything."

"It changed everything, Shaman. It altered your landscape." Glorianna linked her arm through his. "Come on. Sebastian and I need to check Tryadnea's border. Then we'll all sit down and decide what is going to be done."

Chapter Twenty-seven

It wasn't any aspect of Sholeh Zeela a Zhahar who came to help him clean up the stones in his mother's garden. It was Morragen Medusah a Zephyra who knelt beside him, watched him for a moment, and then began picking out the same kind of stone.

"How did these get here if your mother doesn't want them?" Zephyra asked.

"Strength makes stone," Lee replied. "And anger makes stone." He held one up before tossing it into the pail. "These stones were made by anger."

"Zeela's anger. And mine."

"Yep. I guess most people in the world don't make the connection between the feelings their hearts send out and their physical troubles, but when you live around a Landscaper, you learn fast—and you learn to fix what you can."

"Our reservations about Zhahar being involved with a man of single aspect aren't a judgment about you."

"You mean if I were one aspect of a Tryad, I would be considered acceptable for a mate, but being a man of single aspect, I can't be trusted?"

"We didn't say that."

"You didn't use those words," Lee agreed. "But that's what you meant. What happens when Tryad mates with single aspect? Are the children Tryad? Triplets with individual bodies? One body with three personalities? A higher percentage of insanity? Are they ostracized for being different?"

"We *never* speak of this!"

He couldn't tell their voices apart yet, but he knew he was now talking to Morragen or Medusah. Probably both. "Just wondering why you're so opposed to Zhahar and me finding out if there can be anything between us."

He thought for a moment. Wasn't his business, but it kept bothering him that it had been *Zeela* who wanted to walk away from her people. "Did you know Zeela was wounded recently? Wounded badly enough that the injury was showing through on Zhahar?"

The woman beside him sucked in a breath. "She didn't tell us. None of them told us."

"Stabbed," he said, before she asked. "In the side. The wound bled a lot, but the knife didn't slice into any internal organs. She was just getting on her feet when Danyal disappeared and we made the decision to run from the wizards."

"To get *you* away from the wizards."

"I may have been the one the wizards wanted, but their lackey was holding a knife on Sholeh, not me."

Tense silence.

"I could have left the Asylum, Morragen Medusah. I could have gotten to a landscape where any enemy coming with me wouldn't have survived for long. But as I got to know Zhahar, I recognized the significance of the triangle of grass in my sister's garden, and I understood how much it meant to Zhahar and her sisters to keep Tryadnea connected to another piece of Ephemera. I had the means of doing that, so we helped each other get home. You can think what you want about that."

When there was no response, he rose. "May your heart travel lightly, because what you bring with you becomes part of the landscape. Sholeh Zeela a Zhahar wasn't happy in Vision. They were surviving, and I think if they had allowed Danyal to know what they were, they would have had an easier time of it."

"One person's acceptance doesn't mean acceptance by everyone," she said.

"Depends on the person." He carried the pail over to the barrow and emptied it.

When he set it down, Zephyra called out, "There are still more stones among the flowers."

"I know, but they aren't mine to clear," he replied. Then he walked away.

Glorianna tapped Sebastian's shoulder. He signaled the demon cycle to slow down before he turned his head toward her.

"Let me off at the end of the street," she said.

"Any particular reason?"

"Several. One being that I need some time to think."

"But you are going to be sharing these thoughts, aren't you?"

She heard the tension in his voice, felt the resonance of it in his heart. The last time she'd gone off alone, she hadn't expected to find her way back to friends and family. Even so, she waited until they reached the end of the Den's main street.

"I'm going to Sanctuary," she said. "I'd like you to ask Michael, Yoshani, and Danyal to meet me there. Tell Danyal to bring the wind chimes."

He studied her. "Tell those three? No one else?"

"No one else."

"Why?"

"I can't explain it yet. I'm not sure yet."

"Yes, you are. You may not want to explain it, but you know why you're going to Sanctuary."

She kissed his cheek. "Opportunities and choices. What happens to the city of Vision is going to depend on opportunities and choices."

"What about the border?"

"It's solid. Checking on it was an excuse to get away from the house. Morragen wants to get back to her people, and she needs to get back. She has an enemy there. Maybe more than one. Escort her to the border and watch her cross over."

"Travel lightly, Glorianna," he said.

Smiling, she walked away from him. Then she took the step between here and there—and breathed in the Light of Sanctuary.

She walked past the guesthouse and glanced toward the small island that split a stream—the island that had resonated with Lee. Michael's aunt Brighid led a couple of people toward the guesthouse. The older woman smiled at Glorianna and raised a hand in greeting, but continued on.

Glorianna wandered over the grounds a few minutes more, then settled on the bench in front of a pond and watched the koi, letting the water and the movement of those graceful flashes of gold wash away troubling thoughts.

"Ephemera, hear me," she whispered.

???

Closing her eyes, she recalled the sound of that wind chime. The sound of Light.

not yours

"I know. It's the Place of Light that resonates with Voiceguide."

yes

"Can I visit there, like I visit the Music's landscapes?"

She felt Ephemera's currents of power gently flowing around her and beyond her. She waited until the world returned with an answer.

visit

So she could help Danyal return home. And she could help him explain to the other Shamans what had happened to their city. She could do that much. The rest would be up to Danyal—and Lee.

She was thinking of going to the guesthouse for a glass of water and something to eat when Michael, Danyal, and Yoshani hurried toward her. Each carried a wrapped bundle and had a daypack slung over one shoulder.

"Hey-a," she said, smiling as she linked her arm through Michael's. "We have some things to discuss."

I'm not ready to leave this place or these people, Danyal thought as he watched Glorianna unwrap each wind chime and lift it to hear the chime sing. Michael and Yoshani smiled in response to the sound of each chime in turn, a sign that their hearts were touched by the joy that flowed out with the sound. But Glorianna looked more and more puzzled.

"Is there something about the sound that bothers you, Glorianna Dark and Wise?" Yoshani asked.

She pointed to each wind chime. "Restful. Peaceful. Joyful. But not an access point."

Danyal felt an odd relief, swiftly followed by shame. The Shamans needed the knowledge he could bring back to them. The people in the city needed whatever help he could bring with him. Would he ever forgive himself if something happened to Kanzi, Nalah, or the baby because he did something that delayed his return?

"But it *was* an access point, yes?" Michael asked. "Back in Aurora?"

Glorianna handed Michael one of the chimes. "You ring them." After he set each one to chiming, she shook her head. "Yoshani?" She shook her head again after he rang each chime. "Danyal?"

He began with the one that had the brightest sound and ended with the one he had picked up in her mother's house, the one he thought would help her heart remember joy.

Glorianna nodded and pointed to each of the chimes. "Restful. Peaceful. Place of Light. It's not just the wind chime. We have those here in Sanctuary, and plenty of people hang them around their homes. It's a wind chime made in Vision in the hands of a Shaman." She gave Danyal a sharp look. "Or perhaps in the hands of a particular Shaman. These other wind chimes are just chimes—pretty sounds that lift the spirit. But *that* one is an access point."

"How can that be?" Danyal protested. "I've walked the Asylum grounds with this one many times and nothing unusual happened."

"Perhaps unusual things happened all around you," Glorianna replied gently, "but there was no one who recognized their significance. Or maybe it was your resonance combined with Lee's that demanded a new way to express heart wishes."

Voice-guide maker

Danyal jerked, setting the chime ringing again.

"Maker," Glorianna said, nodding.

"I can use this to travel to other places?" he asked.

"I'm thinking that chime takes you back to the place it came from," Michael said.

"But only you and whoever takes that step with you between here and there," Glorianna added.

Danyal closed his eyes. His heart trembled.

Just tired, he thought. *Just heart weary and tired.*

"Shaman?" Glorianna said quietly.

Shaman. The title, not the man. He opened his eyes and replied, "Guide."

Her smile told him she understood perfectly why he used her title too.

"It's time to go," she told him. Then she turned to Michael. "This may take a few days, but I'll be back, Magician."

"If you lose your way, just listen for the music." Michael kissed her and stepped back.

"Should we take all the wind chimes?" Yoshani asked.

"Yes," Glorianna replied. "These chimes belong to Vision."

Two of the chimes were wrapped into a bundle Yoshani could easily carry. Danyal held the one that would take him home.

Glorianna linked one hand with Yoshani, then linked her other hand with his.

"Ephemera," she called softly. "Hear me."

When she squeezed his hand, Danyal set the chime to ringing. Within seconds, the ground in front of them filled with light, and he could smell the spice trees that grew in the Shamans' compound.

"Now," she whispered.

The three of them took a step. They took another step, and Danyal's breath hitched as he stared at the building where the Shaman Council met and also mentored the older students.

Glorianna released his hand and smiled. "Welcome home."

Lee turned his back to the kitchen door and windows, removed his dark glasses, and rubbed his eyes. As if *that* would change what he'd just heard. Putting the glasses back on, he looked at Michael. "She's gone? Glorianna is *gone*?"

Michael nodded. "She left with Danyal and Yoshani. They're going to the inner temples or whatever it's called where the Shamans live."

Lee's hands curled into fists. "Guardians and Guides, man. Why didn't you go with her?"

"I couldn't."

"No one but Yoshani and Danyal could go with her and reach Vision through that access point," Sebastian said.

Hurried footsteps. Some coming toward the kitchen from outdoors; others from the front rooms of the house.

"Now what?" Nadia asked.

"Lee?" Zhahar said.

Tryad. One who is three. Three who are one.

"You and Sebastian are the other two sides of Glorianna's triad now," Lee shouted at Michael. "She shouldn't be traveling without at least one of you."

"She felt she was ready—" Michael began.

"I agree with Lee," Sebastian interrupted as he hitched a hip on the kitchen table. "Glorianna has plenty of heart, but the Light isn't all that good at self-defense. Maybe that will change over time, but that's the truth of it now. And Belladonna can defend anything she pleases, but it's not always easy for her to let go of that power over the landscapes. After all, she answered to no one in the place she created for the Eater of the World."

"Which is exactly why one of you should be with her!" Lee roared.

"It wasn't our choice," Michael said tightly.

"Whether Glorianna has any help this time isn't the Magician's choice or mine," Sebastian said. "It's yours, Lee. That's what Glorianna meant when she talked about opportunities and choices before she went to Sanctuary. If you think we need to be there, then figure out how we get there."

"I—" Lee braced a hand on the table. There was a way. Or there used to be.

He walked out of the kitchen and across the lawn. He crossed the footbridge that was nothing more than a footbridge over the creek at the back of Nadia's personal gardens. Then he closed his eyes and extended one hand and pictured the little island.

You were a piece of Ephemera that came from my sister's heart. She gave you to me because you resonated with my heart. Currents of Dark and Light. They flow through Glorianna Belladonna and me. Different and the same. She is different. And she is the same. She is my sister. In the Dark, in the Light, she is still my sister. You are a piece of my sister's heart that used to answer to me. I need you to answer again. Please hear me, Ephemera. Please.

Nothing.

He rocked forward—and his fingers brushed against the bark of a tree.

Hardly daring to believe—and knowing that he could lose everything if he *didn't* believe—Lee pressed one hand against the tree as he shifted his feet and stretched out his other hand. When he touched the other tree that flanked the path on his island, he stepped between them and knew by the feel of the ground beneath his feet and the different scent to the air that he was on the island.

It was his again.

He slipped off the glasses, then put them back on and wished he'd brought the walking stick and the slouchy hat. The trees softened the light, making it too dark with the glasses, but his eyes were too sensitive without them. No matter. With one hand in front of him and one out to the side, he made his way to the center of the island where the fountain provided him with fresh water.

Lee drank, savoring the taste of water that came from Sanctuary.

"Lee?"

"Lee!"

He made his way back to the edge of the island. Michael and Sebastian were a few paces from him, searching for something they couldn't see.

Watching them made him think of something Danyal said about Shamans being able to remove parts of Vision from sight. When he shifted his island, it existed in that other landscape on the bridge of his will, and *he* decided whether it was visible to the people in that other landscape.

It seemed his island had something in common with Vision after all.

"Lee!" All three voices of Sholeh Zeela a Zhahar.

She almost walked into him as he stepped off the island.

"Daylight!" Sebastian snapped as he strode toward Lee. "Are you *trying* to upset everyone?"

"No," Lee replied, keeping his voice calm and quiet. "I didn't intend to upset anyone. We can use the island to travel to Vision. We just have to figure out how to get to the part of the city we need."

*   *   *

Glorianna wandered the wide stone pathways. Strong currents of Light, as she expected in the part of The Temples where the Shamans nurtured those currents. There were also threads of Dark currents. Those, too, were necessary in any landscape.

Different architecture. Different taste in the air. She could almost believe food was seasoned by holding the bowl under the spice trees.

Danyal, Yoshani, and the Shaman Council sat outside in the shade. It wasn't prejudice against her gender; two Council members were women. She had the impression that the Shamans didn't wish to trouble her with discussion. So she wandered, staying in sight so that Yoshani especially wouldn't worry.

And she thought about how to find a darkness the Shamans couldn't see.

"I could get us back to the Asylum, but that's a full day's journey or more from The Temples," Lee said, bracing his hands on the kitchen table. "And there's no way to know what we might find at the Asylum. Hopefully, the wizards left the people alone, but they might be waiting there in case Danyal or I return."

"They sent Clubs after you," the Knife said. "Whatever they intended when this began, I think they want you dead now. You can tell too many people what they are."

"So can the two of you," Lee replied, turning his head toward the Knife and the Apothecary.

"True. And other shadowmen will listen to us, especially those who have had their streets disappear in a darkness they can't see. But the Shamans will listen to someone like you, and they speak for the world—and to the world. That's a power those wizards don't have. Isn't that so?"

"Yes, that's so. But I don't know how to work that to our advantage," Lee said. He looked across the table. "Mother?"

Nadia shook her head. "A Landscaper keeps her pieces of the world balanced so that it reflects the resonance of the hearts living there. If a place turns darker—or lighter—than her own heart's resonance, she has to let that landscape go, let it be taken up by someone else."

"If there is someone else," Sebastian said. "But so many

Landscapers were killed by the Eater, and their landscapes must be ripe for the taking. Why didn't the wizards take over one of those?"

"They may be trying to turn some places into dark landscapes that they control," Nadia admitted. "But Ephemera is more unpredictable these days, so maybe the wizards *can't* take over."

"If Ephemera lets dark or dangerous *things* grow in wizard-controlled places, ordinary people will flee if they're aware of the bridges," Lee said, turning all those thoughts over and over. "And that will leave the wizards in a landscape they control, but it doesn't leave them with *people* to control."

"The wild child learns from the Guides," Michael said. "What's to say that the bridges out of places that have reached a certain level of darkness still work? In this part of Ephemera, if the stationary bridges stop working, that leaves the resonating bridges."

"And if that resonating bridge takes you to a place that doesn't have these bridges?" the Knife asked.

"You can walk or ride or make your way to a port and buy passage on a ship sailing in the direction you want to go," Lee replied. Then his attention focused on Zhahar, who stood near the table but hadn't been participating. Probably because her mother *was* sitting at the table for this meeting. The a Zephyra Tryad had returned to Tryadnea, but whatever they had found had brought them back to the Den in a hurry.

He had a bad feeling it had something to do with Zhahar.

He heard the buzzing that meant Zhahar and her sisters were having a fierce discussion with each other.

"Something you want to add?" he asked.

Zhahar froze a moment before Sholeh came into view. "Scattering seeds. Michael said the world is learning from the Guides, and it's the *world*, so what if this was a kind of seed scattering?"

"The wizards spread themselves through the world to poison other parts of Ephemera?" Lynnea said, hugging herself.

Before Sebastian could rise and go to her, Teaser threw an arm around her shoulders.

Lee stared at Sholeh. "What if the wizards weren't the ones who did the scattering?" He felt a fizz of excitement when she nodded. "The number of wizards to Landscapers was pretty much even in this part of Ephemera until the Eater changed the balance by killing the Landscapers and Bridges—and Glorianna restored the balance by taking Wizard City out of the world. The wizards have the lightning, which is a deadly weapon, and even if the Landscapers know what they are now . . ."

"Not all the surviving Landscapers believe the wizards are a danger to them," Nadia said, sounding bitter.

"And not all wizards *are* a danger to them," Michael countered, tipping his head toward Sebastian. "But I think I'm following Lee's tune here. Ephemera manifests the human heart, but it also *wants* guidance. If the wizards keep destroying Landscapers when they find them, who knows how much of the world will be in turmoil? Any one of you might know only a double handful of places, but those places are located all over the world. Hearts fearful of an enemy that might gather again and strike down the rest of their kind. Or enough hearts fearful of the loss of the Landscapers. Can't move the Landscapers, but it seems like the wild child can make or break bridges on its own."

"If it can't relocate the hearts that keep it balanced, Ephemera scatters the dark hearts that are a threat," Lee said.

"And makes them a threat in more places," Sebastian pointed out.

"How does any of this help us get back to Vision and stop those bastards?" the Knife demanded.

"It's the nature of Vision that has gotten in the way of you holding on to your piece of the city," Lee replied. "And it's gotten in the way of the Shamans protecting the city. There are a lot of shadowmen and only a handful of wizards. If you don't let them change your pieces of the city, they'll be there trying, but they'll be in sight."

The Knife made a frustrated sound and moved away from the table.

"Pretty words," the Apothecary said, "but they're still just crap."

"No, they aren't," Michael replied. "One of my landscapes is a place called Foggy Downs. A dark landscape because of the number of Dark currents that flow through that part of Ephemera. And yet it's not a dark landscape, because the people keep it on this side of the Light. Generations of them living out their lives in that village and not knowing the importance of being there until Glorianna saw the village and the people and explained it to all of us. If your part of Vision is what you want, you can hold it against the wizards, be an anchor for it like Sebastian is the anchor for the Den. You can get back what they've taken. I'm not saying it won't be a fight, and I'm not saying all of you will live through the fighting, but you can take it back."

Silence.

"Maybe this cleared the air some, but it doesn't get us any closer to Glorianna," Sebastian said.

"What do you need?" Sholeh asked.

"We need a resonance," Lee replied. "Some kind of connection."

"When you found me in the bonelovers' landscape, you didn't know me," Caitlin said.

"But I had a tail of your hair," Lee said. "That provided enough of a link so that I felt it when you needed help."

Kobrah stepped forward. "Does this resonance need to be some *thing*, or can it be a person?"

"A person would be better. Do you know someone at The Temples?"

"The Voice," she said, hunching her shoulders. "I know The Voice."

Chapter Twenty-eight

L ee stowed his pack and Michael's in the wooden shed
Jeb had built a few years ago. It wasn't big, but it held
all his gear when he was traveling, and had plenty of
shelves for jars of food and other cooking supplies. And
while it didn't have heat, he could spread his sleeping bag
on the floor in bad weather instead of getting wet.

Now it would hold all the gear for several people who
hoped Kobrah's memory of someone called The Voice
would resonate strongly enough to bring them near the access point where Glorianna, Danyal, and Yoshani crossed
over to Vision.

Even though he wouldn't be gone long, he closed the
shed's door out of habit before he strode back to the spot he
thought of as the island's front door—that space between
two trees where the path into the island's center began.

As he stepped off the island to get the next packs, he
noticed the woman hurrying to reach him before he disappeared again. The red hair stood out, even with his diminished eyesight.

"Sholeh," he said, offering nothing and asking for nothing.

"We want to help."

She sounded breathless, but he couldn't tell if that was
because she rushed to reach him or was nervous about being seen talking to him. It was clear to everyone that there
was a serious problem between the mothers and daughters,
but none of the Tryad were willing to discuss the reason

Zeela had tried to sabotage the border between Tryadnea and the Den.

Of course, he didn't think any of the Tryad realized Zeela had been influenced by another heart.

"Please," Sholeh whispered.

"Grab that pack." He pointed to one he hoped she could carry. If she couldn't, Zeela would lend some muscle.

Settling the strap of one pack over his shoulder, he picked up another and held out his hand—and felt her hesitate, saw her body turn as if checking to make sure no one saw her touch him.

"Maybe you should go back to the house," he said.

"No."

He huffed out a breath. "Then you're going to have to grow enough spine to take my hand, because you're not going to get on the island any other way."

She hesitated a moment too long, but when he turned away, she grabbed his hand.

He stepped up on the island and heard her gasp as he—and her hand—disappeared.

"Take a step up, like you're climbing a stair," he said.

She did. When she appeared, he drew her a couple steps farther along the path, then released her hand.

He headed for the shed. The island wasn't big, but the trees and plantings kept areas of it private. "Say what you came to say."

"We want to help," Sholeh said, puffing as she struggled to keep up. "Kobrah trusts Zhahar more than anyone else here. And when I was attending school in Vision, I found a map of the bazaar and the part of The Temples that is open to everyone, so I can help you find the inner parts of The Temples. And Zeela can help if there's a fight."

And all of you really want to get away from Morragen Medusah a Zephyra. Why? "Tell me why Zeela tried to break the border. Then we can talk about your helping."

He heard that buzzing that indicated the sisters were having a furious discussion. Letting them fight it out, he opened the shed's door and went in to store the two packs. When he turned, she was blocking the door, and he could tell by the way she held the pack with one hand that he wasn't dealing with Sholeh anymore.

"It wasn't just me," Zeela said. "It was all three of us. But

Sholeh would be more wounded than me by our mothers' wrath, and if Zhahar were blamed . . ." Her voice caught.

"Why?" he asked quietly.

"Because Zhahar loves you," she replied, heat and temper in her voice now. "She loves you, and we *want* her to be able to love you. But Sholeh and I didn't want to die! If we were somewhere the Tryad couldn't reach, if we were somewhere our laws didn't have to be upheld . . . And why should that terrible law be upheld? Why should two aspects be condemned because the third has a chance to be loved?"

He understood the words, but he couldn't make sense of them. What *was* clear to him was that Zeela had her own reasons for taking the blame for the border fading, regardless of whether she was contaminated by someone else. "What law? What are you talking about?"

"We are Tryad," Sholeh replied, her voice trembling. "We are one who is three and three who are one. But if an aspect loves deeply enough to become a . . . wife . . . of a man of single aspect, by law the Tryad must be merged so the three are truly one."

A chill went through Lee. "But you're not three facets of a single personality. You're three people, three *sisters*, who share a physical core but are distinct in every other way."

"Some things remain," Sholeh said. "Knowledge, mostly. Information. Sometimes physical skills, to some degree."

He shook his head. "You're talking about killing two of your sisters in order to have a man. That's . . . Guardians and Guides, do you realize how cruel that is?"

"Of course we do!" Zeela shouted. "But it's Tryad law, set down generations ago."

"Why?" he demanded. "Because long ago two sisters had the same man for a lover and ended up killing or destroying the third when they fought over him?"

"That's one reason. Another is that your kind considers us an abomination, a freak of nature at best. At worst, we're a breed of demon."

"My kind? So far *my kind* has made every effort to welcome you."

"Limited exceptions," she snapped.

He scrubbed his fingers over his head. "So what happens? You have sex with a man who isn't Tryad and wake up the next morning as one person?"

Sholeh came back into view, shaking her head. "Some of us have the magic to merge aspects. The Medusah aspect of the a Zephyra Tryad is one of them. But the sisters who are going to be absorbed can't fight the merging. If they do, the merging doesn't always take properly." She wrapped her arms around herself. "Sometimes they become like single-aspect people who have more than one personality but only one body. We saw one at the Asylum before Shaman Danyal came to be Keeper. At first we thought it was a damaged Tryad, but it wasn't."

"What happened to that inmate?"

"They died. One of them got angry and stabbed another, and they all died."

Bits and pieces of information shifted into a new pattern. "One-face," Lee said grimly. "You use it as an insult for those of single aspect, but it was originally a label, a condemnation, of a Tryad who sacrificed her sisters for a lover."

Zhahar came into view. "It still is."

He moved closer to her. "Why didn't you tell me any of this?"

"I told you being with you was taboo."

"Yeah. You did. I guess for someone who has spent half his life around the Den of Iniquity, 'taboo' doesn't have much meaning without context." His throat tightened. "But I understand now, and I'm sorry my actions put you in the position of thinking you had to choose."

He couldn't see the tears in her eyes, but he saw the shine of them on her cheeks.

"I love you enough to consider it. Even between Tryads, there are few partnerships like your people have. There is loyalty to the children produced from a mating—sometimes—but not being able to get away from our siblings doesn't mean we don't feel all the wants and jealousies and other things people feel. Love doesn't touch any of us often. Maybe that's why we're punished for finding something the rest can't have. I do love you, Lee. I love you enough that I would break with my sisters if I could."

He leaned forward and brushed his lips against hers. "And I love you enough to step back and let you go. I almost lost my sister, so I know how it feels. I'm not going to be the reason you lose yours."

"But . . ."

"No, Zhahar." He took the pack resting on the ground beside her and set it inside the shed. "Come on. No doubt there are supplies and people piling up, and we need to get moving."

"It's getting late in the day," she whispered.

"Here. Could be dawn in Vision, or it could be the middle of the night." He nudged her out of the way, slipped out of the shed, and strode for the island's "front door."

"Hey-a!" Sebastian yelled. "Lee!"

Lee stood between the trees and sighed. *Oh yeah. Plenty of people out there.* Michael and Sebastian. The Apothecary and the Knife with his horse. Kobrah. And—wasn't this going to make the whole thing sweet?—Morragen Medusah a Zephyra. His mother, Jeb, Caitlin, Lynnea, and Teaser were also milling around, but they weren't going on this journey.

"Stop yelling," he said as he stepped off the island. "I was just getting something else settled."

"What . . . ?" Sebastian looked over Lee's shoulder and lowered his voice. "Oh. Really? Now?"

"Not that." Lee closed his eyes and counted to ten. Then he opened his eyes and shifted a little closer to his cousin. "Let's just say some things have been decided, and the a Zephyra Tryad doesn't have to worry about their daughters anymore."

"Oh."

He found some comfort in the regret and understanding in Sebastian's voice.

"Let's get the rest of this gear on the island. If I bring you and Michael onto the island, you can reach over and bring the others. I know the Knife wants to bring his horse, but I'm not sure how to get the animal to step up in a way that will put it on the island."

"Jeb suggested planks. Bring them on the island, then set them down at the edge. He thinks it will work like a common bridge."

"It might. Give it a try. I want a word with Mother before we go."

Brushing past Zhahar, aware now why her mothers watched him so closely, Lee stepped onto the island, then brought Michael and Sebastian over before he returned to the land around Nadia's house.

"I'll give the boys a hand with these planks," Jeb said. "Travel lightly, Lee."

"Thanks, Jeb."

"You have everything you need?" Nadia asked. "The eyedrops?"

He nodded. "All stored away." He hugged her, holding on a little longer than he used to when he headed out to check bridges. "I'll find Glorianna and bring her home."

Nadia eased back a little. "It's as easy as taking a step between here and there for Glorianna to return to the Island in the Mist."

"Even a Landscaper can get lost in the landscapes."

She pressed a hand to one of his cheeks and kissed the other. "Travel lightly. And if you can't find your way back to this home, build another. Build a good life for yourself."

"As long as the island and I resonate with each other, I'll find my way back, whether I build another home or not. Count on it." He hugged her again, then hugged Lynnea and Caitlin—and even Teaser, because the incubus was looking oddly vulnerable.

When he returned to the spot where the island rested above Aurora, everyone else was gone and Jeb was removing the planks.

"Horse did just fine," Jeb said. He hesitated, then added, "You might want to emphasize that a tangle of emotions isn't going to help you get anywhere."

"Ah, daylight." Lee stepped up and almost smacked into Morragen.

"We're coming with you," she said.

"What a surprise." He started to brush past her, then stopped. "'Let your heart travel lightly' isn't just a phrase, Morragen. Not here. If your heart can't do that right now, get off the island. We don't need to end up in one of the dark landscapes."

"We've seen dark landscapes."

"You're still alive, so you haven't seen anything."

He left her standing there as he made his way to the center of the island. Hopefully, the sound of the fountain would help Kobrah guide him to The Temples—the place in the heart of Vision where the Shamans lived.

*   *   *

After a short break, the Shamans and their visitors reconvened in an open-air pavilion that had netting instead of walls.

Sitting between Glorianna and Yoshani, Danyal told the Council about coming face-to-face with the wizards and the Dark Guide, and how Ephemera had shifted him to another landscape to escape them, and how that, in turn, led him to meeting Glorianna, Yoshani, Michael, and Sebastian. He told them how the wind chime provided a way back to Vision.

When he finished speaking, he saw hope in close to two-thirds of the Shamans' faces. He saw bright excitement in Farzeen's eyes, despite his mentor's calm expression. He saw caution in the other faces—and suppressed resentment on the face of the Shaman elder whose apprentice had not been successful in completing the training and had settled for a job as a groundskeeper in order to continue living in the Shamans' compound.

Farzeen and Jasper had been rivals when they were young men beginning the Shamans' work, although Farzeen had always said it was a friendly rivalry. But when Jasper had taken Racket as an apprentice at the same time Farzeen had taken Danyal, it seemed the merit of the students became another proving ground, another avenue for the older men's rivalry.

"Was it ever a friendly rivalry?" he whispered.

"Perhaps on one side," Glorianna whispered back. "But not on the other."

He looked at her and wondered what she heard in this place that he didn't—or couldn't.

Jasper straightened up and sniffed loudly. "A pretty story that tries to justify Danyal's neglect of his duties, but it doesn't provide *any* information on how to rid ourselves of this evil that now walks among us."

"Hardly a pretty story, Jasper," Farzeen said. "And it seems to me that Danyal has done what we asked him to do. Find answers. Find help." He smiled at Glorianna and Yoshani. "The wisdom our guests bring is a blessing on our city."

Other council members shifted uncomfortably when Jasper twisted to stare at Farzeen.

"Shamans!" Racket yanked the netting aside and bounded into the pavilion. "It's happened again!"

"The council is still meeting on another matter, Racket," Farzeen said, his voice gentle.

"Of course," Jasper snapped. "Make sure *your* favorite is heard and ignore everyone else!"

"What has happened?" Yoshani asked.

"I filled six pails full of water, and when I turned away *for just a moment*, they were gone. Six pails!" Racket pointed at Danyal. "This didn't happen before *he* was given that *special assignment*."

???

Danyal closed his eyes. Twenty-five years and some things didn't change. Maybe they couldn't change.

"I regret that the pails were lost, Racket," Danyal said.

"Be careful," Glorianna whispered.

"They weren't *lost*, they were *taken*," Racket snapped. "I wasn't careless, Danyal. I'm *never* careless."

Now wasn't the time to remind the man about his behavior as a youth. One of the reasons Racket didn't become a full Shaman was his assumption that the truth wasn't necessary if it became inconvenient or might require him to accept responsibility for his actions.

He shouldn't allow it to matter, but his hip ached from sitting on a hard bench, and he was tired. And that made him imprudent, despite Glorianna's warning.

"I regret that the pails were lost," he said again, then raised his voice to drown out Racket's immediate protest. "I wish I had a basket of coins to give you so that you could buy new ones, but . . ."

Glorianna sighed as the first coin broke through the pavilion's flooring between his feet.

"Ah." Danyal looked at Glorianna, considered the heat in her green eyes, and leaned toward Yoshani while coins continued to wiggle out of the break in the floor.

"Shall I fetch a basket?" Yoshani asked as he rose and walked to the end of the pavilion that held a table of food and drink.

"A small one," she replied. Then Racket darted forward to grab some of the coins. A plant unlike anything Danyal had ever seen shot out of the flooring and covered the coins. It looked like a delicate green netting until he noticed the short, hair-thin needles that would easily pierce skin.

Sinuous thorn trees, their branches dipped in thunderous Light.

His breath caught. This was what Michael and Sebastian had feared—that something would happen that would call to the dark side of Glorianna Belladonna.

"Those are not for you," she said.

"But Danyal said . . ." Racket began.

"Not. For. You."

Danyal saw Yoshani whirl at the change in her voice, saw the holy man pale. But Yoshani grabbed a small basket, emptying its fruit into another container before hurrying back to them.

The plant pushed against Danyal's shoes, as if poking at the seams to find a weak spot it could slip into. He didn't want to think of what might happen to his feet if the plant did reach skin.

"Guide of the Heart," he said quietly, "I am your apprentice. I have erred and ask for your forgiveness—and your help."

There was no heat in her eyes now. They were filled with a cold indifference that frightened him more than if he saw active cruelty.

"I have the basket, Glorianna Dark and Wise," Yoshani said.

She breathed in slowly. Breathed out slowly. And whispered, "Ephemera, hear me."

The delicate green netting receded into the break in the floor, leaving the coins exposed. Moments later, a small, bedraggled violet pushed out of the floor.

Smiling, Glorianna leaned over and brushed one of the violet's flowers with a finger. Then she picked up a coin and said, "A blessing on the person who gave us this coin, whether the giving was done knowingly or not." She put the coin in the basket Yoshani held and looked at Danyal.

He reached for a coin, hesitated long enough to make sure the violet wasn't going to turn into something else and hurt him, then picked it up and repeated her words.

She picked up another coin. "A kindness to the person who gave us this coin, whether the giving was done knowingly or not."

Again, Danyal picked up a coin and repeated her words. They continued this until all the coins had been picked up.

She studied the last coin, then closed her hand around it and sat up.

Danyal hadn't dared look at the members of the council while he followed her lead. Now he looked at Farzeen. The old man was pale and trembling but still more composed than the others.

Jasper wiped a shaking hand across his mouth as he stared at Danyal. "What are you?"

"A Voice-guide," Glorianna Belladonna replied. "A true voice of the world. The Shamans are the bedrock and the sieve for this part of Ephemera. Their hearts keep the world balanced." She looked at Jasper, then at Racket. "But when *their* hearts are out of balance, shifts can occur in a landscape."

The council members looked at one another, but no one spoke. So it was Yoshani who asked, "Are you saying the Shaman Council brought the wizards and the Dark Guide to Vision?"

"This council allowed it to happen, but it was these men"—Glorianna pointed at Jasper and then at Racket—"who fed the Dark currents in this Place of Light. When the current couldn't expand to hold those dark feelings, Ephemera channeled that darkness to another part of the city, changing the resonance there just enough to let in something that also resonated with that kind of darkness."

"The wizards," Danyal said, feeling chilled.

"The wizards," she agreed. "And once they were able to put down roots here, the resonance changed a little more—enough for the Dark Guide to cross over."

"Lies," Jasper spat. "All *lies*!"

"Your heart has no secrets, Shaman," Belladonna said. "That your heart keeps calling to this side of me is clear warning that you do not belong in a Place of Light. Can't belong in a Place of Light. *Won't* touch this Place of Light anymore."

???

"Glorianna!" Yoshani shouted, dropping the basket and reaching for her.

Danyal felt the ground sway as air rushed over him. He grabbed for her hand, not sure if he wanted to protect her or if he wanted contact because some part of him knew she was the one constant in the world at that moment.

Then . . . nothing. Except the place didn't feel the same. Not so bright. More ordinary.

It's no longer a Place of Light, he thought, stunned by how quickly she could reshape the world—and terrified when he realized this was the same power that had awakened inside him.

"Glorianna." Yoshani knelt before her and took her other hand. "The Light needs to be nurtured. It needs Guardians."

"Those who should find it will find it," she replied.

Danyal relaxed enough to breathe again when Yoshani smiled and said, "Ah. So it will be."

Glorianna stood up and smiled at Farzeen. "Has anything else changed in your city lately?"

"There is the place of sand that appeared a few days ago," he replied. "Part of the retaining wall around the southern end of The Temples broke, and when men went to repair it, they found the sand."

Her smile faded. "What kind of sand?"

maker

Danyal frowned. "Maker sand?"

yes yes yes

She huffed out a sigh. "All right. Let's go see this sand." Then she added, "And I hope you and Lee reached some agreement about what you're doing."

"I . . . We . . ." When had he and Lee ever talked about sand? And what was *maker sand*?

"I would like to accompany you," Farzeen said. "Your words have stirred up much, Guide. I strive to understand."

"We should get a pony cart," Danyal said. "It's a sufficient walk to reach the southern end of our community."

Glorianna nodded. "All right."

"Abomination," Jasper said, taking a stagger-step toward her.

Danyal tensed as he felt something dark swirl past him.

"Don't," Glorianna whispered.

Jasper pointed a shaking finger at her. "Defiler of the Light! You should be locked away where—"

A thorn tree with sinuous limbs burst out of the floor at the same moment a violent wind shook the pavilion and ripped tiles from the roof. In a heartbeat, a limb coiled around Jasper as the tree swiftly grew toward the ceiling.

"No!" Glorianna yelled. "Ephemera, no!"

Jasper screamed as he hung above the floor.

Danyal stared. The coils were still loose; the thorns barely penetrating beneath the skin. But if those coils tightened ...

"Let him go," Glorianna said firmly. "He has no power over me. He has no power over Voice-guide. He can't take either of us away from you."

Danyal jerked when she elbowed him in the ribs. "Yes," he stammered. "Shaman Jasper has no say in what I do with my life, and I have chosen to be Voice-guide and learn from the Guide. We do not want darkness here. Let this man go."

Slowly, the limb uncoiled, lowering Jasper to the broken floor. When the last coil released him, the Shamans glanced at Glorianna, who nodded, before rushing over to Jasper and half dragging him out of the thorn tree's reach. Yoshani ushered the other council members out of the pavilion.

"Now take the thorn tree back to its dark landscape so that I can look at this sand you made for Voice-guide," Glorianna said when she and Danyal were the only ones left.

A moment's resistance, as if the world still wanted to lash out. Then the tree withdrew, like the plant had withdrawn, leaving no trace of what had broken the pavilion's floor.

"Where does that tree come from?" Danyal asked.

Silence. Then she said, "It comes from a landscape that belongs to the Eater of the World." She walked out of the pavilion.

Danyal remained, staring at the broken floor.

The Shaman Council had sent him out to find answers, and he had found them.

Voice of the world. Shamans had been called that for generations, but he truly was a voice of the world.

And the world was not always gentle or kind.

He walked out of the pavilion and joined the others, painfully aware that he no longer belonged with the other Shamans and would never again be considered one of them.

Chapter Twenty-nine

The first time Lee tried to guide the island to Vision by following Kobrah's memory-feeling of the person called The Voice, they ended up in the bogs that belonged to the Merry Makers—one of Glorianna Belladonna's dark landscapes. The second try landed them in Foggy Downs, one of Michael's dark landscapes. The third try . . .

"Guardians and Guides, Lee!" Sebastian shouted from his post at the start of the island's path. "Get us out of here! Now!"

Aurora, Lee thought. *Take me and my companions back to Aurora.*

"The Lady of Light was watching out for us," Michael said, looking pale and shaken as he and Sebastian joined the others.

Lee looked at the two men. "What . . . ?"

"Bonelovers," Sebastian replied grimly.

"Where are we now?" the Knife asked.

"Back where we started." Lee shook his head. "This isn't working. Too many conflicting feelings and dark resonances. Oh, don't look at the shadowmen as if they're at fault," he snapped when Morragen turned her head to glare at the Knife and the Apothecary. "They're clear on where they want to go and why. You two"—he wagged a finger in the space between Morragen and Zhahar—"or you six, or however damn way you count yourselves, are the problem. We're back in Aurora. I'll get your packs. You can stay with my mother until we return."

"No!" Zhahar shot to her feet. "We want to help."

Morragen rose as well. "There are things that must be done. Our daughters will remain in our custody."

"She's not a child," Lee snapped. "Zhahar, come with me. We need to speak. Privately."

She rushed to stand beside him.

"We—" Morragen began.

"—don't want to find out what wizards' lightning might do to a Tryad," Sebastian finished as he rubbed his thumb against the first two fingers of his right hand.

Morragen stared at Sebastian. "You're *threatening* me?"

Sebastian gave her a savage smile. "Just helping you remember to be a good neighbor."

Wrapping a hand around Zhahar's arm, Lee hustled her to the shed.

"Lee," she said when he released her and opened the shed door.

He turned back to face her. "I don't know what's going on between you and your mothers, but it's apparent to everyone that *something* happened in the short time they were back in Tryadnea."

"You wouldn't understand."

"Since none of you are inclined to tell anyone anything, that's a given. What I *do* understand is that the turmoil and anger between your Tryad and hers landed us in the bonelovers' landscape. That landscape is locked away in the place Belladonna made for the Eater of the World. Do you have any concept of how much anger and dark feelings had to be resonating from the people on this island to land us there? And those feelings aren't coming from me or Michael or Sebastian or Kobrah or the shadowmen. Just you and your sisters and your mothers. So you're getting off the island and waiting for us in Aurora."

"Please let me go with you," Zhahar begged.

Fear. Oh, the anger was there too, and that was probably leaking out from Zeela, but there was so much fear, he barely recognized Zhahar's resonance.

"What will happen if you're not surrounded by other people who aren't Tryad?" he asked. "If you're not surrounded by witnesses?"

"The a Zephyra Tryad is our leader," Zhahar said, sounding broken. "She must uphold our laws."

"That's been settled. I'm stepping back. No one is going to be forfeited because of me."

"What you decide doesn't matter now. We wished Tryadnea would end up adrift again. We didn't believe we could really make it happen, but we wished it for selfish reasons, and it almost did happen."

"Hate to whittle down your feelings of self-importance, but you couldn't have broken that border on your own. *Didn't* break it on your own," Lee said, hoping his words would sting enough that she would hurl the truth at him.

"But Zeela . . ."

"Was being influenced, almost poisoned by someone else's thoughts, into believing you needed to have that border broken in order to choose a life beyond your homeland."

"But . . ."

"No, Zhahar. From what Glorianna said, your desire to get away from the restrictions in your homeland was strong enough that you no longer resonate with Tryadnea and aren't going to be able to cross that border. But that's you. That has nothing to do with the rest of the Tryad. So why don't you tell me what's really going on. Let me help you if I can."

He heard the humming of their three voices, could almost hear Zeela's anger and Sholeh's panic.

Daylight! What was going on between them and their mothers?

Zhahar wouldn't look at him. "Someone else came across the border last night. We thought we saw her, but we weren't sure, and there was so much to see in the Den, we didn't tell Morragen or Medusah right away. The one . . . The person went back to Tryadnea, told the people at the camp that there were *abominations* on the other side of the border, that we had locked Tryadnea to this place in order to have one of those men as a lover, were already indulging in carnal obscenities, and all three of us had pledged our hearts to a one-faced man. After stirring up the camp at the border, she rode to the village because some of our more influential citizens were waiting there for the a Zephyra Tryad to return with news. By the time our mothers arrived, the judges who pass sentence on Tryad behavior were all furious and accused us of betraying our people."

Lee rocked back on his heels. "That person lied to them, and may have influenced them the same way Zeela was influenced."

"It doesn't matter," Zhahar cried, cringing at the volume of her own voice. "Allone claimed we did the same thing she had once done—and if our mothers refuse to punish us in the same way, it is proof that the a Zephyra Tryad is not strong enough to be the leader of Tryadnea, that they will ignore our taboos when their *daughters* commit the crimes. So in order to hold the Tryad people together, we will be punished."

Something deep and terrible here. "What's the punishment?"

"We will be merged," she whispered. "We will be merged so we have only one one face."

A chill went through him. "Two of you will be required *to die* because someone falsely accused you of breaking a taboo? Zhahar, that's insane."

"Perhaps. But Allone has been vigilant about pointing out anyone who breaks taboos—especially those whose actions are punishable by merging."

That sounded too much like the influence the wizards had used on the Landscapers who ran the school in order to cull out the students whose abilities might have been a threat to them. Like Glorianna.

"So, basically, in order to satisfy the ravings of this woman and the outrage she can produce in other Tryads, your mothers will have to kill Sholeh and Zeela, and you'll be left alone to carry the guilt of their deaths?"

She nodded.

He leaned against the shed, feeling sick. A different people with different laws and customs, but it seemed to him that their laws were terrible and harsh—which might explain why Ephemera had linked Tryadnea with another dark landscape.

Zhahar and her sisters hadn't broken their people's laws or taboos or any other damn thing. Falsely accused since Zhahar hadn't acted on what her heart may have wanted, but that didn't seem to matter. And there wasn't anything a one-faced man could do about it.

Or was there?

"You intended to run, didn't you?" he asked. "That's why

you wanted to get back to Vision. The Tryad weren't anchored there anymore, so you intended to slip away from the rest of us and disappear into the city."

"Yes."

He entered the shed, found Zhahar's and Morragen's packs, then stepped out and handed Zhahar her pack while he shouldered the other. "You're not running, and you're not going to lose your sisters."

"There's nothing you can do."

"That is true," he agreed. "But I know someone who can do a great deal. You're going to ask for a justice that overrules every other kind of law. At least in this part of Ephemera."

They walked slowly, giving him a couple of minutes to coach her.

"I don't know," Zhahar said.

"Then you'd better decide, because once this is begun, there is no turning back." When they were just about to join the others, he said, "Which is it? Yes or no?"

She hesitated. Then all three voices said, "Yes."

"Magician?" Lee said. "Justice Maker? Sholeh Zeela a Zhahar has something she wants to say."

He felt the change in Michael and Sebastian when he used their titles. They turned toward Zhahar, and power flowed from them into the currents of the world that touched the island.

"We'll listen," Michael said.

"I have been accused of giving my heart to a man of single aspect," she said quietly, staring at Sebastian's shoulder. "That is taboo among the Tryad people. But I did not act on my feelings, so I believe that merging my sisters into me, which is the traditional punishment, is too harsh. Therefore, I ask that Glorianna Belladonna perform Heart's Justice to decide my fate and the fate of Zeela and Sholeh."

Silence.

Then Morragen and Medusah snapped, "That is not acceptable. The Tryad will never accept."

"It's done," Sebastian snapped back. "And as long as Glorianna Belladonna holds Tryadnea in her keeping, the Tryad *better* accept it. I can't break the border, but as the Den's anchor, I can damn well make sure none of you find my piece of Ephemera ever again."

Lee watched Morragen—and saw Zephyra's face for just a moment. For just long enough to know that Morragen and Medusah would argue for form's sake, but at least one of the mothers was relieved that there might be another solution.

"Wild child," Michael said softly as he stared at Zhahar. "Keep these hearts safe until the Guide returns. No magic will touch these hearts. No power will harm these hearts. Sholeh Zeela a Zhahar's fate is in Glorianna's hands now. Do you understand?"

yes yes yes

Lee shouldn't have felt Ephemera's answer, but he did. He didn't need Michael's nod to know the a Zhahar Tryad would be safe while he and the others were gone.

"I'll escort these ladies to Aunt Nadia's house," Sebastian said. "Then I'll be back."

Lee slipped the pack off his shoulder and offered it to Morragen. Then he turned his head toward Kobrah. "What about you? I need to find The Temples some other way, so you can stay here if you want."

Kobrah glanced at Morragen and hunched her shoulders. "I'll go with you."

"Go on," Lee told Zhahar. "Nothing will happen until Glorianna comes back from Vision."

They stood around, saying nothing until Sebastian returned.

"Can't say Auntie appreciates the houseguests you dumped on her," Sebastian said as Lee helped him onto the island, "but she'll make sure things remain civil."

"Civil is good enough," he replied.

"You have another idea how to get to Vision?" Michael asked.

Lee nodded. "One I should have thought of in the first place. You. Glorianna made this island, and you can find her through the heart music. Instead of trying to reach Vision, let's find Glorianna."

"I thought we couldn't reach the part of Vision where she'd gone," the Apothecary said.

"We couldn't have gone with her using the way she crossed over, but the island should be able to impose itself over that place," Lee said. "Even if it's not prudent to leave the island, we should be able to spot enough landmarks to shift position to a part of the city that's nearby."

"Glorianna I can find," Michael said. He pulled his tin whistle out of an inner coat pocket and began to play.

"What should we do?" the Knife asked quietly.

"Nothing," Lee replied as he felt the island begin to resonate with the music. *Follow the music. Lead us to Glorianna Belladonna.*

The island lifted, as if riding a gentle swell. Then the sensation faded.

"We're here," he said as he headed for the start of the path. But when he reached the two trees he used as his entrance, he hesitated, not trusting his diminished eyesight to show him the truth of their location. "Michael?"

"Sand," Michael said grimly. "Not rust colored, but there's nothing but sand."

"And a tall hedge creating a wall around the sand," Sebastian said, holding on to a tree and leaning out. "Any idea where we are?"

"None at all," Lee said.

Danyal stepped up to the break in the stone wall and stared at the sand surrounded by a tall hedge.

"Well," Glorianna said cheerfully, "you are now the caretaker of a couple acres of playground."

"Playground?"

yes yes yes

"I do not understand," Farzeen said as he stepped up beside them.

"Some strong heart wishes went out into the world," she replied. "And this was the world's answer."

"Sand?" Danyal tried not to sound skeptical, but . . . sand?

"If this was the entrance of a place for the heart, what would you want the people entering to see first?" she asked.

So many possible answers, but the first thing he pictured felt right and true. "There was a plant at the Asylum. It just appeared one day. Lee called it heart's hope. People made a point of walking along that path every day because seeing the plant made them feel better. If I could, I would have one of those plants on the right-hand side of the entrance to lift the spirits of everyone who entered this place."

Sand squirmed. It wiggled. Farzeen gasped. Danyal stared.

"Not that close," Glorianna said. She stepped onto the sand and pointed. "Over here so it won't be harmed when the hearts put a proper doorway in the wall."

The sand quieted, then began squirming in the spot she'd pointed to.

Moments later, a small plant pushed out of the sand—a delicate thing with one tiny bud.

Glorianna looked at Danyal and smiled. "Heart's hope."

He swallowed hard. "It needs good soil. Rich soil."

The sand around the heart's hope changed to soil.

Glorianna tipped her head. "Strength makes stone. Let's make some of the stone that comes from the part of the world that made Voice-guide."

Stones formed around the heart's hope, piling up as the soil around and beneath the plant rose until the plant was growing on a raised bed. More stones, bigger stones, rose out of the sand behind the bed, reminding him of the mountains that backed the northern community where he grew up. The crevices that formed between the stones filled with soil.

"Would any of the flowers that grow around your home village thrive in this part of the city?" she asked him.

Before Danyal could admit he didn't know, young plants pushed out of the soil in the crevices.

"Oh, those are lovely," Glorianna said. "Voice-guide, you will learn their names."

"Of course." Danyal glanced at Farzeen. The old man's face held wonder and a touch of fear. To see someone change the world so radically would make anyone wary. To understand that the power also had a dark side that could just as easily destroy . . .

Glorianna Belladonna was the earthquake that had come to shake the Shamans' understanding of their world.

"Glorianna, what is this place?" he asked.

"A very large playground," she replied. "Apparently, you felt you needed one this big."

"I? But I . . ." He caught the warning look in her eyes and gestured toward the heart's hope. "This is lovely."

more more more

"Not today," Glorianna said firmly.

Danyal felt the currents of the world circling around them. Sentient in its way. Like a child in its way, craving guidance, craving someone who could help it shape its ever-changing self. He thought of his grandniece and the fun of being a doting uncle—and gave in to the desire to create a little mischief.

"Maybe one more *little* thing?" he said, smiling at Glorianna in the same way he intended to smile at Nalah someday.

Glorianna tried hard to give him an intimidating stare, but her lips kept twitching with the effort not to return the smile. "A *little* thing."

"A path of grass." He spread his arms to indicate the width.

He felt the sand change beneath his feet, then saw a ribbon of green race across the sand at a speed that took his breath away. When it reached the halfway point, the grass stopped. Little clumps of violets popped up—and a gold pocket watch wiggled out of the ground to lie on top of the grass at his feet.

Glorianna stared at the watch, then at the point where the grass ended. "Michael?" She cupped her hands around her mouth and shouted, "Michael!"

Michael suddenly appeared on the sand, turned toward her voice, and waved. "Glorianna!"

"Michael!" She ran down that ribbon of grass as Michael hurried to meet her.

Danyal took a couple of steps to follow her, then stopped and looked at Farzeen.

The old man smiled, but there was still a touch of fear in those eyes. "You have brought us a way of seeing that will change our piece of the world, Danyal."

"I know. I'm sorry."

Farzeen shook his head. "You did what we asked of you, but I don't think any of us understood what that was going to mean to Vision or its people." He smiled again and added gently, "Go, Danyal. She is your mentor now."

As Danyal headed for Glorianna and Michael, Lee and Sebastian appeared on the sand out of thin air. Moments later, Kobrah and the two shadowmen appeared.

A single heart could change a landscape. What would his city look like when all the changes were done?

Lee stepped away from the others and raised a hand in greeting. "Hey-a, Danyal."

"Lee. You found a way back. One of your bridges?"

"The island. It's mine again. And I didn't find Vision so much as I found Glorianna."

"Ah."

He looked around. "What is all the sand for?"

"It's a playground."

"Big playground."

"So I was told."

Something in Danyal's tone—part challenge, part bewilderment—made Lee think about the word. "Playground? As in a playground for Ephemera?"

play with Voice-guide and Lee-heart

He heard that. He thought hearing Ephemera on the island was a fluke, but he heard that. And . . . *Lee-heart?* *Guardians and Guides.*

"Why did you ask for something so big?" Lee asked Danyal. "Why ask for it in the first place?" Although, after Vito's reaction to that grotto vineyard, hadn't he wondered about using something like the playground Glorianna had on her island to help hearts that didn't know what home was supposed to look like?

He might not be able to see well enough to know the color of Danyal's eyes, but Lee deciphered the expression in them just fine. And *that* look in *those* eyes could strip off skin.

"Some strong heart wishes went out into the currents of the world, and this was the world's answer," Danyal said.

He winced, since that answer sounded more like Glorianna than Danyal. "Ah. Hmm. Well, it couldn't have been just me thinking along these lines."

Danyal sighed. "No, it wasn't just you. But now there are many decisions to be made and—"

A staggering variety of plants sprang up around them, some with flowers as big as dinner plates and others that spread out over the ground and were covered with delicate color.

The Apothecary ran up to them. He clamped his hands on either side of his head and practically danced in place as he stared at the plants.

"They weren't here a minute ago," he said. "You can *make* the plants? Just make them here?"

"No one is making anything else today," Glorianna said firmly as she and Michael walked up to them.

!!!

"No," she said.

The flowers sank into the sand. Lee thought the Apothecary was going to break down and cry. And he thought of the work a Landscaper put into her walled garden in order to keep her pieces of the world in balance. This part of the world was already sufficiently out of balance. The people living here didn't need him adding to the potential chaos.

Apparently Danyal reached the same conclusion, because the Shaman said, "You are wise, Guide of the Heart. Lee and I are your apprentices now and will benefit from your experience and guidance while we learn to speak to the world."

"When did I become an apprentice?" Lee asked out of the corner of his mouth.

"Five minutes ago," Danyal replied just as quietly.

"Good to know." He wasn't sure he liked being considered an apprentice again, but it was a prudent decision. Maybe it was the loss of so many Landscapers in his part of the world that had made Ephemera more aggressive in manifesting thoughts and feelings. Or maybe need had awakened something dormant in people who already had some kind of link to the world. Either way, he was beginning to have an idea of just how careful Glorianna had always been when expressing idle thoughts and comments. "Is anyone else hungry? Shouldn't it be time for the midday meal?"

"Closer to time for the evening meal," Danyal said. "Shaman Farzeen, this is Lee. We met at the Asylum."

He hadn't noticed the old man moving toward them until Danyal spoke. He couldn't read Farzeen's expression, but he noticed the way Glorianna and Michael turned to study the Shaman.

"Danyal is correct," Farzeen said. "We should return to the compound now, if the Guide has seen enough on this day."

"I have," Glorianna replied. "There isn't enough room in the pony cart for all of us."

"I can shift the island as long as someone can give me a clear idea of where I'm going," Lee said.

"Island?" Farzeen asked.

Lee closed his eyes. *It's safe to be seen in this place.*

Farzeen gasped. "You have the Shamans' gift of deciding what can and cannot be seen?"

"Only for that island."

"And that piece of the world moves? Like a boat on a river with you acting as tiller?"

"I hadn't thought of it that way, but I guess it is." He didn't need Danyal's nudge to know what he should do. "Would you like to travel on the island to return to the compound?"

"I would very much."

"Perhaps Michael would ride back with Glorianna and me," Danyal said. "It would give him an opportunity to see some of The Temples."

"We'll meet you at the compound," Lee said.

As they walked the short distance to the island, Farzeen linked his arm with Lee's.

"Danyal mentioned you in his letters to me and told me some of what was done to you by our common enemy," the old Shaman said as he studied Lee's face. "Your eyes are healing?"

"They are." *In more ways than one.*

"That is good." Farzeen patted Lee's arm. "That is good."

Danyal wondered if he should tell Michael about the incident at the pavilion, but decided he would talk to Yoshani first, since the holy man knew the Magician far better than he did. So he kept his comments general as he explained the use of various buildings.

They drove into the Shamans' compound. Instead of the usual peace and order, there was chaos as people dashed around.

"There's Sebastian," Glorianna said, sitting up straighter. "And Yoshani."

"And Denys, one of the Handlers from the Asylum," Danyal said. Recognizing the Handler, he began recognizing other people. Inmates. Helpers. "Stop here." He tapped their driver on the shoulder. "Stop."

Scrambling out of the pony cart, he hurried toward Denys and Yoshani, with Glorianna and Michael right behind them.

"Denys?" Danyal raised his voice to be heard over the shouting and weeping and querulous demands.

"Shaman Danyal!" Denys moved toward him, limping a little. "We made it, but I was just telling Yoshani that I didn't know if Nik and Meddik Benham got out."

"Got out?"

"The Asylum," Yoshani said. "The wizards and the Dark Guide gathered men of dark hearts and attacked the Asylum."

They worked to mend the injured and soothe the minds that couldn't cope with the fear shaped by a savage attack. Kobrah settled into her role of Helper and assisted Denys. The Apothecary offered to brew up some tonics that would sedate distraught minds and hearts, and whatever plants he needed, Glorianna and Ephemera provided. But what Danyal noticed was how often the inmates watched the men and women who wore the white robes of a Shaman, how often they looked at *him* for guidance, for the assurance that they were safe now. And he noticed how often the ones he'd considered borderline tried to catch Lee's attention.

Several hours later, Helpers and inmates were all fed and settled down for the night, each one clutching a white stone that Yoshani assured them would absorb their fears and sorrows while they slept.

Finally, the Shaman Council, Lee's people, the Knife, the Apothecary, and he sat down to a late meal of chopped dates and nuts mixed into balls of brown rice.

"They arrived shortly before Lee, Farzeen, and the others stepped off the island," Yoshani said, tipping his head to indicate Denys.

"Can you tell us what happened?" Farzeen asked.

"Not much to tell," Denys said, breaking up the rice ball on his plate but not eating any of it. "The two men who had claimed to be Lee's uncles showed up less than an hour after Lee and Zhahar took off with Kobrah and the Apothecary."

Denys glanced at Lee, but Danyal shook his head to indicate now wasn't the time to ask about Zhahar.

"We told them that Lee had run off with one of the Handlers," Denys continued. "Said we weren't sure when they'd slipped away from the Asylum, because things were in a bit of a twist with the Shaman missing and all. They were wicked mad to find out Lee wasn't there to be plucked up and taken away, but they left. What else could they do?"

"They sent Clubs after us," Lee said. "Maybe that's why it took so long before they returned to the Asylum. No reason to until they received word that we'd gotten away."

"Guess so," Denys said. "Had some warning, though. Not much, but enough to save some inmates." He knuckled away a tear. "We saved some."

"What kind of warning?" Danyal asked softly.

"Stinkweed and turd plants." Denys's face scrunched up even as he smiled. "Stuff began sprouting everywhere. The stink was so bad you couldn't get away from it. That's when Nik realized he hadn't smelled any of that stinkweed lately except when those two uncles showed up, so it had to be a warning. Meddik Benham had taken some inmates to the little temple, because ringing the wind chimes made them calmer, so Nik ran to warn Meddik while I gathered the people who had been working in the gardens.

"I was out with a dozen inmates, close to the gate that opens onto that weedy park, when I saw those two men heading for the main building with a couple dozen men carrying clubs or knives.

"Our guards came out to challenge them and . . ." Denys took a sip of water. "Those men raised their hands, and the guards were struck by lightning. Killed that fast. Just . . . that fast. Then inmates were pouring out of the residence and running in all directions. Helpers and Handlers were being clubbed again and again even after they fell. The gate was there and I had the keys, so I made a choice to save those I could.

"Couple of the Clubs saw me as I was pushing the last inmate through the gate. Wasn't time to lock it behind me, so I ran." Denys shook his head slowly, as if he wasn't sure what he'd seen and even less sure he'd be believed. "Wasn't time to lock the gate, but when I looked back, the opening was filled with thorny vines that no one could cut through easily.

"Kept everyone together and moving as best I could, taking alleyways and the more winding streets. Got far enough from the Asylum to risk going back to the main road. Had some luck there, since I spotted some city guards close to the stop for the omnibus. I told them the Asylum was under attack and that I was heading for The Temples to inform the Shamans. One of the guards wrote a travel pass for me and the inmates, allowing us to use any conveyance at the city's expense.

"Took the better part of two days to get here," Denys finished with a sigh. "Don't expect there will be much left of the Asylum."

Or the people? Danyal wondered.

"No one feels easy about the Asylums," the Knife said, "but the city guards wouldn't back off and leave the people there under attack. And my guild keeps places on shadow streets all over the parts of the city that we can see. As soon as word reached them that the Asylum was under attack, they would have joined forces with the city guards. For this, they would."

"Until the darkness filling the Asylum changed it so that the men coming to help could no longer see the place," Danyal said.

"And those already inside that darkness would be facing wizards' lightning as well as familiar weapons," Sebastian said.

Michael looked at Glorianna. "If these wizards changed the feel of the place so much that no one can get in, can those ripe-bastard wizards get out without the help of someone like a Bridge or Landscaper?"

"I don't know," she replied.

Danyal heard the words and wondered if anyone else had heard the lie.

Chapter Thirty

A nger burned in him, hot and fierce, until it consumed everything except itself.

Danyal slipped out of the building that housed visiting Shamans and other guests. Everyone else was asleep now, and in the deep hours of night, no one would notice his absence.

He understood now how the wizards and their hired weapons had changed shadow places into places too dark for the Shamans to see. They had spilled innocent blood, killed the young, the old, the ones who couldn't defend themselves. One death creates a shadow. A dozen lives taken at the same time? Darkness.

Like shadows, darkness also came in many shades.

He put on his plain white robe. As a Shaman, he was the voice of the world.

The world had many voices.

Avalanche. Earthquake.

Danyal walked away from the buildings.

Hurricane. Tidal wave.

In the city of Vision, if you can find only what you can see, can you also see what you truly want to find, need to find?

"Ephemera," he whispered. "It's Voice-guide. I need your help."

???

He closed his eyes and pictured the Asylum, pictured the open ground between the inmates' residence and the reflecting pool. "I need to go back to the Asylum. I need to reach this place. Can you help me?"

He caught a whiff of stinkweed. "I know, but I have to go there."

The smell got stronger. Danyal opened his eyes and saw a patch of sparse grass smeared with dark stains. He swallowed hard as he considered what he was about to embrace — and what he would have to leave behind.

Then he stepped onto the patch of sparse grass that was the temporary access point to the Asylum.

"Lee." His name whispered, followed by a pause. "Lee!"

He could have — and would have — continued to ignore the whisper, but not the thump on the shoulder that followed.

"Daylight, Glorianna," he muttered. "Why don't you bother the Magician? You wouldn't even have to get out of bed to do it."

"He offered, but I need you," she replied, giving his shoulder another thump.

Knowing a third thump from Glorianna would be hard enough to leave bruises, he propped himself up on one elbow. "What if I'd had company?"

"She could go back to sleep. You need to get up and come with me."

"Where?"

"The Asylum."

"That's not a good idea. The wizards and Dark Guide might still be there."

"If they aren't there now, they will be."

Some change in her voice told him he was no longer talking to Glorianna. "Why?"

"Voice of the world," Belladonna said with a kind of dreamy viciousness that made Lee shiver. "Someone who speaks for the world touches the Dark as well as Light. In his fury over what happened at the Asylum, Danyal is reaching out to touch dark currents that shouldn't be touched."

"The Eater's landscapes?"

"Belladonna's landscape."

Swearing, Lee flung the sheet aside and nudged her out of the way, glad he hadn't stripped down completely when he dropped into bed earlier.

"Do you need help?" she asked.

He wasn't sure if that was Belladonna or Glorianna asking, but the answer was the same. "At this point, I probably can find things in the dark better than you can."

He could almost feel her annoyed shrug.

"All right, then. I'll—" A thump.

"Glorianna?"

"I found the door."

He shoved his feet into his shoes and rammed his arms into the short sleeves of a shirt. "Let's go."

"Glasses," she said.

He patted the side table until he found the dark glasses. Slipping them into the shirt's pocket, he joined her at the door.

They moved through the hallways quickly and quietly, not out of stealth but out of the habit of trying not to disturb other people.

Outside, Lee called to the island—and breathed a sigh of relief when he stretched out his hand and felt the familiar bark of one of the trees. Keeping one hand on the tree, he reached back with the other and stepped onto the island, bringing Glorianna with him.

"I'm not sure how to guide us to the Asylum," he said. "My eyesight wasn't good most of the time I was there."

"Don't see with your eyes, Bridge. See with your heart."

He nodded to indicate he understood. Not the early days of his time at the Asylum, but those last few days when he walked the paths and had regained a measure of independence, when his Bridge's gift had helped some inmates travel to the places their hearts called home.

At the last moment, just as he felt the island begin to resonate in a way that indicated it was about to shift, he hesitated—and the island remained within the Shaman's compound.

"Are we going to the Asylum to stop Danyal from doing whatever he intended to do?"

"No," Belladonna replied. Then Glorianna added, "We're going to help him with what comes after whatever choice he made."

*   *   *

The dead had been left out, exposed to heat, insects, and carrion eaters.

Inmates, Helpers, Handlers, Asylum guards and city guards, shadowmen from the assassins' guild. Whoever had entered the grounds didn't make it out again. But they weren't alone. There were plenty of men among the dead who looked like hired Clubs, so despite their damn lightning, the fight hadn't been completely in the wizards' favor.

The inmates' residence and the building where he and Benham had living quarters had been burned to the ground. The two-room temple was gone. Just gone. Danyal didn't try to enter any of the buildings that were still standing. He wandered the paths, alone among the dead.

When he finally stopped walking, he took a position in front of the burned residence, no longer a man. Not even a Shaman. Now he was merely the forge that would shape the weapon.

No caution now. No timidity about what he was going to do.

Danyal raised his arms shoulder high, his palms turned skyward.

"Ephemera," he said in a voice that carried a thousand storms. "The men who did this, who violated the trust of the damaged hearts who lived here. The men who darkened this place with pain and blood. Bring them to me. *Bring all of them to me.*"

His fury, burning so hot and fierce, must have scared the world, because the ground beyond him changed, and as a two-story house appeared, it tipped and settled awkwardly, one corner of its foundation missing. Moments later, a brothel appeared, its sign swinging madly as the ground under it turned to mud from the water spilling out of broken pipes. Moments after that, he heard a man's vicious cursing as an outdoor privy appeared in the reflecting pool that now had more things fouling it than stagnant water.

While he waited, Danyal pictured the next step and thought, *This. When I tell you, make this.*

Ephemera didn't answer.

The wizards Pugnos and Styks came out of the house first. A few Clubs came out of the brothel, and one from the privy. More wizards came out of the house—a dozen in all. Then the Dark Guide stepped out of the house. No hood to hide the inhuman face. Not anymore.

"Ah, so you did survive," the Dark Guide said, smiling. "And now you've returned. Have you come to avenge the feeble, Shaman?"

"Yes," Danyal replied, lowering his arms.

"Alone? Against us?"

He saw Pugnos and Styks rub their thumbs against their first two fingers, so he didn't bother to answer. He just snarled, *"Now."*

Thorn trees with sinuous limbs erupted out of the ground. The wizards didn't have time to raise a hand against him before limbs coiled around them and lifted them off the ground. Long thorns pierced clothing and flesh, digging deeper as the coils tightened.

The Clubs thrashed and screamed. The wizards and Dark Guide unleashed their lightning against the trees. The trees screamed and the ends of the limbs sprouted bulbous pods that split open to reveal hundreds of sharp needles.

The pods hovered for a moment. Then they snapped closed over the heads of every man except the Dark Guide. Wizards and Clubs thrashed and screamed as the pods released digestive juices and began consuming the flesh on the faces of their prey.

"Shaman!" the Dark Guide howled. "Do you think you'll be rid of us? You'll never hide your city from all of us. Not ever again!"

"I know," Danyal said. "Your kind may be able to find us, you may be able to enter our city, but you won't make this place your own. We know you now."

The Dark Guide smiled a terrible smile and said gently, "As long as you walk in this city, there will be dark places where malevolent hearts can hide."

"But not your heart," Danyal whispered as a pod split above the Dark Guide's head.

Glorianna stood between the trees that marked the island's path and tried to study the land beyond.

"You used to be better at this," she finally said. "I don't think we're even close to the Asylum."

Lee shouldered her to one side. "Well, daylight, Glori-anna. It's the middle of the damn night. Even if my eyesight was perfect, I still couldn't see where we are. And it's not like we want to set a lantern out there to see what might get curious about us." He cocked his head, listening. "And I don't think I'm that far off. The Asylum grounds had different areas."

"So the vegetables we landed in on your first try . . . ?"

"Could have been the home farm. They grow what they can, and it gives some of the inmates work and keeps them active."

"And this?"

"Does that sound like a brook or stream to you?"

"Definitely water," Glorianna agreed. "Could be a stream."

"There was a stream at the farthest edge of where bor-derline inmates were allowed to walk without close super-vision. There was a footbridge. I avoided it because I was afraid the bridge would respond to me and change into one that provided access to other landscapes." Lee blew out a breath. "Ephemera is bringing the island as close as we can get to the buildings, isn't it?"

"As close as you can get," Glorianna said quietly.

He couldn't see her in the dark, but he reached out and touched her hair. "What's that supposed to mean?"

"It means we're probably close to that bridge, so I'll take one of the shielded lanterns and walk the rest of the way to the grounds around the buildings."

"No." He shook his head. "No, you don't go in alone this time."

She linked her fingers with his. "I'm not going in to save the world this time, or even this city. I'm going in as a Guide of the Heart. To help Danyal. I don't know if I'll be coming back to the island with him or without him, but I'll be com-ing back."

"Do you promise?" Not a small question, because Glo-rianna Belladonna wouldn't make a promise if there was any doubt in her mind that she could keep it.

"I promise."

"Do we have any time?"

"A little."

"Then I want one other promise." His fingers tightened

on hers, and it took effort to relax his hold instead of squeezing harder, holding on harder. "The Tryad have a way of merging aspects. Medusah has the ability to do that to someone."

Glorianna nodded. "Yes, Zephyra mentioned it. She thought the Tryad's magic might be able to put the Light and Dark halves of my heart back together so that I'll always be Glorianna Belladonna instead of Glorianna or Belladonna."

"Don't do it." He hadn't meant to sound so harsh or so demanding.

She pulled her hands away from his. "I thought you, of all the family, would be anxious for me to try this."

"A few months ago, I probably would have been—and I would have been wrong to want it. *Was* wrong to want it. You cast out the Light in your heart in order to trap the Eater of the World and the creatures and landscapes It made. You were split *for months*. And I've realized only recently that you are merging those two sides of your heart, using Michael's music to weave them together. It will take time, and maybe there will always be distinct aspects that people will recognize as Belladonna or Glorianna, because they'll feel that you're standing more in the Dark or the Light. But you're healing in your own way and in your own time, and when you're done, you'll be whole again."

"But not the same," she said quietly.

"Ever changing, like the world."

"Why your change of heart?"

"Lots of reasons," he replied. "The biggest being that I don't trust Medusah right now. She doesn't know you, and while her magic might be able to merge your aspects, it doesn't mean you'll be whole." He hesitated. "And she's not happy with you at the moment, so I don't want her messing around in your head or your heart."

"Why is she annoyed with me?"

"Because I helped Zhahar ask for Heart's Justice instead of accepting the Tryad's punishment for loving a man of single aspect."

"Lee!"

He stared at her. He thought about fetching one of the lanterns, but if the light was bright enough for him to see her face, he'd end up wearing the damn glasses to cut the light and wouldn't be able to see her anyway. At least they were both in the dark this way.

"If Zhahar and I had become lovers, the only way Tryad law would allow her to remain with me is if her sisters were merged into her. One body. One face. Two people trapped inside and unable to experience the world except vicariously through her—if any part of them survived at all. They say it's a merging, but the end result is the death of two of the sisters, with the remaining sister looking at that one surviving face for the rest of her life. What kind of life could she have? What kind of relationship could she build?"

"But asking for Heart's Justice," Glorianna protested.

"Zhahar doesn't deserve that punishment. Neither do Zeela and Sholeh. And I don't think this has much to do with Zhahar or me, but it does seem like someone wants to use us as an excuse to strike at the a Zephyra Tryad's authority. 'Prove you're our leader. Kill your daughters.'"

Glorianna said nothing, just stood looking out over the land beyond the island. Finally, she asked softly, "What do you want for Sholeh Zeela a Zhahar, Lee? What are you hoping Heart's Justice will do?"

"I'm hoping it will give them a chance to have a life in a place where they can be accepted as Tryad and still explore choices that their people aren't ready or willing to accept. They were changed by their exposure to the city of Vision and by working at the Asylum. By meeting Danyal and me. I want Zhahar and her sisters to find the place they were meant to be."

"Even if it's not with you?"

The question made his heart ache. "Yes. Even if it's not with me."

Glorianna sighed. "All right. That's a problem for another day. It's time for me to find Danyal."

"I'll fetch the lantern."

As he made his way to the shed to fetch the lantern, he wondered what Glorianna expected to find that she didn't want him to see.

The living fruit struggled a while longer. Danyal watched them, feeling nothing but a heavy satisfaction. Some part of him knew that feeling meant he was in danger, but he couldn't bring himself to care.

Then something shimmered through the currents of Light—and something far darker than the darkness he'd found in his own heart slid through the Dark currents as she suddenly appeared.

She looked at the thorn trees and their fruit, then looked at him—and smiled.

"It's easy to become a monster, isn't it?" Belladonna said. "So easy to become the terrible and sublime when you can give shape to every dark dream the human heart has ever known. Fear can be a seductive kind of worship, and when you can do *anything*, it's hard to demand that the monster go back to the can't-do-it rules everyone else lives by."

Danyal turned his back on the thorn trees to look at her. "You did it. You turned away."

"I *do* it," she corrected. "I could find that landscape again, that place Belladonna ruled." She lifted her chin to indicate the thorn trees. "Just as you found a piece of it to-night. The memories of people I loved, people I had cast out of my heart in order to survive in that landscape, gave me a way to return to the Light. But I remember what it felt like to *be everything, do anything*. I remember, and every day I choose not to do the things I did in that place. Every day I choose not to let the monster walk in the landscapes that are in my keeping. Every day I choose to hold on to both Glorianna and Belladonna, to stay among the people I love and who love me. I choose, Danyal. Every single day. And now that you've had a taste of what you can do with your connection to the world and what you might become if you allow yourself, you will also have to choose—every single day."

"Have I forfeited the Light?" he asked, looking back at the thorn trees.

"Some pieces of it," Glorianna replied. "Not all of it. You didn't cast it out; just smothered it for a little while. I don't think you'll be able to find the Place of Light in the Shamans' compound, but you can still walk in Sanctuary."

His heart hurt from the relief her words gave him.

"I need a teacher," he said softly. "I need a Guide to help me learn what I'm becoming."

"I know," she replied just as softly. "Let your heart travel lightly, Danyal. Right here, right now, let your heart travel lightly."

He closed his eyes and used his training to empty his mind and heart of all the fury, all the dark thoughts.

Who was he now? A voice for the world. A Shaman. But those things didn't mean the same thing as they had a few months ago. Who was he now—and what could he become that would help the people whose lives he touched?

"Well," Glorianna said with a soft laugh, "not so far from the Light after all."

Danyal opened his eyes and looked around. The Asylum's dead were still all around them, but the thorn trees and their terrible fruit were gone. So were the brothel, the house held by the wizards, and the privy.

And something now glowed where the temple had been.

"Wind chimes," he whispered, moving toward the glow. "I hear wind chimes." Joy.

As he and Glorianna approached the small building, the chimes rang louder, almost changing to something harsh.

"Nik?" he called. "Benham? Are you in there?"

The door cracked open. "Danyal?" Benham said. "Is that you?"

He laughed, his heart soaring with relief. "Yes, it's me."

He passed through the glow as Benham pulled open the door. But the Meddik looked past him and stiffened.

"Fog hides," Glorianna said softly, stepping up beside Danyal. "The people in here don't need to see what is out there."

He looked at Benham and nodded. Benham stepped back from the door. Danyal started to move aside to let Glorianna enter first, but she put a hand on his back and pushed him forward as she said, "They're your people."

Eight inmates, plus Benham and Nik, whose left arm was in a sling. The inmates bobbed their heads at him but stayed on the other side of the room as he, Glorianna, Benham, and Nik formed a tight circle.

"We were just leaving the temple when Nik rushed up to warn us," Benham said, keeping his voice low. "Nik was sliced in the arm while defending the door until I got everyone back inside. It was the strangest thing. The door shouldn't have held, but a couple inmates grabbed up wind chimes and began ringing them, and it was like this building went away from the fighting."

A queer shiver rushed down Danyal's spine.

"You saw the glow when you came up?" Benham asked. "That's all we saw. Then it began to fade and someone tried to break down the door, so we all grabbed wind chimes and rang them."

"Joy," Glorianna said. "Dark hearts couldn't see a place filled with the Light released through joy."

"Odd things happened," Benham said. "The glow gave us a little ground all around the building. Enough to make a toilet outside. And the other day, when we were feeling desperate for water, pails of fresh water appeared outside the door."

Danyal glanced at Glorianna, who tipped her head in the briefest nod, confirming his suspicion that the pails would be the ones Racket had reported missing from the Shamans' compound.

"We need to leave, Danyal," Glorianna said.

Nik and Benham looked as alarmed as he felt. "We can't leave them here."

She huffed. "Of course not. We'll gather up the wind chimes and any lanterns you might have in here. Lee's waiting for us on the island. We'll take everyone back to the Shamans' compound and figure out the rest later." She turned toward the door, then said over her shoulder, "You might want to bring some of the pails back too."

Glorianna led the way, holding her lantern high as a beacon. They found two other lanterns that had a bit of oil left. It wasn't much light, but it was enough. The inmates each carried a wind chime and filled the dark with their sound.

As Glorianna reached the footbridge, another lantern suddenly appeared and was lowered to the ground.

"Hey-a," Lee called.

Murmurs, both happy and tearful, as Lee helped each person step onto the island.

Danyal, as the last one, hesitated and looked back. Lee and Glorianna stepped off the island.

"Problem?" Lee asked.

He shook his head. "That little temple. I don't think I'll miss anything else about the Asylum's grounds or buildings, but I'll be sorry to lose the little temple."

He felt Glorianna staring at him before she looked at Lee.

"Does the building have water pipes or anything else that would cause a problem?"

"I never saw any," he said blandly.

"You're no help. Danyal? Does the building have any attachments?"

"No. It was just a simple building. No water, no drains."

"In that case . . ." she said. "Ephemera?"

???

"The little building Voice-guide uses to help the hearts. I want you to shift it to Voice-guide's playground. Just the building, not any of the land. Do you understand?"

yes yes yes

"Wait a minute," Lee said. "You're encouraging the world to take buildings now? You're going to let it start rearranging villages? If neighbors are quarreling, they'll wake up one morning and find their houses on opposite ends of the street?"

"Ephemera knows better than to shift a building in any of my landscapes without my permission," Glorianna said sweetly. "What the two of you let the world get away with here in Vision is up to you." She stepped up on the island and disappeared from view.

It took Danyal a moment to realize his mouth was hanging open.

"What just happened?" he finally asked.

Lee sighed and guided him onto the island. "The world has been given a new toy, and you and I are in charge of supervising playtime."

Chapter Thirty-one

Danyal, Lee, and Yoshani meandered around another part of The Temples.

"A walking meditation," Danyal grumbled. "Why are we doing a walking meditation?"

"So that you can look and think and, finally, *see*," Yoshani replied, sounding less patient than he had when they'd started this a couple of hours ago.

"I'll point out that whatever I'm looking at is still blurry enough that I'm not actually *seeing* much of anything," Lee complained.

"And we've been walking too long. My hip isn't able to do this much," Danyal said.

"Then start using your head so you can spare your feet," Yoshani replied sharply. "And you." He pointed at Lee. "If you can't see anything, it's because you're being willfully blind."

Lee stopped walking. So did Danyal. Yoshani continued on a few steps before turning back to join them.

"That was harsh," Danyal said.

"What you hear as harsh, I hear as an end of patience," Yoshani replied. "The Guide *you* both asked to stand as your mentor gave you the task of considering what you would need to do your work in the world. I'd had the impression that you both made some decisions already about what you would need, and that this would simply help you determine the physical shape. Instead of following your assignment, you have muttered and complained like cranky children until Glorianna had no desire to listen to either of you. Which is why you are out here walking, and why I, who have no stake in this, offered to accompany you."

A man his own age had just told him he sounded like a whiny six-year-old. Danyal didn't like it—especially because he suspected it was true.

"I'm frustrated," he admitted. "I want to comply with Glorianna's request, but I don't understand what she wants from me. From either of us." He tipped his head to include Lee.

"Yeah." Lee scrubbed his fingers over his hair. "I heard what she said, but I can't get the words to form a pattern I understand. And I've *always* understood Glorianna, even when my brain didn't."

"A first step," Yoshani said. "What do you need in order to do your work? Danyal, admittedly, has a better sense of the buildings, but you both lived at the Asylum for a while. We've walked around the compound that makes up the residential part of The Temples. We've walked around this main avenue that is the public part. You've both lived other places and seen other buildings. What do you want?"

"Not an Asylum," Danyal said, sure of that much. "Not a place for those who will never be whole and need a kind of care I'm not suited to give them. Not anymore." He had admitted to himself that he'd become too dangerous to work with heart-cores that might pull him too far into the Dark. "But I would like to work in a place that could help the ones who are weighed down by the world because they lost their way."

"A building or buildings that could provide housing for two or three dozen people at a time," Lee said. "Fifty people at the most. And a separate building for the staff—suites of rooms or apartments that would give them a home rather than just a room. And private residences for Danyal and me. With a screened porch. I did like sitting out on that screened porch."

"The little temple," Danyal continued. "And a building that could provide space for work and study."

"You would also need a reference library. Would you not?" Yoshani asked quietly. "And someone to do research for you and provide the information you need to shape pieces of the world in the playground?"

"Yes," Danyal said. He closed his eyes for a moment to picture it better. A swimming hole would be lovely. Maybe not on the grounds itself, since that might be too dangerous for the more emotionally fragile . . . students. Not inmates. No, these would be students who came to the school to prepare for the next part of their journey.

"The Apothecary could share a building with Meddik Benham. Then a person wouldn't have to walk far for a tonic after getting some stitches," Lee said.

"No more than an hour's ride from the bazaar and The Temples," Danyal said, looking in the direction of the archway between The Temples and the bazaar. "That would make the school about a day's journey from any part of Vision."

"And not as hot as the southern part of the city," Lee added.

"Definitely not as hot," Danyal agreed.

"Grounds that would include flower gardens and a kitchen garden that everyone would help plant, tend, and harvest. And we'd need enough room for that two-acre playground," Lee said.

Danyal didn't want to think about what they would find at the playground when they returned. He didn't know if the world was ignoring the rest of itself or if it was responding placidly to people's hearts and feelings everywhere else, saving its energy for the place where it could make things without restraint. It *was* treating the little temple like a toy, moving it around to different parts of the playground and creating a variety of trees and vegetation around it, like a child putting different outfits on a doll. Apparently, Glorianna had set *some* limits, because Ephemera wasn't allowed to bring into the playground anything from a dark landscape unless she was with it to help shape the making.

Ephemera's playground. His training ground.

"So," Yoshani said. "For men who thought you knew little, you actually know a great deal about the physical shape of your heart wishes. Lee, why don't you call your little island, and we'll see if there is a place in Vision that comes close to what you and Danyal desire."

The place was run-down and in need of all kinds of repair, but it had residential buildings that would work for the students, and others that could be fixed up for the staff. There were even two large cottages connected by what must have once been a screened patio. Another building could serve as infirmary and the Apothecary's shop, and the second floor had separate living quarters that shared a kitchen. There was a barn large enough to house a handful of horses and a couple of dairy cows—if anyone wanted dairy cows. One of the stalls held an assortment of discarded tools and equipment. They found an old bicycle and a pump for the tires. Between them they got the tires pumped up and the bicycle wiped clean enough to ride. Then Yoshani headed down the lane to find out where they were.

Danyal walked out of the barn and looked around again. "It could work, couldn't it?" he asked Lee.

"It could work," Lee agreed. He adjusted the brim of his hat to shade his eyes a little more. "With your connection to the world and my abilities as a Bridge, we could help people find what their hearts need to see."

Danyal hesitated. "Before I was given the assignment of Asylum Keeper, I had been promised a year's leave to rest and travel and decide if Vision was still *my* piece in the world."

"And now?"

He sighed. "I saw glimpses of life beyond my city. I would like to see more. But this work is more important."

"No reason why you can't do the work and also do some traveling," Lee said, smiling. "Spending an evening in the Den can be as simple as crossing over a bridge. And anyone who works here would benefit from having a few days in Sanctuary each season."

Danyal studied the other man. Madman and teacher. Now the companion and partner he had also hoped to find?

They resumed exploration of the buildings until Yoshani returned with the news that they were less than a mile from a small community that was an hour's ride from the heart of Vision.

After Yoshani returned the bicycle to the shed and joined them, Danyal looked at Lee. "Well. Shall we return to the Shamans' compound and discuss this with our Guide?"

"Yes, I think we should," Lee replied. "And if Jeb is able to come to Vision, I'd like him to take a look at these buildings. He can tell us what will have to be done and how to get started."

They stepped onto the island and returned to the Shamans' compound. The rest of the afternoon was spent talking—describing the place they had found to the Shaman Council. Jasper would have opposed creating such a place, but the man was noticeably absent. Glorianna, Sebastian, and Michael asked a lot of questions for which he had no answers, but Danyal heard no opposition to the idea itself. And Lee joined in, countering their questions with questions of his own, making it clear that as a group they were used to hashing out physical boundaries that could turn fluid with a wish. By the time they were done, they had a crude map of the buildings and some thoughts about the land that would be part of the property.

We're going to do this, Danyal thought. *We're going to do this, and whether we succeed or fail, the city will change because of it.*

When they separated to wash up for the evening meal, Glorianna signaled for him to linger.

"Funny thing about landscapes," she said when they were the only ones left. "Sometimes you cross a bridge and end up in a place unlike anything you'd seen before. New life. Fresh start. Can't mistake the signs. But sometimes you cross a bridge and the world around you looks exactly the same. Except it isn't. Same place, but a different landscape. New life. Fresh start. But it's easy to miss the signs, easy to think you're still where you were."

"Did I miss the signs?" he asked.

She smiled. "No. You didn't miss the signs." She pressed her hand against his chest, over his heart. "But when you destroyed the wizards and Dark Guide the way you did, you altered your landscapes more than you intended, Danyal. So every day for the rest of your life, you will have to choose whether you heed the lure of the Dark or stand in the Light. Every single day."

"Every single day," he repeated.

As she lifted her hand and walked away, it occurred to him that the woman who was Guide to the World might not leave her brother's future to chance. "Did you and Ephemera already find that place before Lee and I started looking?"

Her laughter floating back to him was her only answer.

Chapter Thirty-two

Using the island, Lee brought Glorianna, Sebastian, Yoshani, and Michael back to Aurora. He shifted the island so that it rested near his mother's walled garden.

"I'll have a quick word with Jeb and see when he can come back with you," Michael said.

"I need to have a quick chat with Teaser and Philo," Sebastian said. "Make sure nothing in the Den needs my attention."

"Go home, Sebastian," Glorianna said. "Go see your wife and make funny faces at her tummy."

Sebastian snorted, but Lee noticed his cousin didn't deny making funny faces.

The rest of them left the island, but when Lee tried to leave, Glorianna stepped in front of him.

"No," she said quietly.

"I just want—"

"No, Lee. Not until Zhahar is gone."

"I just want a minute." *Just want to tell her about the place in Vision.*

"You urged Zhahar to ask for Heart's Justice instead of accepting the penalties her own people would have demanded."

"Harsh and unfair penalties," he snapped.

"And Heart's Justice may end up being just as harsh," she snapped back. "You have to let her go, Lee. You can't have anything to do with where her heart takes her."

"Why not? Lynnea was there when Sebastian needed her. You were fine with that."

"Lynnea's heart. Sebastian's heart."

"My heart. Zhahar's heart."

"Sholeh's heart. Zeela's heart. What about them? Did you consider how dangerous this will be for a Tryad?"

He rocked back on his heels.

Glorianna made a growling squeal that perfectly conveyed angry frustration. "Zhahar loves you. You love Zhahar. What about Sholeh and Zeela? Are you going to be three women's lover? Do they *want* you as their lover? Isn't that what the punishment of merging is designed to prevent? Jealousy between sisters caused by wanting the same man?"

"Daylight, Glorianna! It's not like that." It wasn't like that, but Glorianna's words reminded him of why he had to walk away from Zhahar—and the Guide shouldn't have needed to remind him.

"Zhahar wanting to love you is what put her in this position," Glorianna said gently. "Her sisters are at risk because of it. When I release Heart's Justice, Sholeh Zeela a Zhahar's hearts have to be united. Maybe they'll each want a different aspect of something, but they all have to want the same thing. If they don't . . ."

"They would run the same risk as if they'd crossed a resonating bridge while quarreling with each other," he finished.

"If one of them is split from the other two, will she have a body? Or will she die?"

Lee sagged against a tree. "Guardians of the Light and Guides of the Heart. This isn't any better than what Medusah would have done to her."

"If her aspects are in conflict when Heart's Justice is released, it won't be any better," Glorianna agreed. "In fact, it might be worse, because if the sisters get divided, they'll never know if the others are dead or are surviving in some way in other landscapes."

He'd said he would let Zhahar go, would get out of her life. But some part of him must have hoped that he wouldn't have to mean it. Now . . .

"How did Michael let you go?" he asked.

"You would have to ask him," she replied.

"What should I do?"

She kissed his cheek. "Go back to Vision. Start setting up that school with Danyal. Help him deal with the playground and make up a list of rules."

Lee made a face. "Like 'Don't move the temple when someone is inside it'?"

"That's a good rule. Make sure the two of you enforce it."

He wasn't sure how they were supposed to do that, but Glorianna wouldn't be interested in excuses. "I suppose I should see about making a stationary bridge or two, since you'll be traveling to the school a couple of times a week."

She hesitated. "For now, let's plan to meet in Sanctuary. We can use the island to travel back to Vision."

"Yeah. Okay." He tried to resist the words, but they wouldn't be held back. "I guess I was ready to love someone, and it felt right with Zhahar. Maybe I couldn't have handled the intimate details of living with someone as unique as her, but I wish we'd had a chance to try."

"I know." She kissed his cheek again. "Travel lightly, Lee."

"Travel lightly, Glorianna Belladonna."

He waited a few minutes after she left, telling himself it was to be sure Michael wasn't coming back with a message, or his mother didn't want to have a quick chat.

When he finally admitted that he wasn't going to get a glimpse of any aspect of Sholeh Zeela a Zhahar, he sighed, hoping to ease the ache in his chest. Then he shifted the island to the city of Vision and the new life waiting for him there.

Chapter Thirty-three

Zhahar sat in the dining room of Nadia's house, cupping a mug of peppermint tea. The day was pleasantly warm—perfect autumnal weather—but she felt cold inside. So cold. As if she would never thaw.

::I'm scared,:: Sholeh said.

So am I, Zhahar replied.

=We're all scared,= Zeela added.

::What's going to happen? Why won't anyone tell us?::

No one is supposed to tell us about Heart's Justice until Glorianna returns. *And why is that?* Zhahar wondered. Lee had sounded urgent when he'd told her how to ask for it. Why hadn't any of them noticed how he'd avoided telling her what it was or what it would do? Now *no one* would speak of it.

The dining room door opened. Zephyra slipped inside the room and sat across from her.

"Glorianna has returned," Zephyra said quietly, urgently. "She's talking to Nadia and will be here in another minute. Zhahar, ask to be released from this Heart's Justice. Come back to Tryadnea with me."

"To be merged because I dared to love someone who wasn't Tryad?" Zhahar asked bitterly. "Glorianna said we couldn't get back to Tryadnea now, and we wouldn't go back even if I could. Zeela wasn't the only one who wished the border would break and leave us here. We all wanted it. Even Sholeh." Out of the corner of her eye, she saw the door open a crack—just enough for someone on the other side to hear what was being said.

Let them listen.

"That's the trap, isn't it?" she said. "In order to keep Tryadnea sufficiently connected to another piece of Ephemera, the ones sent into the one-face lands have to make an effort to live there, *build a life there*, until we're exposed for what we are and have to run to avoid being locked up or killed. 'Make friends,' we're told, 'but don't let them get too close. Find work, because that hooks you in a little deeper to that place. Be a good citizen but never forget your true loyalty.'"

Zephyra looked devastated by her words, so Morragen came into view.

"Hundreds before you have made the same sacrifice for our people and our land," Morragen said. "Including me and my sisters."

The Morragen aspect had always intimidated her, just as the Medusah aspect had frightened her, but Zhahar was glad it was no longer Zephyra in view. It made it easier to hold on to a hard truth when she wasn't speaking to the aspect whose heart was breaking right now.

"You tell the Tryads who do this work that it is important work, valuable work, *vital* work."

"And it is."

"But you never tell them that making a real connection to a one-face land will change them, *damage* them. Because they will make friends, or begin to care about the people they work with, or fall in love. Tryadnea will no longer have their complete loyalty—until they are revealed for what they are. Until they are betrayed so they have to come home."

Betrayed. Yes, there was truth in that word.

"You will not speak of this," Morragen warned, her voice turned to ice.

"The leader can't be the betrayer. That would tear the Tryad apart. But someone else? Someone who is the living proof of what it costs to love outside our own kind? How many ears within the governing circle hear her whispers?"

"Zhahar, don't." Zephyra came back into view, tears spilling down her face. "You don't know what you're saying."

"Perhaps not," Zhahar conceded. "Your mothers and Allone were rivals for the leadership of Tryadnea before she gave up her sisters in order to love a one-face man."

"Who left her as soon as it was done," Zephyra said. "She became a one-face and was no longer considered for the leadership. But she was always on the fringes of the governing circle, always pointing out the dangers of getting too close to anyone who wasn't Tryad."

::Tell her,:: Sholeh urged.

"When you get back to the capital city, you should go to the archives and check some of the family lines. There might be a reason Allone is as persuasive as she is."

Medusah came into view, but before she could respond, Glorianna walked into the room. Or was it Belladonna?

Zhahar's hands tightened around the mug. She couldn't release it until Zeela loaned her the strength to let go.

"Now," Glorianna said as she took a seat at the head of the table. "Heart's Justice."

Morragen came into view. "That isn't necessary. The a Zhahar Tryad can return with us to Tryadnea."

"I thought I'd made it clear that their returning to Tryadnea was no longer possible," Belladonna said with an icy sweetness that made Zhahar shiver. "No. Zhahar and her sisters asked for Heart's Justice, and that is what they will have."

"As leader of the Tryad people, we must be the judge of that!" Morragen shouted.

"Not this time. Minor wrongdoing and disputes between people are settled through common justice, and the decisions are made by magistrates," Belladonna said. "Until we learned the nature of the wizards and where they came from, acts of violence were punished through Wizards' Justice, and the penalty was usually death by wizards' lightning. But when someone's actions require more than common justice but don't deserve death, a Landscaper is called to perform Heart's Justice." She looked at Zhahar. "Heart's Justice will forge a direct link between you and Ephemera, and you will be sent to the darkest landscape that resonates with your heart. It will be done tomorrow, at sunrise." Now she looked at Morragen. "You will return to Tryadnea *now*."

"No!" Zephyra pushed into view. "We're going to stay and support our daughters!"

"You don't want the same thing they do. All you'll do now is confuse their hearts. Wait for me outside."

"We are the leader of the Tryad," Morragen Medusah a Zephyra said as they rose. "Who are you to speak to us that way?"

"I am the monster that Evil fears," Belladonna replied softly. "I am the one who can take Tryadnea out of the world. Not just set it adrift. *Take it out of the world.* Or, worse, I can have Ephemera connect your land to the place that is feeding the Dark currents swelling in your homeland. You think you're a demon, Tryad? You haven't yet seen the worst demons that walk in our world."

Zhahar sat perfectly still, too afraid to move and call attention to herself.

"We will wait for you outside," Morragen finally said. She left the dining room, closing the door behind her.

"Now," Glorianna said. "What I told you about Heart's Justice is true. At least for a person of single aspect." She reached over and closed a hand around Zhahar's wrist. "Listen well, Sholeh Zeela a Zhahar. A link will be forged between you and Ephemera, and the world will send you to the darkest landscape you deserve. You may end up in a familiar place—even back in Tryadnea, despite not being able to reach it otherwise—or somewhere unlike anything you've seen, where you'll spend the rest of your life hiding what you are. The heart has no secrets. Take this day to think about who you are and what you truly want."

Glorianna pushed back her chair.

"What about Lee?" Zhahar asked, feeling her face heat. "Do you know where he is?"

Glorianna looked at her. "Lee is no longer a consideration. Where he is doesn't matter. What you and your sisters want for yourselves is all that can matter now. Remember, Sholeh Zeela a Zhahar, Ephemera is going to send you to the darkest landscape that resonates with your heart." She walked to the door, then looked back. "Let your heart travel lightly, because what you bring with you becomes part of the landscape."

Zhahar sat at the table a long time. No one came in to check on her. No one disturbed her. She knew there were other people around, but she felt alone. So terribly alone.

::She used our full name,:: Sholeh said slowly. ::Twice.::

=So?= Zeela growled.

::So this Heart's Justice will take us to the darkest landscape that resonates with the heart of Sholeh Zeela a Zhahar.::

Zhahar felt her heartbeat quicken. *Not the one who is three, not the individuals who might be split if considered separately, but the three who are one. She was telling us she can work it so the world considers all three of us together.*

=If we're united, the darkest landscape that would match Sholeh will balance out the darkest one that would match me,= Zeela said, sounding hopeful.

Someplace all three of us could survive, Zhahar agreed. *Put aside the rest,* she thought as she took the mug out to the kitchen. *Let your heart travel lightly.*

Lee was gone; she was estranged from her mothers and from her people. All she and her sisters had were each other. She hoped that would be enough.

Glorianna walked out of the kitchen and stood near the door. Sebastian had taken Lynnea home to rest. Her mother was in the keets' room, taking care of her birds, and Jeb was helping her. She didn't know where Caitlin and Teaser were, but they wouldn't have gone far. Neither would Yoshani. Not until they had witnessed the Heart's Justice that would determine Zhahar's fate.

That left Michael, who was sitting on a bench, playing a tune that was full of bitter weariness and a few turns of phrase that sounded hopeful.

It was the music he heard in the heart of Morragen Medusah a Zephyra.

She walked over to where Morragen stood, looking at the flowers blooming in Nadia's garden. Looking but probably not seeing.

She would make no apology for eavesdropping. Zhahar had known she was at the dining room door and had most likely drawn some courage from having someone besides her mothers hear her words. But some things about the Tryad had fallen into place because of those words.

"Whose voice whispers through the Tryad's dreams?" she asked when she stood beside Morragen. "Is it the voice of Guides who stand for the Light, or do you listen to the voices that were shaped in the Dark?"

"You speak in riddles," Morragen said harshly.

"Do I? How many generations have your people drifted? How many of the strong were lost when they were exposed to people who were primed to see them as demons or monsters? Tryads have mated outside your race. You have a young man who is a Bridge—at least one of his aspects is. What other talents have been brought into your race?" When Morragen said nothing, Glorianna continued. "Who decides who leads? The a Zhahar Tryad is disgraced, so they won't follow you when you step down as leader, the way you followed your mothers. Disgraced because one aspect wanted to love a one-face man, not just use him to bring in fresh blood to the race."

"She may be disgraced, but she doesn't have to go through with this Heart's Justice of yours."

"What kind of life do the disgraced have among your people?" Glorianna countered. "Why are your customs so harsh? I ask you again, Morragen Medusah a Zephyra. Whose voice whispers through the Tryad's dreams?"

"What does Allone spreading rumors now accomplish? It would have been years before Zhahar would step up and take our place."

"Adrift and bitter, the Dark currents in Tryadnea grow stronger," Glorianna said. "A successful union between a Tryad and a man of single aspect might strengthen the bonds between your people and another, might nourish hope that could create other bonds. The Dark Guides and wizards did a similar thing to the Landscapers. Over the years, they persuaded the instructors at the school to view as dangerous the students who were stronger than usual or who had more connection to the Dark currents. And we were dangerous—to the wizards. So they destroyed those among us who were the Guides and destroyed the strongest among the Landscapers under the guise of protecting Ephemera. They whisper in the dark, Morragen, and I think they've been whispering in Tryadnea for a long time now."

She waited while Medusah came into view.

"These wizards are people of single aspect," Medusah said. "How . . . ?"

"If one aspect of a Tryad can be a Bridge, one aspect can be a wizard," Glorianna said, feeling the sudden wash of power in the currents of the world. "A betrayal and death long ago, like the one in the story about the sisters, could have tipped the resonance of Tryadnea enough to let the wizards in. Their females couldn't wear human faces, but mating with another race that might have been spawned in the darker currents could give them offspring that *could* hide. Change the resonance of Tryadnea and set your land adrift. Become an essential part of what is needed to connect the land to another place, but keep the connection only if there are wizards influencing that place. Those wizards provide shelter in the other lands while they mate with Tryad, especially the Tryad who already have some of their bloodlines. And the power that shaped the Dark Guides and their progeny is reinforced in your people."

"If any of that is true, then we have been betrayed over and over," Medusah said. She swallowed hard. "What Zahar said was true. Every Tryad who goes out to connect our land returns damaged in some way." She frowned. "You think that's why we were able to connect to Vision? Because the wizards were already there?"

"Yes, I think that's why. But there were enough hearts that wanted something different. I think that's why, even though you were anchored to Vision, Ephemera made me aware of you. The moment Tryadnea began resonating with me, it was no longer within the wizards' ability to control the currents of Light and Dark. They can influence the currents by influencing people's hearts, but they can't easily set you adrift again."

"So the enemy is among us, wearing the face of a friend."

"The most dangerous enemies usually do," Glorianna said softly. "That's why I'm not going to establish other borders or boundaries between Tryadnea and my other landscapes. If there are wizards hiding among those who govern the Tryad, I can't risk them reaching my pieces of the world—especially Sanctuary. I can't risk them finding Caitlin when she's tending her landscapes. We won't even know a wizard is there until . . ." She clamped a hand over her nose and stepped back from the flower bed as a stinkweed poked out of the ground. "All right, we *will* know now that there is a plant that will warn us. Ephemera, get that out of my mother's garden and shift the wind so the smell blows away from the house."

Medusah stared at the flower bed. "Could that plant grow in Tryadnea?"

"At this point, I think it will grow anywhere." Glorianna lowered her hand and sniffed. The plant hadn't been there long enough to stink up the area too much. "If no one else understands the significance of it suddenly appearing, you'll have your warning that a wizard is nearby."

Medusah hesitated, then submerged as Zephyra came into view. "Is there nothing you can do for Zhahar and her sisters?"

"Their life, their journey, their choice." Glorianna lightly touched Zephyra's arm. "It may take them a while, but they'll find the place their hearts recognize as home."

"Then we will return to Tryadnea to consider all we have learned. And we'll hope that someday we will have news of Sholeh Zeela a Zhahar."

"Travel lightly, Morragen Medusah a Zephyra."

"And you, Glorianna Belladonna."

Glorianna wasn't sure if the Tryad wanted to say more or just didn't know how to leave after everything that had happened in the past couple of days. She did notice how Yoshani and Teaser were suddenly available to escort Zephyra back to the border between the Den and Tryadnea. And she noticed that her mother didn't come out of the house until Zephyra was gone.

"What do you think?" Glorianna asked, linking her arm with Nadia's.

"Are you asking a fellow Landscaper or your mother?"

"My mother."

"She's hurting for her children. As a leader, I think she recognizes that her people might be harboring a deadly enemy—and that must be a terrible and frightening realization. And as a woman, I think she's hoping that, by being cut free of their people, Zhahar and her sisters will find the heart magic that has been eluding the Tryad for so many years."

"If Zhahar does find it, the Tryad who were merged or forced to sacrifice siblings because of some archaic law will be bitter, maybe even destructive." *Especially if some part of them answered to the Dark.*

"Yes. I don't envy the a Zephyra Tryad."

"Nor do I." Glorianna hesitated, struggling to say the words. "Do you mind that I have two aspects?"

"Aspects." Nadia smiled. "We have a way to describe it now, don't we? No, I don't mind, and even if I did . . ." She shrugged. "Your life, your journey, your choice."

She felt the currents of Light become a little stronger, so she laughed and said, "How long are you going to wait before you give Lee one of the young keets as a housewarming present?"

"He doesn't want a keet."

"He didn't want a keet. Now I think having one would be good for him."

Nadia said nothing. Then, "The youngsters I have now will be leaving for their new homes in a few days, but Jeb is building a couple of cages that might suit Lee's new residence."

"So he should be settled in well enough by the time you're looking for homes for the next brood?"

"Exactly."

Laughing, the two women walked back to the house.

Chapter Thirty-four

They didn't sleep that night. They simply stared at the big traveling bag that would hold everything they could take with them.

Twice Zhahar pulled out the Three Faces and the Third Eye, the spiritual symbols of her people, intending to leave them behind. But it wasn't the spirit of her people that had failed her; it was the people themselves. So she tucked the Three Faces carefully into the bag, then studied the three-eyed goddess. One eye to see intentions, one to witness actions, and one to see the heart.

"Watch over us," she whispered as she tucked that into the bag too.

=It's almost time,= Zeela whispered.

Where is Sholeh? Zhahar asked. *She needs to be with us when this happens.*

=Let her rest a little while longer.=

She won't have much of a life in a dark place.

=Probably not. But we'll do what we can for all of us.=

A tapping on the guest room door. When Zhahar answered it, Nadia stood on the other side.

"Ready?" Nadia asked kindly.

No. "Yes, we're ready." Zhahar hefted the bag, grunting a little at its weight. *I hope we don't have to lug this very far.*

Zeela didn't answer.

"You already have plenty to carry, but I made up a pack that has water and enough food to last you for a day or two." Nadia handed her the pack and briefly touched Zhahar's cheek. "Travel lightly."

=She says that and then weighs us down a little more,= Zeela grumbled.

Or maybe it was an attempt at humor, since Zhahar could feel Sholeh's presence now.

"The others are waiting outside to say good-bye," Nadia said.

She didn't want to see them, but it occurred to her that people fated to receive Heart's Justice usually didn't get a send-off. So she thanked Nadia for the food and walked outside.

Michael and Yoshani were waiting just outside the door. Michael held up another pack. This one was big enough to hold the food pack and more. When he slipped the food pack into it, she heard the clink of coins.

"Yoshani and I were doing a little weeding last night and unearthed this stash of coins. We thought having a bit of gold would smooth the way once you get to where you're going."

"Be well, Sholeh Zeela a Zhahar," Yoshani said. "I hope we meet again."

She blinked back tears and walked over to where Lynnea and Sebastian waited.

"Here," Lynnea said, holding out a book. "I know you can't carry much, but this is my favorite book of stories. I thought Sholeh would enjoy them."

"Glorianna is waiting for you at the edge of the road," Sebastian said. "I'll walk you up there."

He took her elbow before she could decline the offer. As soon as they rounded the corner of the house and were out of sight of the others, he stopped and slipped a small cloth bag into the pack.

"One-shot bridge to the Den," he said. "Heart's Justice is supposed to take you where you're meant to be, so you're supposed to handle whatever hardships come your way. But if you're in danger, Zhahar, if your lives are at risk, Sholeh or Zeela can use the bridge to cross over, and we'll deal with the consequences."

"Thank you," she whispered. "All of you."

He kissed her cheek, then led her halfway to where Glorianna waited.

She walked the rest of the way alone—and not alone. One who was three. Three who were one.

There were a lot of things she wanted to say to Lee's sister, but none of them were appropriate—and probably didn't matter now.

Our life, our journey, our choice.

"Let your heart travel lightly," Glorianna Belladonna said. "Because what you bring with you becomes part of the landscape."

What do we want to bring with us? Zhahar asked her sisters.

::Hope,:: Sholeh whispered.

=Courage,= Zeela said.

Heart, Zhahar added. Then she said to the Guide of the Heart, "We're ready."

Glorianna smiled. "Yes, you are. Ephemera, hear me."

The wind blew over her skin, under her skin. The ground felt soft, fluid. The world faded and became a white sheet where images flashed by almost too fast for them to see. A dark lake and two huge black stones rising out of the water. A desert of rust-colored sand. A harbor town that made them uneasy. Another harbor town that looked bright and happy. A valley full of fog. Bobbing lights and music.

Images pulled at one or the other of them, but not all of them. And then . . .

Zhahar felt something snag her as the ground became so fluid it disappeared. She screamed—and heard Sholeh and Zeela scream too.

She stumbled and almost stepped on a dead, bloated cat, scattering the rats that had come for a meal.

Zeela came into view, steadying them as they walked out of the alley and looked around.

=Late afternoon, if I can trust the position of the sun and the feel of the day,= she said.

Then we're nowhere near Aurora, Zhahar said. *But it has the cool feel of autumn here too. Sholeh? Are you all right?*

::Yes.::

Zeela wasn't sure of that, but being the one in view, she had to pay attention to where they were and leave Sholeh to Zhahar.

A dark place. She could feel it. It looked like a poorer section of town, but that wouldn't have made it dark. Sometimes the fanciest parts of a town were also the darkest. This felt more like a shadow street that had gone septic.

Shadow street? Zhahar asked.

=Couldn't be.= *But it feels like one.* Blowing out a breath, Zeela headed for a group of men working around an empty lot in the middle of the block, then veered toward the women who were watching the workers from across the street.

"What happened?" she asked a middle-aged woman.

"Strangers took over a house a while back," the woman replied. "Nasty pieces of work, every one of them. Then one night they disappeared—and the house with them. Pipes were ripped open and we had water and sewage filling up the house's cellar and pouring out into the street. Was worth a demon's ransom to get the city workers to come out here and begin fixing things. Had to petition a Shaman before we got any help, and had to hire the Knife Guild to protect the workers, because some bad things had happened on this street. Wasn't like that before the strangers arrived, even if it was a shadow street."

Zeela swayed and wished she'd taken time for a sip of water and a bite of food. Not that she would have taken either in that stinking alley, but . . .

Shaman. Knife. Shadow street.

"What is this place?" she asked. When the woman, who had sounded friendly enough, gave her a less-than-friendly look, she added hurriedly, "I just arrived. Was left here, actually, and wasn't told the name of the town."

The woman bobbed her head once. After a minute during which they both watched the workers, she said, "This is part of the city of Vision. You've heard of Vision?"

Zeela nodded, not sure if her heart was pounding so hard because of her feelings or because of her sisters. "In the city of Vision, you can find only what you can see."

"That's right." The woman looked her over. "There's lodgings at the end of the street. Not the cleanest place, but it won't cost you much to stay there."

"Appreciate the information. I'll go down and see if they have any rooms available." She narrowed her eyes and studied the man who didn't look like he was doing anything useful, but his eyes never stopped scanning the street. He wasn't the Knife who had helped them get out of Vision, but having that much of an introduction couldn't hurt. "But first I need to talk to a man about a job."

Chapter Thirty-five

L ee settled the island a few steps away from the cottage he now called home, picked up the cloth-covered bundle that contained his new roommate, hurried off the island, and rushed to get inside.

But he still wasn't quick enough.

"Lee?" Danyal called from the large screened patio that connected their cottages.

Sighing, Lee changed directions and joined Danyal on the patio. It was too chilly to sit outside for pleasure, so Danyal must have been waiting for him to return.

"We're going to have to get a hook for that door." He jerked a thumb over his shoulder to indicate the patio door and tried to ignore Danyal's palpable curiosity. Then he sighed again, set the bundle on the table, and removed the cloth covering partway.

The lavender and white keet began a muttering scold—the same sound he'd been making since Nadia put the traveling cage on the island and left.

"Watch him, will you?" Lee said. "I have to get the other cage."

"There's more than one keet?" Danyal asked.

"No, but Jeb made him a big cage to live in. That one is a traveling cage so that, in warmer weather, he can come with me when I'm spending the day at the playground station. That will give him a chance to socialize." He rolled his eyes—a wasted movement, since he was wearing the dark glasses and no one would see it.

He went back to the island, gathered up his pack and the big cage, and took those into his cottage. Then he returned to the patio. Since Danyal seemed interested in the bird, it was tempting to say the keet had been intended for the Shaman, but he could picture sitting down to dinner at his mother's and having *that* little tidbit slip out during a conversation. And now that a stationary bridge linked their school to Aurora, Danyal was a frequent guest at Nadia's home—and Sebastian's—so it was bound to come up.

"I have his food, his dishes, his toys, and things for him to chew," Lee said, knowing he sounded a little more sour than he felt. "And once he settles in to his new home, he'll be able to play with his favorite toy."

"What is that?" Danyal asked.

"People."

Danyal laughed. "What is his name?"

"Haven't come up with one. My mother doesn't name the babies that are going to be given away, because she says the names should be chosen by the new families."

"That makes sense. So you have no thoughts?"

"One." Lee leaned close to the cage and said, "Featherhead."

He regretted it as soon as his eardrums started vibrating. How could something that small be so loud?

When the keet went to the back of the cage and resumed muttering, Danyal said with a straight face, "I don't think he likes that name." He gave Lee a puzzled look. "If you didn't want him, why did you take him?"

"My mother presented me with the cage and the keet and told me it was time for me to have one. My sister, along with Caitlin and Lynnea, agreed." And a man who had lived with Landscapers his whole life didn't argue when three of them said it was time. Especially when one of those Landscapers was a Guide of the Heart.

"Perhaps I can help you with the name," Danyal said. "Maybe something more traditional to this part of the world?"

Lee studied the Shaman, who was also a Guide. "Thanks."

"I was waiting for you because the Apothecary dropped these off." Danyal picked up a small case from the woven table beside his chair.

Lee took the case and opened it.

"Try them," Danyal said.

Slipping the dark glasses into his shirt pocket, he carefully removed the other glasses and put them on. Then he took the book Danyal held out and opened it to a random page.

"They work," he said after a moment. "I can read again."

"Good," Danyal said, smiling.

Over the past few weeks, his eyesight had continued to improve, thanks to the more potent eyedrops the Apothecary had made. His eyes weren't as good as they used to be, but he could see again. And now, after a visit to the eyeglass maker's booth at the bazaar to have a special pair of glasses made, he could read again.

He removed the glasses and put them in their case.

"What are you going to do now?"

Lee listened to the muttering in the cage that sounded more unhappy now than bitchy. He sighed—but he also smiled because the keet was a living reminder of home and the people who loved him. "I'm going to figure out the best place for his big cage—and then I'm going to make him some toast."

Chapter Thirty-six

Zhahar sat at the wobbly kitchen table, rolling a glass of firewater between her hands. The cheap, rough-tasting alcohol didn't appeal to her, but lately Zeela always had a bottle stashed in a bottom cupboard behind the pots and pans that weren't often used.

The seasons were changing. The autumn days still held some warmth, but the night air had the crisp scent of winter. She had to find warm clothes—mostly garments appropriate for Zeela, but also garments she and Sholeh could wear. And tomorrow she would have to face the market and the increasingly suspicious looks from the vendors and the people in her neighborhood.

=Zhahar?= Zeela sounded groggy.

You need to rest, Zhahar said, not wanting to get into an argument and knowing she would if Zeela didn't sink back into rest.

=We all need to rest. We need to *sleep.* It's been too many days since we got real sleep. I missed a couple of easy blocks today and have the bruises to prove it.=

You missed those blocks because you forgot that Sholeh is taking that medicine to calm her nerves, and it's strong enough to affect all of us, Zhahar snapped. *You forgot, so you went out last night and got stinking, fall-down drunk, and I had to clean up the puke after you passed out. You forgot—*

=I haven't forgotten anything,= Zeela snarled. =And you gulping down a glass of firewater isn't going to help.=

A brittle silence filled the little kitchen.

We were sent to the darkest landscape that resonated with the heart of Sholeh Zeela a Zhahar, Zhahar said wearily. *When you connected with that Knife and got work so fast, I thought it was a sign that this was where we were supposed to be, that Sholeh and I would find something here too. I thought it was a sign that we ended up on a shadow street that had been touched by the wizards, that our presence might do some good. But after you started reporting for training every day and Sholeh and I could come into view only in our room or when one of us went out to the market, I began to realize what it had been like for you and Sholeh when I worked as a Handler, how limited your lives were. How limited our lives would be from now on, no matter which one of us is supporting us.*

=We were all able to have a bit of a life when you worked at the Asylum, at least for a while.=

Zhahar hesitated, but this wasn't something she had a right to hide from the warrior aspect of their Tryad. *The last couple of times I went to the market, there was talk—people commenting about how they never see us together, and isn't it strange that we're doing washing and such late at night when two of us are home during the day and could be putting that time to use.*

=Busybodies,= Zeela grumbled. =All *they* do is talk.=

But Zhahar heard the uneasiness under the grumble, so she said the rest. *A story has started going around about a kind of demon the wizards brought with them to act as their servants and spies—a demon that can wear more than one face but has only one body.*

Now Zeela swore. =We need to go. Sholeh needs to get off that medicine so her head is clear and she can help us. Then we need to pack up and go.=

Not yet. Not yet, she repeated when Zeela started to protest. *If you can finish your training with the Knife Guild, you'll have a better chance of finding work in another part of Vision. I'll push Sholeh to remember what she learned about other parts of the city, parts that weren't directly touched by the wizards. We can hold on long enough for you to get your journeyman's badge."

=How many other Tryad held out too long?= Zeela asked grimly.

Because she knew the answer, Zhahar said nothing. She waited until Zeela drifted back down to rest. Then she reached into her pocket and took out the little bag that held the one-shot bridge Sebastian had given them. She stared at it while she sipped the firewater, hoping the alcohol would pull her into sleep.

They could use that one-shot bridge to leave Vision, and she would insist that Zeela use it if they were in life-threatening danger. But every time she looked at the bag, she knew with a certainty she couldn't explain that if they used it, if they tried to slip around this part of the journey that Heart's Justice demanded of them, they would get a glimpse of what they needed at the moment it disappeared from their lives.

Tucking the bag back into her pocket, she got up, rinsed out the glass, and went into the bedroom to try to give them all the sleep they needed.

Chapter Thirty-seven

Answering the summons, Zeela stepped into the doorway of the guild-house room that served as Primo's office. A swarthy man with a long scar on his left cheek, he was First Knife, the leader of the Knife Guild in the northwestern part of Vision. When she had been brought before him, he had been sufficiently impressed with her fighting skills to make her a guild apprentice, and she had worked hard every day since then to earn a guild badge. Judging by the look on his face, whatever he had to tell her wasn't something she wanted to hear.

"Come in, Zeela," Primo said. "Have a seat."

She sat because he was First Knife and he had earned that title.

He settled on the corner of the old desk. Funny to think of him doing accounts and paying bills, but the guild was a business like any other. They were just selling a different kind of skill.

"You need to find another place, Zeela," Primo said kindly. "The shadow streets around here turned dark and mean while those pus-filled wizards fouled our city, and even with the Shamans assigned to the northwest, it will take some time to turn it back to what it was."

"I can help you," she said quickly. "I know I was late and didn't go out with the rest of the team this morning, but—"

"Your sister was crying again," Primo said. "The youngest one. Sholeh. I see it in your face." He leaned toward her. "If it was just you, I'd let you stay. You've got skill, girl, and you would have made a good Knife one day. But it's not just you, is it? And this part of Vision is no place for your sisters. Especially young Sholeh. And even Zhahar was roughed up when she went to the market, and could have gotten more than a black eye if you hadn't shown up to help her carry the bags home. Yes, I heard about that."

Zeela looked at the floor. Ever since Zhahar was assaulted, they were barely able to convince Sholeh to come into view, even in their room. And the Sholeh they knew was fading away a little more every day, hardly interested in existing, let alone living.

But Zhahar still believed they could hold out a little longer, *needed* to hold out a little longer, even if she couldn't explain why.

Primo leaned back and studied Zeela in a way that made her want to fidget.

"There are rumors spreading in the streets around here about a three-faced demon who slipped into the city with the wizards. You've heard these rumors?"

Not with the wizards, she thought as her heart pounded. *But that won't make any difference. Not now.* "I've heard them."

"I contacted brethren in other parts of Vision, asking if they had heard these rumors. Most had heard nothing, but one had met a trio of sisters he called a three-sided heart and spoke well of them." Primo looked pointedly at Zeela's left bicep. The tattoo was covered now, but all the Knives had seen it during the training sessions. "His words carry enough weight with me that I would have let you stay, and will still tell the rest of the brethren what he told me so that they will know the rumors are false. But that won't help your sisters. That won't keep them safe in the market."

No, the guild believing she wasn't a demon wouldn't keep Zhahar and Sholeh safe. By the triple stars, they had tried to hold on long enough build a life here. Hadn't they tried?

"Got you a ticket on a passenger coach," Primo said. "It leaves in the morning."

"Going where?" Zeela asked, feeling weighed down by emotions.

"Going to the heart of Vision." He leaned toward her.

"Go to The Temples if you can find them. Talk to some of the Shamans there."

"I could talk to the Shamans who come around here."

"No, girl. You and your sisters need to be somewhere else." Primo leaned back. "I do have a couple of things for you." He picked up a small bag from his desk and handed it to her. "Everyone tossed in a coin from his last job. Travel money."

"You gave me my pay from my last assignment."

"I know. This is from your brethren. Our way of wishing you good fortune on your journey. Then there is this." He picked up the brass badge that was worn by a journeyman Knife. "In the ordinary way of things, I would have waited a couple more months for this, had you working with someone a while longer. But you've earned it. Any First in the city will consider your credentials if you want to keep training and working with the guild. Even if you don't, that badge would help you get guard work."

"Thank you." She took the badge—and swallowed tears.

Primo stood. "You'll find your place." He looked a little uncomfortable. "I'll take it as a kindness if you let me know where you settle."

She stood too. "I'll do that." She lifted the ticket, the bag of coins, and the badge. "Thank you for this."

He offered his hand—something he rarely did. She gripped that hand, then stepped back.

=Aren't either of you going to say anything?= she asked when she reached their lodgings. =I did my best.=

We all did, Zhahar replied. *But he's right, Zeela. It's time for us to move on.* An odd note came into Zhahar's voice as she whispered, *It is time.*

=Do you think our relocating to another part of Vision will make any difference?=

Primo thinks it will. And if we go to The Temples, we can ask for Shaman Danyal. Maybe he could help us, or at least give us advice, based on knowing we're a Tryad. We have to hope it will make a difference.

=Why?=

That odd note came into Zhahar's voice again. *If we don't hope, how can we change anything?*

Zeela had no answer, so she and Zhahar took turns packing up their things. They didn't ask Sholeh about her books. They simply packed them, accepting the sore muscles that would come from hauling the extra weight. The books were as close to life as Sholeh had seen lately. They couldn't ask her to leave even one behind—especially when they were afraid they were losing her.

Chapter Thirty-eight

They reached the bazaar at the center of Vision after a day's travel. Instead of pushing on to find The Temples, they had to take a room when Zeela suddenly became dizzy and couldn't seem to hold on to her thoughts. That's when Zhahar realized that Sholeh had been submerged for so many days that she and Zeela had ignored the necessity of regular meals. Now Sholeh's aspect was physically out of balance to such a degree that Zhahar considered what would happen to them if she had to take Sholeh and Zeela to a clinic.

She got them to the room and went out again for food, hoping that she would get back before Sholeh's disorientation began to show in her too.

She bought flatbread filled with soft cheese, dates, and chopped nuts; a ball of brown rice carried in a paper shaped like a flower; and a stick of cooked meat. Back in the room, she took a mouthful of each type of food, eating slowly. Then she prodded Zeela to come into view and do the same thing. Once Zeela felt steadier, the two of them managed to get Sholeh into view—and forced her to stay there until she took a bite of each kind of food and drank a glass of water.

Throughout that evening, Zhahar forced the rotation until the food was gone. By then, Zeela was exhausted but back to normal, and Sholeh, while sounding frail, was lucid again.

The next morning, Zhahar went out to the food stalls for

another flatbread. Once she was back inside, she divided the flatbread into three pieces. When Sholeh resisted, Zahar became insistent.

We're going to find The Temples today, she said. *But *not* until we've all eaten and washed up.*

::I don't have to wash,:: Sholeh said faintly. ::No one is going to see me.::

=You still have to wash,= Zeela said. =It's been too many days since you had a full bath.=

Which we can't do today, Zahar broke in when she felt Sholeh start to protest. *The room has only a sink and a toilet, so we're all taking sponge baths.*

They finished up so late in the morning they had to take all their bags with them or pay for the use of the room for another day. After wandering the bazaar for a couple of hours, Zahar wished they'd kept the room.

=The entrance is supposed to be here,= Zeela snarled. =At least, this is the direction everyone we asked pointed to.=

In the city of Vision, you can find only what you can see, Zahar thought. *So who would be able to see The Temples?*

She lugged their bags into an open space between two stalls. *Be quiet for a minute. Let me try something.*

Holding on to the straps of her bags, she closed her eyes and thought of Danyal walking the Asylum grounds, holding a wind chime because it was the sound of joy.

The wind chime, singing in the air and lifting the heart.

She opened her eyes and looked at the archway between the stalls. THE TEMPLES was carved into the arch.

Found it, she whispered. Settling the bags over her shoulders as best she could, she crossed into the part of Vision that belonged to the Shamans.

She paused in front of the Temple of Sorrow, then spotted a figure in a wheat-colored robe standing outside another building farther down the road.

"Good day to you," Zahar called. "Could you help me?"

The person—a woman, judging by the shape of the face—smiled and lifted her hands as if to say "Maybe" or "I don't know."

"Do you understand me?"

A nod.

"Can you speak?"

Fingers touched the material covering her throat, followed by a head shake.

"Oh." Zhahar caught her lower lip between her teeth. The woman *did* understand her, so if she phrased her questions carefully, she might still get answers. "I need help. I came to The Temples for guidance."

The woman spread her arms wide, as if to say there was help and guidance all around them.

"Yes, there are many Shamans here, but I was looking for Shaman Danyal. Do you know him?"

A nod.

"Is he here?"

Head shake.

Zhahar sighed. Could she trust another Shaman with the secret of what she was?

The woman pointed to her own eye, then patted her chest.

When Zhahar said nothing, the woman did it again.

::Could I see?:: Sholeh asked.

Zhahar hesitated. *It would be hard to explain your coming into view.*

::I just need to be close enough to the surface.::

The woman made the two gestures again.

=Eye and chest?= Zeela suggested.

::No,:: Sholeh replied. ::Seeing and heart. I think.::

"Seeing and heart?" Zhahar asked.

Nodding, the woman raised two fingers and brought them closer together.

::Seeing heart,:: Sholeh said.

When Zhahar repeated the words, the woman's smile widened—and Zhahar understood.

"Shaman Danyal is at a place called Seeing Heart? Do you know where it is?"

More hand gestures, patiently repeated over and over.

::One hour. Riding. South.::

"An hour's ride south of here?" Zhahar asked.

The woman clapped her hands, indicating delight.

"Thank you." Smiling, Zhahar blinked away tears of relief. "Thank you."

=We can go back to the travel station where we arrived and find out if there are any coaches going south,= Zeela said.

After thanking the woman again, Zhahar lugged their baggage back to the archway. Then Zeela came into view and took over and got them to the station.

They had to wait a couple of hours for the next south-bound coach. Not liking the look of most of the food being sold at the convenient stands, Zeela settled for a piece of fruit and small jug of water.

The possibility of seeing Danyal again had perked up Sholeh enough for her to pay attention to their surroundings. That allowed Zhahar some time to submerge and rest—and think her own thoughts. Shaman Danyal was an hour's ride away, and that was good.

But where was Lee? If she asked, would Danyal tell her?

Chapter Thirty-nine

The wooden sign at the top of the lane was well made but small enough to be easily overlooked. Under the words SEEING HEART were symbols for the eye and heart. That indicated not everyone who came searching for this place could read.

You can find only what you can see, Zhahar thought. *And you can see only what you truly want to find.*

She and Zeela had debated for the entire ride south which of them should approach whoever was in this place. She had experience as a Handler, but the people in the small community where they had disembarked had said it was a school. A Handler wasn't a teacher. On the other hand, a journeyman of the Knife Guild probably wouldn't find much work at a school either.

In the end, they decided Zhahar would be the one to approach and ask for Danyal.

The lane was still rutted in places and was bordered by frost-killed weeds, but it showed signs of someone making slow but steady effort to make it more passable. Zhahar caught glimpses of buildings between the trees but couldn't see much. Then she got close enough to see why.

A living green wall that topped out a finger's length above her head stretched out in both directions. On either side of the lane were tall metal posts. The metal bar gate was open now, but she thought it was probably locked after sunset—a good assumption, since there was a bell on one of the posts that could summon someone if there was a late arrival.

Shabby buildings that looked like they were being fixed up. Grounds that looked like they were being cleaned up. And . . .

That's Nik, Zhahar said. *And over there. That's Kobrah!*

As she hurried forward to catch up to Kobrah, she noticed other people. Denys. Some of the borderline inmates from the southern Asylum. And Danyal.

She changed direction and hurried as best she could, wanting to drop all the baggage and be free of the weight. "Shaman!"

He turned toward her voice, and for a moment she thought he wouldn't acknowledge her—or didn't recognize her. Then he strode toward her, swiftly closing the distance.

"Zhahar?"

::I don't think he wants to see us,:: Sholeh whispered.

"I should go," she said, stepping back.

"No." Danyal grabbed the handle of one of the traveling bags. "No. I'm just surprised to see you. You were given Heart's Justice. How did you get here?"

"We ended up in the northwest part of Vision."

"The northwest absorbed a lot of the wizards' kind of darkness," he said, studying her.

"Yes. We tried . . . Zeela did the best there, but Sholeh and I were too much of a burden."

=My sisters are *not* a burden,= Zeela snapped.

"Why are you here, Sholeh Zeela a Zhahar?" he asked gently.

"We came looking for work."

"But why here?"

"We went to The Temples and asked for you, hoping you'd have some suggestions or advice. A woman told us about this place and that you were here."

"I see. So you're looking for work. All of you?"

Remembering how little time Sholeh had been in view over the past few weeks and what that had done to their youngest sister, she lifted her chin as a small defiance. "Yes, all of us."

"Is Sholeh still interested in scholarly work?" Danyal

asked. "Because we've got stacks of donated books that need to be organized, and everything from fine prints of paintings to rough charcoal sketches of places that all need to be sorted in a way that will help us figure out *where* those places might be. We have two Supervisors—meaning Nik and Denys—and a couple of Helpers, but we're looking for some help with sorting out the students and working out what each of them needs in order to take the next step in the journey. And the Knife is looking at people from his guild to stay here as guards to help keep order."

We? Zhahar wondered as her heart gave a funny little jump.

::I still like books,:: Sholeh said. ::Tell him, Zhahar!::

She swallowed hard. "Sholeh is very interested in working with the books and pictures. And Zeela earned her journeyman's badge in the Knife Guild."

"What about you, Zhahar?" Danyal asked softly. "What do you want?"

Love. "I think I could learn to be a counselor."

"Is that all you want?"

"I don't know." She hesitated. Then, because it was Danyal, she blurted out the truth. "I'm so scared. We almost lost Sholeh, and I'm scared to want anything but a safe place where we can all survive."

Danyal studied her. Then he nodded. "All right. If you want the work, we could use the help."

Her legs felt weak with relief. "We want the work."

He took the big traveling bag off her shoulder and slipped it over his. He pointed behind her. "The staff has suites of rooms in that building. They're clean and repaired, but they're not pretty. We'll be feeling the full touch of winter soon, so we focused on getting the functional done first. If you want to paint walls or anything else in your free time, go right ahead."

He headed toward the building. She fell into step.

"If we're all working . . ." she began.

"Everyone gets a full day off from the work rotation and a half day of personal time," he said. "The three of you together will put in the same hours as any other person, so you'll have to split the time off between you, but you'll get the same as anyone else here."

"All right."

"There are suites still available on the first and second floors. Any preference?"

"First is fine," she said at the same moment Zeela said, =Second floor is safer.=

"Who's arguing for what?" He smiled. "You've got a look on your face."

"Second floor is safer, but I'd still like the first floor."

"You can always change suites if you don't like this one," Danyal said easily. He stopped at a door and opened it. "We haven't locked the ones that weren't occupied. The key is in the office. I'll ask my partner to bring it to you." He stepped inside, set down her traveling bag, and turned to leave.

"Shaman? Do you wish we hadn't found this place?"

He didn't say anything for a long moment. Then: "This is a new life, Sholeh Zeela a Zhahar. There are no taboos here from your homeland unless you bring them. What you make of your life is up to you."

"I don't know how to begin."

"Getting unpacked is a good place to start. When we meet for the evening meal, we can tell you about this place and what we hope to do here." After giving her hand a friendly squeeze, he left.

She waited until she heard the outer door close. Then she looked around.

=Pretty dingy,= Zeela said. =But nothing some paint wouldn't fix.=

::The furniture isn't any better than what we had in the room near the Asylum,:: Sholeh said. ::But it isn't any worse. And I can study again.::

It sounds like you're going to be doing more than studying, Zhahar said.

=Did we get stuck in the northwest part of Vision because we were scared?= Zeela asked. =Or because I needed to earn some credentials that would help us?=

The heart has no secrets. *Maybe a little of both,* Zhahar replied. *Or maybe we weren't ready to come here.*

::If we had reached this place too soon, we would have brought the taboos with us,:: Sholeh said thoughtfully. ::Even though we believed they were wrong.::

Opportunities and choices. New life, fresh start.

They unpacked. Deciding which shelf would hold Sholeh's books was easy. Deciding where to put Zeela's weapons ended in a lively discussion that wasn't completely settled. When Zhahar unwrapped the Three Faces and the Third Eye, she automatically opened a drawer to hide them away.

"We're done hiding," she said as she set the Tryad's spiritual symbols on the dresser. Between them, she placed the little bag that held the one-shot bridge Sebastian had given her—a reminder of acceptance . . . and possibilities.

That much done, she stopped so they all had time to wash up for dinner.

Just when she began to wonder if Danyal had forgotten about the key, someone knocked on the door.

She opened the door and couldn't do anything but stare.

His black hair had gotten longer, and when he removed the dark glasses, his green eyes were clear.

"Lee," she whispered, filled with so much hope it felt painful. "Lee."

Smiling, he held out a hand and waited for her to slip her hand into his.

"Hello, Sholeh Zeela a Zhahar," he said. "My name is Lee. I'm the Bridge at Seeing Heart. I hear we're going to be working together."

Yes, we are, she thought as he drew her into the hallway, locked her door, and handed her the key. *Yes, we are.*

And maybe, if his feelings for her hadn't changed, they would be able to do more.

ANNE BISHOP

The Voice

An Ephemera Novella

Dear Readers,

Some stories haunt you until you write them. That's what happened to me a few years ago when the first sentence of this story wouldn't let me go until I wrote the rest of it. "The Voice" was my introduction to the city of Vision, one of the landscapes of Ephemera. I'm pleased to be able to share it with you now.

Travel lightly,
Anne Bishop

Chapter One

They called her The Voice because she had none. Fat, mute, and dim-witted, she was an orphan the village supported, providing her with a house and caretakers. And she was always included in village life. Oh, she wasn't invited into people's homes—everyone went to The Voice's house when a visit was required—but every time someone had a "moody day," as my mother had called them, every time something happened that was less than pleasant, a special little cake was made. The "moody" person took the treat to The Voice's house, waited until she took her special seat in the visitors' room, then handed her the food.

She never refused a moody cake. Never. She would smile at the children when they handed her the treats, and sometimes she smiled at the adults. She never smiled at the village Elders, but she also never refused their offerings when they came to visit. You always knew that she didn't refuse because that was part of the ritual—you stayed and watched her eat what you had brought, and when you left, you felt better. The moody day was gone and you went back to your ordinary life.

I never considered the oddity of an orphan having a visitors' room that bore a resemblance to the audience chamber in the Elders' Hall. I never wondered why having a moody day required making a treat that was given away. And I never wondered why an adult provided escort and oversaw the visit until a child was considered trustworthy enough to take the treat to The Voice and not eat it herself.

I never felt anything but a smug pity for the girl—and being just ten years older than me, she was barely more than a girl at the time—who always wore these strange hoods that covered her head and neck and was provided with simple smocks and trousers as covering for her body because, despite being young, there was no need for her to dress in pretty clothes that would attract a male eye, as the other girls were doing.

So I lived quite happily—and innocently—in the village that supported The Voice until the summer I turned ten years old. That was when I had my first glimpse of the truth.

It had been a hot summer, and there had been little rain. Men were wearing their summer garb—sleeveless tunics and lightweight pants that were hemmed above the knee. Some of the younger men—the bachelors in the village who were looking for a wife—were even bold enough to cut off their trousers to midthigh length, which delighted the older women; mortified the older, knobby-kneed men; and scandalized the village Elders. It wasn't until women began fainting on a daily basis while doing housework in the heat that the Elders were forced to revise their strict dress code for our female population and permit short sleeves on the tunics and trousers that were hemmed just below the knee. The Elders reasoned that it was simply too hot for strenuous activity, so the sight of female limbs would not excite male flesh.

The number of women who became pregnant during that summer—and the number of bachelors who were required to make a hasty contract of marriage—showed everyone how embarrassingly incorrect the Elders' reasoning had been. And, according to the whispers of a few sharp tongues, it also proved how old the Elders really were.

But those were insignificant things to a ten-year-old girl who was relishing the feel of air on her arms and legs when she was outside playing with friends.

That's where we were when I had the first glimpse of the truth—outside in the shade of a big tree, lazily tossing a ball between the three of us: Kobbi (who was Named Kobrah), Tahnee, and me, Nalah. Then The Voice plodded by, her tunic sleeves and trousers full length, of course, since the sight of her fat limbs would offend the eye. And then the boys came, with a glint in their eyes that made the three of us huddle together like sheep scenting a pack of wild dogs and instinctively knowing that separation from the flock meant death.

The boys weren't interested in teasing us that day, not when The Voice, looking back and recognizing danger, began lumbering toward the nearest house, no doubt hoping to be rescued.

They moved too fast, surrounded her too quickly.

"Aren't you hot?" they taunted The Voice. "Aren't you hot, hot, hot? We'll help you cool off."

They grabbed at her, pushed at her, and she kept turning, kept trying to move, no different from some poor, dumb beast. Until one of them grabbed her hood and pulled it off, exposing her neck for the first time in our young memories.

The boys scrambled away from her, silent and staring. Then she turned and looked at us girls. Looked into my eyes.

I didn't see a poor, dumb beast. There was intelligence in those eyes, as maimed as her body. And there was anger in those eyes, now unsheathed for everyone to see.

Some adults finally noticed us and realized something was wrong. The murmur of concerned voices changed into a hornets' buzz of anger when the adults realized what we had seen—and why. The Voice was solicitously returned to her house, the boys were marched to the Elders' Hall to have their punishment decided, and we three girls were escorted to our homes, where our escorts held whispered conversations with our mothers.

I spent the rest of that afternoon in solitude, keeping my mind carefully blank while I watched the play of light and shadow on my bedroom wall. But my mind would not remain blank. Thoughts seeped up and got tangled in the shifting patterns of leaves on the white plaster wall.

The Voice had not been born mute. Had the injuries that had healed into those horrific scars happened at the same time she lost her parents? Was there a time when she had been called by another name? Even if her voice had been damaged and could not be repaired, the healers could sew better than the best seamstress and took pride in the health of the whole village. Why had they patched her up so badly?

The pattern on the wall changed, and another thought drifted through my mind as the words spoken by the teachers each school day seemed to swell until I could think of nothing else—until I could hear the threat under the words that were intended as thanksgiving: *Honor your parents. Give thanks for them every day. Without them you are orphaned, and an orphan's life is one of sorrow.*

The Voice was cared for by the whole village. She had a house.

But it's one of the oldest houses in the village. Is she the first who lived there? If you ask your mother or grandmother, will they admit that another mute orphan had lived there before?

Everyone brought her food and treats; even little children, helped by parents, presented her with treats.

Did she ever truly want them?

Why does she have those scars?

I didn't have an answer. Didn't want an answer. I hurt for myself, and I hurt for The Voice.

An hour before dinner, I emerged from my room. My mother studied my face carefully, then said, "I'll make you a moody cake. You take it to The Voice. You'll feel better."

"No," I said, my voice rough, as if something were eating away at my throat. "I'll make it."

Mother studied me a little longer, then nodded. "Very well. You're old enough."

So I made the little moody cake while Mother went into the garden and made no comment about her dinner preparations being delayed (it was considered bad luck to prepare other food while a moody cake was being made). And if a few tears fell into the mixture, I didn't think it would spoil the taste.

As soon as it was cool enough to be placed on the little plate that was always—and only—used for food presented to The Voice, I left the house. The fact that neither of my parents commented or demanded that I wait until after our evening meal told me how concerned they were for me.

She was already in the visitors' room, sitting in the oddly proportioned chair that looked as if it had been specially made for a much fatter person. Since she was there, I was not her first visitor. Probably Kobbi and Tahnee had already been there with their mothers. She was alone, which wasn't unusual. There was always a caretaker in the house, but visitors usually meant the caretaker had a little time for herself.

I approached the chair until I was standing at the correct, polite distance. But I didn't extend the plate. Even though she had been bathed and carefully dressed and a new hood covered her head and neck, I looked into her eyes and remembered those horrific scars.

Tears filled my eyes as I touched my own neck and whispered, "I'm sorry."

To my amazement, since she never showed emotion beyond a simple smile, her eyes filled with tears too. Then she smiled—a true, warm, compassionate, loving smile—and reached out, took my little moody cake, and ate it.

Feeling so much better, I wiped the tears from my face and smiled in return. "I have to go now."

She didn't respond in any way when I turned to leave. She never did.

Before I reached the door, ready to skip home to my family and dinner, the boys who had taunted The Voice entered the room, followed by stern-looking fathers and nervous mothers. I jumped out of the way and pressed myself against the wall to avoid notice, but no one was going to notice me at that point.

And considering what happened, no one even remembered I had been there.

The first boy stepped up to the chair and extended the plate with its little offering.

The Voice picked up the offering and threw it on the floor.

There were shocked gasps from all the adults in the room, and the boy's father hurried to the doorway that led to the rest of the house, calling for the caretaker.

The second boy made his offering. She mashed it in her fist, then smeared it on her clothes. But the third boy, the one who had pulled off her hood, revealing a secret, exposing her pain . . .

She moved so fast, no one could stop her. One moment she was sitting, just staring at the boy; the next she lunged at him, grabbing the cake in one hand and his head in the other. As he started to yell, she shoved the cake into his mouth, forcing him to swallow or choke. So he swallowed—and the look in her eyes haunted my thoughts for years afterward.

Shortly after that, the boy contracted Black Pustules. These were painful boils that developed deep beneath the skin. Sometimes it took weeks before they reached the point where they could be lanced. And a single lancing never cleaned out a pustule, no matter what the healers tried. The pain of healing was endured over and over while new eruptions developed and needed to be lanced. It took several sessions before the hard nugget that was the core of the pustule could be extracted and the body finally healed.

But no matter how carefully the healers dealt with their patients, the final extraction left scars.

It always left scars.

In the weeks that followed, I didn't see The Voice walking around the village, but I'd heard my parents whispering to friends that The Voice had been refusing all offerings, and the Elders and healers had accepted the necessity of taking measures—for the health of the village.

My curiosity got the better of me and, pretending to have a moody day, I prepared a little cake and took it to The Voice.

No child should know so cruel a truth as what I saw that day.

She was no longer left unattended, and one of her caretakers was a burly young man. She was dressed in a robe with a matching hood. The design of the robe's sleeves was clever but didn't quite disguise that her arms were bound to the chair. The fact that she no longer had even the illusion of freedom was bad enough, but ...

They had done something to her so that the caretaker, applying pressure on a dowel of wood attached to something inside her mouth, could force her mouth open enough for the offering to be pushed inside. Then her mouth was forcibly closed so she couldn't spit out the treat.

They had taken away all her choices. She would consume what the villagers wanted her to consume.

She looked at me, and I felt as if I had betrayed her by coming here and forcing her to take something she didn't want. But I couldn't tell her it wasn't a real moody cake, not with the caretaker standing right there, listening. And I couldn't say I had changed my mind and The Voice didn't need to accept my offering. That wasn't done, ever. So in the end, I watched the male caretaker force her mouth open, shove in my little cake, and seal her mouth shut again.

I didn't cry until I was safely home. Then I hid in a sheltered spot in my mother's garden and cried until I made myself sick.

I avoided The Voice's house as much as I could. Oh, I still made the moody cakes when some telltale sign warned my mother that I was not in harmony with the world. I was still trusted to go by myself, so my parents didn't know that once I was safely out of sight, I found a hiding place . . . and ate the moody cake.

There was nothing in the making of it, nothing in the ingredients that could explain the sour, gelatinous, grape-sized lump that I discovered was in the center of every moody cake. Break it open and you'd find nothing, but put it in your mouth and you could feel that lump growing in the center of the cake. And yet you couldn't spit it out. You could spit out the cake, but then the lump remained with nothing to sweeten it.

The first time I ate the moody cake, I was sick for a day, but my mother concluded that I had eaten something that didn't agree with me and, fortunately, didn't press me to find out what it was.

The second time I ate a moody cake, a Black Pustule developed on my belly. It was painful and frightening, but I was more afraid to tell my parents and admit I hadn't been taking my moody cakes to The Voice, so I dealt with it in silence, learning that a warm, wet cloth brought the pustule to a head quicker and a sewing needle was a sufficient lance. Extracting the core is something I do not care to describe, but the substance was a harder, thicker version of the gelatinous lump in the moody cake.

Perhaps if I had been older, I would have understood. As it was, seven more years passed before I reached that moment of understanding.

Chapter Two

"**Y**ou really did it?"

It was the disbelief and admiration in my older brother Dariden's voice that had me creeping a little closer to his open window. I was seventeen; I knew better than to eavesdrop on my brother's conversations with friends. I found out too many things about him that diminished my feelings for him and gave me no liking for his friends. Especially Chayne, who had recently married Kobbi and was now one of The Voice's caretakers—or guards, as I thought of the people who controlled her.

"Wasn't easy, since Vision is such an unnatural city, but I managed to slip away from my father for an evening and find a particular shop."

"And the stuff works?" Dariden asked.

Chayne laughed softly. "She's pretty to look at, but when you spread Kobrah's legs, she's a cold piece. So I put three drops of this drug in her wine, and she falls into a sensual haze. I can do almost anything to her. She's passive on the drug, but her body is so hot and willing it doesn't matter that her brain isn't in the bed."

"A wife needs only enough brains to know when to spread 'em," Dariden said with a smirk in his voice.

I didn't dare move. Hardly dared to breathe. If Dariden found out I had overheard this, he would make my life a misery. Or more of a misery than it was.

"Will she do . . . *that* . . . when you give her the drug?" Dariden asked.

"No," Chayne replied, sounding disgusted. "Even with an extra drop of it—which is all I dare give her, because I was warned that too much will make a woman's brains go funny permanently—I can't make her do *that*. But it doesn't matter, because . . ."

Chayne lowered his voice, so I leaned a little closer to the window, still not daring to move my feet.

". . . I put three drops on *her* tongue, give her a glob of that mixture we feed her when we aren't stuffing her with the offerings, then close her up and wait a bit. Once the drug is working, I can spend hours in her mouth, with her tongue lapping and licking. And I know just how far to open the lever for the right tightness."

"And then she does *that*?" Dariden asked, sounding breathless.

Chayne laughed softly. It was such a cruel sound. "Well, swallowing is what she does, isn't it?"

They left Dariden's room, and I said a hasty prayer to every goddess and god I could think of that they wouldn't come around to the back of the house and realize I had heard them. My prayer must have been answered, because they left the house through the front door, and I was able to slip in through the kitchen door and reach my room undetected.

My father was a good man. I was sure of it. How could he have raised a son who would think such horrible things were exciting?

Is your father truly a good man? some part of me asked. *He goes to The Voice's house with moody cakes when he's unhappy about something. Does he really not know what he's forcing her to eat?*

He couldn't know. Couldn't. But if he did know, that might explain the worry I had seen in his eyes over the past year.

I had kept my secret for five years, dutifully making the moody cakes when my mother felt I needed to visit The Voice, and just as rebelliously eating the cakes myself. During those years I learned that eating pieces of regular cakes and breads that we made at home and gobbling the pastries I bought at the bakery with my spending money absorbed the worst of the effects of the Black Pustules. I still got them whenever I ate a moody cake, but they weren't as big or as painful. On the other hand, I had plumped to what my father had initially, and teasingly, called a wifely figure—meaning my fat-softened body was not the sleek shape a man looked for in a bride but accepted in a wife after the babies started arriving. After all, a man had to make some sacrifices in order to have children.

Then Tahnee blundered one evening when she told my mother she hadn't seen me at The Voice's house at a time when I should have been there. Realizing her error and believing that I must have been sneaking out to meet a boy and had used The Voice as an excuse, Tahnee did her best to deny her own words, but her suddenly vague memory about where she had been on a particular evening didn't fool my mother, who then saw my days of being slightly ill in a totally different way.

After that, I had an escort for each visit to The Voice's house, and when I watched the caretaker feed her the moody cake, I felt sick inside—because I felt better. But until I made the trip to Vision, I still didn't know why.

Chapter Three

Dariden was wild to go to that place that was considered an unnatural city and something even more, even stranger. In the end, I was the one who went to Vision with Tahnee and her parents.

Despite my mother's efforts to control what I could eat when I was in the house, and despite the bakery, in an effort to help me regain my maidenly figure, agreeing not to sell me anything unless I had a note from one of my parents (which I never was given), my body remained stubbornly plump. My father, in an effort to be helpful, had taken to whispering to me whenever he escorted me to visit The Voice, "If you don't stop your foolish eating, you'll end up looking like that."

She was huge. When her mouth was forced open to receive an offering, her eyes disappeared within the folds of fat. It hurt me to see her and know I was adding to her pain. It hurt me to hear my father say something so cruel to the daughter he professed to love.

But on the particular day that led to my going to Vision, Chayne was the caretaker on duty when my father whispered his encouragement—and I had what the healers described as a mild emotional breakdown.

I screamed. I wailed. I wept. I sat on the floor and howled with a pain that filled the visitors' room and frightened all the grumpy-faced children who wanted to feed a moody cake to The Voice so they could leave and be happy, happy, happy while she . . . while she . . .

In the end, I went with Tahnee and her parents because they had already planned a week's stay in Vision and I could share a room with Tahnee—and also because when my brother offered to escort me, I started screaming that he fornicated with barnyard animals and molested small children, and every time my father got near me I began making guttural noises that, my mother told me when I was calmer, sounded like they were coming from a savage animal.

My mother was correct about that. Something was building inside me, and I didn't know why. All I truly knew was that I hated the village I lived in and hated participating in something that not only violated another person, but violated something in myself as well.

I needed to escape, but I didn't know how.

Sometimes all it takes is a change of vision.

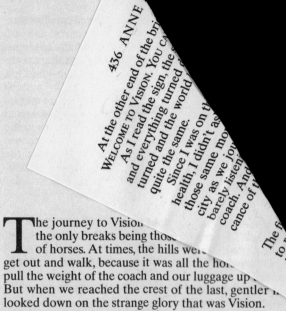

At the other end of the bri...
WELCOME TO VISION. You ca...
As I read the sign, the s...
and everything turned ...
turned and the world ...
quite the same.

Since I was on t...
health, I didn't as...
those same mo...
city as we jou...
barely listenin...
coach. And...
cance of t...

The journey to Vision ...
the only breaks being thos...
of horses. At times, the hills wer...
get out and walk, because it was all the hor...
pull the weight of the coach and our luggage up ...
But when we reached the crest of the last, gentler ...
looked down on the strange glory that was Vision.

It was a patchwork city that spread out across a vast plain, backed by old, rounded mountains cloaked in the restful green of living things. Some parts of the city dazzled the eye, while others seemed lost in shadow—and still other places must have been farmland and pastures. Not one city, but many. And so much more than I could have imagined the first time I saw it.

So we descended the hill, passing the last crossroad that would lead to other places. After that, there was no destination but the city, which was reached by a bridge that had a peculiar but carefully made sign posted a coach's length before the bridge itself: ASK YOUR HEART ITS DESTINATION.

Upon seeing the sign, Tahnee's father muttered about the need to avoid the "peculiar" folks that inhabited the city. Then, in a heartier voice, he reassured his three ladies that we would not be visiting any of the peculiar places.

But I looked at the sign and, even though I thought it was foolish, shaped my answer as the horses stepped onto the bridge: *Escape. Freedom. Answers.* If my heart had a destination, it was shaped by those three words.

...dge was another peculiar sign:
...N FIND ONLY WHAT YOU CAN SEE.
...sun went behind a bank of clouds
...dark and chilling. Then the sun re-
...looked fresh and dazzling—and not

...his journey because of my lack of mental
...k if any of my companions had witnessed
...ments of dark and light. I just watched the
...rneyed for another day to reach its center,
...ng to the comments of the other people in the
...while we journeyed, I considered the signifi-
...he words if that sign meant exactly what it said.

...rst two days, I found nothing of interest and tried not
...esent the hearty comments that came too often about
...w a change of scenery could do a person good. I *wanted*
...change of scenery. I had been searching for that change
for two days.

And I almost missed it when it finally appeared on the third afternoon of our visit.

The bazaar in the center of the city took up entire blocks, almost ending on the doorstep of the rooming house where we were staying. Having tramped through it with us the first two days, Tahnee's parents left us on our own that third afternoon, convinced that two girls from a small village would come to no harm despite the cacophony of sights and sounds. And no harm *would* come to us, because the white-robed Shamans walked the crowded streets. Their pace steady, their faces serene, they walked among the buyers and sellers, sometimes stopping to accept a slice of fruit or a cup of cool water. They seldom spoke to the people around them, but when they smiled and said "Travel lightly," it always sounded like a blessing.

So on the afternoon that changed so many things, Tahnee was cheerfully haggling with the son of a merchant, more to have a reason to remain close to the handsome boy than because she was seriously interested in whatever she had found to haggle over that day. I wandered down the row of booths just for something to do while I waited. Then I saw a flash of white disappearing between two booths. No, more than that. In a place that was crowded and where every merchant jealously guarded his allotted space down to the last finger length, there shouldn't have been a space that would have easily fit four booths.

That was the moment I realized I had passed that gap in the booths more than once each day without really seeing it—or wondering about it.

I stepped into that gap and saw something else that had eluded my eye during those first two days.

The bazaar backed up against a white wall. The gap in the booths matched the width of the archway leading into . . .

The streets, gardens, courtyards, and buildings might have been another world. For all I know, they were. The place was white and clean, and with every breath I breathed in peace. And with every step I took, a pain grew inside me, as if a Black Pustule had formed deep within my body and was festering.

Still within sight of the archway, I stopped moving. Then I looked up and something shivered through me, as if I were a bell that had been struck and somehow retuned to match the resonance of the building in front of me.

The Temple of Sorrow.

I walked up the steps and pulled the rope beside the door. Heard the bell calling, calling.

A Shaman opened the door. His hair was grizzled, his face unlined. I have never seen anything before or since that matched the beauty of his eyes.

He smiled and stood aside to let me enter.

"Is this your first visit?" he asked.

I just nodded, struck dumb by the odd sensation of feeling too gaudy and too plain at the same time. It was my first experience with having a crush on a man, and I didn't know what to do or say.

Then I remembered I was wifely plump rather than maidenly sleek, and there was something festering inside me.

"I see," he said softly, and I was terrified that, somehow, he had. Then he said, "This way," and led me to a pair of doors on the left side of the building.

He opened the doors and the sound . . .

"No," I gasped. "No. I can't. That is—" *Obscene. A violation.*

Something that sang in my limbs.

He closed the doors. "That is sorrow." His voice was quiet, gentle. "That is why this temple is here. To give it voice. To set it free. Sorrow should not be swallowed. It will linger in the body, cleave to the flesh, long after the mind and heart have forgotten the cause."

Each word was a delicate blow, a butterfly tap that reverberated through my heart.

"What do I do?" I asked.

He opened the doors again and we stepped into the room.

It sounded like the entire city was in that room, but in truth, there was no more than a double handful of people, and the room could have held twice that many. Some were wearing a hooded robe that had a veil over the face, which allowed them to see and breathe but obscured their identity. Others sat with their faces exposed to the world.

The sound in the room rose and fell, sometimes barely a hum and other times crescendoing to be the voice of sky and earth and all living things.

In one of the quieter moments, the Shaman whispered, "The gongs provide a tone. If the first one you try does not fit the voice you need today, try another."

"Then what do I do?"

His hand rested on my shoulder for a moment, the warmth of it a staggering comfort. He smiled and said, "Then you release sorrow."

Too self-conscious to really try the available gongs to test their sound, I chose one based on the pleasing simplicity of the frame that held it. It did not produce a sound quite as deep as what I wanted, but having timidly struck it once, I wasn't about to get up and move to another place in the room.

I kept my eyes fixed on the floor just in front of my cushions, sure that it would be terribly rude to look at the other people in the room. I hummed, fearful of being heard, while something inside me swelled and swelled until it was ready to burst.

The voices around me rose and fell. Sometimes a gong would sound and one voice would be raised in a wordless cry. Other times each gong was rung and the accompanying voices filled the room. Over and over until, at last, there was only one voice still keening, only one heart not yet purged of sorrow.

Mine.

But I, too, fell silent, too exhausted and hollowed out to go on. I had lanced my well of sorrow, but I had not extracted the core.

One by one, the other people stood up and left. I was the last person in the room, and by the time I reached the door, the Shaman stood there, a question in his beautiful eyes.

"If you need us, we are always here," he said. Then he escorted me to the outer door and added, "Travel lightly."

"Oh, my friends and I are staying in the city for a few more days," I said, wondering if that was considered flirting or too bold—and wondering if Shamans even had such interests in the flesh.

His eyes smiled, though his expression remained serious. "Some journeys can be made without setting a foot outside your own room." He paused. "If you need us, we are here. Remember that."

It wasn't until I returned to the friendly cacophony of the bazaar that I noticed the sign above the archway. It said THE TEMPLES, as if nothing more was required in identifying that island of peace.

"Nalah!" Tahnee rushed up to me. "Where have you been? I almost went back to the rooming house without you, but . . ."

The day before I might have stammered something or become defensive because I was unwilling to tell anyone where I had been. But that day, I saw something in Tahnee's face, in her eyes.

"We've spent the afternoon wandering around the bazaar, looking at so many things."

"Yes," Tahnee said, wary but willing to hear me out. "We have. But . . . you haven't bought anything."

"I don't have as much spending money as you, so—"

"Oh, I can give you some if—"

"I'm looking very carefully before deciding what gifts to purchase for my parents and brother as a way of thanking them for allowing me to see Vision."

"Oh." Tahnee nibbled her lower lip. "It would be better if we both came to the bazaar, don't you think? Safer that way. Ah . . . how much longer will you need to decide on your purchases?"

"There is still so much to see, I think it will take at least another day or two," I said, linking arms with Tahnee as we headed in the direction of the rooming house.

She gave me a sidelong look. "You are all right, though, aren't you?"

"Yes," I replied honestly. "I feel better than I've felt in a very long time. Perhaps the best ever."

"I feel the same."

I didn't think we had the same reason for the feeling, but I was glad to hear her say it. And for me, it was true. I felt better. Much better.

I felt the same way I used to feel after making a moody cake and bringing it to The Voice. But that was something I didn't want to think about. Not yet. So Tahnee and I returned to the rooming house and endured a mild scold from her mother about almost being late for the evening meal. But her father looked at us and said with a wink, "Had a little adventure, did you? Nothing wrong with a little adventure—as long as it doesn't go too far."

Too far? I thought about what the Shaman had said about making a journey without leaving your room and realized I already had gone too far—because now there was no going back.

The next two days were deceptions tacitly permitted by Tahnee's father, since he knew we were up to something but figured that being together, neither of us would go too far in our little adventures. And there was a tacit agreement between me and Tahnee that neither of us *would* go too far and put the other's "little adventure" at risk.

I don't know where she went, but I guessed that a handsome young man had been given some time off from work in his father's booth. I went to the Temple of Sorrow.

The gongs reverberated in the air. Voices rose and fell. And the sounds and the tears lanced a pain deep inside me that had been growing and festering since the first time I had eaten a moody cake and had gained an inkling of what it meant to be The Voice.

I lanced the pain, knowing there would be scars. But I

wasn't able to extract the core of that pain until later that evening when Tahnee and I were in our room, not saying much as each of us contemplated how to spend our last day in the city.

"The boys at home," Tahnee said, curling up on the bed and fixing her gaze on the wall rather than look at me. "I mean no criticism of your brother. He seems nice enough, although it will be years yet before he is considered of marrying age. The ones who *are* of marrying age . . . They're all like Chayne, and I don't want to live with a man like Chayne. Kobbi . . ." Tahnee licked her lips, a nervous gesture. "Kobbi thinks Chayne is doing something to her when he wants to do the marriage thing. You know. In bed."

Since she seemed to expect it, I nodded to indicate I understood.

"She's not sure, and it isn't every time they . . . do things. But sometimes she doesn't feel right in the head the next day. Chayne was real worried the day she had a bad spell after one of those nights, and that's when she began thinking that maybe he was doing something. Before she could get up the nerve to tell her father, Chayne began making cutting little remarks, especially around her father, saying that a good wife would not begrudge giving her husband little pleasures when he had to work hard to provide her with a home and clothes and food. So when Kobbi finally got scared enough to tell her father . . ."

"What did he say?" I whispered, feeling as if the world itself held its breath while waiting for the answer.

"He hit her." Tahnee's face had a bewildered expression, as if everything she had known and trusted had changed suddenly and betrayed her. "He said she shamed him by being a poor wife and he would denounce her as his daughter if Chayne continued to have cause to complain."

In the silence, I heard the patter of rain. I looked out the window and watched the sky weep. Lulled by the sound, Tahnee fell asleep. I stayed awake much longer, letting thoughts drift and form patterns.

Honor your parents. Give thanks for them every day. Because an orphan's life is one of sorrow.

There was no ingredient used in the moody cakes that wasn't used in other foods. So what made the cakes a vessel for feelings we didn't want? And who had decided that one person would be sacrificed for the health of the village? Who had decided that the people in my village would not have to carry the weight of their own sorrows?

Maybe there was no one left to blame. Maybe no one truly knew anymore.

But the Elders continue it, my heart whispered. *They see her; others care for her. Are there Black Pustules festering all over her body, always hidden because she had been trained to keep her body covered? Someone stripped a child of the ability to speak and scarred her so she would be ashamed to reveal the reason for her silence. The people who did this still live in the village.*

We all did this. Day after day, year after year, we handed someone a plate of sorrow disguised as a treat and expected her to swallow it so that we could feel better instead of carrying the weight—and the scars—ourselves.

Welcome to Vision. You can find only what you can see.

As something inside me continued shifting and forming new patterns, I wondered if I had changed enough to see what I needed to find.

The following afternoon, I turned a corner. It was that easy.

The Apothecary was on a street that is one of Vision's shadow places—neither Dark nor Light, since it is a street that can be reached by hearts that resonate with either.

On another day, the looks of the man standing behind the counter at the back of the shop would have scared me enough to abandon my plan. That day, I studied him in what light came in through his grimy windows and decided if looks were a measure of a man, this one could do what I needed.

So I told him what I wanted, and I paid him what he asked, relieved I had enough coins for the purchase and a little left over so that Tahnee would not end up paying for my family gifts completely out of her own pocket.

"Enough for three people, you said?" he asked when he returned from the curtained back room and handed me a small bottle.

"Yes, three." I was almost sure that there was only one caretaker in the later hours, but I had to be certain I could deal with whomever was there. Because there would be only one chance.

"I am curious," he said as I turned to leave. "Do you seek revenge?"

I slipped the bottle in my pocket and carefully buttoned the pocket flap. Then I looked at him. "I seek another's freedom."

He studied me a moment longer, then raised his hand and scribed a sign in the air. I didn't know if it was a blessing or black magic—and I didn't care.

The next day, we began the journey back to our village. Tahnee and I gave each other sly looks and pokes in the ribs that were followed by giggles, which confirmed to her parents that we had gotten up to some mischief. It also made them relax, confident that nothing much had happened during our visit.

My parents, too, were relieved by the sly looks and the giggling. I was once again the daughter they knew.

Only my brother noticed something different. Or maybe it was just envy trying to bare its fangs.

"You look good, Nalah," he said. "Rested. Almost like a different person."

I just smiled. I didn't tell him he was right. I *was* a different person.

Now I was dangerous.

Chapter Five

I could no longer live in this village and participate in the cruelty of destroying someone else in order to keep myself clean of all but the "good" feelings, and I was afraid of what might happen to me if the Elders decided I was no longer in harmony with the rest of our community. There must have been others before me who had seen and understood what we had done by not having to live with the weight of our own sorrows. What had happened to those others? Had they tried to change the heart of a village, or had they slipped away one day to escape what they could not change and could not endure?

Or did they lie beneath the blank markers that festered in the thorny, weed-choked part of our burial ground that was set aside for the Un-Named—the ones who had done something so offensive their names were "forgotten" in the village records and family trees.

Alone, I could escape, could vanish into the vastness of the world—or, at least, vanish into the streets of Vision. I was certain of that. But if I tried to help The Voice and was caught . . . I would suffer a tragic—and fatal—accident and be buried under one of those blank markers, just one more of the Un-Named. I was certain of that too.

So knowing what was at stake, I spent a week watching, looking, seeing. And the more I focused on the need to leave this village, the more things subtly changed.

An Elder, claiming his cart horse had turned vicious and had deliberately knocked him down into a pile of manure, had taken to leaving the poor animal tied up to the hitching rail behind the Elders' Hall, still harnessed to the cart without a handful of grain or a sip of water. Anyone who looked could see the horse was mistreated, but everyone averted their eyes and didn't disagree with the Elder's right to discipline his own animal, even though I'd heard my father mutter that, most likely, the poor beast had been doing nothing more than trying to get to its feed bucket when it had knocked the Elder down.

The men muttered, the women made moody cakes, and everyone pretended they couldn't see the horse and, therefore, couldn't see its misery.

I saw the misery. I also saw a horse and cart that would be easy to steal.

Then there was the blank marker stone that suddenly appeared behind The Voice's house, far enough from the kitchen door not to be a nuisance and close enough that it could be used as a step up into the cart.

Every day I watched the village and the people. Every day I tucked a few more things into the traveling bag that looked like a small trunk made of cloth stretched over a wooden frame. I had bought it at the bazaar, using my purchases as the excuse to acquire it. Dariden laughed at me when he saw it, saying the cloth could be torn so easily, I might as well not use anything at all. True, the cloth wasn't as sturdy as a wooden trunk, but it had one important advantage: I could carry it by myself.

By the time everything was ready, my biggest worry was Tahnee. She tried to act as if nothing had changed, but I could tell by the leashed desperation in her eyes that *everything* had changed—and I realized that she, too, had been waiting for something to happen and had been growing more and more anxious with each passing day.

I could not wish her scheme to fail because, like me, she was no longer in harmony with the village and staying would only do her harm. But I did wish with all my heart that her scheme was delayed just a few days longer, even though I knew my own disappearance would make her escape all but impossible.

Which is when things began going wrong. Just little things. Just enough things for me to realize how easy it had been for me to move forward with this plan.

"Nalah, what are you doing with that skirt?" Mother asked, catching me as I tried to sneak out of the storage cupboard that held our out-of-season clothes.

"I—" My father's mother had made it for me two years ago, before she got funny in the head and died in her sleep one night. The dark green material was of good quality, which Mother had declared a waste, since it couldn't be worn in decent company, and the needlework was exquisite. My grandmother had kept all the beads, spangles, and tiny mirrors that had decorated her own wedding dress and had gifted them to me on a skirt.

When Mother protested, my father's only comment was that it was more practical to have the beads on the front of the skirt than on the part I sat on. Which proved that the male part of my father's brain had been asleep when he looked at the skirt, because the beaded vines and mirrored flowers were intended to draw the eye to the untouched flower between my thighs. It was a skirt a girl wore when she was ready to attract a husband.

I had been too young to wear it when my grandmother had made it for me, and there was no one in this village whose attention I wanted to attract. But I wanted to take the skirt with me. I wanted the hope that I would wear it someday.

"I was going to take it over to Tahnee's tonight, along with a few other things," I said, suddenly inspired. "We're going to try on clothes, see what we still like. Maybe trade." I said this last bit in a low mumble, which made Mother sigh but also made her shoulders relax.

"The three of you used to trade so often, half the time I wasn't sure if I was washing your clothes or theirs," she said.

I nodded, then looked around to be sure I wouldn't be overheard, even though I knew Mother and I were alone in the house. "Tahnee's a little unhappy about the way Kobbi has been acting lately. I guess married life changes a girl?"

Mother's face softened with understanding as she put an arm around my shoulders. "It can be a difficult adjustment for some girls." She hesitated, then added, "Maybe you should make a moody cake."

I shivered and knew she felt that shiver, but I wrinkled my nose and said, "I'd rather try on clothes."

"You're my daughter, Nalah, and I do care about you. You know that?"

I looked into her eyes and felt the pain of love. She did care. And that was why she couldn't afford to see. And why I would stop looking if I stayed. If I held a little daughter in my arms, would I let her flesh carry the weight of sorrow? Would I let the Black Pustules form and listen to her scream in pain when they were lanced—and see the scars that would mark her when the hard cores were extracted? Or would I make a moody cake and teach that little girl the proper way to present it to the person whose sole purpose in our village was to swallow such offerings?

I kissed her cheek. "I don't need a moody cake."

I hurried to my room to pack the skirt, then hurried out to find Tahnee and let her know my mother thought I would be at her house tonight. But when I found her sitting under the big tree where she, Kobbi, and I used to play on hot summer days, everything changed again.

"Kobbi's father denounced her," Tahnee said in a hushed, tearful voice. "She tried to tell her mother that Chayne was doing something bad to her, something that made her head feel funny. Her father overheard her and dragged her to the Elders' Hall. He denounced her and demanded that her name be struck from the family record."

My chest felt so tight, I could hardly breathe. "She's an orphan?"

Tahnee nodded. "And I heard that Chayne is so shamed because she's an orphan by unnatural means that *he* may denounce her as his wife, since he'll no longer receive the other two parts of the dowry."

"She can't inherit because she no longer exists in the eyes of her family." And I could see Kobbi's fate if I went ahead with my plan—because an orphan's life is one of sorrow.

"Listen," I said, grabbing hold of Tahnee's arm. "I'm coming over to your house with a bag of clothes. That's what I told my mother."

"Oh, I don't—"

"You're going to pack a bag of clothes—basics and the things too dear to leave behind. But don't pack a bag that's so heavy you can't carry it. You're going to tell your mother that you and I are going over to Kobbi's house. We're going to try on clothes like we used to do when we were girls, and we're going to make moody cakes to help Kobbi feel better because she's our friend. After a denouncement, a man has three days to change his mind if he spoke in haste or out of anger, so if Kobbi comes to her senses, her father might restore her to the family. That's what you're going to tell your mother."

Tahnee wiped the tears off her face and gave me a long look. "What are we really going to be doing?"

"Escaping. We're going back to Vision."

Her breath caught, and for a moment I wondered if I had been wrong to tell her. Then the fire of hope filled her eyes.

"The three of us?" she asked.

I hesitated, and felt as if the world itself waited for my answer. "Four of us."

At dinner that night, even Dariden was subdued, although he rallied once when he heard I was going over to Kobbi's house with Tahnee.

"You shouldn't be friends with the likes of her," he told me, glancing at our father for approval of such a manly opinion.

"What happened to Kobbi could happen to anyone," I said, helping myself to another spoonful of rice. Then I looked my brother in the eyes. "If I had ended up married to someone like Chayne, it could have happened to me."

My father made a tongue-cluck sound of disapproval for my criticism of Chayne, but Dariden paled as he realized I knew what Chayne had been doing to Kobbi. And as he stared into my eyes, he understood that, with the least provocation, Tahnee and I would spread that information to every female in the village, and any standing Chayne had in our community would be crushed under the rumors that he drugged his young wife in order to do unnatural things in the marriage bed.

"You're looking pale, Dariden," I said, putting enough concern in my voice to draw Mother's attention. "Perhaps you should stay in tonight."

"You're not feeling well?" Mother asked him.

Cornered, Dariden just stared at his plate. "Been working hard," he mumbled. "Guess I should turn in early tonight."

So I was free to leave the house, secure in the knowledge

that Dariden and I wouldn't cross paths tonight. Even if he retreated to his room, he wouldn't be able to sneak out the window, because Mother always checked on us at regular intervals when we weren't feeling well. Dariden had learned this the hard way as a boy when he had lied to Mother about not feeling well in order to sneak out with his friends, and had found our father waiting for him when he snuck back in.

I left the house with my travel bag and stopped just long enough to slip into our little barn and take a small bag of feed and an old round pan that could hold water. I didn't have a water skin, and that was a worry. It turned out to be a foolish worry, because Tahnee had bought a water skin at the bazaar and hidden it under her other purchases.

We didn't see many people on the way to Kobbi's house, and those who saw us looked away when they noticed the bags of clothes and realized where we were going.

The woman who opened the door . . .

Tahnee and I stood there, too numbed to speak. Our friend Kobbi was gone, and in that moment when my eyes met the crazed wildness in Kobrah's, I knew that even if we got her away from Chayne and the village, we had lost her forever. But we would still try to save her.

"I was going to burn down the house," Kobrah said, as if that were the most ordinary thing to say. "But it can wait until later. Maybe I should wait until Chayne is home and sound asleep. Yes. That would be better."

She stepped aside to let us in. We slipped into the house and closed the door before daring to say anything.

"We're leaving," I said hurriedly. "We're running away to Vision. You can come with us."

She'll destroy us, I thought as I waited for her answer. *Chayne has burned out the goodness in her, and if she comes with us, she'll destroy us.*

But I didn't take back the offer. I just waited for her answer.

"Yes," she finally said, softly. "Yes." She turned and went into the kitchen.

Leaving our bags by the door, we hurried after her. "We didn't dare take any food from home . . ." I began.

"I have food," Kobrah replied. She pulled out her market basket. "I boiled eggs this afternoon, after I got back from the Elders' Hall. Chayne doesn't like hard-boiled eggs. Maybe that's why I made them."

Her voice sounded dreamy—and insane. But she moved swiftly, storing the eggs, wrapping up the cheeses, taking all the fresh fruit.

Then Tahnee, in an effort to help, reached for a loaf of bread still cooling on the counter.

"No!" Kobrah snarled. "*That* is for Chayne."

Tahnee stepped away from the counter, white with fear. She looked at me, her thoughts clear on her face: *Do we dare eat anything that comes from this house?*

Kobrah smiled bitterly. "The rest of the food is safe." She went into the bedroom, and we listened to her opening drawers and slamming them shut, followed by a cry of triumph and the rattle of coins in a tin box.

Kobrah was packed in no time, and even after we told her about having a cart, she refused to add anything to the small travel pack she used to carry when we spent the night at each other's houses. After the second time we urged her to bring more clothes or at least a few sentimental trinkets, she said, "I want no reminders of this place."

The hours crawled by until, finally, we had reached that in-between hour when all the family men were dutifully tucked in with their wives and children and the younger men were still at the drinking parlor or carousing elsewhere with friends.

We crept out of Kobrah's house, lugging our traveling bags and other supplies, always watchful, always fearful of discovery. But something watched over us that night, because whenever we passed a house with a dog, the wind shifted to favor us and the dog, never catching our scent, remained quiet.

So we made it to the tree where we used to play and where, in many ways, this journey had begun ten years before on the day we had seen The Voice's scars. Kobrah and Tahnee remained there with the bags while I went on to the Elders' Hall, now carrying nothing more than the old pan, a water skin, and the small bag of feed. If caught, I could truthfully say I had felt sorry for the horse and had snuck out to give it some food and water.

But there were no lights shining in the hall except for a lamp in the caretaker's room, and that provided me with just enough light to make my way to where the horse watched me.

"Easy, boy," I whispered when he began making noises. He was hungry and thirsty, and I was holding what he wanted. He would be making a lot of noise soon if he didn't get some.

Staying just out of reach and keeping one eye on the lighted window, just in case the caretaker looked out to see why the horse was fussing, I poured water into the pan, then held it out for the horse. He drank it down and looked for more, but I scooped out a double handful of feed and gave that to him next. Another pan of water and another handful of feed. Not much for a big horse, but all I could do for now. I put the water skin and bag of feed in the back of the cart, but I held on to the pan, afraid it would rattle and draw attention.

"Come on, boy," I whispered as I untied the horse from the hitching rail. "Come on. You're going to help all of us get to freedom."

He came with me without noise or fuss, and when we were far enough away from the hall that the *clip-clop* of hooves and rattle of the cart wheels wouldn't draw anyone's attention, I began taking full breaths again.

We paused at the tree just long enough to haul the traveling bags and supplies into the cart and have Kobrah and Tahnee hide in the back. One person leading a horse and cart might go unremarked. All three of us out at this time of night with this particular horse and cart . . .

Our luck held. We got to the back of The Voice's house and got the cart positioned so the blank stone marker could be used as a step. Now the rest of the plan was up to me, and if I failed one of us, I failed all of us.

It didn't occur to me until much later that Kobrah and Tahnee never once suggested abandoning this part of the plan. I suppose that, more than anything, proved none of us belonged in the village where we had been born.

The plan was simple. I would go in on the pretense of consoling Chayne on the loss of the dowry and the embarrassment of Kobrah's behavior. I would slip a third of the drug I had bought into a drink, avoid any amorous advances Chayne might think to make before he drank down the drug, and then get The Voice out of the house and into the cart so we could be far down the road before anyone realized we were gone.

I just didn't know how to do any of that. So I prayed hard and with all my heart, because five lives were at stake now. The horse had become a conspirator with us, and even though he was a poor, dumb beast, I was sure the Elder would blame him for following the girl who had offered him food.

Tahnee held the horse, petting him to keep him quiet. Kobrah remained in the cart. I went around to the front and rang the visitors' bell, still wondering what to say to get myself inside at this hour.

That wasn't a worry. Chayne answered the door looking sleepy, rumpled, and surly, and I suspected he had been drinking, even though he wasn't supposed to when he was on duty. Then another expression slithered into his eyes as he looked at me, and I felt a thread of pure fear roll down my spine when I realized I wasn't the only one who had a drug that had been purchased in some shadow place. Chayne had *his* bottle with him, because he used it on The Voice as well as on Kobrah.

And he intended to use it on me. I looked into his eyes and knew it.

"I heard what happened this afternoon," I said, sounding a little breathless. "I thought . . . maybe . . . you would want to talk to someone."

"Talk?" he laughed softly, and I heard the sound of a heart turning evil. He stepped aside to let me enter. "Sure, we can talk. Come back to the kitchen. I was having a bite to eat."

There was bread and cheese on the table, as well as half a bottle of wine. Looking at Chayne's flushed face, I had a feeling that wasn't the first bottle he'd opened tonight. Which explained why he hadn't paid attention to the sound of a horse and cart.

"Let me get you some wine," he said, picking up the bottle and taking it with him to the cupboard that held the glasses.

Watching him to make sure he wasn't paying close attention to me, I slipped a hand in my skirt pocket and took out the vial of potion. I worked the cork with my thumb, loosening it while I glanced at Chayne's glass of wine and then back at him. He would see me if I reached across the table, and if he saw my hand over his glass . . .

Then he turned toward the kitchen window, and I thought my heart would stop. Had he heard a noise? I was almost certain he wouldn't see the horse and cart unless he went right up to the window and looked out, but I couldn't take that chance. And I couldn't waste the opportunity he provided by turning his back on me. So I pulled the cork off the vial and dumped some of the drug into Chayne's glass, heedless of how much I was using.

"Is there anyone else here tonight?" I asked, tucking my shaking hands in my lap while I worked the cork back into the top of the vial.

He stopped moving toward the window, but he still kept his back to me.

He hadn't heard a noise. He wasn't interested in looking out the window. That was just the excuse he had used for turning away from me while he slipped his drug into my glass of wine.

He came back to the table, set the wineglass in front of me, and smiled the kind of smile women instinctively fear. "No, there's no one else here tonight. Except The Voice. She's the perfect chaperone."

I would have been a fool to come here alone. I hadn't been a friend to Kobrah when I had kept silent after overhearing Chayne tell Dariden about the drug. Now all our fates came down to whether I could avoid drinking from my glass without arousing Chayne's suspicion.

"Drink up," Chayne said, raising his glass in a salute as he watched me.

He knew I knew about the drug—and he didn't care. He was between me and the door. We were alone. He wasn't so drunk that I could get away from him.

Then a door slammed, making us both jump. A moment later, Kobrah stood in the kitchen doorway, breathing like a bellows, looking as if she'd run here all the way from her house.

"Are you going to poison Nalah too?" Kobrah asked. "Isn't it enough that you ruined me?"

"Go home," Chayne said coldly, turning his back on her to look straight at me. "Go back home while you still have one. And if you say anything else that causes trouble, I'll be looking for a new wife, and you'll be grateful for any place that will take you in. You know what they say about an orphan's life."

He didn't see the rage on her face, but he smirked when I, trembling, whispered, "An orphan's life is one of sorrow."

Looking pleased, Chayne said, "That's right," and drank all the wine in his glass.

The Apothecary assured me the drug would work fast. Even so, agonizing hours filled the space between each heartbeat before Chayne staggered, grabbed at the table to keep his balance, then collapsed on the floor.

I caught Chayne's wineglass before it rolled off the table, righted the bottle before the rest of the wine spilled out, then got around the table in time to stand between Chayne and Kobrah.

"I was going to kick his face until it was all smashed and broken," Kobrah said in that dreamy, insane voice. "He deserves to have his face smashed. You don't know all the things he's done."

I held up a hand to stop her, then crouched beside Chayne. His eyes were open, but his mind was swimming in some dream world and his limbs wouldn't work for a few hours.

"You," he said, drawing out the word.

Inspired, I stared at him. "Us," I said, raising a hand to draw his attention to Kobrah, who was standing behind me. "We are the goddesses of justice and vengeance. Tonight we wore the faces of women you know in order to test you, human. And you failed."

Kobrah laughed, a chilling sound.

"When the sun rises tomorrow, you will stand in front of the Elders' Hall and tell everyone about the drug you gave your wife. You will confess every harm you have ever done to any living thing. If you do not, we will come back every night for the rest of your life. We will come back in a dream, night after night, and peel the skin off your face so that everyone will see who you really are."

I stood up and walked out of the kitchen. Kobrah followed me.

"If he doesn't confess all the things he's done, will he really have that dream?" she asked.

"Yes." When I bought the drug, I had emphasized the

need to hide the memory of my presence and had been assured that, in the first minute or two after the drug was taken, the person would believe anything he was told.

Kobrah smiled. "That's better than kicking him in the face, because he'll never tell the Elders *everything* he's done. He would end up among the Un-Named."

We opened doors, searched rooms. Most people never went beyond the visitors' room, never saw this part of the house. Judging by what could be seen by moonlight, the rooms set aside for the caretakers were better furnished and had more luxuries than any of them knew in their own homes. But there were two rooms that had the basic furniture of bed, chair, and dresser. No rug on the floor. No sketches on the walls. Not one pretty bauble to delight the heart.

There was no need for such things when a person had been silenced and could not voice her pain, when she had been kept uneducated so she could not give shape to her thoughts. When she was caged within her own flesh so that she couldn't escape other kinds of cages.

The first of those sparse rooms was empty, and Kobrah stared at it for a long time, shuddering, as we both realized that room had been readied for a new occupant.

In the second sparsely furnished room, we found The Voice.

"It's me," I said, hurrying to the side of the bed. "It's Nalah."

The wheezing, labored breathing eased a little, and the reason squeezed my heart until it hurt.

Hearing someone at the door, she had expected Chayne to come in and do things to her after he'd given her the drug.

But seeing her in the bed, I realized how big she was—and I also realized the flaw in my plan.

I didn't know if she was capable of walking far enough to reach the cart. And if she wasn't able to climb in by herself, even the three of us weren't strong enough to lift her.

"We're running away," I said. "You can come with us. I know a place that can help you. You'll be safe there." I swallowed hard to say what had to be said. "We have a cart behind the house. You can ride in the back of it. But if you want to get away from here, you have to walk to the cart, you have to climb in the back. If you can't do that . . ."

She struggled, flailed. I grabbed a wrist and pulled to help her sit up. When that wasn't quite enough, Kobrah wrapped her arms around my waist and leaned back, adding her strength to the effort.

We got The Voice on her feet. Got her walking. By the time we left the bedroom, she was wheezing. By the time we got to the back door, her lungs sounded like damaged bellows, and I wondered if she would collapse before she reached the cart. She couldn't open her mouth, so she sucked in air through her teeth.

How much time had passed? How much did we have left before someone noticed the horse was gone? Since we hadn't come home by now, and knowing Chayne would be working tonight, Tahnee's mother and mine would assume we had stayed with Kobrah and wouldn't be expecting to see us until after breakfast. The second stage of the potion I bought was supposed to produce lethargy, so hopefully Chayne would fall asleep and not wake up until the daytime caretakers arrived.

Desperate, determined, The Voice took one step after another. I stayed beside her, having no idea what I would do if she fell, while Tahnee held the horse and Kobrah ran back into the house. She returned with a bundle, which she tossed into the back of the cart.

"Clothes," she said.

Up to the blank marker stone that provided The Voice with the step needed to get into the cart. She grasped the sides of the cart and pulled. Kobrah and I pushed. Tahnee held the horse steady.

Then The Voice was in the cart, on hands and knees, panting from the effort.

"Lie down," I told her, while Kobrah ran back into the house a last time to fetch a blanket to cover The Voice until we were out of the village.

I took my place at the horse's head and sent up one more prayer to whoever would listen to me. *Please, let the cart be strong enough to hold her. Let the horse be strong enough to pull the load. Please.*

The horse leaned into the harness, straining to take that first step. But he did take that first step. And the next one. The cart moved. The axles didn't break.

"Good boy," I whispered. "You're a brave, strong boy. Step along. That's it. Good boy."

Clip-clop. Clip-clop. That was the only sound besides the rattle of the cart's wheels. No other sounds disturbed our village's silence.

Two days' journey to Vision in a coach with a team of horses that could maintain a trot for miles at a time. How many days with a half-starved horse who could do no better than a steady walk?

We had gotten out of the village, had left the last house behind us, and I was just starting to breathe easy when we heard *clip-clop, clip-clop, clip-clop* coming toward us.

I kept walking, kept up my whispered encouragement to the horse. Kobrah darted to the far side of the cart and hunched over to avoid being seen, while Tahnee remained near the back of the cart.

The man rode toward us, leading another horse. He seemed vaguely familiar, but it wasn't until Tahnee let out a stifled cry of joy that I recognized him as the young man at the bazaar whom Tahnee had haggled with and flirted with.

And fallen in love with?

I doubt he knew who I was—or cared. He dismounted, shoved reins into my open hand, and leaped at Tahnee, snatching her off her feet as he held her tight.

"I'm sorry," he said. "I'm sorry. You must have thought I failed you, that I wasn't coming. The world . . . There were delays. I . . ."

Kobrah came around the side of the cart, her eyes on the horses.

"Do you need both horses?" she asked, and there was something in her voice, something in the way she moved that made us all tense.

"I . . ." He looked back at his horses, then looked at Kobrah—and then tried to shift Tahnee behind him without being too obvious about what he was doing . . . or why.

We've lost her, I thought. *If we don't let her go, she'll destroy us.*

I think Tahnee realized that too, because she looked at her lover and asked, "Could we ride double?"

We didn't know what we were asking of him, didn't know what the loss of a horse would mean to him or his family. But he knew, and he still went back to his horses, untied the second one, and walked it over to where Kobrah waited. Handing her the reins, he said, "Take the horse."

After she mounted, she looked down at him and said, "May the gods and goddesses of fate and fortune shower your life with golden days."

Then she rode back to the village. I didn't know what she intended to do, but I knew the rest of us needed to get as far away as we could.

"You two go on ahead," I said. "Tahnee's travel bag is too big to carry on horseback. If I bring it to your family's booth at the bazaar, will it get to her?"

"It will." He looked in the direction of the village. "But that will leave you—"

"We got this far by working together," I said, cutting him off. "Now we have to separate." Thinking about the sign before the bridge leading to Vision, I looked at Tahnee. "Now we have to let our hearts choose our destination."

Tahnee hugged me. Her lover studied my face, as if memorizing it, then said, "Travel lightly."

He mounted his horse and pulled Tahnee up behind him, and the two of them cantered down the road, heading for Vision . . . and freedom.

I stood there, feeling so alone. More so because I wasn't alone. But I couldn't look at her just then, couldn't offer any promises or comfort. I would save us—or I would fail.

"Come on, boy," I said softly. "Come on. We've got a ways to go."

The horse leaned into the harness, straining to take that first step.

One step. Another. And step by plodding step, we got a little closer to a dream.

Chapter Six

I have since heard that Ephemera takes the measure of a human heart and helps or hinders what that heart desires. I don't know if that is true or not. I do know the horse shouldn't have made it up the hills I remembered as being so steep. But he did make it. Sometimes I thought he'd break under the strain if he had to take another step up an incline, but somehow the hill always leveled out before that last step, and the descents were gentler than I recalled. I'm sure someone would tell me my mind had exaggerated some things on that first journey in order to make it a grander adventure.

I don't think I exaggerated anything. The world changed itself just enough to give us a chance. Just as I believe the world changed itself that first afternoon when I spotted riders in the distance and knew they were men from the village, looking for us. We kept walking, and my prayer became a chant: *Please don't let them find us.*

They should have found us, should have caught us. They never did.

Several days after leaving the village, in the hushed hour before the real dawn, I stopped the exhausted horse in front of the Temple of Sorrow. Standing on tiptoes, I peeked over the side of the cart, not wanting to stand at the back. The Voice looked at me, a question in her eyes.

"We made it," I said. "I'll get help."

She couldn't get out of the cart. For anything. I realized we had a problem the first time I smelled excrement. But when I went around to the back of the cart, dithering about what to do, the plea in her eyes was more eloquent than words. Every minute I spent caring for her was the minute that might make the difference between getting to Vision or getting caught. So I made my heart as hard and cold as I could make it, and I kept us moving until I saw the bridge and felt numbed by the knowledge that we had reached the city.

I hurried up the broad steps of the temple and rang the bell. Rang and rang and rang.

"There is someone on duty," a voice grumbled as the door opened. "You don't have to wake up the whole tem—"

The moment he saw me, the Shaman stopped his complaint.

"Please," I said, feeling the tears well up now that I didn't have to be hard and cold. "Please help us. She's in the cart. She can't . . . I can't . . . Please."

He touched my arm, giving the warmth of comfort. Then he went down the stairs. The sky had lightened enough that I could see his face go blank with shock when he looked inside the cart.

He ran back up the stairs and disappeared inside the temple, leaving me standing there while something savage raked its claws inside me until I thought I would bleed to death without anyone seeing a drop spilled.

Now that I wasn't hard and cold, I couldn't think, couldn't move, didn't know what to do.

The Shaman returned, rushing past me with six others in his wake, two of them women. One woman, the last out the door, stopped and touched my face gently.

"Do you know where to go?" she asked. "Which door leads to the room for sorrow?"

I nodded.

"Then go in. Find your place."

I felt sluggish, dull. I looked toward the cart. "Horse."

"We'll take care of him. Go in now."

Even at that early hour, there were five other people in the room. I chose a place that spared me from sitting next to anyone else. I smelled of horse and sweat and exhaustion. The cushions were soft, and the minute I sat down, my legs and feet began to throb. The last time I had rested had been unintentional. I had leaned against the horse, too tired to stand on my own, and woke up sometime later to discover that the horse, too, had fallen asleep, his head resting on my shoulder.

Voices rose and fell. Gongs sounded and faded. I drifted.

Then the doors opened and the Shamans walked in leading The Voice. I thought they would take her to a room where she could be cleaned or at least change her out of the filth-encrusted clothes. They had done none of those things, just led her to a spot and helped her lower herself to the mound of cushions.

The voices of the other people in the room sputtered into shocked silence. All through the journey, I had seen without seeing. The Voice wasn't wearing her hood. The scars on her neck were clearly visible.

The Shaman picked up the mallet, struck the gong in front of The Voice, then slipped the mallet into her hand. The gong's deep sound filled the room. The Voice rocked back and forth, clearly in pain.

Then another gong sounded, and a male voice, low but clear, sounded a note. Another gong and another voice rose to fill the room. Another. Another. Another.

A sixth gong and a sixth voice, raw and keening.

Mine.

She had no voice, so we gave her ours, singing the sorrows until finally, in one of those moments when the sound was hushed and spent, the Shaman said, "That is enough for now."

Those five people stood up, looked at The Voice . . . and bowed. Then they left the room, and the Shamans came forward to help her stand.

After they led her away, one Shaman remained.

"You must be tired and hungry. If you want, I will show you to one of our guest rooms right now. But if you can wait a little while longer, I would like you to come with me."

I followed him to a room that, at first glance, contained little more than a small table and two chairs and yet felt so restful to heart and mind, there was no need for anything else.

On the table was a pot and two cups. We sat, and the Shaman poured the tea. I stared out the window, watching bright-colored birds flit around a tiny courtyard where miniature trees were growing in stone pots.

"Now," the Shaman said after a silence during which we had done nothing but watch the birds and drink tea. "Can you tell me how this happened?"

I told him about our village. I told him about the saying we learned in school. I told him about that awful day when I was seven and first began to understand the truth about The Voice. I told him everything, even the things I had done that shamed me. All through the telling, he kept his hands loosely wrapped around the teacup and his eyes on his hands.

I finished my story at the moment when I rang the bell that morning, looking for help.

Those beautiful eyes remained lowered for a moment longer. Then he looked at me.

He wasn't human. Not like me. He was the fury of storms and the laughter of a cool stream on a hot summer's day. He was flood and drought and slow, soft rains that woke up the crops and gave us an abundant harvest.

He was the voice of the world—and the world would do his bidding.

In that moment, I understood why the Shamans walked the streets of the city and why they were respected—and, sometimes, feared. In that moment, I feared for the people in the village I had left behind, especially my family.

"A strong will and loving heart," he said quietly. He pushed back his chair and stood. "Come. It is time for you to rest."

The luxury of a tub full of hot, scented water, where I soaked and washed until I felt clean. The pleasure of a clean bed in a simply furnished room that made no demands on body or heart or mind. And if, in the moments before sleep, I found myself yearning for someone who wasn't quite a Shaman, there was no harm in that.

For the rest of that day, I floated among gentle dreams.

For two more days, I remained in the Temple of Sorrow. Sometimes I sat in the sorrows room to purge myself. Other times I, and the others who happened to be in the room, would raise our voices on behalf of The Voice. Her pain was huge, and because I felt some responsibility for causing it, her pain was killing me.

I suppose that was why the Shaman was waiting for me when I came out of the sorrows room that last evening.

"You did a good thing bringing her here," he said. "Now you must take the next step in the journey."

"I don't understand."

"She needs to stay. You need to go. Tomorrow."

I hadn't thought beyond reaching here, hadn't considered what it would mean if I couldn't stay at the temple.

The Shaman smiled. "There is a community in the northern part of the city. It is a full day's journey from here, nestled in the foothills. Beautiful land. Good people. Artistic in many different ways. I have family up there. You will be welcomed."

"I could find work there?"

"I think that someone with your heart could find a great many things."

For a moment, I thought a blush stained his cheeks, but the sun was setting, so it must have been a trick of the light.

Which is how I ended up driving the cart, which had been scrubbed and freshly painted, to the northern part of Vision and the community of people who were not Shamans but understood more about the world than I had ever imagined.

Chapter Seven

For the first six months, news about the village trickled in to me. After that, I never heard about the village or its people again.

The night we ran away, the Elders' Hall was set on fire, and while the caretaker managed to get out unharmed, the building itself burned to the ground. The other building that burned that night was Chayne's house.

As for Chayne, he screamed himself awake for a week. Then he stood in front of the ruins of the Elders' Hall and confessed his offenses against all living things. He disappeared shortly after that, but Dariden claimed to have seen him behind the orphan's house, looking bloated and hobbling around as if crippled while the caretakers watched him. Dariden also claimed Chayne must have been in a horrific accident that no one wanted to talk about, because in that moment before the caretakers noticed him and hurried to block his view, Dariden saw terrible scars on Chayne's neck.

Tahnee and her lover reached Vision. While his parents were not pleased to have a son make a hasty marriage to a girl who feared being found by her own family, they stood witness at the marriage and helped the young couple set up housekeeping.

I haven't seen Tahnee since the night we ran away. Despite having mutual friends, our paths never cross. Maybe we aren't meant to meet. At least, not yet.

I don't know what became of Kobrah. I don't know if she

reached Vision or even tried. The horse, however, was returned to the merchant's booth in the bazaar by a grateful young man who had needed a ride in order to reach the city. By all accounts, the horse had been handed over to several riders during those months, each person needing a mount for a little while—and each one promising to assist in getting the horse back to its owner in Vision.

I sent one letter to my parents, assuring them that I was safe and well but not telling them enough that they would be able to find me. I cannot change the customs of our village because our village does not want to change. Until the magic dies that allows one person to become the well of sorrow for so many, the village will look away while the Elders maim someone in order to make that person's flesh a vessel.

I cannot change the village. But I saved the people I could.

Chapter Eight

Two years to the day, I stood on the bottom step of the Temple of Sorrow. I had a letter to deliver—and a teasing scold to deliver as well, if I had the courage. I now knew why the Shaman had blushed the day he told me about the community in the north. My lover's eyes are not quite as beautiful as his uncle's, and while he has a fine sense of the world, Kanzi is not a Shaman. Despite those "flaws," he is a talented artist and a good man.

Our marriage was arranged to take place at the end of harvest, and the letter I was delivering was a nephew's enthusiastic invitation and plea for his uncle to attend the wedding and stand as a witness.

So I stood on the steps, wondering if it was a Shaman or an uncle who had been playing matchmaker the day he sent me north, when the sound of finger cymbals caught my attention and I wandered over to a temple that was a little farther down the street.

A woman, dressed in the wheat-colored robes of a Shaman's apprentice, was playing the finger cymbals in a happy little rhythm while a dozen children stood on the steps below, swaying to the rhythm and then freezing when the cymbals stopped.

A game, I decided, smiling as I moved closer, because there was something about the woman . . .

She turned and looked at me. I didn't recognize her face, but I knew her eyes. She wore a hood that covered the hideous scars on her neck, but the robes covered a slimmer body that no longer carried sorrow.

She looked at me and smiled. And in her eyes I saw warmth, compassion, gratitude. Love.

Raising my hand in a small salute, I walked back to the Temple of Sorrow. A moment later, the finger cymbals picked up their rhythm.

I rang the bell, and he answered. His look of delight faded when he saw my face.

"What's wrong?" he asked, stepping back to let me enter. "What's happened?"

"I need . . ." What did I need? I hurt so much, but I didn't know why. "She's . . ."

Understanding. "She's not here anymore," he said gently.

"I know. I s-saw . . ."

"I see." His warm hand cupped my elbow as he led me toward the sorrows room.

"No," I said, pulling back. "Wrong . . . sound." I knew that much.

He closed his eyes for a moment. When he opened them, they were shiny from tears. "Of course. I understand now."

He led me to a room on the other side of the building. It was set up the same way as the room of sorrows, but instead of gongs set before each placement of cushions, there was a wind chime hanging from a stand.

The Shaman stepped out of the room and closed the door.

I stepped over to the nearest wind chime and jostled it. Bright notes filled the room. Bright notes . . . like the radiant face that had been hidden for so many years.

Stepping into the center of the room, I brushed a finger against each wind chime, moving from place to place, faster and faster, until the room was awash in sparkling sound that squeezed my heart until the tears flowed, faster and faster. Until I collapsed on the floor in the center of that room and shed tears that were a bright, sharp, cleansing pain.

They were the last tears I ever shed for The Voice, and they were not tears of sorrow. They were tears of joy.

NEW IN HARDCOVER

from

New York Times **bestselling author**

ANNE BISHOP

WRITTEN IN RED
A Novel of the Others

Enter a world inhabited by the Others, unearthly
entities who rule the Earth and whose prey are
humans. As a cassandra sangue, or blood prophet, Meg
Corbyn can see the future when her skin is cut—a gift
that feels more like a curse. Meg's Controller keeps her
enslaved so he can have full access to her visions, but
when she escapes, the only safe place she can hide is in
the business district operated by the Others.

Shape-shifter Simon Wolfgard is reluctant to hire the
stranger who inquires about the Human Liaison job.
He senses she's keeping a secret—and she doesn't smell
like human prey. Yet he decides to employ Meg
anyway. But when he learns the truth, he'll have to
decide if she's worth the fight between humans and the
Others that will surely follow.

Available wherever books are sold or at
penguin.com

facebook.com/acerocbooks

r0138